fatal
FAVORS

Carol
Bartolet

Copyright © 2009 by Carol Bartolet

All rights reserved. No part of this book shall be reproduced or transmitted in any form or by any means, electronic, mechanical, magnetic, photographic including photocopying, recording or by any information storage and retrieval system, without prior written permission of the publisher. No patent liability is assumed with respect to the use of the information contained herein. Although every precaution has been taken in the preparation of this book, the publisher and author assume no responsibility for errors or omissions. Neither is any liability assumed for damages resulting from the use of the information contained herein.

This is a work of fiction. Names, characters, places, and incidents either are the product of the author's imagination or are used fictitiously. Any resemblance to actual events or locales or persons, living or dead, is entirely coincidental.

ISBN 0-7414-5184-0

Published by:

INFINITY
PUBLISHING.COM

1094 New DeHaven Street, Suite 100
West Conshohocken, PA 19428-2713
Info@buybooksontheweb.com
www.buybooksontheweb.com
Toll-free (877) BUY BOOK
Local Phone (610) 941-9999
Fax (610) 941-9959

Printed in the United States of America

Printed on Recycled Paper

Published March 2009

For my two *favor*ite guys, Don and Matt,
always willing to help.

This book's for you!

fatal
FAVORS

CHAPTER ONE

While stark white walls surrounded the single bed in the hospital room, shafts of dusty afternoon sunlight cross-examined the spotlighted occupant. Kamila, however, was not alone as she sat propped against her pillow, huddled in a nest of rumpled bed sheets. The young woman, dark-eyed, and still astounded by the miracle, gazed at her perfect baby. Tentatively, her manicured fingertip touched the face of her newborn daughter, tracing a gentle line across the infant's downy cheek and leaving a soft path in the delicate baby fuzz. The new mother's untested heart filled with tangled emotions as she absorbed the sleeping infant into her soul.

"Sofah, my own little star, I love you…too much," murmured the new mother, as she held the baby girl tenderly to her breast and kissed the top of her head. She smelled so clean, so innocent, all fresh and new. After the birth, when the nurse had placed Sofah in her arms, Kamila's breasts had filled and leaked instinctively even before the rooting mouth had touched her skin. At last, she was a mother. This feeling was much more than she had dreamed possible, and now how could she do this thing? Do this for Sajid? Do this for Allah?

As tears threatened to cascade from her filling eyes, Kamila quickly blinked them back. Heavy male footsteps approached her room from the hallway. She heard a man speaking and looked toward the door. The recognized voice was not boasting the paternal pride usually heard in the maternity ward. Her husband, Sajid, and his brother, Hassad, filed through her door at New York City General and stopped. Not looking up, Kamila felt their unspoken disapproval as the bearded men stood there silent, watching her cradle the baby. Still damp-eyed, her cheeks flushed with tenderness and a hint of unusual defiance, she pulled Sofah even closer and covered the baby's face with the blanket. Her husband, walking as mechanically as a soldier, came to her bedside. His eyes were black with warning. Sajid stood beside Kamila's bed for a moment looking at his wife and infant daughter, his arms folded close to his chest. Kamila tried to read his mood, but kept her eyes low and focused on her child. She knew he had just come from work and was tired. His wrinkled, stained shirt smelled like the ethnic foods served at his downtown restaurant …a combination of spices, hummus, and lamb kabob. His stale breath held the odor of many cups of strong Arabic coffee. Ordinarily, the familiar aromas of home would have comforted Kamila.

"How are you feeling, Kami?" Sajid asked, placing a cool hand on her shoulder.

Kamila shrugged, not trusting herself to speak. Sajid lifted the blanket ever so slightly to reveal Sofah's plump, pink face. Hassad also glanced at the baby, but then turned away. Suddenly Sofah's eyelids popped open, revealing huge eyes, bright and sparkling sapphires framed by long, black lashes. She was a beautiful baby. First her rosy lips puckered, then her mouth circled as if in amazement, as the baby's inexperienced eyes struggled to focus on her surroundings. Then, seeming to siphon strength from the heavens, Sofah scrunched up her face, prune-like, clenched her little fists, and opened her mouth as if preparing to scream. But no sound emerged. Instead, an O-shaped yawn consumed her expression and the tiny girl squirmed, closed her eyes, and again fell asleep, cuddling contentedly against her mother's breast.

"She's such a good baby, my husband," said Kamila, finally able to speak, her eyes again filling with passion for her infant daughter and dread for what was to come.

"Kami. Are you feeling you can soon leave the hospital?" Sajid demanded in near perfect English, his dark eyes expressionless. He ran his fingers up and down her arm as he spoke, his hand reaching beneath the cotton hospital gown to rub her shoulder. Hassad stood in the corner by the window, his hands shoved into his pants pockets, staring at the traffic in the busy street several floors below. Kamila looked away from the men. Words formed in her mind, but her tongue and lips were paralyzed by distress. Again, she couldn't answer her husband. Sajid's caress of her shoulder became a squeeze, his fingers pressing harder and harder into her soft skin.

"Kamila!" he whispered harshly, bending close to her ear. "When can you leave?"

"I don't know, I don't know," murmured Kamila, pulling her arm away, but averting her eyes from his stare. She still held Sofah tightly to her breast, and protectively covered the tiny head with the pink flannel blanket. Fear was clouding her thinking, but she responded quietly, "I will ask Dr. Fleming tomorrow, Sajid, tomorrow morning."

Satisfied with the answer, Sajid bent towards Kamila, kissing her forehead, before his lips again formed a hard, thin line. "She will be a martyr. She is the only way we can accomplish our goal. What greater end for all of us?" he breathed into her ear, leaning on the bed with his elbow, and adjusting himself to be closer to her face. His fingers outlined her jaw line, working their way to her neck. Pushing aside her long black hair, his thumb felt her throbbing carotid artery, pulsing in fear, pulsing in grief and sadness.

"Try not to become too attached, my wife. You are only making things more difficult."

"Yes, I know," whispered Kamila, bowing her head until her chin nestled gently in the baby's dark hair.

"I love you, and the baby…and Allah. We will all be together after the hell storm, I promise you," said Sajid.

Kamila didn't voice an answer. She nodded and squeezed his hand.

A female voice on the overhead intercom system announced that hospital visiting hours had ended for the afternoon. Sajid kissed Kamila's hand and turned to look at his brother.

"We can soon go forward with the plan. Praise be to Allah," said Sajid, hands tented into a gesture of prayer toward the other man.

Hassad's eyes fell once more on the wife of his brother and he said, "Good night, Kamila. You've done a good job.

Praise be to Allah." With a dismissive wave of his hand, he turned away following Sajid into the hallway.

They were gone and Kamila's shoulders sagged as she dared to breathe again. She gently peeled back the blanket and watched the face of her sleeping daughter. *Yes, praise be to Allah.*

CHAPTER TWO

In the delivery room, a thirty-something woman screamed and a wet, bluish-red, slippery mass slid from between her stirruped legs onto Dr. Ronnie King's waiting forearms. The ultrasound done months ago had foretold the story. The infant was alive, but still and quiet. The malformations of the skull and spine were obvious to even the untrained eye. The newborn daughter of Evie Krantz would never learn, never walk, and never talk. But after an aggressive assault on the infant's airway by a nurse with suctioning equipment, the baby began her life with a gasping breath and a weak cry. Evie, upon hearing the newborn's feeble but brave attempts to live, hugged herself and began to sob.

Another nurse held Evie's folded arms and wiped her tears with a tissue, consoling her, "I'm sorry, so sorry."

"Like we thought, it's a girl, Evie. Did you have a name picked out?" asked Dr. King, as she pressed her hands down hard on the mother's uterus. There were more sobs from the distraught mother. The placenta was delivered easily, and the doctor examined it as she spoke, "I know it's tough going through this, but the chances are about a zillion to one of anything like this ever happening again."

After a brief and silent interlude, Evie sobbed, "I don't want to go through this even once. I can't even love the baby, knowing she'll die soon…it's just too hard." This statement was followed by another barrage of tears.

Evie's baby was placed in a warming incubator after being weighed, measured, and getting a cleansing bath. She struggled to breathe on her own, air supplemented by oxygen, as her tiny chest heaved with every inspiration. Blood tests were done and drops were placed in her eyes as per state required protocol. Baby Krantz was hastily written on a pink identification card and attached to the clear plastic incubator. She weighed five pounds, seven ounces, and was eighteen inches long, as best she could be measured. Her spine curled at a strange angle and neck torsion pulled her misshapen head toward her left shoulder. Her parents, Evie and Jack, had already decided that no heroic measures would be taken to prolong the life of their imperfect daughter. Nothing to prolong her misery...or theirs.

Once the infant's breathing had improved, she was placed at the rear of the nursery in a small alcove not readily visible through the public viewing windows. Evie was taken back through the obstetrical wing into a private room to recover from the delivery. As her gurney rolled past another room, she glanced through the door and saw a pretty, young girl sitting in bed, gently rocking her baby. She was crying too...perhaps another dying child? A tinge of guilt grabbed Evie in the belly, or maybe it was the cramping post-partum uterus, but it made her think more clearly. Then she saw Jack standing by her room. He'd been faithfully waiting all morning.

"Hi, Honey. Are you okay? Please don't cry," he said. Jack looked pale and worn as he reached out to cup her chin and kiss her on the cheek. He took a wad of smashed-up Kleenex from the pocket of his Levi's and wiped her wet face. "It'll be okay, really. We'll get by this. Things will be fine. Please, please, don't cry."

"Jack, I didn't even hold her. I couldn't, I just couldn't," Evie sobbed, eyes refusing to meet his. "I'm a terrible parent...that's our daughter." Two nurses in green scrubs were helping to slide Evie smoothly onto her hospital bed.

"I know, I know. It's just real hard right now," consoled Jack, his own eyes moistening. He helped the nurses pull up the sheet and raise the bed rails. "Maybe later, we can have her brought to your room?"

"Sure. Maybe that'd be best. Just love her for the short time that we have her."

"Exactly. Let her know somehow, in our own way, that she was a loved child of God," replied Jack. "The church is praying for us right now. I called Cal and let him know our baby was born. They'll expect me to say something in the pulpit this Sunday. I'm having a hard time deciding on the right message."

"The congregation needs you, needs you to be strong. We need to be strong for our baby and for everyone in the church," agreed Evie, holding his hand and staring down at her now empty belly.

Later, after the nurse had checked Evie's blood pressure, the baby was brought to her room to stay. As Evie held her daughter for the first time, she caressed the sandy brown swirls of soft baby hair and could feel the sharp pain of the coming loss. She would never tie long curls into pigtails or help her fix her hair for the prom. She held the baby close and named her Rebecca Anne. Rebecca Anne Krantz. She passed the flannel-wrapped bundle to Jack. With two boys at home already, Evie had always wanted a baby girl. Now she had her daughter at least for a while. Jack sat with the baby in the comfortable bedside chair and began to rock, humming a Gospel favorite. For this afternoon anyway, father, mother, and infant would be a family. They would try to make the best of whatever life threw at them. No one knew what lie ahead.

CHAPTER THREE

By late afternoon, Sofah was also rooming-in with her mother and Kamila was planning their escape. Kamila would risk Sajid's violent anger to save her child. This evening's hospital meal, including meat loaf and a baked potato, had become part of the plan. She had carefully unwrapped the potato and placed the aluminum foil aside. After dinner, she took the foil to the bathroom and rinsed it, pressing it flat as she washed. Kamila was not sure this would work, but she had remembered the SunPass transponder her husband kept in their car's glove box. It was placed inside the windshield to automatically pay highway tolls whenever they visited Florida. When not in use, it was protected in a shiny silver bag from accidental consumption by some other electronic device. Kamila hoped that the potato foil, wrapped as a shield around the baby's identification alert bracelet, would prevent the alarms from sounding as she left. It wasn't fail-safe and she needed to get away undetected. She needed a back-up plan. If she could access the alarm system at the nurses' station, she could try to disable it. She would wait until everything was quiet later in the night.

At 10:00 P.M., after the evening baby feedings, Kamila quickly dressed in her black abaya and headscarf, and was ready to slip away. The only jewelry she ever wore was a watch with an expandable band. She had slipped that onto her wrist and glanced at the time. She wrapped her baby snuggly in the pink blanket issued by the hospital and gave Sofah a quick kiss. This was not the time for emotion, but for stealth and cunning. She picked up her baby, gently rocking her and chanting soft love-nothings. Sofah smelled so good, so sweet. Kami could understand the sacrifice of herself...but a tiny baby? She hoisted her overnight bag across her right shoulder and cradled the baby in the crook of her left arm. Kamila could hear that some of the new mothers had their televisions on, but most were probably already asleep. It was temporarily quiet in this part of the hospital and Kamila was getting away now, before her husband could find her. She had set her idea in motion. She would walk out of the hospital with Sofah and go to the nearby New York Crowne Hotel to check in and wait until dawn. Routinely, Sajid went to the restaurant every morning to check on his employees and then tomorrow he would come to the hospital to get his wife and daughter. With good timing in the morning, she could take a taxi home from her hotel while he was at work, get her passport and their financial account numbers, and head for their bank. And with good luck, she could be out of the state, if not out of the country, by tomorrow night. She would go to her mother, now a widow, who could use her grandfather's power and wealth as a shield. She could be in Riyadh soon and she and Sofah would be safe.

Kamila peeked into the dim hallway, now filled with shadows and brief white flashes of prime time coming from open doorways into the corridor. She had never watched much television, since Sajid said most of it was against Islam and against God. She had agreed that the advertising was stupid and dumb, but privately enjoyed some of the programs when Sajid was busy at work. He wasn't a bad husband and he took care of her. But this time he was asking too much.

Some of the nurses had left for a last break before the new shift came in at 11 P.M. A few were attending a new arrival in the delivery room. The lone remaining nurse was pushing a cart filled with drawers of pills far down the long, tunneling hall. Kamila could hear a new father laughing and talking on his cell phone, spreading the good news from his wife's room.

"Mom! It's a boy! It's a boy! He's a beauty...looks like Melissa, thank God!" he exclaimed.

A pinch of jealousy for their happiness, their new baby, their celebration, almost overcame Kamila, but she moved past them toward the elevator, just six doors from her own room. No one would see her leave, alone and carrying her baby. Quietly, but with purpose, she strode toward the big steel doors. Keeping one eye on the nurse, Kamila inched towards the empty workstation. It was easy to see the lighted alarm board at the back of a long desk. It was situated beside the copy machine. She also saw that all the exit doors were marked on the board with a number and a small green light. She worried that if she went through an armed door or even the elevator, the foil wrapping on Sofah's ID bracelet might not prevent the trigger of a loud, beeping alert.

Kamila crept into the nurse's cubicle area, crouching low and trying to balance Sofah and her overnight bag. Suddenly she tripped on the hem of her abaya and reflexively caught herself, but not before her shoulder fell against a cupboard under the counter. The small *bang* echoed down the vacant hall and the medication nurse turned to look back. The nurse stopped and watched for a moment, but she was too busy to investigate.

Kamila ducked farther below the counter and exhaling with relief, saw the switch to disengage the door alarms. She quickly flipped the lever off, holding her breath. The alarm board remained silent, but now it began to flash a blood-red warning! All the lights were blinking red! Creeping, half crawling, back into the corridor, she stood slowly and carefully, not sure of the nurse's position. Fortunately for Kamila, the nurse had gone to check a patient in a room far down the hall. Kamila's heart hammered her ears and she felt light-headed. The telltale red flashes continued to bounce off her face and clothing, pointing accusingly to her predicament. She heard nurses talking in the stairway and realized their last break was over. They were standing behind the closed exit door gossiping about something, but soon the door would open and everyone would see the disabled alarm board. Kamila had to move right now! She edged along the wall towards the elevator, slowly and deliberately. She almost made it.

CHAPTER FOUR

Kamila jerked still in shocked reflex as she heard the muted musical *bong bong* of the elevator announcing a late night visitor. Only steps from her escape, she stood inanimate, frozen with terror. Reflexively she backed quickly into the dark of the nearest room, avoiding detection just as the elevator doors swooshed open. Just one quick peek and she knew she had to revise her plan.

Oh no, Allah! It's him! Heart racing in panic, Kamila looked around the unfamiliar room for a place to hide. She quickly felt her way around a corner into the bathroom. Kamila's heart was pounding her ribs, seeming to want escape as much as she. She began to breathe in rapid pants, and a queasy sense of dizziness threatened. Clutching the door handle for balance, she saw that there was one occupied bed in this room. It was the woman she'd seen earlier. Her sick baby was lying soundlessly in a bassinet along the wall. The room was very dim and the television was off, so both mother and infant were sleeping. Kamila tried to quiet her nerves and calm herself. It was hard to see in the darkness, but her eyes adjusted quickly. With only seconds to think and act, she carefully placed Sofah into the bassinet and picked up the woman's baby. She began to rock it, simultaneously removing Sofah's aluminum foil to place on this child's alarm anklet. Kamila felt a wave of nausea grip her throat as a vaguely medicinal smell replaced the sweet fragrance of her own child. She glanced quickly at the nametag on the little bed, *Krantz.*

"Don't wake up, don't cry, little one," she whispered, as she hugged the flaccid infant. The baby's mother continued to sleep. Kamila mouthed, *I'm sorry,* in the slumbering woman's direction. She ventured one more glance at Sofah, who was starting to wiggle and squirm defiantly at the loss of her mother's safe and warm embrace. Quickly Kamila stood erect and brave at the doorway, timing her entrance into the hallway. She saw that Sajid had passed and had just reached the door to her own room.

"Kam? Kamila!" he was beginning to shout, seeing the empty bed.

"I'm right here," said Kamila, rushing up from behind him and holding a finger to her lips to try to quiet him. "You must have received my call, Sajid. Good. I am ready to go. The doctor stopped by and said it was okay to leave. Look, I have my bag ready. I was walking the halls hoping you would come soon."

"I didn't get a call. What are you doing? What are you up to?" he demanded, eyeing her up and down, looking for something.

"I was ready to get out of here and I called the restaurant. I knew you wanted me home as soon as possible. I left a message there with Naja."

"I received no messages."

"I'm ready. Let's go. It's good, right?"

"Yes," said Sajid slowly, watching Kamila's face. "It's very good. Instead of a late night visit, I'll be taking my family home. Tell the nurse you're ready."

"I don't want to go out in a wheelchair like an old lady. Please, let's just leave."

"But don't you have to check out with the nurses?" asked Sajid, glancing around for someone to help them.

"I've done that. They're busy. Lots of babies being born tonight. Please, let's go."

Peripherally, Kamila could see the medication nurse finishing her work. She was writing on a clipboard and getting ready to turn the cart back down the hall towards them. Sajid stared at Kamila again, looking for some clue. Something wasn't right, he knew, but finally he just shrugged and walked towards the elevator. As he pushed the button to go down, Kamila prayed to Allah for the first time in many months. *Just get me out of here, please, please, please!*

Allah or God or someone may have heard her plea, since the lift arrived in record time, and they stepped inside. No alarm sounded. Kamila let her breath slowly release through pursed lips. She knew she'd been hyperventilating. Sajid took the bag from his wife as the doors shut. As Kamila held the strange infant tightly, her legs felt wobbly, and the small space began to close in. She could not, would not, faint. She would get out of here and her baby would be safe and have a good life with *someone*. Once outside in the fresh air, empowered by fear and adrenaline, she walked courageously to the curb, clutching the abducted Rebecca Krantz. Sajid summoned the hospital valet for his Lexus. Just make it home, she thought, just make it home. After that, Sajid would know she had switched the babies, but it would be too late to go back. The hospital would have alerted the authorities and they would be looking for them. Sajid wouldn't take any chances that they would be caught or even detained for questioning. They would have to leave immediately for Miami. And just a week from now on Monday, they would all be aboard that fateful flight…just as planned.

CHAPTER FIVE

Mikelle Walsh was grateful that she had clipped her long hair to the top of her head as she tossed the last pitchfork of manure into the old, rusting wheelbarrow. She rested in the stall for a moment, leaning on the handle of the plastic-tined rake, and wiped her forehead on her arm. She was so wet with sweat that barn dust had turned into little mud rivulets streaking onto her neck and the creases of her arms. However, Mikki guessed that her gelding, Cajun Clown, wouldn't care a bit that he now had a clean and fresh-smelling stall. She had boarded her horse at Palm Pines Equestrian Center for over a year, ever since she bought the Quarter horse from the Roberts family. He was a retired Western Pleasure champion and his quiet and calm nature made him the perfect mount for Mikki. She just didn't want the stress or hassle of a horse that needed constant training or visits with Mr. Lunge Line. The Clown, as he was called by everyone in the stable, never needed warm-up or tone-down by going in aimless circles at the end of a long nylon exercise line. He was always ready to ride, no funny stuff, no bucking, no spooking at his shadow on a sunny day. Mikki, an excellent equestrian, could have ridden about anything. In fact, she used to play with the Junior Team at the Palm Beach Polo Club until she went to college. This was the first horse she had owned. He was all hers to ride and care for and she loved that. She even enjoyed picking up the poop. As she worked in the stall, she felt the stress of her engineering job fade away. It was Saturday afternoon and it was plenty hot. This was summer in Florida after all, but the horses, the barn, even the stable smell…well, minus the damned flies, she thought, were the best psychotherapy a person could ask for.

"Hey, girlfriend!" called Julianne Connery, the dressage trainer at the barn. "Are you ready to take some more lessons?" She was walking toward the stall where Mikki stood sweating. Julianne was a tall, lanky blond with a casual attitude that seemed to calm horses.

"Hi, Jules," answered Mikki, smiling. "Sure, maybe we can start up again next week?"

"Well, Clown whispered to me that he wanted to do something new," said Julianne, also damp with perspiration, her hands propped on thin hips in tight gray riding breeches. "I just saw him out in the paddock. Where've you been anyway?"

"Mostly still getting Gran up and running. She's doing really well since her stroke, but you know that's why I moved back here from Orlando. Gotta keep an eye on the old girl. She's always up to something…something more than she should be doing at her age, anyway."

"Tell me about it. My grandfather wants to go back to riding on some sort of Masters Polo Team. He's eighty, for God's sake! He said the team is for age sixty and over. I asked him if the team was sponsored by some funeral home or something!"

Both girls laughed hysterically, then Mikki picked up the handles of the wheelbarrow and shoved it over the concrete edge of the stall with a grunt. The two young women walked towards the barn exit together, both glistening with sweat. "Hey Jules, maybe we should get them hooked up…our grandparents, I mean."

"I think Gus Delano would be too much for your grandma. Grandpa's too wild and crazy. The rumor was that he and his brother used to be in the Mafia. Shit, maybe a hit man or something! Who knows? Probably would still want sex, too!" said Julianne, squinting her eyes wickedly and giggling.

Mikki started to laugh so hard that tears came. She gave the wheelbarrow a toss and flipped the contents out onto the growing pile of manure accumulating behind the barns. After replacing the wheelbarrow in the equipment storage area, both girls headed for the air-conditioned lounge.

Wiping her moist eyes, Mikki said, "Geez, the reason I was laughing so hard is that if my Granny knew that…about the sex…she would want his email address and they'd be text messaging, having phone sex, meeting at the club for lunch, and then having rolls in the hay. Really! When she was younger, she used to tell Brigetta and I that all her out-of-town trips were to visit some sheik and do sexual favors for him. She said that this sheik was in love with her and that she refused to join his harem. The story was that she just wanted to ride his Arabian horses through the desert. She told us he might try to kidnap her at any time. My mom used to get so mad at her for telling us all this junk, but we loved it. I think we half-believed her, too. After all, she did have all the extra security around her estate."

"Sounds like just his type! He thinks he's still an Italian stallion!" said Julianne, as she wiped her hands on her breeches.

Mikki paused, still smiling, and then said, "What the hell, give Gus the phone number for the Pink Flamingo! I'll give Gran a warning and she can do what she wants if he calls her."

Both girls burst into gales of laughter once again as they stripped and headed for the ladies showers adjoining the rider's lounge. As the warm spray hit her face and hair, Mikki watched as soapy rivers of brown water flowed towards the drain. "Doesn't this barn business just make you feel so beautifully feminine?" she called to Julianne in the next shower stall.

"Yeah, well, think about how good we'll look when we clean up! It's like we're two different people. We don't even need aliases. The grime twins first and then these two gorgeous, undiscovered swimsuit models appear. Huh, Mikki?"

"Exactly," answered Mikki, drying her long auburn hair with a fat, fluffy towel. "As long as we don't have to do any nail polish ads. Look at this manicure!" Mikki stuck out one hand towards Julianne, reaching around the plastic shower curtain. The French tips were no longer smooth, white, and even. Ragged cuticles reigned supreme. It was just too hot for work gloves and horse chores took their toll on hands.

"Well, at least they're clean," said Julianne, as she examined a torn nail on her own finger. "But who has more fun, and of course...we are *stable* people!"

"Sometimes I wonder about my mental stability, but this sure does help. I don't think I could make it through the work week without coming to the barn for my R & R."

"I've got lessons starting at 7:30 A.M. tomorrow and a date with Bryce tonight, so I'd better get dressed and get going. You still seeing Erik? Wanna join us for a movie?" asked Julianne.

"Nah. That's kinda over and done with. He bores me to where I would rather be home watching the news. All he wants to do is talk about his multitude of cars, his big house, blah, blah, blah. He just has nothing to say. As far as all the bragging goes, I'm not impressed. Been there, done that stuff. He just doesn't get it."

"Certainly with your grandmother living in the Pink Flamingo and having a Jaguar in every color..."

"Uh...no red one."

"Oh yeah, right. I remember you had a little accident."

"She hasn't quite forgiven me, either. All the same, I'll take a rain check. New man, another time, okay?"

"Sure," said Julianne, as she combed conditioner through her hair.

As the girls finished dressing, they caught up on all the latest stable gossip...who bought what horse, who was dating who, and the latest relationship rumors. Both women were transformed, looking clean, refreshed, and beautiful as they tossed lipstick and make-up back into their riding bags.

"Seeya next week, Mikki," said Julianne, as the girls left the locker room and headed for their cars in the grassy lot adjoining the barn. "Maybe it'll be a little cooler."

Mikki got into her BMW, started the engine, and twisted the air conditioning control all the way. Before she reached the pavement, the little car's vents were blowing icy air onto her face and into the neck of her blouse. Turning onto Atlantic Drive, she headed towards her grandmother's beachfront estate. She felt good, physically tired and relaxed, but had a strange feeling of unrest and anticipation.

CHAPTER SIX

"Gran, are you sleeping? Hey, there's a fly on your nose…wake up!" Mikki chuckled, as she gently stroked her grandmother's tousled and windblown gray hair. It felt damp from the ocean mist despite the warm sun on the veranda of the Pink Flamingo. Mikki loved her grandmother more than any one else imagined.

Emily Vanderhorn had been dozing outside with her cats on a cushioned lounge chair for about an hour. She wore a neon pink swim tunic and was lying semi-reclined with a white beach towel covering her thighs. It was late afternoon and the corner balcony facing the Atlantic was slowly becoming shaded and more comfortably cool. The air was full of unshed rain. Emily wasn't quite ready to cast off her pleasant reverie for real life.

"Very funny, and no, I'm not sleeping. I'm awake…now," she answered, barely opening her eyes. "I hope you have a good reason for waking me. Is George Clooney at the door or what?"

"Not quite, but it's interesting. I just came from the barn and yes, I showered."

"Good. You smell nice…like a lady."

Mikki, who was now barefoot and wearing clean denim Capri's and a blue silk blouse, sighed and continued, "I just walked up to the workroom and the pink line was beeping, so I read the message on the computer."

"The pink line? On Saturday? Don't people know we don't work on weekends?" But Emily was pulling herself into a more upright position, immediately awake and interested.

"Since when was that a rule?"

"Since today. Since I was having the best sex dream I've had in a year that was rudely interrupted by my wonderful, but annoying granddaughter."

"Oh. We'll definitely talk about that later. In fact, speaking of sex, I was just talking about you. I may have found you a man. Julianne's grandfather. I understand he's still quite spry. Not that anyone could keep up with you, but he just might be your type."

"At my age, if a man can still fog a mirror, he's my type. Did you warn him about me?"

"I gave fair warning to Julianne. But if that doesn't scare him off, he might call, so be prepared. His name is Gus Delano."

"Consider me prepared. So now what about the pink line?"

"Yes, anyway...this was a very weird message, Gran. Seriously."

"Okay, get me my cane and we'll go up there. Better be good to spoil my wet dream," said Emily. She gently pushed the two sunbathing cats, which doubled as afghans, from her belly as she rose to stand. She draped the towel around her waist and tucked it in, creating a skirt. She was still muttering about her dream as she hiked up the one floor of pink marble steps to the office. At age seventy-nine, and two years past her stroke, Emily was doing very well. Dr. Blakely said now she only needed a cane to help with steps or uneven pavement. She had been warned about falling and breaking a hip, so however reluctantly, she had promised to follow her doctor's instructions, at least on this matter.

The office had dual computers and monitors so each woman could watch from her own comfortable chair. Mikki latched the security door behind them with a solid snap. There were no maintenance personnel scheduled for today to worry about, but there was always the potential for a walk-in family member to appear from nowhere. When both women were seated, Mikki brought the message back up on the screen. Both read and reread the typed information and then sat silently, both thinking about the text.

Leaning back in her chair and rubbing her eyes, Granny Em was the first to speak, "Did you check out the government chatter line info? Before we go crazy about this, we should see what other channels are getting. Anything vaguely related to this?"

Mikki shrugged and said, "Yep, I got the White House channel and there's been some talk, but nothing to raise us to orange or red. Want me to check the other sights?"

"Better do that. I'll check my instant data line," replied Emily, eyes glittering with anticipation as she began punching the keyboard, reading glasses halfway down her nose.

Mikki and Emily pursued all their lines of secretly hacked intelligence and began to highlight any codes or repeated phrases. Finally Mikki said, "Something is going on. Seems like what we've got here could be legit to me. But there's nothing official. I don't get it. Why this personal message to us? Where's this coming from? This isn't what we do, not our expertise."

"Too many loose ends for fed action, I guess. Protect the economy by keeping everything running as usual? Otherwise all the anti-terror units would be handling this. I don't get it, either. Where's Homeland Security? Close your eyes and hope it goes away?"

"So it's me," stated Mikki with an exaggerated sigh, as she sat up straight in her chair, and looked at her grandmother. "One more pro bono life-saving mission to accomplish."

"No, it's *us*," answered Emily firmly, standing up, still wearing her swimsuit, and pointing the tip of her cane towards Mikki. "Us with a capital 'U.' This could be nothing or it could be something really big and awful. You'll need me along. 'Ms. Oldie but Goodie.' "

"Gran. I've been training for this stuff now for two years. *You've* been training me. My last client was very happy with the job I did. I made more money on that favor than my entire last year's salary at the new engineering firm. All went great!"

"You've been training for two years? Ha! That's nothing! And what about your driving? What about *my* Jaguar?"

"Oh."

"Yeah, oh."

"That was a minor bobble. But true, sorry about your car, but the situation demanded immediate action. This time I'll use a rental...just like you always tell me in the first place."

"Yep, a rental. That is what *we* will use, just in case. One that can pack my wheelchair and our equipment. We have to travel in a big hurry."

"I guess you're right again. Your expertise...but my wit, charm, beauty, athletic ability, training..."

"Yes," interrupted Emily. "You may be a valuable asset. Just like me. Let's get moving." With a push of a button on the keyboard, Emily started the process to raise the concealed panel to the workroom. There, in the cupboards, they would gather their supplies. "If this guy's for real, we don't have much time."

CHAPTER SEVEN

By late Sunday afternoon, the women had driven from Hertz Rental Car in West Palm Beach and parked at Miami International Airport. They chose a room at the Hilton Grande Airport located inside the terminal building. The hotel was comfortable and afforded direct access to the airport, the parking areas, all terminals, and a view of the runways. In the parking garage Mikki and Emily unloaded the rented Lincoln Towncar. They got Emily situated in her old wheelchair and hauled their equipment bags, that all looked like luggage, to the lobby. Their room was on the second floor and had an indoor balcony to the airport lobby atrium and another to an outdoor view of the tarmac. They unpacked in silence as Mikki used the remote to tune in a local news channel and then *CNN*, as Emily unfolded the *Miami Herald* across one of the beds. Emily sat cross-legged, Indian-style, at the head of the bed and scanned the newspaper for anything unusual, even the smallest clue. Both women were fastidious about knowing current events. It didn't pay to be out of the loop for even a day. Any interesting facts seen or heard were delegated to memory or recorded via scanning in bits and pieces in Mikki's personal digital assistant device. Sometimes she used her cell phone camera to photograph news clippings to later file by category in the bank of office computers at home. Mikki linked her laptop computer to the hotel's wireless connection and double-checked her PDA. Several news items of interest caught her eye, but nothing rang alarm bells for this particular circumstance. People were always doing something weird or totally outrageous, and/or illegal.

"Ready Gran? Let's do some reconnaissance and get some dinner. I'm starving," said Mikki. She had taken a quick shower and was combing her hair into a practical ponytail as she spoke.

"Just gotta gargle and I'll be all set. You never know, in the Miami airport we might see George," answered Emily, from the bathroom which now smelled like Listerine.

"You and your fixation on George Clooney. Really, Gran. He's Mother's age! He could be your son," said Mikki, "but I admit it would be fun having him as my Grandpa!"

"We're all entitled to our little obsessions. Keep that in mind. I remember the guy from that band...Bon Jovi? You bought every album as a kid, and played them over and over. I thought I'd go nuts. That summer I knew why Susan sent her daughter to live with me for the month. She had to get away from 'Bad Medicine.'"

"Point taken. Let's go, okay? I've got the chair all set."

Emily had donned a housedress and flat 'sensible' shoes. As the two traversed the corridors, they looked like any other common, ordinary travelers. Others saw a dutiful granddaughter pushing her invalid grandma in her wheelchair. First they checked the ticket counters. They needed to purchase tickets for Flight 6598, leaving Miami tomorrow afternoon at 2:05 P.M. That flight was headed to Los Angeles and was non-stop. The tickets would give them access to the gate area. They had no intention of actually going anywhere except back home, but in this business one never knew what would happen next.

"Sir, is the flight full? We were hoping for first class seats," asked Mikki. "With my Grandmother in a wheelchair, she needs to have a roomy seat, and close to the bathrooms if possible." Mikki felt the not-so-gentle jab of Emily's elbow into her hip.

"The flight's nearly full, but I'll see what we can do. We could put you in the front row coach? That has extra room for your legs and is close to the restrooms, too," the counter attendant answered, smiling at Mikki knowingly. The sign behind him read, "USA Skyway Aims to Please." It was a new airline trying to fill big planes with luxury service and extras at no charge to passengers.

"That's fine. Thank you," said Mikki, rubbing her hip and giving Gran the evil eye.

Emily now sat quietly, watching and looking at her surroundings from the wheelchair, a crocheted robe hanging over her lap. Mikki took the tickets and pushed Emily away towards the atrium hub of the airport. Busy passengers with their own agendas paid no attention to the two as they weaved in and out of people, heading toward the section of trams, gate entrances, and the shops. After looking around, they chose the Runway Grille for dinner and ordered a bottle of Pino Grigio, garden salads, and the special, Chicken Scampi. They ate, talked, and observed everyone and everything. As they sipped their wine, they discussed the message again and again and its many possible meanings. They had to get this one right.

Someone was smart and desperate enough to search the Internet to find and contact ExtremeFavors.com. This was Emily's and now also Mikki's, difficult to find and impossible to trace, web site. At home their message notification system via a flashing and beeping pink light was set up to look like a smoke alarm in the office at the Pink Flamingo. Their web site could only be found by diligent searching on the Internet. Maybe someone with enough hopelessness and misery to look for keyword phrases like "Need Justice?" or "Hopeless Situation?" or "Life Unfair?" Sometimes someone errantly asked about party favors, looking for wild and crazy wedding, birthday, or bridal shower specialties. They were automatically transferred to the FAVORS.com link for the gift and party shop web site. The exclusive Palm Beach store, Favors, had been Emily's retirement business venture for many years. Its innocuous setting had also served as a base for the lucrative and much more adventurous enterprise of actually *doing* favors. Favors done for money, lots of money, and also the pure pleasure of fixing something that was unfair or going wrong. Both would admit that doing risky favors was exciting, but the favors requested were not always the favors that would be done. Mikki had learned, for instance, that sometimes an errant wife wanted her rich husband knocked off so she could pilfer his finances. Those types of messages were handled discreetly and anonymously via FBI or police notification. The women would do many kinds of clandestine favors, even fatal favors, but they had their standards. It wasn't as if they had no moral values, but rather that they weren't standard issue ethics. The women could be classified as pit bulls with PMS by someone who had the misfortune of becoming the object of one of their obsessions. There were rules...their rules.

After receiving a message, in most cases there was a way to contact the sender and follow-up was done via obscure disposable cell phones. But this time they had determined that the email message came from a library computer with no reply or trace possible. Why hadn't the sender just emailed or called the police anonymously? Was the writer actually part of a planned attack? Were they worried about being caught by authorities? Perhaps they just didn't trust police to get it right. Mikki and Emily were not in the anti-terrorist business, but they were always on the side of fair and certain justice.

This time the message was, "Cannot speak to you. No phone. Watched 24/7. 100% serious. Miami Flight 6598 Monday. No police. Discretion. Help. Baby. Bomb."

CHAPTER EIGHT

The next morning the women awoke at 6:00 A.M., dressed, rechecked the news channels, and read the *USA Today* that was outside their hotel room door. After coffee and a double check on their equipment, they again made their way to the inner corridors of the airport. They easily found their way to the terminal that housed the gate for their flight. A calm facade belied inner anxiety as they approached the security checkpoint.

"G' mornin', ladies. Do you realize your flight isn't leaving for another six hours?" asked a security guard as he checked their passports and boarding passes.

"My grandmother insists on being early for everything," replied Mikki, winking at the man. "I'm just going along for the ride, sir."

"I know what you mean. My parents are the same way. Really afraid of missing their plane, their bus, their 'ticket to ride,'" continued the guard, bobbing his head in understanding. "Oh well, there's lots of coffee shops—Starbuck's and all that—very close to your gate. Pretty good muffins, too, if you like those big meal-sized ones."

Leaning closer to him, Mikki, green eyes dancing, whispered, "Yeah, that's another thing, she really likes to eat, too!"

"I'm not deaf, you know!" announced Emily with a wagging finger aimed at Mikki and the guard. "Let's go. I'm hungry. I hope you're not going to strip search me! You're not, are you? And I'm not standing in front of those cameras that see through your clothes! I'm way too old for your shenanigans! And I haven't had my breakfast!"

"See what I mean? And crabby, too!" said Mikki, with a shrug of her shoulders.

The guard just smiled and handed the documents back to Mikki, saying, "Have a good flight." Mikki pushed Emily through the glass-enclosed air-sniffing booth that scans for contraband of all sorts and then through the metal scanning archway. Both sighed silently and rolled through the security devices with their best and most innocent smiles super-glued on their faces. No alarms went off. Daring to breathe again, they grinned at each other as they headed for Gate Seven, just two more passengers ready to travel.

"Good one, Mikelle, good one. *Crabby?* Take advantage of a little old lady in a wheelchair? Just keep pushing," muttered Emily, as she was rolled along, talking under her breath.

By the time they reached the gate, Emily had cocked her head to one side, pretending to be dozing. Her head rested on her hand, which had just adjusted something in her ear. The device looked just like a large old-fashioned hearing aid, but was actually a two-way radio. For the women to be effective, Emily would need to be in constant communication with Mikki, who wore a Bluetooth wireless connection over her ear. As her granddaughter adjusted the knit afghan over her lap, Emily also discreetly placed a small video monitor into the folds of the lap blanket. The camera could be adjusted by the smallest movement of her finger to give Emily a perfect view of everything around her, all without the slightest movement of her head. With another touch on the back of the camera case Emily could raise the volume of her listening device, and with a twist she could decide which spyware gadget to use for observation. After apparently seeing to her grandmother's comfort, Mikki stood and began to walk around the gate area. She would begin placing the four wireless sound bugs in appropriate areas. They must not only watch, but also listen. She checked the clock near the check-in desk. 8:30 A.M. At least their informant had given them the date and time, but who was it and how were they involved? If the women had guessed correctly, the bad guy would have already done his homework. He wouldn't arrive at the gate until close to departure time. Less time to draw attention to himself. They knew he already had a plan, and because of that he was many steps ahead of them.

After placing the sound mikes and assuring that they were in working order, Mikki needed to walk to the restroom, more of a reconnaissance mission than potty break. She carefully went to every stall, taking her time and looking around when no one was there. She found nothing unusual in the toilet facilities and she left one of the bugs under a sink. Mikki exited the restroom area and decided on two caramel lattes with whipped cream at Starbuck's. She took the long way back to a seat next to Emily's wheelchair. Emily had aligned her chair to face the incoming people traffic from the corridor. Waiting passengers in adjoining seats were now getting up to board a plane to San Juan and most were Hispanic teens, maybe on summer break from school, going to visit relatives in Puerto Rico. They were all laughing, shoving and pushing each other, and were oblivious to anything but having a good time.

A new group of passengers was trickling in to the gate area and the departure sign had been changed to read "Chicago, Departure 10:35, On Time." A blond female desk attendant saw the two women and approached.

"Hello! Which flight are you on? Going to Chicago? We can make sure you get advance boarding with the wheelchair, ma'am."

Mikki shook her head, "Thanks, but we're going to Los Angeles. The 2:05 flight, Number 6598? I know we're early."

"Oh wow, you're really early! If you need help with anything, we'll sure try to oblige, though," said the blonde.

"Nope, we're fine, just early," said Mikki and standing behind her grandmother, rolled her eyes and pointed an accusing finger down towards Emily's head.

The woman smiled with comprehension and kindly said, "There's only a sandwich being served on the non-stop, so you might want to get some lunch later before you board. That flight won't start boarding until...hmmm... maybe 1:30 or so."

"We'll certainly do that. Thank you so much for your helpfulness," answered Mikki as she watched the woman turn and head back to the desk where a line was forming. "Hear that, Gran, everyone is concerned that you won't get enough to eat."

"You did get me a strawberry Danish, didn't you?" said an uncharacteristically feeble little voice from the wheelchair. Emily was really good at playing her part.

Mikelle gave the chair a little shake and said, "Sure, later," but her voice faded away as something caught her attention. A man.

"What is it?" whispered Emily, head still down towards her lap and using the camera to scan the crowd.

"Not sure. I'm going to sit down beside you for a minute." Mikki began digging in her purse and pulled out a paperback and her glasses. The eyeglasses had prism lenses that enabled the wearer to position face down but still see what was in front of her. Now both Mikki and her grandmother were facing books in their laps but actually looking up and around them, thanks to the glory of technology. She watched as the man with dark wavy hair and a creamy tan complexion leaned against a pillar, stuck his hands into his pockets, and began to scan the seating area. There was a ticket or boarding pass stuck in the pocket of his navy sport coat. He wore a white polo shirt with an open collar and some sort of silver chain at his neck. Tan khakis. Very attractive. Very... Mikelle noted, as she took a deep breath. Her pupils widened as her brain soaked up his image, everything about him. He was alone, but looking for something or someone. Mikki looked away but felt his searching glance briefly pass and then come back to her. She met his gaze, but not noticeably, head still bent towards the historical romance novel in her hands. He stared at Mikki and then at Emily, and glanced at his watch. He appraised the women again, and tucking a newspaper under his arm, walked away towards the bar.

All at once, Mikki realized she'd been holding her breath. She adjusted her ponytail and straightened her tank top reflexively. *Well, that guy certainly got my attention.*

"Gran, what do you think? What was that about?" Mikki exhaled.

"Not sure. Try to cool off!" whispered Emily. She had also been watching. "I could feel the heat and it wasn't this damned afghan, either! Keep focused. This isn't like you! You want to get everyone killed? Of all the times to finally decide you want a boyfriend."

"Gran, just because he's attractive, doesn't mean I can't be objective. God, I hope he's not some stupid, depraved, lunatic bomber. Should I follow him?"

"Hell, no! Think! He's obviously Mid-Eastern descent. Maybe Saudi or ...well, I'm not sure. He noticed us--or you--but why, is the question. Mikki, you have to learn. There are many pieces of the puzzle. Just because one falls off the table, you don't jump off the chair like a maniac, tipping the table over to find it. Just quietly put more pieces together, and when you need that piece, it'll still be there for you."

"Yeah, if the cat doesn't find it and eat it first. God, he was so gorgeous. But you're right. I'm focused. You know me; I just don't get that excited about men in general. It's just that once in a great while, one does make me want to grab his ass."

"Oh, shit."

"I'm cool, really, Gran. I'm just rattling your cage. I'm all business now."

The two continued to observe the area for another couple of hours as passengers arrived and departed their respective planes. At noon, Mikki helped Granny Em to the bathroom via wheelchair. They chose the companion restroom as it afforded more privacy and more space. Once there, Emily disassembled her cane, refitting it with a double-action taser in the detachable tip. After she unscrewed the curved handle of the cane, she twisted open a compartment in the lead-lined right arm of her wheelchair to pull out her hidden ammunition. She checked the trigger mechanism hidden in the handle of her cane and loaded four 45-caliber rounds into the makeshift barrel. Mikki helped Emily put the innocent-looking cane back together and placed it on her lap. Locked and loaded on both ends. Emily deftly lifted the left arm of the wheelchair and revealed the other lead-lined compartment. The five-milliliter glass vials were still lined up and perfectly packed into the lining like fluid-filled little soldiers. Emily picked four volunteers and stuffed them into her lunch bag cooler. She placed the cooler onto her lap with the cane.

"No one had better mess with my cheeseburger or they're done for!" said Emily hoarsely to Mikki, with her best bad-guy sneer. "One finger on my French fries and I blow them away!"

"I know you well enough to guess that isn't even a joke. Are you ready?" said Mikki, checking her own travel bag for essentials.

"Good to go," said Emily as she hopped back into the wheelchair, pulling the lap robe back over her legs. She was feeling younger and more energized by the hour.

CHAPTER NINE

This time, after leaving the restroom, the women chose seats near the window at the outer edge of the seating area. This afforded a full view of the plane, the expandable gateway, and the gate seating area. Mikki could also see into the corridor and could watch the incoming human traffic as people approached the gates and looked for their correct boarding area. It was noon and time for their triage and assessment to begin. No one would be above suspicion.

A family of five had settled near Mikki and Emily. Three children, all within the age of forgiveness, were running around the seats yelling and chasing each other. The father talked on a cell phone while the mother made timid, apologetic attempts to get them to settle down. She finally pulled out some Cheerios, a bag of puzzles, two fire trucks, and a Minnie Mouse doll. Then Mom opened a cooler with kid-sized juices, inserted straws into them, and halted the screaming masses. They sat on the floor and were still for several minutes. *No. This was just family time,* thought Mikki, as she looked at Emily who was penciling a "no" on the edge of her *Miami Herald* crossword page. They had agreed in their assessment that this family was not their list of potential suspects.

An older couple, followed closely by a man about thirty years old, approached the desk. The man, apparently the couple's son, had Down's syndrome and was looking around the seating area as something caught his attention. His eyes settled on the snacking children and he pulled on the elderly woman's sleeve, pointing in the direction of the toddlers. His mother gave him a Snickers bar and he busied himself unwrapping the candy. *No. They wouldn't make sense as bomb-wielding terrorists.*

Two African American men who wore their baggy pants in the rap, mobster style were talking and nudging each other as a young, black woman walked by wearing two navel rings and semi-circles of earrings. Her pants were so low cut that soon there would be nothing left to the imagination. Her tight, stretchy top ended just below her braless breasts, revealing a slim, but muscular midriff. *No. This bunch had other things on their minds.*

Rows of summer college students arrived from another gate, dropped their backpacks in front of their seats and promptly began pulling out cell phones, sitting or walking while they talked. All were in various stages of tan or sunburn and wore T-shirts touting Cancun and Cozumel bars, and the Xcaret Nature Park as places to "do it naked." *No. These kids were having too much fun enjoying their lives.*

Mikki saw that her grandmother was taking notes on the edge of her crossword. Mikki steeled herself to see more, watch more. What was she missing that Emily was writing down?

Mikki's neck hairs stiffened and prickled. A group of five bearded men dressed in business suits, ties, and turbans approached the gate. They all carried briefcases and appeared anxious. They kept looking at their watches and hyper-talking among themselves. Emily saw them too and tuned to the listening monitor near them on the back of a tall trashcan. She turned the channel to also broadcast to Mikki's left earring, so they could hear the conversations simultaneously. Mikki had learned several foreign languages in her post grad studies after engineering school. Emily also knew some languages, but was rusty, and her specialty had been European countries. Now Mikki wrote a questioning "No?" on the edge of her paperback novel so Emily could see it. It was Mikki's turn to analyze further. *Doubtful... not sure. The men seem highly concerned about their return trip to Pakistan being late. But most concern revolves around their proposal for a two-story mall in the tourist district at home. It had not gone well with their American investor group. We won't write them off, however. Now is not the time to worry about "profiling" and civil rights.*

Three women arrived from customs pulling stuffed carry-ons and wearing visors from "Glory of the Seas." They were excitedly talking to each other about the jewelry stores discovered on Grand Cayman Island. The three looked like they had enjoyed every buffet and every dessert offered on their cruise ship. They were returning to Ohio and much less pleasant weather ahead. Three summer tornadoes had been reported in the last two days in the Dayton area. *No. Ohio weather, as bad as it can be, is not a reason to kill off your fellow passengers. Besides, the worrisome flight #6598 was going to California.*

Emily was the first to see him this time, then Mikki felt his presence and looked up. *He* was back and his eyes were scanning the crowd of Los Angeles-bound travelers. He was fantastically tall, dark, and handsome. But now there was an aura of danger…or perhaps guarded caution, and he was definitely looking for something… or someone.

CHAPTER TEN

Mikki kept an eye on the suspicious man, but as the boarding time for Flight 6598 edged closer, she watched everyone with equal concern, fidgeting in her chair. *Time is running out and who am I looking for anyway? Is it this man?* Mikki checked her atomic watch again and felt her palms grow moist with concern. Was the call a prank? She doubted that, but where was the bad guy?

Then a family of three with a small infant arrived and sat near the boarding ramp door. They would board early as per usual airline protocol. Two other men arrived with them and seated themselves close by. They all looked to be Mid-Eastern, like the man seen earlier. Were they the answer to Mikki's question? They seemed nervously wary and kept glancing around at the crowd while avoiding eye contact with anyone. Mikki discreetly nudged Emily, but she was watching a group of couples. They had lots of luggage they wanted to carry onto the plane, but the luggage was being tagged at the gate to go into the cargo hold. They were not happy campers.

Emily had been wondering if all these bags had been scanned and searched. Tennis racquets? Golf club bags? How did all this get through the security line? The women simultaneously glanced at each other's faces, eyebrows raised in quiet question.

Mikki's elbow nudged Emily again as she got ready to move. She switched to her necklace mike as she rose to circle the mass of people. The handsome man had moved to a hidden area behind a pillar and was intently watching someone. Mikki picked up her newspaper and handbag and circled around behind him. She followed the direction of his gaze and her eyes fell on the couple with the baby. He was definitely interested in them. The baby's mother had a short and stylish haircut; black hair in spiky tousles framed her small pixie-like face. She wore big red earrings, and a red and orange gauzy tunic over white Capri's. Red Gucci sandals completed her outfit. She looked brand-new, coming right from Saks to the terminal. Mikki recognized designer when she saw it. The mother sat quietly in a chair, silently staring at the baby carrier at her feet. The woman's husband was clean-shaven, and wore an open-necked white cotton shirt, crisp and freshly ironed. Navy pleated slacks, navy socks, and black casual but expensive loafers gave him a well-scrubbed look. He sat beside his wife, his dark eyes were mechanically scanning the area. The infant was wrapped in a large pink blanket. *At last, here was a baby, in fact, the only baby in this gate area! What would a baby have to do with a terrorist attack?* Mikki walked toward them, trying to *feel* something that could help her. Their nationality and the baby were her only clues. She felt something odd and unpleasant when she got closer. *Why was the man by the pillar watching them? Did he know them? Was he part of an evil plan?*

"What should I do, Gran?" asked Mikki, speaking softly into her mike, as she sauntered slowly towards the couple with the baby. The two men were seated close to the family, but were not speaking to them. Both of them had extended their legs into the narrow aisle, leaning back into their chairs. *Were they trying to form some sort of barricade?*

"Something's funny about this. Check the woman's earrings," ordered Emily from the wheelchair, as she began to push herself along the carpet, also trying to get closer to the family, excusing herself along the way.

"Huh? Oh. Will do," said Mikki, as she lowered her chin toward the pendant of her necklace to speak. Stepping over the men's legs and staring hard at their faces as she went, Mikki headed right for the baby. *It did say 'baby' in the message...whatever that meant.*

One of the men quickly raised his right leg as Mikki stepped across. Mikki had expected about anything and was prepared. She stumbled dramatically and aimed herself right towards the infant's carrier that was near the woman's feet.

The young woman gasped as she saw Mikki falling and pulled the infant seat up towards her lap.

"Oh! So sorry!" said Mikki, as she landed on hands and knees exactly where she had planned. She didn't even bother to send any visual death wishes back to the man who had unwittingly sent her to her planned destination.

"I'm fine. A baby? Oh, can I see her?" asked Mikki, now kneeling, as she reached for the edge of the blanket covering the baby's face. "I just love babies!" gushed Mikki, reaching for the infant.

The woman's caramel Mid-Eastern complexion turned pale as she quickly grabbed up the infant from the carrier and handed the baby to the father now seated beside her.

"No, no! She is sick; you can't touch her. Please. Very sick!" exclaimed the mother, her voice squeaky and high pitched. Her English was pretty good, Mikki noted, probably has lived in the U.S. for quite a while.

In that same instant, Mikki saw the clip-on earrings and then the bruising around her eyes that was covered by thick make-up. The wide dark eyes would have been beautiful, but the lids were swollen, the right sclera pink. During the movement of her lips, those few words spoken, Mikki saw her broken tooth and heard the underlying sound of terror. This trembling woman had been beaten. Domestic violence. Mikki had seen the signs before.

"Sorry, I didn't mean to upset you or bother the baby. I hope she'll be all right," said Mikki as she rose to stand in front of the woman.

"No problem. The child has had surgery. We are taking the baby to a hospital in California, you see," interjected the husband quickly, as he handed the infant back to her mother and stood up. Tall and towering over Mikki, he continued, "We're hoping she'll be fine soon. Thank you for your concern, though."

Mikki walked further along the seating row and sat down. She unfolded her newspaper in front of her and whispered into the necklace, "Clip-ons. Nobody wears those anymore. Didn't want me to see the baby. She's been hit on for sure. He's newly shaved, has a few razor nicks and tiny blood marks on his collar. Probably had a beard a day or two ago. But listen to this. When she yanked the kid out of the carrier? There was a spot of blood on the bottom quilt, about fifty-cent-sized. Maybe the baby did have some surgery, but something's up with them for sure."

Emily didn't answer at first. "Check your PDA. Look at all the latest news. Stay there. I've got the potted plant on now." The large plant had a listening bug attached underneath one of the big leafy palm-like branches. "Your man has been watching all of this and pacing like a caged leopard, like he's not sure what to do. He's pulled something from his pocket. I thought his cell phone was ringing, but it doesn't look like a phone, although it looks like he's trying to get a signal or something. I'm sure he's connected to them somehow and so are the two dudes with the big feet. I'm listening to mike number four right now. I'll go there."

Emily got out of the wheelchair, took her cane and began to walk, merely an old lady adjusting her hearing aids as she slowly wound her way through the crowd. She was soon standing right behind the man by the pillar. He didn't seem to notice her. Now Emily could see what he saw and hear what he heard. Suddenly, for no apparent reason, the man was checking the plant's leaves! *What the hell? Now was not the time for Botany 101...crap, he's found the mike!* Emily watched in stunned silence as the man stared at the tiny round audio device.

The man had a half-ass smile on his face as he reached under the leaf and peeled the sticky wireless mike from its hiding place. He looked at it and turned to stare at Mikki in her chair, and then put the tiny instrument in his shirt pocket. Emily crept away, unnoticed.

Suddenly the mother put the baby back into the carrier and began to stand up. Her husband's arm was just as quick. His hand reached out and snatched her elbow, pulling her down roughly. Smiling maliciously through clenched teeth, he whispered coarsely in Arabic, "Sit down. Where do you think you're going?"

The woman had become empowered by the closeness of the many people around her and announced loudly in English, "I must change her diaper right away," as she pointed quickly and judiciously, directing her husband's glare to the red spot in the carrier. She covered it with a small towel and replaced the infant. "I'll be right back."

The father pulled back in surprise when he saw the blood on the blanket and reluctantly nodded permission. He and the two other men intently watched the mother walk away toward the restroom, carrying the baby. Mikki almost missed seeing them leave. She was reading something on her PDA and her eyes grew wide as she caught her breath reflexively.

She engaged Emily's attention as casually as possible, then got up and began to work her way back around the crowd toward the restroom. Emily smoothly moved towards the anxious father. As Mikki slipped through the restroom entrance, Emily saw the young man by the pillar turn to follow the women towards the bathroom. Emily had come to the realization that the man had been holding a bug scanning security device. *What was he doing with that? He was definitely part of whatever was going on today.* She tried to warn Mikki, now in the restroom, but she was getting no response except static from her audio equipment. She had heard Mikki say something about two news reports and that something now made sense. Emily hobbled on her cane until she was directly behind the group of men, now all huddled together, whispering, and nervously looking toward the ladies' room. They murmured quickly in Arabic and Emily could understand nothing. Their faces were grim and tense. That much she could understand.

"I'm here to help you," said Mikki, coming from behind the young Arab woman and pulling on her elbow to bring her face-to-face in the diaper changing area of the restroom.

"You can do nothing for me," replied the young mother dismissively, confused at first and then clearly afraid.

"You wrote to us...we do the favors. It was you, right?" demanded Mikki, green eyes now flashing bright and urgent.

The girl suddenly placed the baby carrier on the floor and fell prostrate to her knees beside it. She began sobbing hysterically into her hands. "You! You are just a girl like me. You can do nothing! You don't know what they are capable of! Oh no, no, no…"

An announcement was being made to prepare for the advance boarding for Flight # 6598 to Los Angeles. The girl continued to wail uselessly on the floor.

"Where is the bomb? What's the bomb you're talking about? Let me help! You don't want people to die. I know you don't," demanded Mikki, pulling and forcing the girl to her feet.

"The baby is dead. Sajid and the others don't know it yet. They have killed the child."

"What are you talking about? What's your name? Let me see the baby!" Mikki insisted, wishing Emily was here right now. She grabbed the infant carrier from the floor, placing it on the diaper-changing table. Mikki pulled back the pink blanket. The young mother shrieked and covered her face with her hands. Luckily the sounds of the airport covered most of her persistent lamentation.

Mikki withdrew reflexively when she saw the baby. The infant's face was bluish, with some reddish mottling on her cheeks and hands. The mouth was open and whitish with foamy drool remaining in the corners. Recovering, Mikki felt for a brachial pulse, like she had learned from her sister, Brigetta, a pediatric nurse. There was no heartbeat and the skin was cold. The baby's eyes were wide-open, pale blue eyes. Something else looked strange about the baby. Her spine was twisted and her head seemed out of symmetry. This was not this woman's child. She had light brown hair, fair skin, and blue eyes. Mikki flipped the baby's body over and yanked off the bloodstained, yellow dress. A huge wound with crude sutures was present below the ribs, encircling almost the entire body. This was so sick that Mikki had trouble organizing her thoughts. A wave of nausea gripped her stomach.

"Who did this? Is this the bomb? You put an undetectable bomb inside a baby? Can I get it out?" asked Mikki, sticky moisture forming on her brow and in her armpits, her hands shaking almost as badly as the girl's. Just then two chatting and oblivious elderly ladies came into the doorway. Seeing Mikki's warning look, they turned away, toward the other toilet stall area. Mikki didn't care to have an audience. Another woman entered, fingers fumbling in her purse. She looked up and stared at Mikki and the mother. She jerked to a stop, eyes wide, as she saw the dead baby. Just as she turned in horror to run for help, Mikki's arm reached out and grabbed her before the woman knew what had happened. Mikki, in a practiced motion, unsnapped the cell phone holder on her waist, pulled the contents loose, and tasered the innocent woman into unconsciousness before she could speak or scream. The woman dropped like a puppet with slashed strings and lay on the floor in a heap of spasms. The young mother recoiled from the violence and velocity of Mikki's attack on the innocent woman and quickly blurted out, "My name is Kamila. Dr. Numair Al Thani. He did this. And no, it's all sewn in. You can't get it out. We came to Miami so this doctor friend of my husband's could do it. If you tamper with it, it goes off. Sajid has the trigger. It's a remote on his key ring."

Mikki stared hard at the girl and circled her hand with increasing tempo, imploring her to continue quickly. "It looks like his car keys with a door opener attached," Kamila stammered, wringing her hands and shaking all over.

"Shit," said Mikki, putting the dead baby back on the diaper changing counter and digging wildly in her purse.

"If I don't come right back, Sajid will detonate the trigger," cried Kamila, her hands squeezing the sides of her head and staring at the little body. "I don't think it matters that much to him if we actually get on the plane. He just wants to kill Americans. His family doesn't matter either...he doesn't care about anyone!"

Mikki was furiously throwing things out of her purse and finally found her screwdriver. She attacked the paper towel holder on the wall like the berserk crazy person that she had instantly become. Stepping over the tasered woman still jerking and trembling on the floor, she cracked open the plastic case as quietly as possible and pulled out the roll of towels.

"Here, wrap this in the blanket. Keep it covered, just like before. Try to act calm and hurry back to the men. There are four of them, right?"

"Four? No, only three. My husband, Sajid, Hassad and Mohammed," replied Kamila, looking confused, but trying to regain her composure and wiping her face on a paper towel.

"Then who is the young guy, the one who has been watching from the hallway?" asked Mikki as she wrapped the dead baby in one of the blankets from Kamila's diaper bag.

"I don't know who you mean! Really! I didn't see anyone else!" wailed Kamila as she frantically placed the blanket-wrapped roll of paper towels into the carrier. The women jumped in unison when they were startled by a man's loud voice right outside the restroom.

"Kamila! Get out here! We will miss our plane!" demanded Sajid, angry, but not quite daring enough to enter the forbidden female space.

"Coming, husband!" answered Kamila, rushing to arrange the blanket to look like it held the baby. "What do I do next?" she whispered to Mikki.

"I've got to get the bomb out of here. Someone will try to help you soon. Just be calm," said Mikki quietly. She held her breath as she waited for Kamila to leave the room. After the girl had left, Mikki checked the groaning woman on the floor and walked quickly away from the bathroom, carrying her bundle. She heard some static and with her free hand, tried to raise the pendant hanging below her neck directly to her lips. This message had to get through.

CHAPTER ELEVEN

"Gran! Can you hear me?" panted Mikki, as she ran down the corridor with the bomb, looking for a stairwell or anything that was mostly devoid of people. Each gate area was equipped with a dumbwaiter cargo carrier. If the stainless steel door could be slid open, she could drop the bomb inside and push the button to send it down to the concrete. Then what? If it went off there, the terminal and luggage area would still be damaged and lives lost...maybe even a plane waiting to disembark. She jogged past a glass-fronted caged smoking area. There was a balcony and the outer walls were just bars and wire, otherwise open to the air. As a last resort she could evacuate the smokers and toss the package out there. Still the glass would blow everywhere and the terminal walls would be compromised. Well, that would be a crude no-smoking reminder to all involved. Her brain was getting short on oxygen, not from running, but from the exertion of thinking. There was the threat of instant annihilation in the form of a bomb cradled by her arm and any second now Kamila's husband would realize there was no longer any baby in the carrier...no baby bomb. As she ran, she saw everything. Mikki hoped the huge windows of the terminal were shatter resistant. *Keep moving. Stay away from people. If I die, I'll never see Cajun Clown again! What a crazy pre-death thought! I'll never see my horse again? What about my family? Run, keep looking, and get rid of the bomb quickly!* When Sajid peels back the blanket and sees his newborn roll of paper towels, he'll push the remote and the gruesome bomb will incinerate much of this part of the terminal, taking many other lives in addition to Mikelle Walsh, she thought as she ran.

"Got you! Where are you!" answered Emily, as a crackling sound was heard in Mikki's ear as she ran.

"Running with the bomb! I've got it! Keep those guys distracted and don't let them get away. Don't let them see...,"

Mikki had to catch her breath, "the baby. It's not a baby now. It's paper towels. Just do it, Gran!"

"I understand. Be careful. Dump it quickly! Save yourself!"

"It's a remote, so watch for him to start handling keys or something like that!"

"I'm there. I'm on it! Just be careful!"

Mikki ran full tilt, stopping here and there at doors leading to the outside, only to find them locked. Finally she saw a door that said "Emergency Exit." The instructions on the lock bar read, "Push Until Alarm Rings—Door Will Open In 15 Seconds." Mikki pushed. A loud ringing bell jolted the senses of everyone in the area. She kept pushing. Someone was running towards her. Maybe someone could help. Maybe airport personnel!

Oh no, it's him! The mystery man had seen her run from the restroom and was following, running easily to catch up. A security guard had heard the commotion and was holding a mobile radio to his ear. Mikki didn't need more people added to the mix. But if she yelled "bomb," she would probably be shot or something and there would be a major stampede. The man was getting close. All her workouts for nothing? And all that jogging? *Please open now*, she begged the door. *What bigger emergency could there be, for God's sake?* The alarm seemed to grow louder, but the door remained a solidly locked barrier.

The handsome Mid-Eastern man, now also breathless, had slid to a stop in front of her. She karate-kicked him hard in the thigh and twirled to kick at his spine and kidney. But he was fast and grabbed her leg during the second spin, and puffed at her, "Hold on! I can help!"

"Get away unless you want to become a million little pieces," she screamed as she wrenched her knee loose from his grasp. He didn't grab again but jammed his hand into his pocket and pulled out keys!

The remote! He's got it and he's going to blow us all up right here! thought Mikki, as she set down her parcel and started to run. He caught her wrist so fast and hard, she fell into a sitting position in front of the door, legs sprawling.

"Help me instead of being so wild and crazy!" he shouted at her over the blaring alarm.

Then she realized he was inserting keys into the door lock. She stood, scooping up the morbid bomb, and helped him by turning the handle as he inserted each test key, one by one. Finally the latch twisted open and while pushing, they fell through the doorway together. The stairs led down and they ran in tandem. He grabbed the wrapped bundle from her and smashed his body against the last emergency door that led to a luggage area leading outside. As Mikki watched from the doorway, he jumped aboard a four-wheeler hooked to an empty luggage cart and pushed the accelerator pedal to the floor. He was heading for the runway and open ground. Racing past a slowly taxiing Air Tran airliner, he careened off the concrete into a grassy opening between runways. Mikki watched, still breathless and still in the panic mode, as he carefully placed the deceased baby containing the deadly weapon on the grass of the open field. Jumping back into the vehicle, he almost drove under the wheels of a Boeing 737, whose surprised pilot was forced to make a sudden turn and begin braking. Security was now everywhere and the mystery man jumped from his hijacked ride and ran toward the chain link fences nearby. He was yelling, "It's a bomb!" to the men following him. Fleeing like a lizard pursued by birds, he climbed the wire fence, agilely flipped himself over the top, and was gone. Mikki, panting for breath, felt this was a good time to ease back into the crowd that had gathered. She climbed back up the stairs and pulled the emergency door shut behind her. The noise of the alarm had stopped but the crowd noise was louder. She tried to calm herself, wiping her forehead with the back of her hand. Some in the crowd stared at her as she strode quickly but determinedly back towards Gate Seven. Behind her she heard and felt the shiver of a huge explosion on the tarmac. The big viewing windows were shaking from the blast's shock waves. People stopped watching her and ran to the glassed-in waiting area to see what had happened. Mikki kept walking, feeling queasy.

CHAPTER TWELVE

When Mikki arrived back at the gate, she was preparing mentally for what she would find. Kamila and Sajid were gone, but paramedics were there. What had happened while she was running with the bomb? She searched visually for her grandmother, trying to quell her fear and nausea. Emergency Medical Technicians were wheeling the woman from the bathroom floor away on a gurney. Mikki ducked away from them and merged into the crowd. Was Granny Em okay? People with worried faces were milling around asking questions. The two men who had been with Kamila and Sajid were writhing on the ground, moaning. Hassad and Mohammed, Mikki now knew. A familiar elderly lady was walking slowly towards her wheelchair, balancing on her cane, evidently needing a rest from all this excitement. A sigh of relief escaped Mikki's lips. Granny Em was fine.

Two of the women from the cruise were talking animatedly about what they'd seen to a policeman and a cluster of airport security guards. Mikki listened on the perimeter of the crowd as they told the cops their version of what had happened.

"This man went to look for his wife and baby in the restroom and we could hear him yelling. Then they all came back. These two men who had been sitting near them...well, I think they were all together because they all looked like they were Arabs...they turned and started to get up and then suddenly, one right after the other, the men fell to the floor like they'd been shot! But there was no sound!" said the woman with the orange hair excitedly, waving her hands in the direction of the fallen men.

"They writhed around like a pair of snakes, moaning and groaning, and this little old lady, who happened to be standing right behind them, came over and offered them some water from her cooler. At that point they seemed to have recovered somewhat. They were still sitting on the floor and shaking, leaning their backs against the chairs. They each drank her water after they became more 'with it' and that seemed to help a lot," said the one with the peeling sunburn.

"Yeah, soon they got back into their chairs, but they seemed dizzy and forgetful. Then suddenly—it was so strange—they both fell writhing and were right down on the floor again. It was so damned strange! This time though they said they had stomach pain."

Mikki walked towards Emily and took her arm. "You okay, Grandma?" She helped her back into the wheelchair.

"Better take me to the bathroom, honey. All this excitement about made me pee my pants," said Emily in a weary voice.

Once again in the locked private companion area of the restroom, Mikki and Emily began to talk at the same time, each demanding to know what the other had done and seen. They only dared speak in excited whispers. Mikki spoke first, "The bomb was in the baby! They used a real baby as a bomb, Gran. I just can't believe it! The evil! The cruelty!" As Mikki spoke she leaned on the wall and melted down to a squatting position, holding her hands over her eyes. "The little baby was already dead. The mother—well, I don't think it was the mother—was in the diaper-changing area of the restroom. I caught up to her there. Her name is Kamila and she was the one who emailed us. She wasn't expecting me, a woman. Probably wanted Superman or some other comic book hero. I followed her when I saw blood in the baby's carrier and also because I had reread some articles on my PDA. Remember when those dope dealers brought some Labrador Retriever puppies into the country and their vet had surgically implanted packages of cocaine into the dogs' abdomens? Some puppies died and some were sick?"

"Sure, I certainly recall that. Was a few months ago, wasn't it?"

"Yeah. Also, do you remember the other day; a hospital in New York had a weird case of baby snatching? Someone purposely took the wrong baby? Switched a healthy baby girl for a sick baby? They actually took the sick baby instead of their own? So far, no one had figured it out. None of it made sense to anyone. But at the hospital this couple with a terminally ill infant finds a healthy baby girl in their bassinet. Their child is gone and the nurses denied knowing or seeing anything unusual. The dad is a pastor with some local church and the parents first said it was a gift from God or something. The hospital authorities were quick to point out that it doesn't work like that, but haven't found the parents who left with the wrong kid. The hospital knew who they were…Muslims with Arab names, but the couple took off and couldn't be found. Dad owns a popular Arabic restaurant on the west side. The whole family just disappeared. Big apartment, nice car…all left behind. Looked like they left in a hurry, but no signs of where they went. Had some family still in town, but no one was talking. I think this sicko family planned on putting an undetectable bomb on the plane. I think the woman left her own daughter at the hospital because they had originally planned on using this pregnancy to take a family trip to the ultimate Promised Land. At the last minute the mother wimps out, but doesn't mind using someone else's baby as a human explosive. Wouldn't their Allah just be pleased as hell with that set-up? Shit."

"Where'd they come up with this stuff? That's enough to gag a maggot," said Emily, with a wince and a shake of her gray tousled hair. She moved to the wall and sat down beside Mikki on the floor.

"Poor little baby never had a chance. And the mother who took the infant had the crap beaten out of her. Once Daddy Dearest got on to the switch, that changed everything and I'm sure that they had to hightail it outta town before the authorities came a knockin'," said Mikki.

"They seem to have gone ahead with their plan, though. Were you close enough to see the bomb detonate? I was worried when I heard the big boom outside. Thank God you got away from it."

"Oh yeah, it went off. That is so sick, sick, sick," said Mikki, tears now welling and ready to spill. She was still sitting on the floor leaning against the wall and holding her chin with her knees.

"Was anyone hurt?" asked Emily, putting her arm around Mikki's shoulders.

"Well, the poor baby is in a million pieces. I don't know about anyone else," said Mikki haltingly, trying not to start sobbing. "I just can't believe it! I'm so sorry we couldn't have helped the baby."

"I'm sorry, too, sweetie," said Emily, clutching Mikki to her chest and hugging hard. "Go ahead and cry a little, but it's not over. They got away. No one said that terrorists play well with others. I wonder how low they can go after that one. What else happened?"

"That cute guy followed me. I thought he was chasing me and he was, but he was trying to help. Had a whole set of skeleton keys he just whipped out of his pocket and once we got the damned door open, he took the baby and the bomb out to the airfield. I ran off after I saw him get away from security. I don't think he wanted to deal with all the questions. I, myself, would have liked to hear his explanation as to his part in this scheme. I heard the detonation, but I think it was too far away to do too much damage. Did you see the bad guy push the remote button?"

"When the mother came back with the supposed baby, she put her baby carrier right down on the floor near her diaper bag. She looked nervous, but smiled at her husband and took his hand. With her foot, I could see she was pushing the carrier away from him and trying to get him to focus on her. The baby was still covered up. The two men who had started to follow the dad seemed satisfied and went back to their seats. I'm guessing they're brothers, uncles, or just other zealots along for the ride to Kingdom Come. Whole family of damned idiots. I was still standing behind their seats just keeping an eye on them. Dad was scratching his chin as if thinking, and suddenly reached for the baby. The mother, Kamila, pulled the carrier away as she made a little whimper. As the first man in front of me started to rise, I nonchalantly touched my cane to his back through the lumbar opening of the seat. I was glad I had the double-charged taser because the second man made a move to jump up after the first and I got him, too. I'm still pretty fast for an old broad. Those tasers were charged to deliver a super cattle prod jolt. No one knew what had happened...of course! I had my cooler pouch over my shoulder and moved to them as fast as an old lady should be able to move. Offered them water as soon as they quit thrashing about and kept an eye on Mom and Dad. Dad was now up and moving, threw back the blanket and saw a roll of paper towels where a baby had been earlier. He was shocked and way beyond furious. He dragged his wife up by the neck and started walking, digging in his pocket... for maybe the bomb trigger? People in that seating section just sat there with their mouths hanging open...like they were at the movies or something.

"The parents were headed for the restroom and I could only hope you were a faster runner than you were in Junior High. I knew that once he saw the baby bomb was gone and not still in the restroom, he would push the detonator immediately. There was nothing I could do about them from my vantage point. A small curious crowd had encircled the downed men as I poured more water down their throats. I am very helpful in an emergency, you know. Soon paramedics arrived and began checking blood pressures and all that cool stuff you see on TV. Brigetta should have been here to critique. So, anyway, I got up and started hobbling back to my wheelchair. And then you showed up...and I thank God for that."

"Well, Gran, I've had enough. I'm wondering why you graciously gave them water, but I need to reorganize my head. I just can't deal with this any longer."

"Yeah, I think it's time to go. I'll tell you about the water idea and the tracer patch I put on Daddy Dearest later."

Tossing their torn-up plane tickets into the nearest trash receptacle, the two women wound their way back through the frantic crowds and tense security towards their hotel room to gather their belongings. They would do their post-event analysis on the way home. This was not neat and tidy.

There were lots of loose ends and untied ropes to tighten up. Too many unanswered questions. But not right now. This was enough action for two ladies on a Monday afternoon.

CHAPTER THIRTEEN

As the security system recognized the identification device behind the front license plate of Emily's car, the huge black iron gates to the Pink Flamingo swung open. The large pink house seemed to glow as it welcomed them. Its windows glittered with light and the huge glass and mahogany doors glistened with prisms of color from the crystal chandelier hung in the foyer. It was 9:00 P.M. and all the entry lights were on, illuminating the pink marble staircase. Mikki used the remote entry and the garage door below the house began to open.

"Who's here?" asked Emily, turning toward Mikki for the answer, and eyeing an unfamiliar vehicle parked in her garage.

"Oh, that's Brigetta's new car. I bet she came to show it off. With any luck she and Mom are here and have brought some dinner."

"I thought you were too upset to eat," said Emily.

"The stomach calls, I answer," answered Mikki, patting her flat belly.

Mikki drove the pearl-white Jaguar reclaimed from a parking lot near the rental agency into its usual spot in Emily's garage. Mikki went to the trunk. Emily climbed from the passenger's seat and headed toward the new red Mini Cooper convertible parked to the left of Mikki's BMW. She inspected the newcomer all over and even gave a tire a jab with her foot.

"What are you doing, Gran? Thinking of taking it for a ride?" asked Brigetta as she stood watching, arms crossed, and tapping her foot. She had come down the elevator as soon as she heard the gate's alarm buzzing in the kitchen. Brigetta walked first to her Granny and then to Mikki and gave them both hugs.

"Well, actually, I was planning a drive along the coast in that little cutie...but I guess we could all go. Seats four? Pretty damned small car, Brig," answered Emily.

"Right now we're bushed from our little excursion. Another vendor expo. We needed new merchandise for the store and we saw some really cool new items we might order," said Mikki to Brigetta, with a sigh. "We should get some convention discounts, since we signed up for a bunch of stuff."

"You two are always running off somewhere. I feel left out," complained Brigetta, with a toss of her pale blond hair. Mikki's younger sister was tan and had some girlish freckles on her nose. Her long, straight hair was almost white from days in the sun. She wore short shorts and a halter-top that accentuated her tall, lean body. She stood with her hands on her hips, lower lip pouted out like a spoiled child.

"It's dull business," said Emily. "Besides, didn't you spend the weekend playing with the kitties and sitting by the pool? That doesn't sound too tough."

"Yeah, and I asked Ryder to come over last night. Hope you don't mind. We watched some horror flicks until we both got creeped out."

"No, that's fine. He's a nice young man. I had him checked out."

"Gran! You didn't!" squealed Brigetta. "You didn't call Lt. Carlton or anything, did you?"

"No, I didn't call anyone. Didn't even have to get his fingers rolled. No need for fingerprints, I just checked his background on the Internet. Easy for anyone to do."

"Oh, no," moaned Brigetta, shaking her head.

Mikki just laughed. "You should be used to it by now. Granny Em is our second mom, well, more like Big Momma watching from the sky. We never got away with anything. Can't you remember back that far?"

"I guess I'm glad you care enough to worry. It's best though, if we don't tell Ryder about his virtual criminal pat down. He'd be shocked at your lack of trust."

"And by the way…did he go home at a decent hour?" asked Emily, wagging her finger at Brigetta. Mikki just stood there smiling for a second, enjoying her sister's discomfort, then shrugged and walked away.

"Of course. With this family of spies, I know I'll never have sex unless I'm in some foreign country or something. Then my life will be private," answered Brigetta.

As Mikki's head disappeared into the trunk of the Jaguar, Brigetta heard her say from the hollows of the car, "Ya think? Don't count on that!"

The three women grabbed bags and wheeled suitcases and headed for the elevator for the ride to the third floor. Brigetta wondered if there were land mines in the heavy luggage. The door opened again near the pantry of the expansive pink granite and marble kitchen.

Susan was at the sink washing Romaine lettuce and placing it on a paper towel. She called back without turning her head, "Hey, welcome home! Dinner will be served in one hour. Anyone care for a drink? Brigetta, your bartender for this evening, has mixed some fresh Mojitos." She pointed at a glass tray with four tall frosted glasses, each topped with a sprig of mint and a lime wheel.

Mikki went behind her mom and circled her in a huge hug. She held on and squeezed, not wanting to let go. "You don't know how great it is to be back and find you and Brig here." Mikki felt herself starting to tear up, so she quickly added, "Hope you don't mind, but I need a shower…right now!"

As Mikki rushed towards the stairs leading down to her bedroom suite, Susan called after her, "Are you okay, honey?"

Emily stepped to her daughter and also gave her a hug. "She's okay. Just really tired. Long weekend and we didn't get much sleep. Thanks for all this, Susan," said Emily as she gave her a kiss on the cheek. Emily reached for one of the icy cold glasses, took a big swallow, picked up her bags, and headed for her own bedroom which was right next to the kitchen.

After a chatty dinner, the women had some pineapple sherbet on the eastern veranda. Around 11 P.M. Brigetta announced she had early shift at the hospital and had to get home. Susan had just finished clearing off the dessert dishes and went to find her purse. In minutes, the two honked their way down the cobbled driveway with the convertible top down and the Mini's headlights flashing. Brigetta still lived with Susan since her dad had taken the job in New York City. She didn't want to leave her mom alone at night too much, but now both of them had their own busy lives. Since graduation Brigetta had a full-time job at Palm Beach Memorial, working rotating shifts.

As Brigetta drove through the night and seeing her mom dozing, she thought about how she loved the Pediatric Department and felt she could dedicate her life to nursing. She talked to herself about soon getting her own apartment. Mikki wouldn't be staying with Granny Em much longer, would she? Granny Em was almost back to normal since her stroke. She just needed someone there once in a while, to make sure she was all right. And there was Carla, the housekeeper, three times a week. There was Ernest, the groundskeeper, twice a week. And the family called Gran all the time. No need for Mikki to have to stay there, unless she wanted to. She'd already given up her job in Orlando for one in Palm Beach, but Orlando was busier...a better selection of men, more stuff to do, more nightlife. Of course, Mikki's got the horse now, and she really seems to be into that. She spends lots of time at the barn and doesn't even mind getting all sweaty and dirty. And those kickboxing lessons, what was that all about? Mikki was always busy with something. But Granny will soon be back in town at FAVORS full-time, selling her party supplies, decorating for all the big charity events, and getting her life back to the way it used to be. Brigetta realized she wanted her own life, too. A new, more adventurous life, something more exciting, something less predictable. Soon we'll all be a regular family again, thought Brigetta, well, an almost normal family.

CHAPTER FOURTEEN

"Gran, do you ever think we'll be normal? I mean, what happened to ordinary, every day, common normalcy? I used to think I was leading a normal life," pondered Mikki aloud, as she sat alone with Emily on the veranda facing the sea. The moon was full and there was an eerie misty fog hovering over the ocean. With barely a sound, foamy waves lapped at the sandy shore, again and again, like a puppy's excited tongue reaching farther and farther. High tide was struggling to touch the sea grass near the dunes. The women loved to sit outside on the open balcony. They could hear, see, and feel the ocean's presence all at once. They sipped herbal tea from delicate porcelain cups, trimmed with violets and edged with gold. The cups were two of many collected as European souvenirs during Emily's lifetime travels.

Finally Emily placed her teacup onto the banister ledge, folded her hands into her lap and said, "Normal is okay, I guess. Is that what you want?"

"I'm not sure. Today was a reminder of all that lurks out there while normal people just try to live their lives. Maybe normalcy is just complacency."

"Maybe."

"I'm not sorry that I'm with you. Not at all. It's just that today was such a bad day. Things didn't go well."

"Not for the baby, you mean. But, no plane full of people blew up. No airport blew up."

Mikki sighed and sank deeper into the lounge chair, clasping her hands behind her neck and tilting her head to look up at the stars, and said, "Even the heavens are hazy tonight. It's pretty, though. All the misty, foggy stuff...hiding the clarity of the stars. You keep trying to see them, because you know they're there, and sure enough, the night clears, and suddenly you can see the Big Dipper. It was there all the time."

"You know you can do anything you want with your life. You have a great job as a civil engineer. You don't have to make your millions this way. I may even leave you something in my will," said Emily with a wink and a little chuckle.

"Maybe that's it. I'm spoiled. Never had to worry about the money thing."

"I think you need a sort of sabbatical. Take a break. Go draw some bridge and road plans, go gallop that gelding, take a nap. Skip a few martial arts classes. Hide the trophy for the Combat Fighting Championship under your bed for a while. You're a smart cookie. You can figure out your life. And you know, whatever you want to do, I'll totally agree with you. Unless you decide you want to be a transvestite prostitute or something, then we'll have to talk again."

"You are the weirdest grandmother a girl could ask for," said Mikki, reaching for Emily's hand.

"I try my best," said Emily, giving Mikki's hand a little squeeze.

"Okay. Tomorrow I'm going to the office and finish the road project assignment. You know, see if I can add a few more ziggy-zaggys to our toll road system? Then, after work, I'm going to the stable, saddle Clown, ride the hell out of him, give him a bath, a good grooming, and go home and sleep. The perfect day. Maybe I'll stop by the new Thai restaurant and get us some carryout on the way home. How's that sound?"

"Fantastic and wonderful, just like you!"

"You're just saying that because you think I'll bring you two extra spring rolls."

"No, not at all. Shrimp and vegetable, please."

"I give up. Okay, and do you want the Peanut Chicken or just soup?"

"Just soup? Darling, it's me, Granny Em. I want food."

"Got it...the works. Will do. Right now, I'm exhausted. Are you going to bed?"

"In a minute. I've gotta make some calls first."

"Gran?"

"Nothing for you to worry about. Just a couple little phone calls. I promise, no calls to the President, CIA, U.N., or pizza delivery. I'll see you in the morning, unless I sleep in."

"I'm going for a beach run in the morning before I shower. I'll grab breakfast on the way to work, so I'll just have coffee here. If you're up, join me. If not, I'll read the paper and see you tomorrow night. I want to see what they write about the airport incident." Mikki got up, stretched, gave Emily a kiss on the forehead, pulled herself through the sliding glass doors, and was gone.

Emily sat quietly, running her fingers through her short gray hair, curly and limp from the sea air. Almost lost in thought, she was startled by the noise of the slider being pulled open again. Mikki was back.

"Hey, Gran. I just realized I wouldn't be able to sleep until I know why you were giving those terrorist dudes some water from your cooler. I know you're not that nice."

Emily laughed and pointed at the chair. "Sit down, this'll only take a minute, but you might as well be comfy."

Mikki sat on the edge of the lounge chair this time, facing her grandmother. "Ready. I know this'll be good."

"Yep. Well, I didn't want these bad guys to get away, but didn't want to give myself up either. I've survived anonymously all this time and plan to continue. So, anyway, I made some specially prepared Dasani bottles at the airport. Not exactly Dasani water...that was long gone. I refilled the bottles with my own concoction."

"And? The suspense is killing me."

"You have to learn to be more patient. I keep telling you that."

"Okay."

"Have you ever heard of Guinea worms?"

"Guinea hens, but not worms."

"Yeah, not the same. The worms are three-feet-long worms that are found in Africa. They're pretty much gone now. *Dracunculus medinensis,* "God's fiery serpents," Numbers 21: 4-9. But the interesting part is their life cycle.

The worm larvae live in water fleas in pools of infected water, for example, in Nigeria. The natives drink the water and digest the fleas. Digestion releases the larvae into the human's abdominal tissues where they mate. They grow and migrate through the body, mostly to the legs but sometimes to other parts of the body, like eye sockets."

"I'm getting freaked, thinking where this is going."

"Well, get ready to freak out, because about a year later or much less in this case, the worms form blisters, well, ulcers, on the body and then the fun part. The worm starts to come out of the blister...all three feet of him. It's really gross and sometimes the natives would have to coil the emerging worm around a stick to help slowly pull it out. The bonus for these guys will be that the migration of these worms and their emergence is very painful and sometimes takes weeks or months! The worm actually dies and then the human body has to slowly slough it out. In Africa, friends and family might help to milk it out of the ulcer. Here in the U.S, I don't think anyone will help these guys."

Mikki was now making exaggerated gagging sounds, but said, "So cool! These guys in a year will get blisters all over and in the middle of the next Jihad 'Creating World Peace' Convention, these giant worms will begin emerging from their feet, eyes, and hey...how 'bout penis?"

"You could imagine about everywhere and anytime. I used maturing larvae in the water and this should take much less than a year of incubation in the body. Also the number of worm larvae was far more concentrated than would be found in a real pond of water in Africa. So if we can't find these guys before a month or so, the worms will get them for us. They might not die from it, but its got to be painful as the blisters burst and as odd as hell. Wait 'til their buddies see all this happening!"

"Ooh...I can't wait! Maybe they'll think the Prince of Darkness has inhabited them as a reward for all their good deeds."

"Yeah, we can only hope we're there to watch. Mostly the African victims try to end the pain by jumping into cool water. That bursts the blister and begins the release of the worm. Maybe they'll drown. I made sure the men got a super-concentrated solution containing millions of growing larvae. I used our centrifuge in the pink room and only used the concentrated sediment found at the bottom of the test tubes. There should be enough worms growing in those guys that it just might kill them in that concentration. And, in that case, neither one will be open-casket material."

"Well, now I know I'm not normal since the thought of all those worms popping out like cuckoo clock birds will just lull me to sleep tonight. Good-night, Gran."

"Pleasant dreams," said Emily.

CHAPTER FIFTEEN

Mikki awoke early, did her beach run, and drove to work thinking of her respite planned for 5:00 P.M. Actually, Mikki didn't punch a time clock, being a salaried member of the civil engineering firm, Bagen and Ford, but she had some catch-up work to do which would easily fill her day. She planned to finish up the planning job for Florida Department of Transportation before the day was over. After the FLDOT work, she would head for the barns to ride Clown and get her head straight. She had tossed her tote containing her jeans and T-shirt into the trunk of her BMW where the clothes would join her freshly polished riding boots.

At 5:10 P.M. Mikki shot from the back door of the building like an escapee during a prison break. As she power walked, she hoisted her satchel strap over her shoulder and began to pull out her car keys. She smiled as she plopped onto the leather seat, thinking of the kudos from the boss for a job well done. The car cooled quickly as she turned onto the expressway and headed toward the stables. Arriving in less than fifteen minutes, she parked by Clown's barn and then walked toward the rider's lounge to change clothes. She waved at Julianne who was exercising a Thoroughbred in the dressage arena. As she turned the corner to the lounge, she heard Julianne calling to her. When she looked back, the trainer was motioning her to the fence where she had halted the sweating mare she had been riding. Mikki saw a big grin on Julianne's face and wondered what was up. She obviously had something to tell her that just couldn't wait. Maybe she was engaged? Pregnant? Bought a new horse? With Julianne it could be about anything.

"Yesss? You summoned?" said Mikki, eyes scrunched up suspiciously as she ambled toward the fence.

"Is there something you wish to tell me?" asked Julianne.

"Huh?" replied Mikki.

"Don't 'huh'me, Mikelle Walsh. You know what and who I am talking about."

"I do?" Mikki was seriously confused. Did she have anything to tell Julianne? Or anybody? What the hell was her skinny blond friend talking about? She couldn't have known anything about her weekend at the Miami airport.

"The guy. The absolutely gorgeous, drop-dead beautiful guy. Where have you been hiding him? No wonder Erik is sooo over," Julianne talked so fast that Mikki couldn't even understand half of what the obviously deranged girl was saying.

"I don't..." was all that Mikki could sputter.

"Fine friend you are...yep...hiding him. I mean, I don't blame you, but I am one of your best friends, aren't I?"

"Yeah," Mikki said so slowly that her brain felt like it was at a standstill. Then suddenly, she was afraid. "Who and what are you talking about? I'm serious. Who?"

Sitting astride the seventeen-hand horse, Julianne dropped the reins, crossed her arms over her chest and just stared down at Mikki. The silence hung there like paint waiting to dry, the only sound being the mare's labored breathing. Mikki stared back, hands on hips. It was like the standoff at the OK corral or something.

"You really don't know what I'm talking about? If you're lying, I'm going to kill you," threatened Julianne.

"If you don't come forth with the info, I'm going to kill *you!* I mean it, Jules. What are you saying?"

"Okay, don't get your undies in the wringer. There was a guy here looking for you. Asking about you. Really, really, really good-looking. Ring any bells?"

"No."

"Tall, dark, and handsome. Maybe Mid-Eastern, but perfect English, hardly any accent. He said his name was Faris and he was looking for you."

Mikki just stared at her, eyelids fluttering as her brain whirled. She forced her mind to absorb this new knowledge.

She needed time to adjust and think. Finally words formed on her lips.

"His name was Faris?"

"You really don't know him?"

"Maybe."

"Maybe?"

"Explain again what he looked like. He asked for me by name? Maybe I met him somewhere."

"Okay, well, maybe I shouldn't have said anything. You seem upset. Is he some sort of stalker or something? But I figured if he knew about the barn and your horse being here, that you gave him the information. And yes, he asked for you. He said 'Mikelle Walsh'."

"My horse? Say again what he looked like, please. I'm not upset, just trying to figure out who he is for sure."

"Like I said, very good looking. Arab, Egyptian? Very good manners and good English. Probably American born and bred or at least educated here. Not someone you would forget once you met him, would be my reaction."

"That's got to be him. I never knew his name. Faris." Mikki let the name roll slowly off her tongue.

"Okay. I've done my duty," said Julianne, picking up the braided leather reins with her gloved hands. "I've got to finish working this horse. Seeya later. Oh yeah, by the way, if you don't want him — your new boyfriend? — send him my way."

Julianne winked at Mikki and turned the mare away from the fence, urging her into a ground-covering long trot. Mikki just stood there a minute and then warily glancing around, hurried to the barn to check on Clown. She was breathless and felt like someone had smacked her in the head with this information. *Calm down. Reason this out.*

Her chestnut gelding was in his stall, safe and sound. He nickered a greeting to Mikki as she approached him to rub his neck. She turned away from him and leaned against the stall door. Protectively she surveyed the area that was Clown's world for most of the day. Many of the horses had been turned out. Clown shared his aisle way with Mini Mee and her newborn foal. She nickered a welcome from the stall next to Clown's and then protectively shielded her foal from viewing. Rows of stalls, a tack room door to his right, and a rubber-matted wash rack beside his stall...nothing seemed out of the ordinary. No sign anyone had been here or touched anything. Clown began to nuzzle her hair and neck, his nostrils softly blowing and searching for his treats.

"Okay Clown, I know I can't ignore you any longer," said Mikki as she dug into her tote bag and pulled out a plastic bag of molasses and oat cubes. The horse's ears pricked expectantly when he heard the familiar rustle of the Ziploc baggie. Mikki picked out three or four cubes and placed them on her open palm. The whiskery muzzle poked and prodded her hand until it had vacuumed them up into the waiting mouth. Clown began to crunch them loudly, eyes half-lidded, in obvious pleasure.

"Yes, you're my good boy," said Mikki as she caressed his face and nose in long, pleasurable strokes. She put her head on his big cheekbone and hugged him, arms encircling the big silky neck. "You'll always be my good boy." She kissed the stubble of his still chewing muzzle quickly, picked up her tote, and turned toward the lounge area to change into riding clothes. The horse had calmed her sense of shock and dismay about Mr. Mysterious for the time being. Right now Mikki just wanted to ride her horse on a beautiful summer evening. She would tell Granny Em about the newfound revelation and together they could figure out what this could mean. Granny would know what to do. Experience still counted for a lot.

Mikki changed quickly and as she zipped her jeans and pulled on her boots, she thought she heard a noise outside the locker room door. Instantly on alert, she felt for the small Lady Smith revolver in her purse. She found the sculpted wooden grip and fingered the safety, still listening. Nothing. Now she was beginning to wonder if her nervousness would make her a bad rider and that alone could make this a bad time to exercise her horse. She knew that's how an accident could happen. She didn't want to get hurt or even worse, see her horse become injured by her mistake.

She put the weapon back into the bag and opened the door. Two teenagers were talking as they walked through the barn, heading to the parking lot. They raised their hands to wave at Mikki as they passed the door. Mikki waved back and shrugged to herself. Then she walked toward the tack room, unlocked her storage closet and pulled out her western saddle, Clown's bridle, and saddle pad. As she rolled her aluminum saddle rack down the barn aisle way, the wheels squeaked and jiggled along the way. Definitely time for some WD-40, thought Mikki.

As she rounded the corner, pulling the noisy contraption, Mikki stopped so quickly the rack rolled into her ankle. There she saw the man, Faris, standing at her stall and petting her horse. Touching her horse! Feeding him something! Panic and fear were in competition for her soul as she raced to save Clown.

"Stop! Don't touch my horse! Don't feed that to him!"

"What, he's not allowed to have a chunk of carrot?"

"Let me see it!" Mikki brusquely grabbed the carrot bag from his hand and held it to her nose. It smelled like carrots. Still, she eyed him suspiciously.

"Where'd you come from and how did you know how to find me?" she demanded rudely, holding the carrots in her clenched fist.

"Nice to see you again, too. Believe it or not, I wasn't following you."

"Uh huh. I've heard that one before."

"Really. It may be the first time some guy didn't chase you all over the countryside, but it's true."

"Uh huh," murmured Mikki, with one eyebrow raised and her arms crossed defensively now.

"I saw your travel bag at the airport when I was walking around. The luggage tag was dangling by a thread like it was ready to fall off, so when you went off to the bathroom for the hundredth time, I pulled it off to give it to you. It had the name of this equestrian center embroidered on the back and your name on the tag. Here."

As Faris handed Mikki the lost tag, she realized that she had screwed up. She had forgotten to change the luggage identification tag on her overnight carry-on bag used at the airport. A hot flush came to her cheeks as she realized how much more she had to learn. Faris was now casually leaning against the stall door and Clown was playfully nuzzling his hair. He reached around and began to quietly rub the horse's forehead.

"Thanks. So you've been around horses before?" asked Mikki, trying to divert his attention from the airport situation and back to the present. She began to absently wipe a rag over her saddle as she watched his interaction with her horse. She meekly handed the carrots back to Faris.

"I'll admit I wanted to know who you were, but I was actually equally intrigued by the emblem for the Palm Pines Equestrian Center."

"Oh, really," said Mikki with more than just a hint of doubt. She was used to guys following her around.

"I'm looking for a place to keep my own horse when he arrives from Saudi."

"You own a horse? And this just happened to be the place to bring him, right?"

"I live in this town. Somehow I don't think you believe me."

"Where would you get that idea?"

"Well, it could be that you're always that unwelcoming and unfriendly to the men who risk their lives to save your ass, but somehow I don't think so."

"Maybe it's just that I usually don't need men to save my ass on a regular basis."

"That I believe. You're a little crazy, yes?"

"Yes."

"So. Now that we have that all figured out. I'm Faris," he said as he stuck out his hand to reach for hers. Mikki hesitantly took his hand to shake it, but he smoothly pulled her hand to his mouth and gave it a light kiss before she could even think about resisting. A devilish grin seemed to overtake the man's face and brought out boyish features that the usually cautious Mikki suddenly found irresistible. Terrorist or not, it was her patriotic duty as a woman to find out more about this man.

"Hello, Faris. I'm Mikki."

"So glad you meet you and your horse, too. A Quarter Horse?"

"Yes, and let me guess. You have an Arabian. Right?"

"Not just an Arabian. The Champion Aljazar Prince Shel. He was used for racing as a colt, and then retired to stud and pleasure riding. Now he's mine."

"You bought him?"

"My uncle gave him to me."

"So your uncle is some big-time Arab sheik and he raises horses?" asked Mikki, eyebrows raised in question and hand propped on hips. "Very handy."

"I could tell you all about the stallion...*my* stallion...but I detect an aura of displeasure and disbelief. You are a very suspicious woman. Why is that?"

"Number one, I have lots of questions for you."

"And I have a few for you, Miss Walsh."

The two faced off, each refusing to give in to the staring contest.

Finally Mikki spoke, hoping to disarm him, "Well, you are cute."

"Yes, I am."

"And modest, too, I gather."

"Very."

Mikki was smiling in spite of herself. She just couldn't stop her face from grinning. Mikki dislodged Faris from the front of Clown's stall by flipping open the latch and pushing open the door. Clown waited patiently for his owner to place the halter over his ears and buckle it into place. Mikki led him into the center aisle crossties and secured him there. She didn't know if she was nervous or crazy, but the usually easy job of grooming and saddling her mount suddenly was hard to do with fumbling fingers.

Faris had moved to the other side of her horse and was helping her center the saddle pad. He watched silently as she expertly hoisted the heavy western saddle onto the big horse's back. He held the lead rope around Clown's neck as she pulled the bridle onto the gelding's head and the snaffle bit slid into his willing mouth. Faris watched as Mikki's tan arms rippled with feminine muscling as she pulled the cinch strap tight. The horse was ready to be ridden. The familiarity of the task had calmed Mikki, but she felt eerily dreamy.

Mikki looped the reins into her right hand and prepared to leave the barn. Faris's hand came out quickly, but gently to stop her. They were again face-to-face.

"Would you have dinner with me tonight?" he asked, as his chocolate brown eyes looked questioningly into hers of emerald green.

She ran her hand over her forehead to swipe at the sweat and smooth her hair, which was beginning to curl in the humidity. Somewhere in her body she felt danger, but almost reflexively from her mouth came, "Okay. NO! I mean, no. Yes, I mean maybe."

His mouth formed the most beautiful smile Mikki had ever seen. Faris' shoulders seemed to sag with relief.

"Thank you for saying yes." He gave the horse a rub on his neck and said, "I have to go now, where should I pick you up?"

"We'll *meet* somewhere."

"Good enough. How 'bout Chez Tammi? Do you like French food?"

"I love all food. And that sounds great. I can be there at 8:00?"

"Wonderful. I'll make the reservation...candlelight and champagne," he said with another big mischievous grin that showed his perfect white teeth.

"Ha ha," said Mikki, starting to grin again, too. "I'm not that easily plied."

"Well, we do have a lot to talk about. And I just figured the champagne would be nicer than, say...torture?"

"Ha ha, again," said Mikki, "I'll see you then. Oh, and by the way, I'll be fabulous-looking by then, so I hope you can recognize me without the barn smell and sweat."

Faris then gently took her free hand and brought it again to his lips. "Until later, then."

Mikki watched as he walked away. Tight jeans molded over a nice butt and a pale blue polo shirt covered his very masculine broad shoulders. She had just now noticed what he was wearing...as he was leaving! What had happened to her powers of observation? The ones Granny Em had supposedly instilled into her little pea brain. She couldn't help it. He turned around halfway down the aisle way and gave her a small salute. Then he was gone. She hoped he hadn't seen drool fall from her still dangling open mouth.

As she led Clown to the warm-up arena, she looked for Faris in the parking lot. Already out of sight. As she walked the horse, her emotions began to crash as reality set in. *What am I doing? This guy is probably some sort of terrorist or at least he knows terrorists. He stalks me to the barn and asks me out on a date and I say yes. I am truly not normal. I'm going crazy!* She mounted the horse and began to do some exercises to loosen up both the horse and rider. Even the riding didn't seem to fade her focus on this new man. Mr. Mysterious. Faris. *Oh my God, what will Granny Em say?*

CHAPTER SIXTEEN

All the way home, Mikki chided herself for her foolishness. In the spur of the moment, she had gone nuts. She was always the one who was in charge of her relationships. These things just didn't happen to her and she never, ever, reacted like this. She had to tell Emily. There was no choice about that. Especially in the light of the events of the past weekend...Faris was involved, no doubt about that. But how?

Mikki pulled her black BMW into its space in the garage and was relieved that there was no Mini Cooper in one of the extra spaces beneath the Pink Flamingo. She loved her sister and her mom, but she needed time to talk to her grandmother.

As she rode the elevator to the kitchen, she clutched the bag of egg rolls and Panang chicken, squeezing the white paper bag in a death grip with her clammy fingers. As the door opened, she called out, "Gran, I'm home!"

Emily was already seated at the table in the nook beside the kitchen. Plates, napkins, and silverware were ready. "Hi honey," said Emily. "Hope you've got the goods, because I'm starved."

As Mikki began pulling the food from the bag and Emily began opening the cartons, she seemed confused. She stopped spooning rice onto her plate and stared at her granddaughter. "Are we on a diet?" she asked.

"I've got a date, but I'm having an appetizer with you. A spring roll. You know how we girls don't like to make pigs of ourselves on a first date." The words had rushed out as if holding them back was no longer an option. Mikki kept staring at the pile of wrapped fortune cookies, not trusting herself to meet her grandmother's steel-blue stare.

"You. You have a date. Tonight. Hmmm, first date," Emily said as she sat back in her chair as if trying to see her granddaughter more clearly. She sat drumming her fingers on her chin. She had abandoned the food to begin the interrogation. To Mikki, this was a bad sign.

"Gran, I do have dates," she ventured.

"Yep."

"Gran, I'm sorry I'm not chowing down with you. Are you upset? I can cancel...I think."

"No, that's not it. It won't kill me to be without you for one night. I'm just dying of curiosity, that's all."

"Well, it's kinda business and kind of a date."

"You're just too darn happy about it for it to be a business date. In fact, I haven't seen that much glow since our last Halloween jack-o-lantern. Is there something more you want to tell me?"

"Yeah."

"Well?"

Mikki bravely just blurted it out. "It's him. Mr. Mysterious."

"What?" squeaked out Emily, caught by surprise. She had been dipping her spring roll in the hot yellow mustard and dropped the whole crispy treat in the spicy sauce. She sat straight up in her chair and grabbed the armrests, holding on so she wouldn't fall from her seat from the shock. After a moment of silence, she took a deep breath and blew out, "Explain, please."

Mikki gave a brief rendition of her afternoon while they ate and Emily had resumed chewing her wonton noodles by the time Mikki had finished.

"Well, say something," demanded Mikki. "Don't just sit there with food hanging out of your mouth. It's very uncouth."

"I'm a little surprised," said Emily reaching for the cup of hot green tea, and slurping a little too loudly. As she set the cup back on the table, she picked up another spring roll. "So, what did he say about the airport and all that?"

"We couldn't exactly talk about that at the equestrian center, could we? I agreed to meet him at Chez Tammi tonight for dinner. At 8:00."

"He followed you from the luggage tag?"

"That's what he said."

"Do you feel safe going to meet him?"

"I'm not sure what I feel, and that's really scary. God, he's so handsome and when he looks at me..."

"Mikki. You could get yourself killed if you're not smart."

"I don't think so. That's not his plan for me... I don't think. I agree, very weird to show up the next day...not a week or month later, but the next day."

"Okay. Just be careful. Let him do the talking."

"He said he's buying us some French champagne."

"Oh, wonderful. You and alcohol. What a combo. Just pretend to drink it, like the ladies at the brothels."

"Sure. And you know all about that because...? Really Gran. By the way, his name is Faris."

"Well, that's better than Mr. Mysterious. Shorter, easier, when you need to call him for dinner or whatever." Waving her hand dismissively, Emily continued, "Go get ready. I'm dying to see what you're going to wear for this business date. Little Miss Espionage, herself. Meanwhile, I'll just sit here all lonely and old.... eating my Thai carryout, all alone. Boo hoo." Emily was dabbing her eyes to wipe away all the pretend, but dramatically presented, tears.

"You're not too convincing, Gran. You're just as anxious as I am for me to find out what's going on with him. Without the hormonal attraction, I mean. Since you already are hot on George Clooney and all that."

"Proceed with caution. But, yes, get the scoop. We still have some bad guys out there that we may need to deal with."

Mikki was heading for her bedroom suite and was undressing as she spoke, "Gotta get moving, Gran. It's impolite to make a man wait *too* long," as she pulled her grimy T-shirt over her head and disappeared down the stairs to the second floor.

"Hey, what's his last name?" shouted Emily, her voice trailing after Mikki.

"I dunno. Will let you know in the morning! Gotta get my shower!"

In record time, Mikki presented herself at the top of the stairway. She had transformed herself into something more like a runway model than a barn waif. She had pinned up her auburn hair onto the top of her head, with tousled tendrils escaping here and there down her neck. Her dress was a basic black Vera Wang with a crisscross front and a sweetheart neckline with tapered straps. The silk-lined skirt was flounced and ended just below the knee. Black heels with just a hint of sparkle completed the outfit. Very feminine and sexy. Mikki had bought the dress on a whim some time ago, but it had remained in the plastic dress bag from Saks for months. Was this a special occasion, she had been thinking, when earlier she pulled it from the hanger?

As her mouth shaped into a rounded, "OOh!" Emily said, "What did you do with my granddaughter?" Not that she hadn't seen Mikki scrubbed up before, but this was something new. She seemed to shine with radiance. And Emily doubted very much that it came from a cold shower. "Come here and let me give you the smell test. "

Mikki laughed and came to her grandmother to give her a kiss and a hug.

"You pass. No more horse poopie. More like Obsession?"

"Yep. And that's just the freebie magazine samples I unfold and put in my underwear drawer."

"Glad to see I've taught you frugality, anyway," said Emily.

"I gotta go. Love you, and I'm sorry I'm rushing off to meet the man of my dreams...but you know how those dreams are, huh, Gran?"

Emily smiled and threw her fortune cookie at the departing Mikki.

CHAPTER SEVENTEEN

Mikki tossed her car keys and an advance tip to the valet, who greeted her by name and promised to keep an eye on her car. Not that she had to worry here at Chez Tammi. Most of the cars were far more costly than hers…the cream-colored Bentley, the red Lamborghini, two Aston Martins parked side-by-side. Mikki smiled as she remembered her first car. A teal-colored Honda with a huge dent in the door. Her ugly learn-how-to-drive car that got her through high school and a few fender benders still brought back fond memories.

Feeling excited but nervous, Mikki headed towards the purple and gold steel door and the awaiting doorman. Stan tipped his hat and opened the door for her. She looked through the foyer to the entrance of the bar. Faris had been watching from a barstool and slid off the stool to come to her side. He gave her a quick kiss on the cheek and squeezed her hand. He smelled like something spicy and citrus, but she couldn't name the cologne. He was clean-shaven and dressed in a tan suit with a pale blue shirt and royal blue tie. Mikki inhaled his scent deeply and thought to herself that it didn't get any better than this. She took his arm and smiled up at him.

"Mr. Busaid?" asked the maitre d', Paul Beauchand. "Your table is ready, as you requested."

"Thank you. Shall we?" Faris answered and looked to Mikki. They followed Paul to their table in a flower-filled quiet corner of the dining room. Although the posh restaurant was often host to the rich and famous in southeast Florida, eyes turned toward the handsome couple as they reached their candle-lit table and were seated.

"Gee, now that we're out in public as a stared-at couple, I'm glad I know your last name. Busaid?" whispered Mikki, as her chair was pushed in and her napkin was placed in her lap.

"Actually, it's Al-Busaid. But I don't use that much."

"Because?"

"Sounds too much like membership in the infamous Al-Qaeda club, doesn't it?"

Mikki just looked at him, smiled and nodded. So much she needed to know. Just then the waiter brought the champagne and poured some for Faris to taste. Then the waiter was quickly gone, leaving them in privacy once again.

"Well, you drink alcohol. You must not be a strict Muslim then, are you?"

"I was never a true Muslim. I was a lot of things. Most of them nothing to be proud of, for sure." He pulled at the gold chain around his neck and a small gold crucifix was revealed. "I'm Christian, a Methodist."

"Go on," said Mikki, as she felt the first wave of relief pushing away her nervous caution.

Faris reached for her hand, making small circles on the back of it with his thumb. They both sipped their wine. "Should I begin with the last time I dined with Osama?" he asked, smiling innocently.

"Of course," answered Mikki quickly, not missing a beat. She squeezed his hand and then pulled away, folding her hands on to her lap, waiting.

"Don't faint or anything, but it's true. I met Osama Bin Laden." He held his breath as he waited for her reaction. Would she run out the door, as he feared?

Mikki's green eyes widened and then narrowed. "Uh huh," she said.

"I knew you would go from shock to disbelief in one easy step. So I'd better hurry my explanation before you turn tail and run. And I'd hate that," he continued, grinning again.

Mikki sat up a little straighter in her chair, remaining calm while her mind began to spin. *Well, this sums up my mental capacity for sure. I am certifiably mad. I'm having a romantic dinner in a French restaurant with a terrorist pal of the big bad one himself.*

As if Faris could read her mind, he reached for her wrist and held it. Firmly, yet gently. "It's a long story, but I want to tell you. I don't know why I want to tell you, but I know I have to. I want to get to know you and for that to happen, I must tell you about myself. It all leads to how I ended up in Florida...with a beautiful red-haired woman that I want very much to like me."

Mikki looked away from him, absorbing what he had said. She was staring at, but not listening to, the piano player in the center of the room. Faris waited. Finally her eyes again joined his.

"Okay," she said.

"I think I'll give you the summary, and then the details. It'll be easier to hear the ending of the story than the beginning."

The waiter brought the menus and they ordered crab-meat cocktails.

"I hope this doesn't ruin my appetite," said Mikki as the food arrived.

"The hors d'oeuvre or my story?"

"Either one. Although, I admit, not much can kill my lust for food," said Mikki as she poked a crab chunk with a little fork. "And I must say, I'm curious. Please go on."

"When I was a teen, I lived in Saudi and went to school with a bunch of boys...some of whom were extremists because they had relatives who were extremists. I was sucked into the peer pressure thing and that was easy. All of us had family money and no immediate plans. Some men went off to Al Qaeda training camps, but my family was more moderate and sensibly had planned for my college education. I went to London for college and not knowing anyone, I found a group of Arab Muslims to hang out with at Cambridge University. They invited me to some clandestine meetings in the Ipswich area and though I was skeptical, I went along with them. I think it was more that I was alone in the city and these men became my friends. I didn't, of course, go out to bars and hang around with the other college kids. I didn't fit in. But part of me wanted to. There was an Italian girl. She wanted to be a kindergarten teacher. She was very sweet and loved children."

"Could you leave if you wanted to?" asked Mikki as she sipped her wine, the empty appetizer plate had been pushed aside in front of her.

"No. And that was when I met bin Laden. He came into our camp one day. It was cold and ugly and suddenly all these men, his bodyguards, swarmed into the camp and searched everywhere. Then they all began shouting that our leader was coming. We all gathered to see him. We sat on the ground on the rocks while his goons stood among us with their AK 47's. We all listened attentively and inserted the proper 'Praise be to Allah's' as expected. The guy had some sort of charisma to draw the crowd to him. When I think back on it..."

Faris had paused in mid sentence.

"What?" asked Mikki, waiting for the rest of the story.

Faris had suddenly begun to eat and had stopped talking. He was facing the remaining crabmeat but his eyes were darting here and there and he was dialing someone on his cell phone. Mikki had seen that methodology before. What was going on? She knew better than to look around the room. Something was up. Faris reached for her arm.

"Dance with me," he said.

"But no one's danc..." she protested, staring at the vacant sheet of oak planking in the center of the room. As soft music played, Faris pulled her from her seat.

"Dance with me," he said more firmly, pulling her to him and beginning to move to the center of the dining room. He held her close and Mikki felt like butter in the microwave, suddenly all soft and gooey.

"Just go with the flow," he whispered in her ear.

Before Mikki could respond, Faris suddenly dropped onto the floor, grabbing his throat! He was making gurgling noises. Was he choking? My God, she thought, what kind of first date was this going to be?

"Faris! Faris! Are you all right?" she yelled at him, as she knelt on the floor beside him. "Are you choking?"

"Call 911," someone screamed nearby and a waiter raced, balancing his tray of drinks, toward the front desk.

"Italian? As in Catholic Italian?"

"Yes. She started talking to me and we went out for tea a few times. My English was very good and so was hers, but quite different accents! I had to meet her secretly and I even drank some Italian wine...that I found quite tasty! Soon one of the members of Force 17, an extremist group, found out that I was seeing the girl and threatened to dispatch both of us. I distanced myself from her for our safety. At our next group meeting many men were being 'volunteered' to go to Afghanistan to the training camps. I still thought I believed in some of the causes for a Muslim world at that point, but not so strongly as the others. But I went to the training camp more out of curiosity than anything. We were drilled and almost brainwashed into believing that the killing of infidels was what Allah would want. But all along, I kept thinking of sweet Francesca and wondering how her death could possibly please our Allah. I learned to fight...fight dirty. And I lived dirty, literally. We had little food, little clean water, and only sandals to wear on our feet on the rugged terrain through a cold, bitter winter. The whole experience was a real eye-opener."

Mikki, still chewing her crabmeat and circling her fork through the air, said, "So you had a beard and turban and all that?"

"I was a towel-head. Just like Americans say... about Arabs in general."

"I guess I can picture it, but it's a far cry from the clean-cut gentleman I see sitting across from me right now."

"So you at least see me as a gentleman? Anyway, thankfully the thinking side of my brain seemed to kick in. I thought about my college education. I knew at some point that I didn't want to donate myself or any of my family to some martyrdom cause that didn't even make sense. I went back to rereading the word of God as I originally learned it. I wasn't sure this was how it was supposed to go. The Jihad thing. But I stayed and I learned."

Mikki knew how to do the Heimlich maneuver, but found that Faris was still able to talk and breathe. As she leaned towards him, he reached behind her neck and roughly pulled her face down to the floor near his. He whispered hoarsely, "Stay down! Go with me in the ambulance! Be sure to take your purse!"

She sat back quickly to look at him in shocked surprise. "Just do it," he whispered, as he pulled her shoulder roughly towards him. As she caught herself to balance on his chest her hand felt the hard lump of a small automatic pistol in his jacket pocket. She obeyed and as she crawled to her chair to get her purse and scarf, EMT's arrived to assist Faris. How did they get here so fast? They must have been right around the corner, Mikki thought.

"To Palmetto Way Hospital!" she ordered, surprising herself with the authoritativeness of her voice. As the patient looked up at her, Mikki could've sworn she saw just the hint of a wink as medical personnel loaded him onto their gurney for transport to the hospital.

Not knowing what else to do or say, she grabbed Faris' hand while walking beside him and said, "You'll be okay."

As the cart rolled between the tables, startled and curious diners watched, unable to resume dinner conversations until the emergency entourage was outside.

The warm, sticky outdoor mist of humidity seemed transformed into a strange carnival atmosphere with flashing red and yellow lights and foggy exhaust from the waiting emergency vehicle. The ambulance attendants quickly rolled the cart through the back doors and Mikki was taken by the arms, lifted up the step-bumper, and tossed into the back with Faris. Mikki thought the hurried treatment was unusual and reminded herself to ask Brigetta about it tomorrow. Why didn't they check his blood pressure or start an IV? Hell, they didn't even ask any questions about what was wrong with him! Mikki sat down hard on the bench seat beside the reclining Faris as the ambulance started up abruptly and, lights flashing, pulled away from Chez Tammi. Mikki knew something was wrong, really wrong, about this emergency situation as she saw another ambulance coming from the other direction, siren screaming and veering towards Chez Tammi.

CHAPTER EIGHTEEN

As soon as the ambulance carrying Mikki and Faris sped away from the restaurant, Faris sat up abruptly from the gurney, flipped off the interior lights, and swung his legs toward Mikki.

"I feel a lot better," he announced, as he hopped up, hanging on to the top shelves. He peered out the back window of the emergency vehicle. It slowed as it rounded a corner and bumped its way over a curb into a dark parking lot just a few blocks from Chez Tammi. Suddenly the bouncing ceased and the vehicle jerked to a stop, sirens and lights turned off.

"Where the hell are we, Faris?" gasped Mikki, as she straightened herself after the jerky stop and reached for her purse, "and what the hell is going on?"

Faris thanked the driver and his assistant, shook their hands, opened the back door and jumped out, pulling Mikki with him. The driver gave them both a thumbs-up and pulled away, leaving his "patient" behind. Mikki correctly guessed that this ambulance must have been on call for any kind of Faris emergency.

Mikki yanked her arm away from Faris and threw her bag over her shoulder with furious irritation. She flew around to face him, her left heel catching in a crack in the pavement, almost toppling her. "Answer me!" she shouted, hands planted on hips in anger. She didn't plan on being kidnapped tonight. This was definitely not on her agenda.

In consolation, Faris went to her and attempted to encircle her body with his arms. Mikki pulled away with a jerk. She was now shaking with fury!

"I had a sudden desire for some Italian food?" Faris attempted.

"You are an idiot!"

"I may be an idiot, but we're safe now. I have saved your life once again. You can thank me later."

Mikki's chin dropped, mouth open enough to show perfectly aligned teeth. In her face, he could see incomprehension, but not fear.

"I'm sorry. Seriously, I am really sorry. Please come with me?" he asked gently, as he tentatively reached for her elbow once again. "I promise, I'll explain. Not out here, we may have been followed. Please come. Quickly!"

Glancing around for possible demons and seeing only ordinary traffic, Mikki obeyed. She was still angry, but her curiosity allowed her to be led to the door of Sal's Italian Kitchen, just seven blocks away from the crab cocktail she'd eaten a few short minutes ago. She needed the explanation for what had just happened, if for no other reason than to tell the whole ridiculous story to her grandmother. Granny Em would be on the edge of her seat for this one. They walked quickly through the restaurant's door and easily found an open booth in the large and noisy restaurant, then seated themselves. Mikki's nostrils inhaled the comforting aromas of garlic, spaghetti sauce, oregano, and freshly baked breads that greeted them.

Faris ordered a bottle of house wine from the waiter that was brought to the table in record time. Soon the vague recollection of expensive French champagne had been replaced by something sweeter that was squeezed from red grapes. They both sipped quietly. Faris ran his finger around the top of his glass for a moment, and then began to speak. He was no longer smiling.

"I saw a woman in Tammi's that I knew. We had to get out before she saw us. She was lurking in the doorway and talking to the maitre 'd when I spotted her. Paul knows the etiquette of confidentiality, but she can be quite persuasive. I always try to have a backup plan in case of a needed emergency getaway."

Mikki swallowed her wine in her mouth with one gulp and exclaimed, "You scared the royal crap out of me, thinking you were really sick or dying or something, and all because you saw an old girlfriend? Geez, Faris!" Her anger was gone now. Actually, inside she was smiling and thinking that this stunt was something she herself could have used a time or two, if she'd thought of it.

"You're jealous?"

"I'm stupid. Stupid to come on this damned date or information session or whatever it is. I'm still wondering what in the world I'm doing here."

"Okay, settle down. Yes, she's a woman I know. But she's not the girlfriend type."

"Oh, the one-night-stand type?" said Mikki, wiping her lips with her napkin and wondering if the steam she felt boiling out from under her scalp would be visible to other diners. Maybe she could just shoot him here and in the chatter and clatter no one would notice. Granny would have a ball with this one. *How dumb could one person be?* Mikki asked herself.

"Have you seen *Kill Bill*…the movie?"

Mikki just stared at him with evil daggers stabbing deathblows from the once calm emerald ponds of her eyes.

"Well, this woman is kinda like that. The *Kill Bill*-type."

Mikki said nothing and began to gaze around the room as if looking for someone, something familiar…or an exit.

"Mikki, do you hear what I'm saying?"

There was no verbal response, but Mikki finally met his gaze with hers.

"It's all part of my story and I thought it would be best if I could tell the story before we both became another statistic. Another notch on her belt or whatever."

Mikki's hands were now clasped in her lap and finger twirling the white linen napkin round and round into a cord, perhaps to be used for strangling someone. She said, "Go on, I'm listening. In fact, you've got about ten minutes more of my time. Then I'm taking off these four-inch heels, beating you to death with them, and walking barefoot back to my car, never to be seen or heard from again."

"Okay, fair enough. Can we order some Ziti? I'm starved."

"Dead men don't need food," she mouthed at him silently.

Faris smiled, but didn't dare reach for her hand again. He should've known when he saw this beautiful, young woman running like a red-haired maniac through the airport, that the clench he felt in his gut was not going away easily. Mikki's body had now sagged back against the back of the booth, and she was holding herself with her arms crossed. Her legs were also crossed and a spaghetti strap draped casually, but seductively over her shoulder. Her red hair was falling from its carefully coifed position into tantalizing curling tendrils on her neck and forehead. Her lips were both pouting and challenging. He wanted to kiss her, but valued his life. He knew he'd better start talking and talking fast.

CHAPTER NINETEEN

They ordered a large antipasto to share, and then decided on baked ziti and sausage lasagna. Mikki was silently jabbing at her salad, amazing even herself with an undaunted appetite despite the situation. She was thinking she must have inherited the hunger gene from her grandmother.

Finally Faris put down his fork. "I like you, Mikki. I find you to be a very attractive lady and because of that, I'm not sure how to tell you all of this. I don't want to drag an innocent young woman into all of my messes, even a crazy young woman."

Mikki had to smile at his description of her as "innocent." That meant he didn't know anything about the Emily-Mikki dynamic duo. *Good.*

"I left the training camp and at the end of our encampment, we were to pledge loyalty to the Jihad cause and vow to become martyrs. No way, I was thinking, so I went home and told my parents I wanted to go to the United States and finish my education. I had been speaking and learning English since I was four years old. My parents were big on cultural diversity and education. This was years before 9/11, of course, so arrangements were quickly made and I left for New York. The men in my group were ecstatic, thinking I would be their way into the U.S. to spread terrorism. I just let them think that. My family arranged everything for my collegiate transfer to America. My parents were, well, are quite wealthy. And wealth is power in Saudi, just like here in the U.S. I was finishing my degree in business at Ohio State and there were Islamic groups there, but most were benign. By this time, I was totally disenchanted with the whole Jihad/Islamic thing. I even joined a fraternity and found out I liked partying like the rest of them. But my old pals hadn't forgotten me. One night as I walked back to my apartment, out of the shadows comes this woman called only 'Aziz.' That's usually a man's name in Arabic, and she was something else for sure. Her real name was Azizah, which means powerful or dear. She definitely is not dear. She confronted me. She said she was from a group who'd been following my progress at school and she told me I had a new assignment. I was to run a fronted charity organization for supposed orphans in Pakistan, which was being funded through the Arab Bank. The Arab Bank is based in Jordan, but has some branches in larger cities in other countries, including here. They wanted me back in New York to run this operation, which was to benefit Hamas. I let them feed me all the information, but all the while I was thinking about all this money actually being used to support suicide bombers and their families. I agreed to move to New York as soon as I had graduated. I'd become so easily Americanized that my accent had almost disappeared. I used English exclusively at college. I was young, but no longer confused about what I wanted."

"But I'm confused," said Mikki, forehead furrowed in puzzlement. "So you agreed to help them, hoping you would fit in easily in New York with your new American personality?"

"I was hoping that was what the Al-Aqsa Martyrs Brigade was thinking. I took the offered position of co-chairman for the charity drive. Since I specialized in finance, I was in charge of all the funds received. I was given all the money transfers, credit card payments, and cash, and deposited them in the Arab Bank each week. Believe me, I was being watched very closely. I didn't do anything to attract suspicion while I schemed against them. To screw up would mean an unpleasant death...most likely just pieces parts of me in a very small body bag sent back to Saudi. You've seen how these guys play the game. Beheading, live disembowelment...that's just play for them. Imagine if they *really* got creative!"

"Pretty scary," said Mikki, who was still eating, but listening intently, now more interested than angry. Faris took a moment to point to her upper lip.

"Oh, sorry. Thanks," said Mikki as she wiped a bit of Italian dressing from her mouth. "Please go on."

"Anyway, to make a long story shorter, I went to the CIA. I was scared shitless, of course, because this Aziz chick was always on my tail. I mean, she found me at Ohio State and that's a huge campus."

"I know. I had a friend that went to school there."

"The C.I.A. didn't trust me at first, but I fed them the data they wanted via a secure connection on a safe house computer. I didn't dare use my own equipment, of course. The agents organized a sting operation and intercepted a huge, and I mean huge, cache of money meant for the Martyrs Brigade. This expose' was also the basis for later lawsuits against the bank filed by families of American victims of Palestinian terror. The money originally destined for laundering and forwarding to the Arab Bank branch in Ramallah was detoured during the C.I.A. sting operation. The bank was later implicated in other terror affiliations and also had repeatedly saved the Palestinian Authority from bankruptcy."

"So then what did you do?"

"The CIA made a big show of arresting me, along with the rest of the charity chairpersons, and hauling us off in big, black government cars."

"Just like in the movies, huh?"

"Right. Only once we got to the federal holding facility, we were all separated and I was released to the custody of Agent Cushman. He's kind of a cool guy. Looks like the stereotyped movie idea of CIA. Blond, crew cut, muscular physique, but not with the robotic personality. In fact, at the time, he was almost fun. He took me to the airport and we flew in a private jet to D.C. where there was an extremely long debriefing. There they discovered I could be of much more value to them in further abating terrorism in the States. Cushman and I flew back to New York and I was put back in the holding facility."

"Why did you have to go back to the jail?"

"Because in a few days, myself, plus the other co-chair were to be publicly released because we had been 'unknowingly' drawn into the charity scheme. They had to release both of us so it wouldn't draw the terrorists' suspicion to me. The other chair was quite guilty and the CIA knew it. They just took a calculated risk that I could continue my relationship with the Martyrs group and the others if they let me go back to them. Both of us released co-chairs would be followed and my life was all about anti-terrorism after that. At least for a while."

"What happened?"

Faris paused as the waiter set his serving tray on the stand near their table. The place was filled with the sounds of clinking glasses, laughing patrons, and recordings of Italian-themed music, so it was doubtful that anyone could possibly overhear any of their conversation. They poured and sipped more wine as the waiter placed the hot plates of food before them. Tantalizing smells of oregano, tomatoes, garlic and onion rose from the food. Mikki was becoming more relaxed with Faris or maybe it was the wine. She didn't know where Faris's story was leading, but she felt confidant that she would soon find out. Meanwhile, she was in the company of a handsome man with an extraordinarily interesting history.

The waiter offered bowls of grated Parmesan cheese and a shaker of dried and crushed red peppers. After he had refreshed their water glasses he left for the kitchen.

"Ummm. Delicious," said Mikki, as she inhaled with her nose close to her plate of steaming pasta, cheese, and sauces. Faris watched her. Usually, the women he dated would only play with their food. All were on diets or afraid of looking as if they enjoyed eating. Not this girl...he could see she loved her food. Faris smiled. She hadn't run off when he mentioned Al Qaeda or his dubious past. She was interested, but not judgmental. After her initial outburst of anger, she seemed to settle into a much more reasonable persona. He loved intelligent women, especially if they were beautiful.

True, she listened and absorbed everything he said. The fact that she was also recording his every word was something he missed in his evaluation of Mikelle Walsh.

CHAPTER TWENTY

Mikki and Faris absorbed themselves with the food for a few minutes, and then simultaneously wiped their mouths with their napkins. They clinked their glasses together, sipped, and sat back to relax in their padded booth of red leather.

"It didn't take long for me to tire of the constant agency surveillance, so I asked for an in-person meeting. Agent Cushman picked me up and took me back to Washington from my New York apartment. We agreed that I would be an official CIA operative since with my background, I could work quietly without interference in many useful ways. They finally trusted me and I gained access to more and more of the CIA data banks. However, if somehow I got my ass in a wringer...they would say they never heard of me, except for my prior arrest record as a bad guy."

"So, that's what you do? Covertly spy on terrorists for the CIA?"

"It sounds so blunt when you say that. But, yeah, I guess that's a way you could look at it. I'm not on their official payroll. I'm more an informant, but I also have access to some secret intelligence files that help me do my thing."

"Your thing? Your thing being looking around airports for terrorists? Where does that come in? What were you doing there?"

"Looking for you."

"Ha. Funny."

"Seriously, I was looking for you. Or someone like you. Actually, I wasn't expecting it to be you and I don't really know if it was you."

"Huh?"

"In any case, I'm glad I found you. I'm glad I followed you and could get the bomb outside in time."

"The baby bomb."

"Yeah. That was pretty horrible. I didn't think even Al Qaeda would go that far."

"So it was Al Qaeda?"

"Oh, pretty sure."

"So what were you doing there? How did you know? The secret Intel?"

"No," he answered, as he looked around the room, dark brown eyes scanning. "No, I was looking for my sister."

"Your sister?" asked Mikki, as she leaned forward so far her breasts almost touched the marinara sauce left on her plate. "Please continue!"

"My sister had been trying to locate me. Her name is Kamila bint Bahir Al-Busaid. She found my cell phone number and called saying that she was in trouble. She couldn't say much, but she told me when and where they were going. Since it was close to me here in Florida, I bought a ticket and went to the gate to see what was going on. I notified Agent Cushman of my fears, but by then I knew it was too late for them to arrive and be efficient. When I saw Sajid with his brother and uncle, I knew something bad was about to happen. I had to stay back where I wouldn't be drawn into them before I could assess the situation. I figured an explosion or other terrorist attack was imminent, but I needed to keep my distance. Sajid's uncle is a member of Intifada al-Quds. That was a given fact I knew. They wouldn't be here all together in the airport for just a family reunion. When I saw Kami, I could see Sajid had beaten the crap out of her again. She looked like a Kewpie doll with the short spiky haircut, the make-up, and new clothes. She never wears that. She's real religious and quiet by nature. No jewelry, no make-up. She was tossed in with Sajid and his family by marriage, but even I never suspected what was going on behind the scenes. Kami and I don't see each other much. She's not allowed to talk on the phone unless he's there to monitor her conversations. That's why I only got a brief message that day, and then a copy of the email she apparently sent to you. She used a library computer in New York for that. That day she told her husband that she needed books on baby care. While he waited on a bench, she said she ran to the bank of computers, signed in, and in desperation, found your site and sent the message. Sajid doesn't allow her out of the house often and would always accompany her wherever she went, even to visit with me. I never saw Kami that much even when I lived in New York, but then the CIA wanted me to move to Florida after the 9/11 attacks. They thought there might be more bad guys down here. I feel partly responsible for what has happened to Kami and how she's become involved in all this."

"So the terrified girl in the airport restroom was your sister? And the baby?"

"Not hers. My niece is still in a New York hospital. Probably will soon be in foster care. Kami can't exactly walk back in there and claim her daughter at this point."

"And you know all this because?"

"As I said, Kamila is my sister. And I have spoken with her."

"Spoken with her…spoken with her when?"

"The last time was this afternoon. She's in hiding at my condo near the Polo Club."

CHAPTER TWENTY-ONE

"That does explain why you were at the airport, I guess," said Mikki, as she unconsciously chewed her lip. Elbows now on the table, she pressed her chin against her hands, which she had pressed together, folded into a steeple. "And you live near the Polo Club?"

"Yes, so now you know all about me. Now it's your turn. Were you the one Kami called to help her?"

"Did she say that?"

"When she called, she said she needed help and wanted to get out of the country. She wanted me to come get her and put her on a plane back to Saudi. When I asked about the baby, she started sobbing so hard that I couldn't even understand her. Plus she was back to talking Arabic and so fast that I had trouble understanding anything other than she was scared out of her mind. She had a chance to tell me their flight number and that she had tried to get someone else to help her. When I asked who, she said she didn't know, just someone she found on the Internet. She couldn't call any law enforcement agencies, since she would have been arrested along with the rest of the family."

"And she didn't say anything else?"

"Nope. Sajid came into the room and pulled the phone away from her. He calmed down when he heard it was me. I told him Kami had called to say good-bye before their trip. He had made Kami pretty much a prisoner in their home. She couldn't go anywhere by herself. I didn't even know she knew how to use a computer and probably Sajid didn't know that either. But he did allow her to go into the library. Was it you she contacted?"

"Why would she call me? I don't know anything about bombs or terrorists or how to get people out of the country."

"Then what were you doing there?"

"Getting ready to get on a plane, like lots of other people. Then after the incident at the airport, we decided to go back home."

"Uh huh. Why did you jump up and follow her into the bathroom?"

"She looked distressed and I saw a spot of blood on the baby's blanket in the carrier. Also I'm observant enough to notice that it looked like the mother had been beaten up. I could still see bruises underneath all that make-up, just like you did. I thought I'd follow her and see if she needed help."

"Well, she did need help. I followed both of you to the restroom entrance and could hear some of what she was saying. Something about 'but you're just a girl like me' is what I remember hearing."

"And I said I would help her, but some other people came in so we couldn't talk much. She had told me that the baby was dead," said Mikki, rapid-fire.

"You seem a little defensive, Mikki. Slow down."

"I'm just trying to remember something I really don't want to remember. The baby and the bomb and running and all that."

"Yeah, like me running after you and saving your ass. I had to leave my position when I saw Sajid get up. Then you took off running and I followed along. Who was the old woman who was with you?"

"My grandmother. We often travel together. She loves traveling and I live with her right now. She had a stroke two years ago, so needs some help. She's in a wheelchair."

"Is she in a wheelchair all the time?"

"Well...no. She's been going to rehab and doing pretty well, actually. Speaking of which or whom, I have to get back home soon." Mikki was uncomfortable now that the questioning had turned in her direction. She felt torn between staying here with this attractive man and getting away before she revealed too much. She knew Granny Em could help her decipher all this, back in the safety of the Pink Flamingo beach house. Mikki needed time to think before she said any more.

"Okay, but I have lots more questions. It doesn't seem fair. It seemed like pretty much a one-sided conversation. Well, can't say I haven't provided an interesting evening, right?" asked Faris, putting his napkin down on the table.

"Let's see. An ambulance ride, although a short one. Scaring the shit out of me. And giving me the 'I'm associated with terrorists' revelation. Oh yeah, pretty interesting evening. By the way, what happened to Sajid? Is Kamila okay?"

"She's fine for now, but Sajid is out there somewhere. I snatched Kamila away as they were heading for the parking lot. Sajid's got a little bump on his head, but that's a whole other story. He's probably out there lurking around with Aziz. Now he knows I have Kamila somewhere and that I'm helping her, so there's no more secrecy."

"How did you get her? What happened? How did you find them?"

"For someone who wants to go home, you don't seem to be quite finished with me," stated Faris with another one of those beautiful smiles. He pulled Mikki toward him over their dinner plates and kissed her lightly. "I know I'm not finished with you," he added with a quick wink. "But I also have to get home and check on Kamila, especially since I saw Aziz tonight and know I'll soon have their whole network looking for us. I don't want to endanger you. None of them know where I live. I have two houses in Florida, a condo, and also an apartment in Orlando."

"In Orlando? I used to work there."

"There you go again...you aren't finished with me."

Mikki smiled, but said, "I really have to go, Faris. It's been...well, it's been different."

"But you like me, don't you?" It wasn't really a question. Faris signaled for the check, the waiter nodded and returned quickly with the tab. As she rose, Mikki pulled her silk shawl from the seat in the booth and Faris reached to help her pull it over her shoulders. His fingers ran the smooth line along her neck and massaged the area below her hairline. Then he wrapped his arm protectively around her and they walked to the exit. Back to a dose of reality, Mikki remembered her car was back at Chez Tammi.

"Want to walk? I think it's safe," asked Faris.

"Sure. It's a beautiful night. Let's go." Mikki took off walking at the pace of a seasoned runner.

"Dear God, woman...slow down. It's not a horse race! Can't we have a leisurely stroll?"

"Sure, sorry. Thank you for dinner and the most unusual evening. I'll go home and write this one down. Hmm. Dear Diary..."

"Be sure to put the diary where no one will read it, okay?" whispered Faris with the suggestion of hushed secrecy. Mikki twisted her fingers to lock her lips conspiratorially.

They silently walked hand-in-hand the three blocks back to the parking lot, neither one knowing exactly what to say next. Back at their original restaurant, Mikki found the attendant who managed the car keys. When he saw them, he blinked twice, perhaps wondering how he missed them coming out of the front door. But between valet assignments, he had been in his little hut with a portable fan running furiously while he played with a hand-held video game. He jumped up and raced toward the lot for Mikki's BMW. Faris and Mikki held hands in the alcove attached to the restaurant until they saw the car appear and jerk to a stop.

"But, where's your car, Faris?" asked Mikki, watching for him to reach for his own keys.

"I didn't want Aziz to spot my car, so my car is parked in the rear lot. I don't think she knows exactly where I'm staying and I'd rather keep it that way for now. I need to protect Kami...and you." He gave Mikki a paper torn from a pad in his pocket. The number was his cell phone. "Please call me. I want to see you again, but I might not be able to return to the stables for a few days."

Mikki frowned and took the paper, stuffing it into her black silk Prada clutch. She handed him a business card with her own cell phone number. She kissed him on the cheek impulsively as Michael stood watching.

"Thank you for a great night," said Faris, as he opened the driver's side door and helped Mikki inside. After she swung her long legs inside and placed her hands on the wheel, she gazed up at him.

"I think we'll see each other again soon," said Mikki as she jammed the floor shift knob into first gear, and showing off the little car's acceleration qualities, smoked the tires out of the parking lot into the quiet street. Waving as she left, she glanced back to see Faris handing Michael his valet ticket. Michael raced for the keys to the Aston Martin Vanquish. The dark blue car didn't stand out in this parking lot for the Florida rich and famous and it allowed Faris a zero-to-sixty in 4.7 seconds response when he needed it. Like now. Faris also pushed pedal to metal as he snapped the two-ton car into gear and tore out of the parking lot. He had an idea where Aziz had gone and he didn't want Mikki around when he found her. He was worried about how the dangerous woman had found him at the restaurant. There would be a later time to introduce Mikki to the Aston Martin, a safer time, when Aziz was out of the picture.

CHAPTER TWENTY-TWO

As Mikki drove home, she had the odd and unpleasant sensation that someone was following her. Aziz? Faris? Who? She turned abruptly into a coffee shop on Southern Boulevard and stopped the car. She sat quietly and watched the traffic through her rearview mirror. She saw nothing unusual as the traffic flowed by like salmon running upstream. Stop and go, fast and slow, with occasional horns beeping and cars shaking and bouncing, seemingly propelled by giant bass speakers. There was at once a surprisingly familiar car that slowed and then merged into the mass of cars and lights and was gone. A white Jag. Just like Granny's. She wouldn't, would she? Follow her on her date? No? Maybe. The phone calls Granny Em had said she had to make were probably to check out Faris. Emily probably knew Faris' last name before she did, if she knew anything about her grandmother.

Mikki jumped from her parked car and raced to order two caramel lattes with whipped cream and chocolate sprinkles. Granny loved dessert coffees. Mikki hopped back into her car and sprang into warp speed. If that was Granny Em's car and she was spying on her, Mikki was now determined that Gran would be caught. Yep, she would be caught and chastised. Mikki likened herself to Dale Jr. as she sped along in her own race against time towards the Pink Flamingo and her errant grandmother.

"Oh, no!" Mikki exclaimed aloud. "Dammit!"

Flashing red and blue lights behind her announced that she had been caught speeding. She pulled the car to the curb, cursing herself. *Yeah, yeah...haste makes waste. Damn! Shit!* Now she just wanted to get the ticket and get going. The officer sat in his car, apparently checking her license tag, for what seemed like hours. Then a rotund male figure approached her car, his right hand was touching the handle of his gun. *Well, yes, I could be a big-time drug dealer or homicidal maniac! Get real!* She had already pushed down on the power window lever and had her driver's license ready when he bent down to the open window.

"Good evening, ma'am," he said, peering into the car's interior and shining his flashlight beam here and there.

God! He ma'am'd me! The perfect evening with Mr. Mysterious was getting less perfect as the night went on. It was only ten o'clock. What else did the night hold in store for her? She had pulled the pins from her hair and stuffed them into a pleat in the leather seat.

"Good evening, officer. Was I going a little fast?" asked Mikki with a flip of her now loosened auburn locks. She gave him her best 'sorry' look as she opened her green eyes to their widest, trying to look as innocent and angelic as possible. He took the offered license and seemed to spend a great deal of time looking at it with his flashlight. Front and back. Then back and front. Then he looked at her hard and long. He still hadn't said anything. After taking out his ticket notebook, he copied some information from her license and handed it back to her.

Mikki had not dared to say another thing. *Don't speak unless spoken to. Try to shut up before all kinds of things spew forth from these lips non-stop. Just relax, sit quietly.*

"Well, ma'am, seems there's a problem here. You were doin' seventy-two in a forty-mile-an-hour zone here," said the officer, talking out of the side of his mouth and leaning into the car just a little too far, a little too close. Mikki could smell cigarettes, some cheap after-shave, and also maybe a little pastrami lingering on his breath.

"I'm really sorry, sir. I don't even have a good excuse," said Mikki, with uncharacteristic acquiescence and her very sweetest smile.

"Well, I could let you go..."

Yes!

"But I can't, due to you also hav'n a taillight out on this hea' little bitty car."

"My taillight is out? Thank you so much for telling me, officer. I'll have it fixed right away. I promise."

"Well, how can I let you drive 'round like that all night? You wanna get killed or kill someone?"

Just you for now, buddy. But the words actually formed were dripping with honey, "Sir, I'm on my way home right now. I have to take care of my sick grandmother. She's waiting up for me, and I can't leave her alone. I'm sure a man like you has a loving family to worry about, too. And you'd understand my predicament, right?"

The officer stood up and scratched his chin. He tore off the ticket and handed it to Mikki. "Get along home now, little lady. Take care of your poor ol' grandma. Slow down or the next time we'll be dancin' 'round like this down at the jail. Ya hear me?"

"Yessir," said Mikki, as she batted her long eyelashes his way and took the ticket. As he turned to walk back to the patrol car, she murmured, "Asshole," and stuffed the ticket between the seats.

She accelerated ever so slowly away from the curb and started home with extreme caution. To calm herself, she left the windows rolled down and opened the top. The stars were bright and twinkling and soon she was relaxed enough to think the night sky was there just for her. She turned on her Beethoven music disc and soon the car seemed to find its own way home.

As she approached the gate, the electric eye read the chip behind the grillwork of the Bimmer and the gate opened. She pushed the garage door opener quickly, screeched to a halt inside, and jumped out of the car. The white Jaguar was in its place and looked untouched. She went to the front of the car and put her hand on the hood. It was still warm. *Gotcha, Gran!* She grabbed her scarf and bag and yanked open the garage door to the stairs. No time to even wait for the elevator. She sprinted up the stairs two at a time.

Granny was casually seated on the couch with a bowl of Ben and Jerry's. She wore a robe and slippers and barely looked up as she heard Mikki come in. She was watching a rerun of *Law and Order*.

"Granny!"

"You don't have to yell!" said Emily, still spooning cookie dough ice cream through open lips. She seemed entirely engrossed with the television. "How was your date?"

Mikki pondered this facade of innocence and wondered if she was this transparent to the policeman who had stopped her for speeding. *Well, I guess I come by that part of me honestly enough. Acting lessons? Who needs 'em!* Mikki's anger was fading, and curiosity was growing.

"How did you do it and why?"

"Huh?" answered Emily, turning to see her granddaughter who was about to plop down on the sofa beside her.

"And where's my ice cream? You saw me stop at Coffee Catch and, of course, you knew I would bring you a latte."

"I saw you...?"

"Don't play dumb, Granny. It doesn't become you. Isn't that what you always said to Brigetta and me when we tried to lie our way out of things?"

Granny just licked her spoon and turned back to the TV. Mikki got up to get her own bowl of dessert. She opened the bag with the two coffees and sat Emily's on the table.

While Mikki was getting a clean bowl from the dishwasher, Emily said, "I guess I need to refresh my reconnaissance techniques?" When there was no answer from the kitchen, Emily continued, "You didn't really think I would let you go by yourself to meet some Arab terrorist that you suddenly went gaga over, did you?"

"You let me go out with Billy McNicoles, right?"

"Who?"

"In seventh grade. Billy? He was the terror of Palm Beach Middle School. He was always in the Dean's office, always had to stay for detention. Finally he was sent to an alternative school. Remember him? Mom said no contact with him, but when I stayed here with you, you said, 'Sure you can go to the movies.' He was really cute and at that age we girls always liked the bad boys. So we went to the movies and we spent the whole time making out. It was fun, really!"

"So, what's your point?"

"The point is that you didn't care about that, but now I'm all grown up and my grandmother, of all people, is following me around town to check up on who I want to go out with. Uh, doesn't that seem a little backward to you?"

"Nope. If you just want to make-out and do a little groping, that's fine and fun. This is something else. There was some serious shit going on last weekend and it ain't over. You know it, I know it, and Faris knows it. And by the way, seems you still like the dangerous bad boys. After you left I checked him out on the CIA website you hacked into. He's a CIA operative, how handy."

Mikki just stared at her for a moment from the kitchen and then she slammed another huge scoop of ice cream into her bowl. After that she flung open the refrigerator door and pulled out maraschino cherries and hot fudge sauce.

"Granny, you're making me so mad, I think I'll eat myself to death in front of you."

"Suit yourself...Ms. Piggy."

"Gee, maybe next time I should just take you along on my date with Faris?"

"So there's going to be a next time?"

"Hope so."

"I'll be in the back seat."

CHAPTER TWENTY-THREE

Mikki had just changed into some comfortable pajamas and the women were enjoying the ice cream and watching the news when Mikki's cell phone rang. Mikki jumped up and pulled the phone from her purse on the kitchen counter.

"See Gran, he can't let me alone! It's Faris calling...you're not the only one with irresistible sex appeal around here!" exclaimed Mikki as she pushed a button to take the call.

"Hi Faris," said Mikki, grinning at Emily who was staring from the couch and holding a hand cupped behind her ear as if to hear better. Emily was motioning for her to put the call on speakerphone.

Mikki, ignoring Emily, began walking toward the French doors leading to the balcony overlooking the Atlantic. She was speaking softly and Emily, unable to listen in, just shook her head and went back to the *FOX* TV report on local property taxes.

Suddenly Mikki was back in the room with the phone still clamped to her ear and looking at her grandmother, her eyes huge.

"Well, where is Kamila? Is she okay?" Mikki was saying into the phone.

Emily's attention was now fully alert and focused on her granddaughter. There were a few moments of pause and Emily waited to hear what was said next.

"That's *our* place!! My grandmother and I are there now!" Mikki was shouting and Emily got up from the couch to go to her. Whatever was happening involved all of them.

"No, don't come over here...well, yes, okay...fifteen minutes? Okay. Bye...I will."

Mikki turned to Emily, biting her bottom lip. She said nothing but sprinted upstairs to the computer room and began to punch buttons like a maniac. Mikki was watching the monitors, green eyes darting from one to the other frantically.

"Gran!" Mikki screamed from the office, "Come up to the safe room! Hurry!"

That said, Mikki raced down the stairs and grabbed her grandmother's arm and began to guide her up the steps. Neither said anything, just worked hard to get quickly up the steps and into the safe room. They had a pact. In time of immediate danger, follow the orders of the other and save the questions for later. Emily felt she was easily able to make the stairs on her own, but conceded to the assistance she was given. To refuse at this point would have been stupid, Emily knew, plus she was carrying both of her cats and couldn't hold the railing.

Both women were securely locked into the main office and Mikki was again at the computer, jabbing at the keyboard keys in rapid succession. Soon the familiar but quiet roll of the wall to the hidden room was heard. This was their sanctuary, their training room, their exercise room…and maybe most importantly, their weapons and equipment room. Mikki assisted Emily onto a futon and when she was safely and comfortably seated, she began to talk.

"It was Faris, like I said. He was warning us to be aware. Aziz, this killer terrorist bitch, found his condo and left him a warning there. A red-stained paper in his bedroom said 9309 Seaside was next on her agenda."

Emily had opened her mouth to question Mikki, but stopped quickly by her granddaughter waving a silencing finger at her.

"Gran, please…time is everything. Let me finish, and then we'll see where this goes. Faris didn't know my address. It was left on the note in his condo when he got home. After he left me at the restaurant, he hurried home to check on Kamila—she's hiding out at his condo—and found that his place had been entered. This Aziz is a really bad chick and may be on her way over here because she may have seen Faris and I together and either traced my license plate or followed me here. She is part of the terrorist group that's not too happy that there was interference in their plan to blow stuff up on Monday. We have to lay low until he gets here."

"Slow down! Faris is coming here? To the Pink Flamingo?"

"He's on his way. He said he'd explain more details later."

"And you trust him enough to let him come here…to my, to our home. My Pink Flamingo?"

"Gran, I feel safe with him. He's protecting us."

"You didn't happen to tell him that we don't really need protecting, did you?"

"Nope."

"So we're huddled in this room with no windows just so you can see your boyfriend again tonight?"

"Gran, there are times you're impossible. Of course not. I couldn't very well say to him, 'Well, don't worry about my little old grandmother and me because we're trained assassins,' could I?"

"You could've thought of something."

"Anyway, we're staying here in the safe room until he gets here, just in case."

"In case of what?" asked Emily, now slumped back into the futon, arms criss-crossed in defiance. "We don't need protection. We *are* the protection, remember?"

"I just know that this Aziz chick is a really bad girl. Kinda like you used to be in your youth. You know, focused and dangerous?"

"I still am focused and dangerous," answered Emily, with a startlingly cool look.

"I agree, we bad. But this is no time for play, okay? Just go along with me for once in your lifetime, please?" pled Mikki, now looking at the security monitor that displayed the driveway. Emily sat silently for another minute and then got up to help view all the security screens. The concrete walls surrounding the villa enclosed the three-acre beachfront estate beautifully, but also securely. Bright spotlights illuminated the walls and every landscaping plant and tree on the property. Lighting around the pink mansion displayed not only the beauty of the majestic home, its white columns, its many balconies, but also each window frame was well illuminated. No burglar would have an easy entry. It would be downright impossible for an uninvited guest to encroach the premises, or so they thought.

CHAPTER TWENTY-FOUR

"He's here!" exclaimed Mikki, as she reached for the entry gate remote. As the heavy wrought iron creaked open, the Aston Martin flashed into the driveway and slid to a stop, James Bond style, in front of the garage. The women exited the safe room and closed the huge wall to the room quickly. Mikki unlocked the office door and helped Emily back down the stairs. They cautiously checked the main floor of the home for signs of intrusion. Mikki had forgotten to shut the door to the balcony when she had returned to the living room, but everything seemed to be in place.

Mikki went to the kitchen hallway and pressed the garage door opener so Faris could hide his car under the house. She heard him drive in and checked the monitor by the elevator. He was alone. She watched as he spotted the elevator door and entered. She called to him on the intercom to press the button for the second floor. He was on his way up in less than twenty seconds.

Emily headed for her favorite chair near the television and turned off the picture. This promised to be better than *Entertainment Tonight* and she wasn't going to miss a minute of it.

Faris arrived at the kitchen via elevator and stepped through the door carrying a handgun in his right hand and quickly assessed the environment. Mikki noted the shiny new Glock 36 Slimline, a .45 caliber firearm she knew from marksmanship classes. *This guy's got it all,* Mikki thought, beaming at him and admiring his choice of weapon. Without speaking, he walked quickly through the kitchen and into the living area. Since there were no window coverings he needed only to walk from window to window and glance outside. Feeling secure enough, he holstered the gun and said, "Nice to see you again, Mikki," and flashed her that fabulous smile. He went to Emily and bent toward her, taking her hand and saying, "I didn't mean to scare you with the gun. I'm Faris."

"I'm Emily Vanderhorn. So when are you two getting married?"

Faris's face went blank. Mikki's face went red. Emily began to laugh.

"Granny!" exclaimed the shocked Mikki. "What in the world are you talking about?"

Faris had retreated into a corner and was hugging himself, trying to control his own laughter. He wanted to stand back and watch this.

"You, Mikki, are the one who has gone cuckoo over this guy. And now he comes strolling in here, carrying a nasty little gun, and you about wet yourself in adoration. And hey, if you like him, so will I." Emily was smiling one of those smiles that said she was very pleased with herself. "Oh, and Faris, I don't really scare that easy."

Mikki was now beet-red and so flustered by her grandmother's cheap shot that she was almost speechless. Was her grandmother trying to sabotage her love life?

"Faris, please excuse my grandmother. She's senile and that's why I always have to hurry home to be sure she isn't burning down the neighborhood or something. She's dangerous," said Mikki, giving Emily one of her famous "if looks could kill" stares. Mikki, now anxious to change the subject, rolled her balled-up clenched fists into the bottom of her pajama top and asked, "Would anyone like anything to drink? Grandmother will be having a Molotov Cocktail."

But Faris wasn't going to let this go so easily. "Mrs. Vanderhorn…"

"Call me Emily…please."

"Emily, Mikki didn't really give me the impression that she was all that excited about me. I wasn't real sure that she even liked me. Thanks for filling me in. Anything else I should know about?"

"Don't let her drive your car. She wrecked mine," said Emily, without missing a beat.

Mikki was now in the kitchen, banging heavy crystal glassware around on the pink marble counter near the sink. As soon as Emily began to speak again, Mikki began running the noisy ice crusher until she had filled a whole bowl with cracked ice. Faris and Emily watched her from the safety of the living room. When it was quiet, they tried to speak again. Immediately came the sound of a very loud blender in the kitchen. Emily thought, *God, what is she grinding, silverware?*

Soon Mikki arrived with a tray and highball glasses mounded high over the top with ice. She returned with two pitchers of iced tea and some lemonade and a bottle of wine. She smiled sweetly and sat on the couch beside Faris. She kicked off her slippers and put her bare feet on the coffee table, picked up one of the glasses and helped herself to the bottle of Pino Noir. She filled her icy glass to the top and drank it down without taking a breath. Then she pulled her legs up and crossed them, sitting yoga style and looking like she needed to meditate.

"She always was quite a drama queen...not as bad as her sister, though," said Emily directly to Faris. "Would you like a snow cone?"

"She didn't mention she was an alcoholic," Faris whispered to Emily.

At this point Mikki began to hum some mantra and closed her eyes, hands on her knees.

"You still smell good and you look cute in your pajamas," Faris ventured, but the chanting continued, followed by a huge and unladylike belch.

Emily was first to give in and break the spell. She needed to know what was going on and the time for joking was over. Time for more of that later. "Earth to Mikki," she said. "Please come back to our planet. We miss you."

Mikki sighed, gave up her chanting, and actually gave Faris a welcome hug. Maybe Granny needed to be embarrassed by seeing her granddaughter in pajamas hugging a guy she just met. And Faris didn't seem to mind the pajama thing a bit.

"So tell us the whole story," said Mikki.

"Yeah, we'll work on the wedding plans later, babe," said Faris, with a wink.

"Okay, I accept your proposal," answered Mikki, with an exaggerated double wink.

"I went home quickly because as soon as you left me at Chez Tammi, I got a call from Kami saying that she had seen someone in the parking lot. From her description, I knew right away it was Aziz. Kami saw her lurking around and looking in car windows and shining a flashlight at apartment numbers. I drove home fast, kinda like the way Mikki does, and when I got to the parking area at my condo, I knew something was wrong. I always leave all the lights on inside and the place was now dark."

Mikki ignored his remark about her driving and asked, "What about Kami?"

"She wasn't in the condo when I got up there. Anytime I leave her, she crosses the hall to a vacant condo. I bought both condos and leave the other one empty. There is a passageway through my pantry to a closet on the other side. I had it built in when I moved there, and now it's working for my present need to protect my sister. Each outside access door to the extra condo is triple locked by deadbolts, which can only be opened from the inside. No one can get in, but someone in there can get out. As a safety measure, there are no lights or other signs that the apartment might be occupied. I just pay both mortgages and write it off as extra security. This time it really paid off. Aziz apparently was able to access my condo, but Kami wasn't there. Aziz left me a threatening note, with the letters of your address written in red. I didn't even know where you lived, but thought of you first. You need to be careful, because she'll show up sooner or later. That's why I rushed over here, to save your life...again," he said, taking Mikki's hand.

"Faris. Here's something to think about. Every time you have to save my life, it's because you or your family have put me in danger," said Mikki, taking her hand back slowly, still entranced by his big brown eyes. "I can take care of myself. I really appreciate your efforts, though. It's just that I'm not as fragile as you think I am."

"What about your grandmother? Don't you want me around to see that she's safe? She looks small and frail…"

Mikki interrupted his speech by chuckling. *Her grandmother? Frail? Little did he know! Yes, she was now almost eighty years old and had suffered a stroke two years ago. But he didn't know about the constant retraining, the exercise program, the knowledge, the history, the past. Yes, the past that she, herself, had discovered only two years ago. Two years ago, after the stroke and hospitalization where everything had been revealed to her. And now the two of us are partners. Yes, Faris, Granny's elderly, but certainly able to take care of herself.*

"…I mean she's pretty smart and good-looking, and I was taught to value and take care of my family. Isn't that the right thing to do, Mikki?"

"Yeah, right, Mikki?" Emily chirped, now rocking on the recliner and picking up some knitting needles enveloped between the cushions.

Mikki noticed that her grandmother was looking for something…yarn? She had never seen Emily knit, crochet, or do any needle work. The things you find out. Her grandmother knits. Amazing. Skeet shooting, target practice, maybe… but knitting? This was another surprising bit of knowledge.

"Right, Mikki?" asked Emily again. If Mikki had been more observant, she would have seen there was a reason for Emily's insistence. She was trying to get her attention. Emily had seen something and the big fluffy cat on the floor by her feet was growling, a low and warning rumble. Badger was staring at the door to the coat closet. Hanging on the closet doorknob near the front door entrance, Emily had hung a pretty glass ornament, a pink flamingo. It always was the damnedest thing. Every time the closet door opened and jostled it, the thing would flip over and its eyes would face backwards instead of frontward. But that's why it was there. It was now flipped backwards and Emily had seen it. Someone had recently opened the door.

CHAPTER TWENTY-FIVE

Before Emily could send any more signals to Mikki or Faris, the door of the foyer closet sprang open, smashing the delicate glass flamingo and sending shards flying across the marble floor. A tall woman with wild looking, black hair emerged. Faris and Mikki jumped to their feet and turned towards the woman.

Emily continued to sit quietly and murmured, "My husband gave me that..."

"Sit now down!" the woman screamed at them in broken English, swinging the barrel of an assault rifle in a semi-circle.

They sat. Aziz was an imposing figure. She was nearly six feet tall and had lean, bulging muscles like a man. At first glance, Mikki thought of her as a commando from a bad movie, or even Xena in warrior garb. But Aziz wore a black sleeveless military jumpsuit and her hair was a mass of unkempt frizz and dreadlocks. Mikki wondered for an instant what insects could be nesting in her hair. She had a roughly handsome face and black eyes that glared with anger and hostility. Her weapon was a thirty-inch, self-loading, military carbine that meant she was not kidding around.

Faris had inched his hand towards the handgun in its holster across his chest, turning his back to Aziz. Mikki didn't follow this action with her eyes, but had noted his intent with her peripheral vision. Aziz missed nothing. With a super quick snapping turn of her weapon, she swung the handle at Faris' head. He fell to the floor with a grunt as the butt of the gun connected with skull bone in an action so fast it was hard for the others to comprehend what had happened. Mikki screamed reflexively, but Emily sat very still, like a quiet river with strong undercurrents. Aziz had eased herself toward the fallen Faris and had pulled his gun from the leather strapping. Blood was oozing slowly from a wound near his left ear.

"You!" screeched Aziz, pointing at Mikki. "Come here...slow and easy." Aziz motioned with her forefinger to a spot directly in front of her. The pajama-clad Mikki rose and went to the spot where she had been directed. Mikki was thinking as fast and hard as she could. *Where were the closest hidden weapons in the house? Faris! Is he okay? Aziz will kill all of us.* At that moment Aziz grabbed Mikki's arm and twirled her around so Mikki's back was to her. Aziz held Mikki in a tight chest grip with her left arm, while the right arm targeted Faris and Emily with the rifle. Mikki's eyes were now darting here and there in the room, looking for something to use as a weapon. Emily continued to sit quietly, seemingly unconcerned, as she twiddled with the silver knitting needles and a ball of pink yarn. This seemed strange to Aziz, but she could not be concerned with the old, apparently senile woman.

"Now, we all go outside to that so pretty balcony. Do not you ever bother to lock your doors around here? Stupid women," said Aziz with a laugh. "You got lots of lights and cameras, so you think you safe?" Aziz tossed back her head and cackling like a mad woman, she muttered something in Arabic to herself.

Faris was stirring on the floor. Mikki saw his eyes flicker as he regained consciousness. He slowly pulled himself to a sitting position, leaning on the couch for balance. He knew his automatic handgun was gone. His head was bleeding and he was fighting an urge to vomit, but fear for everyone's safety superceded the impulse. He struggled to think clearly as he sat quietly, assessing the situation.

Mikki's face was glistening with sweat. The open door to the outside beach deck permitted naïve balmy breezes to blow into the house as if nothing was wrong. The security of the Pink Flamingo had been breached...something that until now the two tenants had deemed impossible.

Aziz was pushing Mikki as she held her with a vise-like grip. They walked in tandem towards the French doors. Aziz was not worried about the old woman knitting on the couch. She would dispatch the girl she held, then shoot her nemesis,

Faris Busaid, so full of bullet holes that his body would more resemble hamburger than a human male. But torture first! The most fun of all and the best revenge for an infidel traitor.

Faris was still too dizzy to stand. He was working hard to make it to his knees. Emily had left her chair, crouching like a hungry cheetah eyeing her prey. At that same moment, Mikki had tucked her chin to her chest and with all the force she could muster, she flung her head back hard, into the jaw of her captor. There was a crunch and a shriek of pain and anger as Aziz felt blood in her mouth from her broken teeth and bitten tongue. Mikki acted fast, turning and grabbing Aziz's weapon by the barrel. The women, now both screaming and panting, were fighting for their very lives. Blood flew from Aziz's mouth as she cursed in foreign dialect and fought to regain possession of her weapon. Then the old woman came from nowhere. Emily leaped onto the back of the intruder like a monkey, legs wrapped around Aziz's pelvis. Emily's hands twirled and then aimed sharp and deadly knitting needles. A brown ball of feline silently pounced from the floor onto Aziz's face and clung there, nails embedded in her scalp. Screaming with anger, Aziz could only see and feel fur on her face, but her arms were helplessly pinned as Mikki gripped them from the front. Then Emily's stainless steel knitting needles punctured again and again, pushed to their full depth in all vital places…lungs, neck, heart. The yowling monkey-woman stabbed ferociously, still attached to Aziz like a refrigerator magnet. The cat jumped free and ran under Emily's chair. Mikki whirled around quickly and with a move learned in the dojo of her Brazilian Jiu-Jitsu class, kicked hard to the enemy's solar plexus. Her right heel battered the spleen of the still cursing intruder and Granny Em rode Aziz down to the ground. Her victim was still squirming, so Emily, deftly and with perfect precision, jabbed a pearl pink knitting needle through her right ear into the brain. *Kill the head and the body follows.* Suddenly all was quiet, except for the huffing of labored breathing. Aziz lay unmoving and face down on the imported Spanish tiles, rivulets of red were bleeding into the grout lines. Faris managed to pull himself to his feet and stood staring at the body on the floor.

Emily rose with some effort and panted, "She was not a very nice person. She broke Pinkie."

Mikki smiled and wiped sweat from her forehead with her arm. "I think I hurt my foot. How 'bout you, Gran?" she said between breaths.

"I think I broke a fingernail. Suppose I'll live…with an emergency call to my manicurist," puffed Emily, hanging on to the back of a recliner. Badger seemed none the worse and strutted, haughty and proud, onto Emily's lap as she sat down. Bubbles, the younger orange cat, peered out from her hiding place behind the couch.

Faris was speechless. Silently he retrieved his handgun from the floor where it had fallen in the fight. He wiped blood from his head onto his sleeve and looking at the two women, he said, "You killed Aziz."

"We're usually much more hospitable than this. I hope you didn't get the wrong impression about us," said Emily to the man who was clearly in shock and still trying to figure out what had happened. "Are you okay?"

Faris nodded speechlessly. He would not admit to his pounding head.

Mikki went to Emily's chair and bent to hug her grandmother. Both were smiling and not a tear was shed between them, causing Faris to wonder what he'd fallen into here at the Pink Flamingo. Maybe this wasn't a nesting spot for chicks, but a roost for birds of prey.

"Now what?" asked Mikki, as she looked from Emily to Faris. "We've got to get her out of here, and soon."

Faris still hadn't found the ability to speak, but Emily said, "Yeah, I hate it when someone is bleeding all over my house. That's so rude."

"I can help," said Faris, finally. "We can take her somewhere in my car and dump her out. Pretty simple. Down the elevator and into my trunk."

"I'll go get a plastic tarp. Wouldn't want to mess up your quarter-million-dollar automobile, would we?" stated

Mikki, as she assessed her pajamas. She was a mess...blood, sweat, and a torn pajama top. If this was considered a second date, she doubted that she had made much of an impression.

Moments later, Mikki had showered and changed to clean jeans and a T-shirt and Granny had gone to her own bedroom to wash up. Mikki had cleaned and dressed Faris' wound using the first aid kit in the main floor bathroom. After washing his face, a Band-aid, two Tylenol, and a cup of coffee, he felt somewhat better. He wasn't sure if it was the headache or the activity here at this beach house, but he still felt a little fuzzy and out of control.

The three pulled the body onto the elevator and went down to the garage. When the trunk lid was lifted, Emily tapped the car's exterior and asked," Is this fiberglass or metal?"

Undaunted by the strange question, Faris replied, "Cold hard steel, ma'am. Do you like her?"

"Is it fast?" asked Emily, as she ran her hand along the fender.

"Sure, zero to sixty in 4.7 seconds, six-speed manual transmission. Not so good gas mileage, however."

"Don't let Mikki drive it," said Emily emphatically. "Remember my red Jaguar. That was the one she wrecked."

Mikki scowled at her as they lifted the dead weight, grunting in unison. Soon Aziz's vinyl-wrapped body was loaded in the trunk and Faris and Mikki were driving away from the beach house in his car. Neither had said much about the incident in the living room.

"Nice car. Can I drive?" asked Mikki hopefully, sitting in the passenger seat, legs crossed and bouncing her sandaled feet to the music on Beach 102 FM.

Faris let his thoughts go for a moment and chanced a look at her. She was freshly showered and smelled like jasmine after a summer rain. She had easily lifted her share of the burden without complaint. The two of them had found some blue tarps in the basement garage and rolled up the body, transporting it without speaking.

"No, you can't drive. I may be a little confused about this evening, but I do remember the part about you wrecking your grandmother's car, a red Jaguar she used to own?"

"Why does everyone keep bringing that up? It has nothing to do with me as a person."

"You're starting to scare me. Care to explain how two lovely women, one in her upper years, shall we say, managed to dispatch a terrorist zealot? A murderous bitch that no one has been able to get near, let alone knock off?" asked Faris, both hands gripping the leather steering wheel in concentration.

"She made us mad and we didn't like her," Mikki responded, still nonchalantly bouncing her foot to the music.

CHAPTER TWENTY-SIX

Faris said nothing, but watched her face as they stopped for a red light on Seahorse Boulevard. Mikki had been silent and was chewing her lip, looking out the window at a darkened shopping plaza near the intersection.

"Mikki? Are you alright?" asked Faris.

"Sure," she answered, but her face clouded with uncertainty and uneasiness. Her mind was filled with the evening's events. Faris had seen what damage she and Emily could do...had seen it in person. There was no denying that. But how much to say, how much to tell? Here they were, disposing of a body wrapped in blue plastic that was now lying in the trunk.

"Maybe you'd care to fill me in on how you knew those moves? You surprised the shit out of me, and certainly Aziz. She wasn't expecting anything like that. Me neither."

"Grandma and I have been going to self-defense classes...a lot. We go to a lot of classes...on self-protection. They're always selling those to women now, you know."

"Yeah, I know. But this was a little more than that."

"We were mad and scared, too. My grandmother always told me that a little adrenaline could help a person do almost impossible things."

"I've heard that," answered Faris, as his right eyebrow raised just a little. His brows knit together in a sort of frown. Then he smiled, unaware of the captivating picture he made. Mikki smiled too, and then Faris took her hand.

"Where are we going exactly?" questioned Mikki.

"Gator Village," said Faris, pulling slowly from the intersection.

"Gator Village? Should you call Kamila?" asked Mikki. "She might be wondering where you are."

"I'll do that in a while. Can we just talk? I really want to know more about you."

"Truthfully, I don't know what else to say. I can tell you I'm an engineer, civil engineer. I work downtown and I live with my grandmother to help out since she had the stroke."

"Umm...she didn't look too physically needy when I saw her throw herself onto Aziz tonight. In fact, she acted like this was something normal and everyday. Afterwards, she just got herself a little glass of Scotch and went to her room to take a shower. She wasn't shaking or calling for smelling salts or fainting or anything. Plus, I didn't see a scratch on her. Pretty tough little old lady, I guess?"

"Oh yeah, pretty darn tough. I could tell you stories. Why don't you want to know about our attack cat?"

Just then a cell phone rang and Faris reached in his pocket. He spoke quietly in Arabic for a few moments. "It was Kami. She just got a call for me. They're delivering my stallion next week. He's been held in quarantine and will be ready to be released on Tuesday."

"Wow, I can't wait to see him! What's the bloodline? Can I ride him? What color did you say he is?" questioned Mikki.

"You seem more excited about the horse than me. He's a blood red bay with hind socks and a star. He's very athletic and confident. I plan to ride him, do some showing on the Arabian circuit, and then stand him at stud here in the U.S. He's a beauty."

"I can't wait to see him, Faris. Can I help with him?"

"Sure, he'll be stabled in your horse's barn. I made sure that's where the equestrian center reserved a place for him. That way I can keep an eye on you."

"Aren't you forgetting something?" asked Mikki.

"What?"

"We'll be spending lots of time together," said Mikki, with an impishly evil grin. "You proposed, I accepted. We're getting married!" She was determined to call out Faris and Emily at their own embarrassing game. "And we have lots to discuss about the wedding, our children, our home. You know, all that stuff!"

Faris said nothing, but slowed the Aston Martin and pulled onto a dark residential side street lined with palm tress and quaint streetlights. He stopped the car and turned off the engine. He reached for Mikki and pulled her closer, until she was almost in his lap. His arms encircled her body and crushed her tight against his chest until she could hardly breathe. His lips came aggressively down on hers and she succumbed to the forceful domination of his mouth. Mikki was shocked by her eager response that was short-circuiting her normal sense of inhibition. Her emotions whirled and skidded out of control as his tongue parted her lips in a soul-searching massage. She felt weak and quivery, lost in the sweetness of his kiss. As the kiss continued, his hand moved gently under her T-shirt in a heated path toward her breasts. Mikki did not resist, even though thoughts of caution entered her mind, she slammed the door shut on them. His touch was light and teasing, like a wonderful form of torture. The danger of the situation was so intoxicating that Mikki felt drunk with pleasure.

"Is this how you kill off women, Faris?" she whispered almost inaudibly, as she broke from his kiss, trying to catch her breath.

"I'm trying out a new method. You're my guinea pig,". he spoke directly into her ear and began to nibble on her earlobe.

"Thanks a lot," she murmured breathlessly, as she circled her arms around his neck and returned his kiss with reckless abandon. There was an almost dreamy intimacy to the kiss now. It was a kiss she had been waiting for her whole life. This man, this time, this night.

Faris now had both hands under her shirt and her breasts rose to the gentleness of his touch. He had eased the lacy cups of her bra aside and was stroking the taut, pink nipples with reverence. His right hand reached behind her and unsnapped her bra and as he cradled the breasts under his palms, he groaned with pleasure. A car's headlights approached them and they stopped for only a moment. The passing vehicle only added to their excitement.

"Mikki, you're everything I ever wanted," said Faris, nuzzling close to her.

"I think I've finally gone over the edge. I'm crazy," Mikki murmured, with just a glance at the car's taillights fading away down the street.

Her flesh felt sleek and smooth beneath his touch as his hands searched for pleasure points. His pants were getting uncomfortably tight as he pulled her shirt over her head, leaving her nearly naked in his lap. Mikki couldn't stop him. Warning lights and sirens were going off in her head, but she shut each one off without another thought.

His hands were exploring her thighs and his mouth searched and found sensitive, swollen nipples. Mikki sighed with delight. She didn't stop him as his hand found the zipper to her jeans, pulled it down, and began to pull the waist. She rose a little and helped him pull her pants off. *What the hell am I doing?* But there was no stopping this madness. She reached for his crotch and found his stone-hard erection to her liking. She pulled at the zipper and his manhood rejoiced and rose with the newfound freedom. Faris' hand slowly crept through uncharted territory to the soft mound of red curly hair until he found her most intimate area. He tentatively touched and rubbed until she all but screamed with pleasure. She had now gripped him and began to move her hand in a tormenting, lustful rhythm.

"I want you," Faris said, hoarsely. He pulled her, now naked, onto him. The beauty of her shapely body rose and fell in front of him. The shadow of it permanently etched into his memory by the soft glow of the street lamp. His mouth explored her breasts as the movement of the two lovers became more urgent, almost frantic. Now his hands reached below her butt cheeks and urged a quicker pace. She writhed above him, their bodies in an exquisite rhythm. With an explosion of fiery sensations, they both groaned as dangerously forbidden ecstasy throbbed through them, seeming to never stop.

Mikki was filled with an amazing sense of completeness. She had never felt this kind of sexual desire. The dormant sexuality of her body had awakened in a most pleasant, yet perilous way. Faris continued to breathe hard in panting gasps. Mikki worried now that while he'd been merely satisfying a moment of male physical desire, she had allowed him to tear into her soul. She had fully responded to the seduction of his passion. Her desire for him had overridden everything else. She was here on a public street, sitting naked on the lap of a man she had just met. Risk and vulnerability had only elevated her desire in the parked car. She had totally exalted in his maleness and was lost in the beauty of him.

As she climbed away from him, she searched quickly for her tangled lingerie, but gave up the chase. Faris watched her, unable to move. Finally he sat up straight and looked around. The windows were opaque with steam. This was a good thing. This was not the time or place, but he hadn't been able to control himself. As he stuffed himself back in his pants, he watched her pull on her jeans and shirt.

"You're beautiful, but then you know that," he said, trying to bring his heartbeat back under control.

Mikki eyed him as she pulled her shirt back over her head and zipped her jeans. She tossed her wavy auburn locks and gave him her sexiest smile. "You ain't so bad yourself, Mr. Busaid."

"So how does next week sound?" he asked her, his eyes shining with purpose.

"That's our next date?" asked Mikki. She didn't want to wait that long.

"Oh no, we'll be doing more of this togetherness stuff real soon. Next week, let's see, the horse arrives Tuesday. How 'bout we get married on Friday? I'm not busy that day."

Mikki watched his eyes for a hint of the joke, but he was studying her intently.

"I'm not joking," he said, his gaze was now intense.

Mikki felt the hysteria of delight rising inside her. He loved her! He must be crazy, too! She was so overcome that she couldn't speak. He had been rubbing the back of her neck and she was hypnotized by his touch.

"I love you," she ventured and snuggled again into his arms, burying her face against his curly chest hairs.

"Does that mean that it's a good day or no?" he persisted.

"Yes, yes, yes!!" she shouted, fully aware of what she was saying. "Do we have to wait that long?"

"Well, it'll take that long to tell, well…warn our families, and of course, I need to buy some rings."

"Faris…you *are* serious! Oh my God!" said Mikki, as she sat back to watch his face. No… he was no longer kidding. He meant it. She had not done anything this nuts since she rescued her grandmother from Citrus City two years ago. What would Mom, Brigetta, and most of all, Emily say? She absolutely did not care. She felt alive and feminine for the first time in her life.

CHAPTER TWENTY-SEVEN

Mikki sat as close to Faris as physically possible with her butt balancing on the console. The bucket seats were comfortable, but she wanted to be closer to him and to never let him go. She was afraid that something would happen to break the spell, to break them apart.

"You know I was kidding, right?"

Jolted by his statement, she jerked away and looked at him, her heart splitting in two pieces.

"Not the wedding! Going to Gator Village!" he said in quick explanation.

"You scared me," said Mikki. "Please, don't ever do that again."

"I promise," he said, as his arm curled around her shoulders and warmly pulled her close to him. "I promise I'll never hurt you. I love you. You and your grandmother scare the shit out of me, but I love you."

"Yeah, we're some pretty scary chicks, alright. Just be nice to us and all will be well," said Mikki, pleased and happy. She squeezed his hand, then pulled away to search for a map in the glove box. "Just where are we going, anyway?"

"Stop digging in there and look under the seat. I have a GPS and we're heading for the Everglades. Aziz will be meeting some gators, but not at a park where kids might find her pieces parts hanging out of Big Tooth's mouth or something."

"I hope you brought insect repellent."

"That's under the seat, too."

"You are certainly one well-prepared man. Are you sure you don't have some wedding rings hidden in here somewhere?" Mikki couldn't help talking about their marriage. It hadn't sunken in just yet. She just knew that her body still tingled from his touch and their impromptu lovemaking. She put her head on his shoulder, finally exhausted and engulfed in tides of weariness and satisfaction.

"Put the seat back and take a little nap. We have about an hour drive. I'll wake you when we're close to a good spot and you can help me get Aziz out of the trunk."

Mikki had almost forgotten they weren't on a road trip to a fun destination. There was a dead person in the back end of the car. They had made love with a dead woman in the trunk. She rested against him, curling into a fetal position, her face against his chest. She slept.

Soon she felt a gentle jiggling on her shoulder and awakened wondering where she was. She smelled that fabulous man-smell and the citrus aftershave. She sat up and then leaned to meet his kiss.

"Let's go. We don't want to be seen here," urged Faris, as he pushed himself from the low-bodied car. When he reached the rear of the car, Mikki was there to meet him. They heaved the rolled tarp from the trunk and dragged it to the edge of the saw grass. His flashlight canvassed the dark area of squishy mud, marshes, and swamp.

"Over here!" he said urgently, as he pulled the body closer to the muddy shore. "Look!" he said, as he pulled Mikki to him and pointed into the beam of the flashlight. There were several twin reflections of light staring back at them. "Alligators! See their eyes?"

"Can we just get outta here? This is too spooky for me," said Mikki, swatting at a mosquito buzzing near her ear. Even in the soggy heat, goose bumps were forming on her arms. Just as she spoke, there was noisy turmoil in the grasses just off shore and some loud grunting. She gasped, realizing a moment of panic. A quick and disturbing thought flew into her mind. *What if all this was a ploy? This man could be a terrorist...what if he meant to leave me here, too? Dead women tell no tales or something like that?*

"Mikki!" Faris said insistently, handing her a spray can of Off Deep Woods. "Come closer to the water and help me!"

Mikki just stood there frozen, sudden icy fear squeezed around her heart like a boa constrictor.

"Hurry! Look!" insisted Faris, turning off his flashlight.

Mikki turned to look and saw headlights coming down the road to the swamp. What if it was the convenient ambulance guys again? She could smell the musty odors of the boggy ground begin to mix with her own sweat. She made a quick decision. She hurried to Faris and together they unrolled the body from its blue plastic cover and heard it splash into the muck. Faris grabbed her arm forcefully and she let out a tiny screech as he yanked her towards him and threw her to the ground. Both were panting from the exertion of moving the body and were listening to the sound of tires squishing down the nearby damp and grassy road. Mikki's nose filled with the loamy smell of wet mud and vegetation as she lay on the ground.

"Quiet! Shssh!" Faris demanded. They were still and soon the car passed. In the glow of the moon, they could see a large alligator inching towards Aziz's body. Suddenly the jaws clamped down on the dead woman's head as the gator dragged her into the watery grasses. Several other gators began slapping their tails and jaws and grunting their arguments regarding ownership of their discovered prize. So close to feeding alligators, Mikki had never been this terrified.

Faris rolled onto Mikki and held her down by the wrists. Mikki's heart was pounding so hard she thought it might leap from her chest, *Alien* style…but this was no Sci-fi movie.

"You okay?" he asked, his face inches from hers.

"You're squishing me. I'm scared. I'm wet and bugs are flying up my nose, but other than that, I'm just dandy."

His weight was pushing her into the softened damp ground. She felt totally powerless.

"Wanna play around?" he said. She knew he was grinning, although she couldn't see his face in the moonlight. His hands loosened her wrists and began to move up her sides towards her braless breasts. As she moved her mouth to reply, he covered her lips with his. His broad shoulders were rolling as he breathed. He was moving himself between her legs. In the distance, the gators were splashing and fighting, dangerously close. The couple lay only ten feet from the edge of the swamp.

Mikki fought to speak, but instead she buried her face in the corded muscles of his chest and began to kiss him. *What is wrong with me?* She heard that thought in her mind. *I need psychiatric help!* Faris was again making dangerous love to her and she was unable to resist. Amid the sounds of splashing gators, the couple was finally still and silent, exhausted. Mikki realized that wet mud was seeping through the back of her top. She could hear the buzz of hoards of mosquitoes dive-bombing her ears. Large alligators were all around them and Faris was snoring!

"Faris! Get up!" she insisted and wiggled her body out from under him. He got up and helped her to her feet. He felt around in the grass until he found the flashlight and then aimed the beam at Mikki.

"Good God! You're a mess! I don't know if I should take you out on any more dates or not!" he said, as he appraised her mud-soaked clothes, hair, and body. Then he began to laugh.

"You! You don't look so great yourself!" she accused, trying hard to yank on her now damp jeans, which were a little tight to begin with. Finally she was dressed and Faris had stopped laughing. The knee areas of his once neatly pressed, pleated Dockers were brown with stuck-on muck and an assortment of brown sticky grasses.

"Uh, yeah. Maybe we can run through a car wash on the way home? You know, get naked again, hose off our clothes…and my very expensive car?"

Mikki glared at him.

"Okay, I give in. No more making love in public places…tonight. Let's go home. And don't sit on my seats! I've got some extra blankets in the storage area in the trunk," he said.

"I'm ready. Let's go," said Mikki, now anxious to get out of here and back home. She was still brushing pieces of weeds off her pants.

But Faris wasn't planning on taking her back to the Pink Flamingo.

CHAPTER TWENTY-EIGHT

Emily showered and put on some lavender sweat pants and an old T-shirt that she usually wore to bed. She couldn't sleep and went back to the office to take a look at the computer. She punched on the monitor and clicked search mode. The tiny round homing device she had planted under the fender of Mr. Busaid's Aston Martin was still working. Emily followed the travels of her granddaughter and this guy who had captured her heart. *I just can't help myself, Mikki. You don't know him and I've got all this spy ware just sitting around doing nothing.* The monitor showed the position of the car on a map, similar to a GPS system. She realized they must have dumped Aziz's body in the Everglades. She wondered to herself what was taking so long. Surely they couldn't possibly be screwing around out there among the snakes and gators. Even she had never done that!

Well, there was the time in Tunisia. Joe had been working overseas for two months and Emily decided to fly to the desert to see him. She smiled as she thought of old times. She and Joe had taken a weekend to drive to Tozeur to have lunch in the Saharan oasis town of Gafsa. The next day they went to the Saharan Zoo and Botanical Gardens. Then they took a train, the renowned "Red Lizard," and rode through the gorges and canyons of the desert. Emily recalled getting a room at Douz that had a romantic view of the Saharan dunes. They had gone on a camel safari and that night, in front of God and a dozen camel eyes, they made love in the moonlight. What happy memories, she thought, as she replayed them in her mind. When Joe had a heart attack, he was gone so suddenly. Surely she couldn't begrudge this young couple their fun.

It worried her that Mikki was so smitten by this man. True, he seemed very likable, certainly good-looking, and also smart. Emily had discovered that he was with the C.I.A., but there was an aura of danger surrounding him. Most likely, Mikki found that part of him also quite attractive. Mikki was just like her grandmother. She, too, loved the adrenaline rush, the sense of peril, the threat of discovery. When Emily discovered just who Faris was, she was shocked to realize she knew someone in his family. A phone call was in order. Still smiling after the overseas call, Emily felt better. But to be sure, Emily decided to wait up for her granddaughter. The knitting needles were sterilized in the dishwasher and the floor was mopped and clean. Mrs. Gambrand from the Civic Association would never suspect that the same spot where she would be sipping tea for next week's bridge game was recently a blood splattered murder scene.

At 2 A.M., the phone rang and Emily jumped up to get it. She had been dozing off while trying to complete the *New York Times* crossword. Rubbing her eyes to awaken herself, she listened.

"Granny! I've been kidnapped!"

"Huh? What!" shouted Emily, holding the phone close to her ear and ready to put a trace on the call.

"Well, sorta anyway. Faris is taking me to his condo for a quick stop before he brings me home. Just didn't want you to worry or wait up. I didn't wake you, did I?"

"I was doing the puzzle," said Emily, with relief in her voice.

"Good. Umm…we got a little messy during the disposal job and we're going to his place to clean up."

"Clean up? Is that what you young folks call it these days?" said Emily with a hint of false indignation.

"Gran! Where do you get these wild ideas anyway? Kami's there, you know. And I kinda wanted to talk to her some more. We need to figure out where her husband might be, before he causes any more trouble."

"And all of this can't wait 'til morning? It's not like I've never seen you dirty. Remember the horse, the barn, the manure?"

"I'm okay, Gran. Please don't worry and I'll see you soon, okay? Lock everything up real tight and leave all the security on, too."

"Oh, well, I never would have thought to do that on my own. What do you think? I'm an imbecile?"

"No, of course not. I'm just worried. Lots of shit going on and you're there by yourself."

"Well, come home. Not now, but soon. Okay? Promise?"

"Yeah, Gran. Soon." There was just a bit of hesitation and then Mikki blurted out, "We have something important to talk about!"

"What something would that be? Of course we have lots of things to go over, not on the phone, but in person. We always have things to rehash and reevaluate. That's part of what we do."

"Nope, this is bigger than all that."

"I'm waiting."

"I'm getting married next week!"

"To whom?" asked Emily, unable to think of what else to say. Surely she had misunderstood her granddaughter.

"To Faris, of course! Who else?" said Mikki, excitement in her voice.

"Of course. Mikki. Come home right now. You must be on drugs. I'm hanging up. Have you been drinking?" asked Emily.

"Bye, Gran. Seeya later this morning!"

CHAPTER TWENTY-NINE

"Were you trying to give her a heart attack?" asked Faris, surprised, but smiling after listening to Mikki's outburst on the phone. "I thought we were going to ease people into the idea."

"This is how you ease my grandmother into things. Say it and run away 'til it sinks in. Let her have time to mull it around in her head, then sneak back home. By morning, she'll just be dying to know all the details and forget about yelling at me."

"Somehow I have a problem believing the part where she forgets that announcement. She might come after me with a gun or something."

"Hmmm...probably not," said Mikki, finger on her chin, thinking.

"Probably not?" questioned Faris, dark eyes rimmed with question.

"Well, you just never know how she'll react to things, but she hasn't killed any of my friends or anything...and only one boyfriend," said Mikki, with a shrug.

"What?" said Faris, staring at her as they sat at a stop sign.

"Just kidding. Geez, you're so gullible, just like a man," said Mikki. "Had you goin' there though, didn't I?"

"Like I said, you scare me. And I always used to consider myself pretty fearless. You know, going to Al Quada training camps and all that. I wasn't nearly as nervous with bin Ladin as I am with you," said Faris, giving her a little peck on the cheek and driving the car away from the intersection.

"Yeah, you look real scared. Hey, where are we going, anyway?"

"My condos are just to the east, near the Intracostal, but not directly on the water. You and your grandmother have a beautiful place. So you're a rich bitch? I mean I saw the clothes, the jewelry, the mansion."

"Well, my job pays okay. But my grandmother has some money. No big secret. I mean that beach house is on three acres of prime real estate, right on the Atlantic. I live with her and she helps me out financially and I help her out physically."

"What does Mrs. Vanderhorn do? Is she retired from big business or did your grandfather leave her well-off?"

"She did get money from Grandpa Joe, but she has her own business. It's a shop on Worth Avenue called Favors. It's a party and gift shop. She does a lot of decorating at all the elaborate bashes of the rich and famous. Also she sells exclusive gifts and custom made party decorations and favors. Just gorgeous stuff. Gran used to design or hand pick most of the items, but now she lets Rosa and Tamille do most of that. She goes to the shop almost every day, since she's still the manager, but she needs more time to herself now. My sister, who's a nurse, and I often help out in the shop. We've done that since we were little kids. We also house sit for her or watch her two cats if she goes away on a trip. Now, though, mostly I go with her when she wants to travel, in case she needs assistance."

"So, will you still be traveling around with your grandmother after we get married?"

"Wow, I never really considered all that. Sure, if she needs me, I'll need to be there."

"Okay. As long as you aren't gone too long. I'd miss you too much," said Faris, as he pulled the Aston Martin into a driveway leading to a gated condominium community. He swiped his key card and the gate swung open. Mikki looked around as they drove along on clay-colored brick pavement. Palm trees silhouetted by strands of tiny white lights surrounded a community pool that was closed for the night. The effect was a dreamy aura. The condos were all Spanish style with stucco and red tile roofing. Some condos had bell towers and the whole complex had a Southern mission look. Very classy and beautiful, thought Mikki as Faris pulled towards the unit on the far end and clicked his garage door opener. *I could live here.* Mikki could see a small light on in the upstairs window.

"Will Kamila still be up? Will she be worried about you?" asked Mikki, touching Faris's arm. She felt a little anxious about meeting his sister in this new circumstance, curious, but a little anxious, too.

"She'll be up. She doesn't like being here by herself. She's afraid that Sajid or Hassad will find her. We can't blame her for that. I can't imagine what they would do to her if they did get their hands on her again."

There was no typical keyhole on his doorknob, but Faris swiped a card to gain entry to his home. Mikki wondered how Aziz gained entry to Faris'condo, but she followed, holding his hand. The kitchen was dark, only a small nightlight near the stove showed them the way to the main floor. The kitchen smelled of strong Arabic coffee and the room was clean, looking almost sterile. Faris led Mikki to a small living room and pointed to a spot on a comfortable striped sofa.

"I'll go get Kami. Wait here," he instructed.

He went to the pantry door near the stairs and opened it. Pushing aside several rolling shelves of canned goods, he knocked and said something in Arabic. The panel lurched and then slid aside. This was the doorway to the adjoining condominium. No one inside or outside the condos would suspect the secret connection. Kami, looking small, frail, and tired, stepped through the opening and into the living room. She wore a typical Arab burqa, but her face was uncovered. She was obviously surprised to see Mikki sitting on her brother's couch.

"Hello again, Kamila," said Mikki, standing and walking towards the girl, smiling and extending her hand.

"Hello," said Kamila, her large mahogany eyes now questioning her brother.

"This is Mikelle Walsh, Kami. You remember she helped you in the airport? Well, she is also my girlfriend."

Kamila's eyes darted back and forth between the two, not understanding. Pensively she looked down, trying to put the pieces together. She sighed and clasped her hands together, staring at her entwined fingers in bewilderment. She was fearful and uncertain almost all the time now. She tried to smile and reached for Mikki's hand.

"Hello, Mikelle. I hope you are well," she said as her voice wavered. "So you were helping Faris at the airport?" she asked cautiously.

"Uh...yes. We had the same goal, I think," Mikki answered, not knowing what else to say. Apparently Faris hadn't told his sister anything about her. Of course, until tonight there wasn't much to tell. Mikki again realized how fast things were moving.

"Would you like some coffee, Mikelle?" asked Kamila, hoping she didn't sound as hesitant as she felt. She had to sheath her inner feelings as inadequacy swept over her. She wanted her brother to help her and not be distracted by this woman, this muddy, disheveled woman. Why were the two of them filthy dirty? They looked like they had been rolling in mud, thought Kamila.

Faris answered for Mikki, "No thanks on the coffee. We need showers. Just go to bed now, Kami. The danger is over. Aziz is gone for good and you're safe. We're all safe. We're going to clean up and get some rest. We went off the road a little and had to push my car out of a messy quagmire. We're both exhausted and dirty, as you can see. We're going to shower, have a glass of wine, and sleep for a while. Then we'll all have some breakfast and Mikki will go home in the morning."

"Whatever you wish, Faris," said Kamila, as she turned away with a swish and began to climb the stairs to her bedroom.

"She won't turn on any lights up there. She dresses and undresses in the dark. I have given her the whole second floor so she'll feel private and secure. I'm not sure she even trusts me. She just wants to get out of the States and back home to our mother."

"Can you get her out?" asked Mikki, looking worried.

"I think so. But it would be best to eliminate those men first."

"She looks petrified. Will she help get rid of her husband?"

"Even though he beat her, she believes she should honor her husband. She has a lot of confusing issues to deal with right now. Plus she's worried about her baby, the one she left in New York at the hospital."

In spite of her efforts to stifle it, Mikki yawned. "Sorry, I can't help it," she said, covering her mouth with her hand.

"Me, too. Let's go to my suite and get cleaned up," said Faris, also yawning.

"We've got plenty of time tomorrow to worry about all this. Right now, I just want to get in the shower…with you."

CHAPTER THIRTY

Mikki awoke to the smell of freshly brewing coffee and turned over to reach for Faris. They had showered and fallen into bed naked and clean, so exhausted that they fell asleep immediately. Mikki awoke alone. She was no longer entwined in a man's arms but tangled in a mass of crisp cotton sheets, her head on a mound of feather pillows. In the morning's light, she surveyed the room, sand-colored walls with glossy white woodwork and window trim. Mini window blinds encased in the glass shielded some of the morning sun from the east-facing bedroom. The furniture had a beautiful cherry finish, simple and manly. The king-sized bed faced a triple-sliding door that led to a deck. She saw Faris sitting outside at a glass-topped table sipping coffee and reading a newspaper. She watched him silently for a minute, but then seeing a terry robe draped over an upholstered chair, got up and put on the robe. In the adjoining bathroom, she washed her face and rinsed her mouth with a swish of his mouthwash. Then she tossed her hair around while surveying her face in the mirror. She found her purse and dug through it until she retrieved a hair band. She bent over at the waist, gathered her auburn locks toward the top of her head and secured them into position with the band. Then Mikki twirled the top of her hair into a knot and pinned it in place. Standing, she surveyed her image. Oh well, she thought, nothing would keep her from her man.

Mikki slid open the doors and Faris stood to guide her to a chair at the table. He kissed her cheek and said, "Good morning, gorgeous. I want to see you wake up every morning I live…from now on. You're beautiful right out of bed."

"Gee…thanks. You don't happen to have a toothbrush, do you? I'm a mess!"

"I love your mess. But, yep, I have a toothbrush. In the off season it works to clean my grout," he said, quickly adding, "just kidding. Let me get you a nice new one from my stash."

"Oh, the stash you save for all the girls you bring home? Umhumm. I've got your number."

"I'm sure you do have my number, but I don't bring girls here. What are you talking about? I'm an engaged-to-be-married-next-Friday man," said Faris, sitting back down.

"Yeah, and I could tell you're a virgin, too," said Mikki.

"Could you tell?" chuckled Faris, looking back to his *USA Today*.

There was a second door leading to the wide deck from the kitchen. It slid open and Kamila stepped onto the cedar planks. Mikki took the time to appraise the woman in the daylight. She looked to be in her mid-twenties and younger than her brother. Now Kamila wore a navy blue long skirt and a white silk blouse and head covering. She was a very stunning young woman with huge nut-brown eyes and a flawless complexion. The greenish bruises were fading to yellow, becoming almost invisible. Kami carried a wooden tray with a glass carafe of very dark coffee, steaming and aromatic. White porcelain mugs, sugar, and thick cream were placed on an embroidered napkin on the tray. Tiny cream-filled pastries and slices of oranges sprinkled with powdered sugar were on a plate.

Mikki was suddenly very hungry. Faris rolled his hand toward the tray and said, "Please, help yourself. May I pour you some coffee?"

"Coffee smells great. Please, yes," answered Mikki as she reached for a napkin and some finger food. "I'm starving. It was a very busy night," she added, daring a glance at the smiling Faris. He nodded and held his cup in his hands, sipping coffee and watching the women.

"Kami, please join us," said Faris as he motioned her toward the other seat at the table.

"I'm afraid to be outside here. What if people see me?" said Kamila, wringing her hands, her eyes darting here and there towards the bushes and trees surrounding the deck.

"Sit," he ordered gently, "You'll be fine. No one can see through all this vegetation. And there's a wall at the front and a gate at the road. Please. Sit and join us. Aziz will not be back. You need to eat, to relax. We need to talk."

For the next two hours, the three of them sat at the little table and talked. Kami had two goals. One was to leave the country and return to her mother in Saudi Arabia. The second was to retrieve Sofah from New York. The first challenge was difficult, yet possibly attainable. Faris knew how to get her out of the United States and Mikki agreed to help if she could. The CIA, the FBI, Homeland Security...they would all be looking for Kamila bint Bahir Al-Busaid and her husband. They had stolen a baby and used it to make a bomb with the help of an Arab surgeon from Miami. None of the men who had accompanied her to the airport had been captured. Those men would be looking for Kamila. She was a traitor to their cause, since she had saved the lives of the infidels and her own baby. A baby conceived in marriage for only one reason...to become a political martyr, to become a human bomb, to blow up a plane full of American passengers. The bomb would never have been detected and the group would have been allowed to board the plane. The terrorists had failed because Kami had not completed her task. She had put herself and her baby above the Jihad, above Allah. This could not be forgiven.

"I really have to go," said Mikki, wiping her mouth with a napkin. She was really wired from the strong coffee. It gave her the strength to go home and try to explain things to her grandmother. "Can you drive me back to the Pink Flamingo?"

"Sure, if I have to give you up," Faris said, standing and brushing crumbs from his pants. He looked like a model for a tennis racquet ad. Bronze skin, black wavy hair, eyes that turned sable in the sunshine, white polo shirt and shorts. He had already shaved and showered before Mikki had even opened one eye to greet the day.

Mikki just wanted to get home and catch up on her usual grooming routine and get a long, hot bath. She felt a little sore and wasn't sure it was from lifting dead weight the night before. Maybe something else, something else more pleasurable had caused this aching sensation in her lower body.

After Kamila was secured into the adjoining condo, Faris backed the Aston Martin out of the driveway and headed in the direction of the beach. Mikki rolled down the windows and told him she wanted to feel and smell "real" air, so he turned off the air conditioner and mimicked her exaggerated inhalations out the window, panting like a Labrador Retriever.

"I know you're making fun of me! But I smell rain, do you?" asked Mikki, still sticking her nose out the window and shutting her eyes. She inhaled the saltiness of the sea as they drove closer to the beach house districts. As they pulled onto Emily's street, clouds were forming to the east and Faris could see a glint of a lightning flash towards the southern horizon.

"If I could drive with my eyes closed, I'm sure I could do a better job of smelling, but if you open your eyes, you can see the thunderclouds and lightning rolling in closer to shore," said Faris, grinning.

Opening her eyes and seeing that they were already at the Pink Flamingo's driveway, Mikki looked around sheepishly. "Oh yeah. It's getting ready to rain."

At that moment, splatters of giant raindrops began to plop onto the windshield. Mikki gave him the code to the security gate and in an instant they were in front of the massive pink marble staircase. The stairs led to the imported mahogany double doors high in the foyer. The etched glass windows sparkled from reflected sunlight bouncing off the crystal chandelier hanging in the entryway. A beautiful and welcoming entrance, looking more like the gateway to a five-star hotel than a beach cottage, but Mikki just sat in the passenger seat. She regarded Faris quizzically for a moment.

"You're not coming in, are you?"

"Hell, no."

"Sissy."

"Hey, she's your grandmother. You're the one who had to tell her everything over the phone. I said we should break it to our families gently. Families are important. God, we have until next Friday, for God's sake."

It was now raining harder. Mikki pulled her purse from the floor and grabbed his arm. She kissed him on the cheek and said, "Good-bye. If she doesn't kill me, I'll call you later. Thanks for the use of your washer and dryer. At least I don't have to explain the mud."

Faris reached for a black umbrella from the back seat and knew he should walk her to the door. But Mikki grabbed it, leaped from the car, and ran up the stairway. Halfway up she looked back, rain now soaking her pant legs, and saw him staring at her as the windshield wipers attempted warp speed. She darted back down the stairs and ran to his window, which he rolled down.

"I love you, Faris Al-Busaid," she yelled through the sound of rolling thunder, and she reached through the window for his face, kissed him quickly, turned and ran for the shelter of home. He smiled, and seeing her slip safely inside the big doors, he circled the car around the drive and headed back to his condo. He would need to remember these happy moments, since he never knew when events would begin to turn against him.

CHAPTER THIRTY-ONE

"You've decided to return, little lost grandchild?" asked Emily, as she wiped off the sink in the kitchen. "How did it go?"

"No problems. We took a trip to the Everglades. R.I.P. That's it."

"That's it?"

"That's it for Aziz. Are you okay, Gran? I mean that was a lot of jumping around for someone with a blue handicapped tag on her rearview mirror," asked Mikki, as she examined her grandmother, eyeing her up and down.

"Do I look any worse for the wear? I took a couple of ibuprofen tablets this morning. I did notice you two left me here to do all the dirty work. Mop the floors and all that stuff."

"And...?"

"And what?" answered Emily, still pretending to be busy in the kitchen.

Mikki just stood there waiting. Then she twirled her butt onto the bar stool at the kitchen counter to face Emily up close. "What did you think...of Faris?"

"Oh, him?" she said, as she wiped the counter closer and closer to Mikki's planted elbows. Suddenly Mikki grabbed the dishtowel from her grandmother and tossed it into the living room. It landed unceremoniously on the back of the sofa.

"Yes, I mean him," exclaimed Mikki, throwing her arms above her head in exasperation. "Do you like him?"

Emily grinned, "Sure, he seems like he's just your type. Very handsome, dark and mysterious, with that certain element of danger. I can see why you like him...and his Glock, the whole perilous uncertainty thing. I find him somewhat attractive myself!"

"Well, you can't have him. He's mine and we're getting married next Friday!" Mikki blurted out quickly before she lost her nerve.

The two women stared at each other as Emily's mouth gaped in surprise. She was unable to speak after this confirmation that she hadn't dreamed last night. Mikki was just happy she had thrown it all out on the table and now they could pick through it, piece by piece. It felt good, like cleaning out your purse. Mikki was relieved that there were no lurking shadows over her heart. She had plopped everything out of her head and the feeling it gave her was euphoric. Emily watched her granddaughter. Mikki was serious. Joy shone from Mikki's eyes and Emily could see she was truly happy. Maybe the happiest she'd ever seen her. She studied Mikki's face, reading just the tiniest bit of uneasiness. Emily knew what she needed to say.

"That's wonderful!" exclaimed Emily, racing around the counter to embrace Mikki.

"It is? You're really okay with it? You're not going to lecture me?"

Emily reached her granddaughter and the two hugged. Emily took Mikki's face between her palms as she looked into those flashing green eyes. "I've never seen you this excited or happy about anything. Even the horse didn't make you glow like this! I'm just so thrilled for you, darling!"

Mikki's eyes became moist and a cry of relief burst from her lips. "I just knew you'd understand. My dear grandma…you'd be there for me."

"Of course! You're no dummy! If he's the one, he's the one! That's it!" said Emily, picking up a clean towel and dabbing at Mikki's eyes. "I trust your choices. I love you. But how in the hell are we going to have a wedding by next Friday?"

"I love you, Gran. You're something really special. Weird and different, too. But so special to me. I just don't know what I'd do without you."

"Sure, all you kids say that when you want something," said Emily, brushing wrinkles off her blouse and going to the phone. "You just want me to break the news to Susan and your father, right?"

"Would you mind?" said Mikki, sounding meeker than she intended.

Emily just laughed and picked up the phone to dial. As her fingers poked at numbers, she said, "I'll make the call, you go change your clothes, fix your hair, put on some make-up, and put that smug I-just-got-out-of-bed look away for now. Remember, we have both of your parents to impress with this situation."

When Mikki just stood there, Emily waved her away with a swirl of her hand. Emily Vanderhorn, champion party producer and wedding planner, was now in her element. There would be no more fatal favors this week, just bouquets of flowers and linen tablecloths. At least that was the plan she had in mind.

CHAPTER THIRTY-TWO

Susan called Michael in New York and Emily left a message for Brigetta at the hospital. Soon the whole Walsh family would be in on the news. Mikki could hardly believe it herself. After the calls were made, Emily and Mikki sat on the veranda and celebrated with a champagne glass of Asti Spumante, complete with a stemmed Maraschino cherry. As they clinked their glasses together, Mikki began to fill in the details of what she'd learned about Kamila and Faris and the events of the last few days. Soon the women of the family would arrive at the Pink Flamingo to plan the wedding event scheduled for next Friday. As best they could figure, Susan was dealing with sensations of shock and awe. She had just mumbled agreement to everything Emily was telling her on the phone. Susan said she would call Michael and be right over. The family would be here soon and there would be lots of questions. Mikki knew her family would drop everything to come over after the surprise announcement. Yes, family was important, like Faris had said. For her, family loyalty was ingrained in her DNA. Family came first, now and forever. And soon, Faris would be part of their family…and she would be part of his. Kami would be her sister-in-law and Mikki wasn't sure how she felt about that. She didn't feel Kamila welcomed her, on the other hand, the girl truly had enough on her mind at this point. But Mikki had the distinct feeling that Kamila Busaid would not be happy when she learned about the wedding plans. Mikki could bring herself to feel sorry for her, but she didn't trust her. Hopefully, she and Faris could work out problems with his side of the family, but now she had her mother on the way to the Pink Flamingo. Susan's mind would be spinning a million different ways. And then her Dad…he was agreeable with almost everything Mikki had done. She hoped he wouldn't be disappointed this time.

More phone calls had been made. Mrs. Yolanda Grimes, they decided, would cater the party with a Caribbean flair. Yolanda and Emily had first been business acquaintances and then friends. Their friendship was sealed with the completion of a favor. That favor really brought Emily and Mikki to where they were today. Yolanda brought tasty menu renditions from her restaurant and catering business "Caribbean Soul" to the Pink Flamingo almost daily while Emily was recuperating from her stroke. She had been right there when anything was needed, from her best jerk chicken dish, to doing the grocery shopping and meal planning. Now she would help with the party. The short time for planning wouldn't bother Yolanda. She was a professional and already knew what the family liked to serve for parties.

Mikki knew, as she sipped her bubbly celebration drink, that her wedding would be wonderful. She and Emily sat waiting for their guests to arrive, rocking and watching the waves on the beach.

"So Kamila wants to retrieve her baby? That would be nearly impossible. She'd be arrested," said Emily, emptying her glass of Asti and digging her fingers in for the cherry.

"I know. The Feds would want to grab the whole family. I'm not so sure they're not back to following Faris around, either. I mean, since she's his sister, that's got to cast some doubt," said Mikki.

"It amazes me that *you* have no doubt. But," Emily quickly added, "I totally trust your judgment. If you say Faris is cool, I'll buy it. Besides, he's nearly as cute as George Clooney."

"Thank you, Gran. I'm worried about Mom, though. Brig will be full of questions, but she'll trust me too. After we three worked together to rescue you when you had the stroke, she's been my best friend and loyal confidante. When you were sick, even Mom came through like a champ. It was amazing. I hope they can still trust me now. With my choice, I mean."

"That's the key phrase right there. *Your* choice," said Emily, closing her eyes and enjoying the afternoon sunshine over the Atlantic. "Besides, it's the whole family loyalty thing. And you know how I am about that. The family sticks together and supports each other, no matter what."

"For sure, we all learned that growing up. What do you think Dad will say?"

"Your father isn't home enough to really notice if you've had a boyfriend for days or months or years. He won't say anything because you're his little girl and he isn't around much. He'll feel guilty because you're getting married and he hasn't met the guy yet."

"I suppose. Will he be upset because Faris is from Saudi?"

"Well, let's not spring it on any of them right away. You know, the stuff about Al Quada and all that? I think we'll wait on that information. Even I'm not brave enough yet for that. Let's let them get a chance to know Faris first."

"Oh, you mean like the introduction to you last night? Like when Aziz shows up and tries to kill us all? And Faris is here with a gun? And he and I have to dump a body in the middle of the night because you stuck a knitting needle through her brain? Is that how you knew Faris would be right for me?"

"We won't mention those things, will we? I knew Faris was right for you when you said he was. Case closed."

Mikki swallowed her last sip of Asti and was getting up to get them both some refills of courage when Mikki's cell phone rang. It was Brigetta. She hadn't been able to reach her mother and didn't know what was going on. She had called Mikki because she was worried about Granny Em.

"Hey, Mikki," said Brigetta. "Is everything okay?"

"Yep. Come over to Granny Em's house...we're planning a party."

"Okaay...right. I'm gonna leave the hospital and come over there for a party planning session?"

"Well, yes, it's a party to plan a party. There's a wedding next Friday!"

"And? I can't leave the hospital to help you guys figure out somebody's wedding! Are you nuts? I have patients to take care of...little sick kids. Why did Mom call me? What's going on?"

Mikki put the call on speakerphone so that Emily, still sitting on the balcony, could hear too. "Well, okay then, if you want to miss hearing about my fiancé?"

After seconds of silence, during which Mikki and Emily could only hear the background sounds of the busy hospital, Brigetta finally screamed, "You! You? You are getting married? When? And to whom?" She was laughing now and Mikki could picture her in the Pediatric Unit, tall and blond, jumping up and down in her Minnie Mouse scrubs with her stethoscope bouncing. Mikki smiled. Her younger sister was happy for her. She knew Brigetta would be excited and dying of curiosity to know all the details. "Are you kidding me, you're really serious, right?"

"Yep! And to answer your questions...it's next Friday and his name is Faris."

"Friday? Faris?" asked Brigetta. "What kind of a name is that? Sounds Mideastern."

"It is. He's from Saudi, originally. And he's very handsome," said Mikki.

Emily was still listening in to the conversation, her eyebrow raising a question to Mikki.

"Want to talk to Gran? She's right here listening to every word."

"Sure. Hi, Gran," said Brigetta. "So have you met this dude?"

Emily took the phone from Mikki and aiming a wink towards Mikki, now standing with her hands on her hips, she said, "Very handsome and knows Osama bin Ladin. That's all I know."

"You both are impossible. I'll be right over," said Brigetta, giggling.

Mikki heard the gate swing open and the rumble of the garage opening downstairs. Her mother was here.

Susan popped through the elevator doors like a kid at the school bell and ran to her daughter and said, "Are you pregnant?"

Both Mikki and Emily simultaneously burst into laughter. Finally Mikki said, wiping tears from her eyes, "Mom, what made you ask that question?"

"Well, because of the suddenness, the immediacy of the situation. I'm happy for you. I just want to make sure everything is all right," said Susan. The laughter of the others was arousing Susan's old uneasiness. She had never been able to maintain the intimacy and closeness that sustained the relationships between her daughters and her mother. She often felt awkward with them, feeling left out somehow.

"Sorry, Mom. I know how it must look. And this is really irregular, I know. In fact, I've just met the guy. It might sound stupid, but you've heard of love at first sight? Well, I think that's what happened."

"But why the quickie marriage? Why not wait?"

"I don't know. I just feel an urgency about him. About us. Maybe like it's now or never or something. I just have to have him. And you know I'm not usually like that."

"Congratulations, darling!" said Susan and reached for her daughter. Mikki felt immediate relief at her mother's acceptance.

"I left the gate open for Yolanda," said Susan, when they heard the doorbell ring. Mikki ran to answer the front door and opened it for Mrs. Grimes.

"Wow, Mrs. Grimes, you look great!" said Mikki, as Yolanda came inside. She was a tall Jamaican woman of her grandmother's age, with gorgeous mocha skin and raven black hair. She wore a magenta silk sheath with a matching wide belt and shoes. A wide brim hat with a huge silk mum and bow was angled stylishly on her head. Today she looked relaxed and serene. Getting both closure and revenge for the senseless and cruel murder of her granddaughter had taken away the signs of worry and unhappiness that had plagued her life in the past. And Yolanda knew she had only Emily to thank for that. Sacrifices had been made, favors had been done, and not a word more would be mentioned by either woman, not ever. Today was time for celebration.

Fifteen minutes later everyone heard the squeal of tires on the cobblestone drive. The little Mini Cooper convertible had arrived with Brigetta at the wheel. The driver flew out of the car and up the stairway and through the door before anyone could even turn around to meet her.

"Hi! Where is the man?" squealed Brigetta, panting from her run up the outside stairway.

"No elevator today? Hope you put your top up because it might rain," said the always practical Susan.

"Wheeere is he?" demanded the breathless girl still in nursing scrubs. Her sense of urgency was confirmed by damp straggles of long blond hair now coming loose and falling from her hairclip onto her shoulders and neck. Brigetta stood waiting with hands on hips.

"The meet-the-groom party comes later," said Mikki. "You're supposed to kiss the bride-to-be now!"

"I'd rather hug Faris," said Brigetta in typical pouty sister fashion, "but you'll do for now!"

Yolanda was already helping Emily in the kitchen with snacks and drinks and soon all were gathered and sitting in a circle in the living room. Susan held the notebook and the planning of Mikki's wedding began.

During all the excitement, Mikki just wanted Faris to call. She wanted to tell him her Dad was coming from New York City and to see if he had told Kami or his parents. She just wanted to hear his voice. Faris would soon call Mikki, but it wouldn't be what she wanted to hear. Something had happened that would change everything.

At 5:30 P.M. the familiar ring tone announced a call to Mikki's cell phone. The caller ID said it was from Faris. She rose from the group and strolled toward the balcony to take the call. The planning party was breaking up anyway, with most of the decisions made and decorations planned. The reception would be here at the Pink Flamingo, if Faris agreed, and the bridal couple would plan the ceremony itself. Only family would attend the wedding but the reception would include lots of close friends. Yolanda insisted on hosting a giant couple's bridal shower and gala party at the

Palm Beach Country Club, because "you need things to get started." With everything planned on the rush, they were lucky to get the Seahorse Dining Room for the shower at this late date. Actually there was a cancellation that worked out to benefit Mikki and Faris. Yolanda left right away to place a deposit on the room and do a reconnaissance of the floor plan for food set-up. While the remaining ladies began to clean up and make a few last minute phone calls, Mikki answered her phone outside.

"Hello? Faris?" she answered. "I've missed you…"

"Mikki. I need you to listen. Kami is gone."

CHAPTER THIRTY-THREE

"I stopped to do some shopping and run some errands and when I went back to the condo, she wasn't there. I think she left on her own. Her clothes are gone. No signs of foul play or forced entry," said Faris.

"Why would she do that? Where would she go?" asked Mikki.

"Maybe she got some idea about going to New York by herself and getting the baby. We all know she'd be arrested right away."

"Yeah, for one thing, her husband will probably be waiting for her to show up."

"Or else she called him and she took a cab to meet him. He could be promising that he'd get the baby for them. She's naive enough fall for that."

Mikki thought silently for a moment and then said, "Come back over here and we'll talk. Granny Em will know what to do. The other ladies are leaving now anyway."

"I don't want to drag your grandmother into this. What are you thinking?"

"You don't know my gran. She'll have some idea how to proceed. She always does."

"Okay, I'll come back. Be there in a few minutes."

"My sister and mom want to meet you. They'll be on their way home soon, so hurry so I can make the introductions, then they'll leave," said Mikki, ending the call.

"Mom! Brig! Faris is on his way over, so hold on just a few minutes so you can meet him, okay?" Mikki asked as she came back to the living room, pocketing her cell phone.

"Now? He's on his way?" asked Brigetta. Susan and Brigetta looked at each other and together said, "We wouldn't miss this for the world!" They both raced for the closest bathroom to begin reapplying their lipstick and smoothing their hair.

Emily pulled Mikki into the kitchen and whispered,

"What's going on?"

"Kamila's missing! I told him that the three of us would try to figure something out. He's on his way back here," Mikki continued, looking around to be sure she wasn't heard.

"Okay, we'll kick out the rest of the family soon after he gets here," said Emily quietly, her forehead wrinkled with concern, as she loaded dishes into the dishwasher. She waved Mikki back into the living room.

Faris arrived within fifteen minutes and the women were suitably impressed with Mikki's fiancé. Faris was as charming and as attentive as he could be considering his growing concern over Kamila's welfare. Kamila could easily become another Al Quada murder statistic. A grotesque beheading or some other graphic bloody scene was playing like a *CNN* video inside his head. He was willing to talk to Mikki about this, but he knew it was his position as protector in the family to find Kami and ensure her safety. Kami had gone along with the terrorist plot, but Faris also knew that she probably would have had little choice in the decision. Kami had been programmed and brainwashed to believe whatever her husband and his group of family outlaws presented to her. She wanted her baby back and he was sure she would do almost anything to find and reclaim Sofah. Besides being worried, he was also angry with her. In leaving the safety of his condo, she had gravely underestimated the ferociousness of the Jihad group and the fact that to them she was now a traitor. The punishment would be terrible and fatal. He had to try to find her before Sajid or Hassad did any more damage.

After the allotted minutes of meet and greet with Faris, Mikki followed her sister and mom down the stairs to their cars. Brigetta turned to lean close to her sister, whispering in her ear, "He's hot...does he have a brother?"

Mikki just smiled and said, "We'll check out all the relatives later. Maybe there's a sheik or prince somewhere in the family line for you, who knows?"

Waving good-bye as she hurried back up the stairs, she

ran to Faris and gave him a big hug. "I'm so sorry. We'll find her."

Pulling Mikki outside to the balcony and eyeing Emily who was trying to busy herself again in the kitchen, Faris said, "I'll find her. I've made the decision. I must find her myself. It's my position in the family to find and protect my sister. There's no way I'm dragging you or any of your family into this mess. This is not a job for ladies. I'm leaving, but I'll be back as soon as things are resolved. We'll get married next Friday, just as planned. And I'll be back in time for the big party your family is planning, I promise."

"But..." Mikki began.

Faris grabbed her and pulled her to him in a tight squeeze. When she began to speak again, he kissed her hard and long, silencing her efforts to speak. When they broke apart, her eyes were misty and she looked sad and worried.

"I want to go with you," she murmured, arms around his neck.

"Listen, Mikki. My mind is made up. Someone needs to finish planning our wedding. Okay? And remember that the horse arrives next Monday or perhaps Tuesday. If I'm not back, can you be at the stable to receive him and get him settled? Can you do that for me?"

"Sure. Okay. Maybe I'll take him for a little spin," answered Mikki in an attempt to lighten the situation, but still hugging his neck. "Will I be able to call you? You promise that you'll be back for our wedding?"

"I promise. I'll call you when I know more and can figure things out. I'll be around gathering information, but I'm staying away from here and from you for now. It's not safe. First Aziz and then who'll be next to follow us around? It's too risky."

Mikki decided this was not the time to question his decision or interfere with his family.

Instead she said, "I'll miss you. Please come back safely and quickly."

"I will," he said, and he turned and walked away.

CHAPTER THIRTY-FOUR

For the next few days, Mikki went to work and waited and worried. Faris had disappeared and there were no calls. Emily tried not to notice as the weekend arrived and Mikki became less communicative and spent more time walking on the balcony and recharging the battery on her cell phone. The wedding arrangements had been completed and quick planning by experts guaranteed a beautiful setting and fabulous food. The hastily prepared guest list would include family and friends of both bride and groom. Faris, thankfully, had given his guest list to Emily before his hasty departure. The shower event would be the night before the wedding at 7 P.M. and the wedding would be Friday afternoon at 2 P.M. There hadn't been time to even discuss a honeymoon.

"He's gone," Mikki announced suddenly. "He's not coming back, is he?"

Emily looked up from her Sunday crossword and put the pen to rest beside her morning coffee cup. She thought for a moment, giving herself time to carefully choose her words.

"Don't you trust him, trust his abilities?" answered Emily. "Give him the time he needs to take care of things."

"But what if he doesn't come back and I'm here, ready for my big wedding...and it turns out like the runaway groom or something?" said Mikki, fighting tears, but trying to be confident. "I remember what happened to you on your last independent adventure."

"Yes, I can remember two years ago. Hey, things happen. But I'm sure he's doing his best. I saw his eyes when he looked at you. You can't fake that. He really loves you."

"But that's almost worse. What if something's happened to him? What if we get a call from some detective saying they've found a headless body? What if they find my phone number on a bloody scrap of paper in his pocket?"

"What if, what if. Life is full of that and full of lessons just waiting to be learned. Everyone just does their best with the cards they're dealt. No guarantees, no lifetime warranties. Give him a chance, Mikki. Remember, he has his family loyalties too. You have to respect that in him."

"I am giving him a chance. I've also made a big decision. He left without me because he thinks I'm some little pansy girl who took a few self-defense classes and couldn't handle it if things got really rough. I've decided I want to tell him everything."

"Do you think that's wise? I mean, think about it. Our little business isn't exactly on the up and up. He is or was a federal agent. Right now he thinks we're a couple of damned feisty chicks. What will he say or do if he knows the whole truth?" asked Emily, sipping her coffee.

"Well, he already knows that his sister found us on the Internet as a last resort to try to help her. So I think I can ease him into the rest of the story."

"All of it? Even about me?"

"I won't tell that part if you don't want me too," said Mikki, laughing. "He probably wouldn't believe all that stuff anyway. Let's see...my grandmother has threatened to castrate a man in a public bar, planned and executed a successful death by peanut butter, shot and killed a fellow Secret Service agent, and ...shall I go on?"

"What makes you think that's so unbelievable?"

"Well, for starters most people think of grandmothers in the kitchen, with an apron and getting the Thanksgiving turkey out of the oven."

"I do that."

"Of course. But what about the safe room and all the weapons and training videos and fake ID's that are right upstairs above the homey little kitchen?"

"So what's your point? If he's joining the family and you can trust him, I guess you can tell him that we help people."

"No. I want to tell him everything, about me anyway, so that he'll take me with him if he gets called for some anti-terrorist duty. I want to help him and he needs to know what I can do."

Emily thought about this for a minute as she got up to get more coffee. "Your classes in martial arts might come in handy, but there's no way you are going to infiltrate a terrorist camp. A woman with red hair!" Emily tossed back her head and laughed as she sat back down. She picked up the crossword again. She shook her head and said, "Where's the Arikok National Park found? Five letters."

"Aruba, I think," answered Mikki. "That reminds me…our honeymoon!"

"You never said where you'll be going. Is it a big secret?" asked Emily.

"No, we just never had time to talk about it. Maybe a cruise, though. You should come too! You always wanted to try a cruise vacation!"

"Just the bride and groom and Grandmother Vanderhorn. How cozy!" said Emily.

"Well, of course, we'd have separate staterooms," said Mikki. "Maybe get some nice balcony suites! Oh, wow! That would be fun! I'll ask Faris if he gets back…when he gets back."

"Here she goes again, folks," said Emily, throwing up her hands. "He'll be back. No matter what, he'll be back."

"Okay, I'm tired of waiting for the phone to ring. I'm going to get on-line and scope out the latest cruise destinations, get some prices, and get ready to book our cabin as soon as Faris comes home."

CHAPTER THIRTY-FIVE

It was just after midnight when the phone beside Mikki's bed rang. Mikki had been dreaming that she was lounging by the cruise ship pool when something interrupted the pleasant sensation of carefree drifting. Was that the ship's bell announcing lunch? The phone! Faris!

"Hello?" she mumbled, her sleep-clogged mind felt soggy as she clamped the receiver to her ear.

"Mikki!" someone shouted. It wasn't Faris. It was a woman. Julianne! Why was she calling at this hour? The horses! Was Clown sick?

"Mikki, wake up! The barn's on fire! Come and help us! Quick!" screamed Julianne and the line went silent.

Mikki's feet were already on the floor as terror filled her mind and tears filled her eyes. She was wide-awake now and running for the bathroom. She grabbed her sweatpants and old Bon Jovi T-shirt hanging on the doorknob, dressing as she ran. No time to wake Granny! She jammed her feet into the canvas barn loafers and ran down the stairs to her BMW. In her rush to back out of the garage, she almost forgot to open the door and squealed to a halt inches from the barrier. She pressed the garage and gate opener buttons simultaneously and pushed the little car to the limit as she screeched out of the driveway toward Interstate 95.

In minutes that seemed like hours, Mikki could see ahead to the red flashing lights and the horrible yellow-orange glow illuminating the smoke-filled sky in the area of the boarding stable. Oh, God! Was her horse dead? What about the other horses trapped in their stalls? Were they being burned to death while she slept, dreaming of traveling on a cruise ship? A sick eruption of guilt became overwhelming. She would never forgive herself. She braked and swerved, sliding sideways onto the road to the stable, James Bond style. Police near the blocked entrance gate immediately flagged her down. Her car screeched to a stop to the right of the gate and then impulsively she gunned the engine and crashed through the once pristine white vinyl fencing. The rails gave way with loud hollow snaps and suddenly she was driving on the grass on the other side. Mikki jumped from the stopped car when she reached the riding arena and ran along the front row of barns that still remained intact. Police yelled at her, but she didn't care. Mikki needed to find Julianne and Clown. A queasy feeling brought her to a stop as she arrived at the smoldering embers and saw something in the charred remains. It was the remnants of a mare's bronze name plaque, tarnished and bent from the heat. The barn that had housed her horse was nothing but fallen timbers and charred roofing. Mikki thought she'd be sick, but she moved on. She could see people through the haze and smell of the smoke, burned wood, and hay.

"Mikki! Over here!" Julianne yelled. Mikki saw her. Julianne's shirt was soaked with sweat and caked with dirt and soot, her face was almost unrecognizable. Some of her hair was singed into frizzy wet strands. She had been crying and pink wet rivers ran from her eyes to her chin through the sooty mess on her face. Mikki ran to her and waited for her to speak, dreading to hear the news.

"We got them all out. Clown and six others are in North Pasture. He's got a big cut on his neck. Some others are hurt. Little Mini Mee is pretty badly burned and her foal has a lacerated tendon from a rafter falling into their stall. We're waiting for the vets to arrive."

Mikki felt she could finally breathe. She began to cry. Clown was hurt, but alive. Some were injured, but no horses were dead. The firemen had things pretty much under control now. They were flooding the area with geysers of water being pumped from the hydrants located in the barn areas. Mikki could see Julianne's arms were shivering. Mikki felt shaky, too. A horseman's worst nightmare, a barn fire. Mikki put her arms around Julianne and they both cried and held each other. Then holding each other up, they briskly walked toward the area that held the injured horses.

When she felt she could talk coherently, Mikki pulled away from Julianne and asked the big question. "What happened?"

"Thank God for the sprinkler system. The sprinklers automatically popped and the direct alarm kicked in. The fire department was here in minutes. Luckily, I was in Barn Ten. I had decided to sleep in the lounge over there because I've been doing poultices and hydrotherapy on a three-year-old filly's foreleg. When I heard the alarm, I shot off that cot like a human cannonball and then saw the smoke. I started grabbing halters and leading horses out of the barn. I was tying them to the fences, just really anywhere so they'd be away from the flames and smoke. The barn roof was already coming down!"

"Thanks for calling me as soon as you did. I want to help."

"Look!" exclaimed Julianne, "There's the ambulance!"

"An ambulance just for horses?" exclaimed Mikki.

The HEART, Humane Equine Aid and Rapid Response Team, was the horse ambulance that had arrived to help the equine victims of the fire. As they watched the vehicle park, Julianne explained that the yellow and red vehicle was equipped with bandages, braces, slings, splints, and a large green sled that could be used as a stretcher for a downed horse.

"This transportation system is superior to a regular horse van or trailer," continued Julianne. "The team of five attendants is on call twenty-four hours a day on radios and a hot line. A horse can be stabilized at the sight of injury or illness and once inside the ambulance, a sling can be used around its belly to help support its weight during the trip to the equine hospital. This set-up is especially useful for a broken leg, which was once a death sentence for a horse."

Immediately the attendants were out of the $65,000 ambulance and running with supplies to the north pasture where the injured horses were being held. The clinic trucks of two local veterinarians were parked in the area. Mikki and Julianne ran to help. Mikki saw Clown tied to a fence post, nostrils wide and front feet pawing the ground. She raced toward him, calling his name. He was trembling and glistening with sweat, but raised his head and nickered a welcome when he heard Mikki approach. She saw a gash about twelve inches long on the left side of his neck. The tear was jagged and ran from his mane to his shoulder. The blood had clotted and lay in sticky reddish-brown clumps on his once pristine and glistening chestnut coat. Mikki went to him and talked softly, rubbing him and telling him what a good boy he was and that he'd be fine. She would take care of him. She untied his lead line from the fence and led him toward the attendant nearby.

"I'll go wash off his neck and bring him back in a few minutes for treatment. Go ahead and look at the others. He'll be okay for now," she said to the man in the gray coveralls. He nodded, glancing at Clown's injuries, and then went back to work pulling out rolls of gauze and Furacin ointment to treat burns on the other horses.

Mikki led Clown to the hydrant next to the field gate that was used to fill the horses' water trough. She dropped the lead line and Clown stood next to her, head down and quiet. He sensed that she would help him and that the burning, painful sensation in his neck would soon feel better. Mikki turned on the water and adjusted the hose nozzle to a fine spray, talking to Clown as she wet his neck, gently at first and then using a more forceful stream of water. The caked blood became soft and she loosened the viscous goo carefully with her fingers, rinsing and cleaning as she worked the water over his neck. As the water ran, she massaged his legs, belly, and face, checking for more unapparent injuries. He seemed to be okay other than the wound on his neck. Julianne appeared with a clean white towel and handed it to Mikki. She used it to dry Clown's neck and then rubbed it over his body to dry and comfort him.

"I think he's okay, but I don't think they'll be able to stitch this one. Too jagged and torn. What do you think?" Mikki asked Julianne.

Julianne inspected Clown's neck closer, pulling a flashlight from the pack on her belt. "Looks much better since you cleaned him up. Probably will heal from the inside out. He'll need some antibiotics for sure and maybe something for pain so he can move around a little easier. He'll have some problems putting his head down to graze if his neck starts to swell."

"That's what I thought, too. I think I'm ready to take him back to the vet and let him have a look," said Mikki, watching Julianne. Something was wrong. Julianne was just standing there, hands on her hips, staring off into the distance.

"Is something else wrong?" continued Mikki. "Tell me."

Julianne just shook her head. "Let's go back and check on the others. Mini Mee's foal is hurt pretty bad, but they're going to try to save him. They might need help getting them into the transport ambulance."

"Okay, I'll take Clown to the doc and then we'll get Mini Mee and Chigger loaded up for the hospital," said Mikki, as she picked up the lead rope and began to urge Clown back to the triage area and the ambulance attendants. Palm Pines had called all their veterinarians and six had already arrived. Mikki saw Dr. Mellonack and headed his way with her horse.

Two hours later, most all of the horses had been united with their panicked owners and their vets, treated for their injuries, and placed into a safe empty barn. The barn had portable stalls and a tent-like canvas roof to cover them. There were four of these temporary barns that were used when horse shows were held in the equestrian center show grounds. Mikki stood protectively at the welded pipe enclosure and watched Clown eating his alfalfa hay from a feedbag hung at the front of the stall. His water bucket had been raised from ground level so he could eat and drink without stretching his neck too much. He was bandaged with rolls of gauze and had received two injections of strong antibiotics. Clown seemed to have totally forgotten about his ordeal, but he followed Mikki's movements with his closest ear and a watchful eye. He was tired and once he had eaten, Mikki was sure he would sleep in the deep straw bedding she had provided for him. As he chewed, his now calm eyes were closing in weariness. Mikki saw Julianne walking through the tented barn checking on the horses and turning out some of the lights. It was time for things to quiet down and for people and horses to rest. For Mikki it had been a long night and it was about to get a lot longer.

Julianne was approaching Mikki as she flipped off the bank of lights on the far aisle way. "Mikki. I need to tell you something. The fire marshal had a preliminary cause for the fire."

"And?" asked Mikki, warily.

"It was arson. Plain old gasoline." Julianne said, staring at Mikki.

"God, no! Who would do that? Innocent horses? Try to burn them alive?" Mikki exclaimed, squeezing her head on both sides with flat palms, as if trying to force the thought from her mind.

"It's worse than that," said Julianne, her eyes avoiding Mikki's. "There's a suspect. He's been here before."

"Who?" cried Mikki, eyebrows raised in question. She couldn't believe it was someone they might know.

"I saw him. There was a man running away from the barn, along the north perimeter."

"Could you see who it was? Who was it?" Mikki shouted, grabbing Julianne by the shoulders. She was now feeling murderous.

Julianne's head hung down. She couldn't look at Mikki at first. Then she raised her chin and looked Mikki right in the eyes. As she spoke, Julianne's tired face filled with rage, and her fists balled up as if she wanted to strike someone or something.

"It was that guy…your new *boyfriend*."

CHAPTER THIRTY-SIX

Mikki's mouth gaped open and her face went pale. A gagging sensation threatened to strangle her as she tried to speak. Her lips moved but no sound emitted.

"Are you sure?" she finally stammered. "I can't believe it!"

"I saw him running along the fence in back, heading toward the north parking area where the horse trailers are stored. It was him. No doubt in my mind," said Julianne, shaking her head and not wanting to believe it herself. "I'm sorry," she added quietly, her own anger abating as she watched Mikki struggling with the unwelcome news.

Mikki reached back to her cell phone secured at her waist and yanked it free from its holder. The aqua glow of the phone's light reflected off Mikki's face as she furiously punched in numbers. She put the phone to her ear and listened intently, her pale bluish face grotesquely twisted in anger, shock, and grief.

"He's not answering," said Mikki, dialing more numbers. Then she said, "Gran! Are you up? He did? Good!" Mikki listened some more as the tightness of her neck and shoulder muscles relaxed. She began to cry, and then said into the phone, "Thanks Gran. I'll be home in a few minutes and fill you in on everything here." Mikki reholstered her phone and turned to Julianne, wiping her wet and grimy face on the bottom of her dirty T-shirt.

"He called my grandmother's house, trying to reach me. He wanted to make sure I was on my way here. He'd been watching the barn. There's someone who's been following us...it's a long story, Jules. But take my word for it, Faris isn't the one who set the fire. He was chasing the guy who did...and trust me, he'll get him."

"Thank God! I'm so glad he's not the arsonist. I didn't want to tell you, but I had to. I was so angry and worried and upset," said Julianne, who was now crying, too. "I'm sorry I thought he was the bad guy."

Mikki reached for her friend and they held each other without speaking. Then Mikki put her arm around Julianne's shoulders and they began to walk towards Mikki's car. "You don't know him. I barely know him, I guess, but I do know he's a good guy. In fact, you'll be getting the invitation by tomorrow."

"Invitation?"

"Yeah. No big deal. It's kind of impromptu, in fact. It's an invitation to our wedding reception. Faris and I are getting married on Friday."

Julianne's dirt and tear streaked face lit up in the smoky atmosphere. Then she grinned, "You're pulling my chain, right?"

"Nope. This coming Friday. I've waited long enough for Mr. Right and now I've found Mr. Right and his first name is Perfect. Mr. Perfectly Right."

"In that case, I'll be there, Mrs. Right. Guess I'll get all the details in my engraved invitation?"

"Yep. Be there, Jules. You can be a bridesmaid or servant girl or handmaiden, or whatever you want to be. Brigetta will be there to help get me ready for this, too. Mom is freaking, of course, but Gran and her catering pals have everything in order."

"I'm in total shock. But I'll be there if I can recuperate from all this excitement on one night. At least there's one bit of good news! I'm really happy for you. You're nuts, of course, but I'm happy to join you in the peanut factory! This will be fun!"

"Yeah, we'll talk later about what to wear, who to bring, and all that. Right now, I've got to get home and get some sleep. You too, okay?"

"Promise me you'll fill me in on the bad guy when Faris gets him, okay? Is Faris some kind of cop or something?"

"Not exactly. But sure, you'll be on the top of my call list."

"Oh shit," exclaimed Julianne.

"Oh no, don't tell me you have a previous commitment

or something! Come on, this is my big day!"

"It's not that. Look at your car," said Julianne, pointing and staring at the BMW's battered front end.

"Oh. I forgot about the graceful entrance I made getting in here."

"And check out the fence!" added Julianne.

"I'd better get out my checkbook. Granny's going to have a good one with this. She's never forgiven me about her Jag. She'll never let me live this down."

Julianne just kept hugging herself and walking back and forth in front of the car, bending to peer at the cracked fenders and smashed grillwork. She touched the hood where black paint was scratched and dents had buckled the metal.

"I guess I won't be able to just ignore this one, said Mikki. "I'll park in our garage tonight, get up early, and take it to the shop on Parker Avenue in the morning. I'll just get a loaner and tell her that the car was due for a tune-up, an oil change, or something."

"Yeah, and if you pay me enough hush money…" threatened Julianne with a wink.

"Good-night, pal. I'll come by tomorrow and check Clown and the others. I'll help you make the rounds. I'll call the vet hospital tomorrow, too, and find out about Mini Mee and her foal. Oh my God! I almost forgot! Faris' Arabian stallion is arriving tomorrow. He was supposed to be stabled in the same barn as Clown. That barn's gone now."

"I'll put some shavings in that extra stall in the tent barn. There's an empty one just two stalls away from Clown that should be suitable for a stallion if he's not too nutsy. Don't worry, I'll figure out something for him. Seeya later in the morning, then. Let's both get some sleep. I'm going back to my cot. Soon it'll be time to get up and start feeding my client's horses. The owners from out of town will all be calling early in the morning, too, once everyone hears about the fire."

Mikki got in the BMW and prayed there was no radiator damage or something else that would prevent her from driving it home. The little car bravely started right up and quietly crept out of the grassy spot, willed by its abusive owner to try to make it home. The front bumper was cracked and wind made a little whistling noise over the car's bruises as Mikki hit the road, but she felt confident that finally the worst of the night was over.

CHAPTER THIRTY-SEVEN

The whole way home, Mikki thought about the horses and the fire. She wondered if Sajid had been trying to victimize Faris' horse in order to draw him to the barn. Those men were dangerous and Faris was trying to find Kamila on his own. Mikki was more convinced than ever that she should tell Faris about extremefavors.com. He needed to know for sure that she was not just another Southern Belle who would vaporize at the slightest sign of danger. What if he thought that the incident at the Pink Flamingo was just a fluke? Granny would just have to trust her on this one.

As Mikki entered the kitchen through the elevator entrance she saw her grandmother sitting in her favorite chair, a hot steaming drink cupped in both hands.

"Want some tea?" Emily asked as she viewed the walking mess that used to be her lovely granddaughter. Mikki's once white T-shirt was wet with splotches of blood, burn ointment, and ashes blended into the design. Her hair was grayish red, like a ghoul from a C-rated horror flick. "You look like you need tea and a hot shower...not necessarily in that order."

"Thanks, Gran. I'll get the shower and some clean clothes. I think I may have to trash these. The smoky smell and the ground-in soot might not ever come out. I'll be right back."

"Are you okay? Is Clown...?"

"Some horses are hurt. Clown's got a big cut on his neck. They took Mini Mee and her foal to the equine hospital in West Palm. We'll know more about them tomorrow."

"I'm so sorry. You should've awakened me. I can deal with a crisis, you know."

"Sure. I was just in a damned big hurry to get there. I'll be right back. I've really got to get that shower and dispose of these clothes. Phew, they stink!"

Mikki left for her room and Emily's thoughts slipped to Faris. What was this guy really about? It wasn't that she didn't trust Mikki's instincts, those were usually right on target. It was her driving that was terrible. Good instincts, bad driving. And everything she had found on Faris seemed to be exactly as he had told Mikki. He was a truthful man, according to her very best technical snooping and a very important phone call.

Within a few minutes Mikki reappeared with a towel wrapped around her wet hair and wearing blue cotton shortie pajamas.

"A+ for improvement, Ms. Walsh," said Emily, "especially the fragrance. What is that? Obsession? I mean, that would fit."

Mikki glanced and nodded from the kitchen where she was pouring herself a cup of steamy water from the kettle. She selected a chamomile tea bag from a wicker basket and went to the living room to sit. On her way, she picked up an open bag of Oreos from the counter and took them with her to the couch. She plopped down with a sigh and pulled up her legs, crossing them Indian-style before she began to speak.

"It was a long night. I was already about to freak out about the fire and then Jules told me she saw the arsonist running away from the barn. It really floored me when she said it was Faris."

"Well, at the time, he was calling and looking for you here. He said that he could've caught Hassad, but he used some pursuit time to find the fire extinguisher nearby. When he saw Julianne running towards the flames, the alarms and sprinklers had already gone off, so then he ran to try to catch up to Hassad. He said he'd been following him for two days, trying to find Kamila's location. He hasn't seen Sajid, so he thinks Kamila is still alive and is being watched by her husband while Hassad wreaks havoc around Palm Beach."

"I tried to call Faris, but no answer. Hope he's okay."

"I'm sure he can take care of himself."

"Yeah, well, I thought you could take care of yourself

and you ended up in Citrus City hospital on your death bed."

"Don't be so dramatic. There was no death bed."

"That's your opinion. I had to save your ass and even had to enlist the aid of my dear sister and mother."

"I still can't believe they helped you."

"I know how to con people into doing my will. I learned that from you."

"Glad you picked up some useful knowledge from your old grandmother."

"Yep, and tomorrow, once my mind's clear, we're going to think this out. We need to help Faris and fess up to our life of crime and indiscretion. Instead of a dynamic duo, maybe we'll become a dynamo trio. Unfaltering, indestructible, indivisible."

"You make it sound like we'll be comic book heroes."

"And heroines, of course."

"Of course."

The two women sat thinking, talking, and drinking tea until Mikki was relaxed enough to try to go to bed.

"I'm beat," Mikki said, rising and picking up their teacups and the now empty bag of Oreos. "It's dark-thirty o'clock by now and way past the bewitching hour for me. Going back to bed too?"

"I'm on my way."

"Tomorrow I'll get Faris' horse and check on the others. I'm sure Faris will contact me. We'll work things out from there."

"Good night, Mikki," said Emily as she switched off the reading lamps, and headed toward her bedroom.

"Good night, Gran. And, by the way…"

"What?" asked Emily, hesitating at her doorway.

"I wrecked my car."

CHAPTER THIRTY-EIGHT

As Emily turned around to comment, Mikki's cell phone rang in the distance and Mikki raced down the stairs to her bedroom. Emily just shook her head and went to bed. She wanted to know about this early morning phone call and the poor car, but was too tired to stay up a minute longer.

Mikki grabbed the phone from the bed where she had tossed it before showering.

"Hello?" she said quickly, hoping it was Faris.

"Hi, wife-to-be," he said.

"Oh God, I'm so glad to hear your voice!" Mikki said, falling backwards onto the bed, a small, cautious smile appearing on her face. "Are you all right?"

"No sign of Kamila, but I've seen glimpses of Hassad and Sajid. I've been following Hassad. The bastard started the fire at the stable. I think he thought my horse was going to be there. Kami must have told him the original arrival date. That says to me that they have her. Willingly or unwillingly, she's with them. She's my sister, but I don't trust any of them, even Kami. I think I've now narrowed the area where they must be embedded."

"I'm sorry all this is happening," said Mikki, wiping a wet drop of relief from her cheek.

"Me too. Are the horses okay? What happened after I left? I pulled the fire alarm by the tack room door. The sprinklers were going off when I took off after Hassad. I told your grandmother I tried to use the fire extinguisher. When I heard the alarms and sirens, I knew help was on the way and the extinguisher was useless at that point. I thought I'd be more valuable trying to catch Hassad and find Kamila. I felt awful leaving the barn and horses, even with help on the way, but I hope you can understand why I left."

"I do. Everything's a mess over there, but most of the horses are okay. The fire department contained the fire to one barn and the equine ambulance service came and took care of the horses."

"Clown?"

"He's injured, but he'll recover."

"Praise the Lord. The smoke wasn't too bad, so I was pretty sure someone would get them out. Now I wish I would've stayed to help. If anything would have happened to any of the horses...especially your horse...I know you'd never forgive me for not saving him before I ran off."

"It was about your sister. She's family. You had to keep up with Hassad. Don't tell Brigetta, but I'd save her before my horse, too. Of course, I'd never forgive myself if anything happened to Clown, but he's going to be all right."

"I want to see you," said Faris softly.

"I miss you so much. Hey, did you say praise the Lord? Not praise Allah or something? You really are a Christian, aren't you?"

"Sure. I told you. Did you think we'd be getting married in a mosque with big gold turrets?"

"I wasn't sure. Remember we're in charge of the actual ceremony? We really need some time together. Come get me. We need to talk. I need you."

"I'm a bona fide Methodist...since I came to America. I love you. I'll be there for the wedding and I'll be there at noon today to take you to brunch. Then we'll go to the barns and check the horses. I got a call from the equine transportation guys. Aljazar's van should arrive around 3 P.M. and we can be his welcoming party of two."

"Sounds great, but maybe we'd better talk here. I'll have Granny Em cook for us. She likes to show off her cheese blintzes. Do you like crepes?"

"I like them just fine, but don't you want some time alone with me? So you can use and abuse me?"

"Oh yeah, but that comes later."

"Good. Get some sleep. I'm going to," he yawned.

CHAPTER THIRTY-NINE

After a few hours of required unconsciousness, Mikki was awake and looking forward to her day with Faris. She planned on telling him everything and also learning more about the man she'd chosen for a lifetime of wedded bliss. They'd have a soul-searching time of truth on the veranda overlooking the Atlantic. They'd share secrets, hold hands, and be a normal engaged couple for the whole day.

Emily was a good sport and had agreed to introduce Faris to her special breakfast, usually reserved for family holiday gatherings. Emily concurred in that this was a special occasion and agreed to give Faris the full guest treatment. Mikki was setting the table outside when she heard the gate alarm. She pressed the opener and jogged to the front door, pulling back her freshly brushed hair into a ponytail as she walked by the hall mirror.

"Come on up here," she called down to Faris. "You don't have to use the servant's entrance today!" She stood waiting at the open door until he was close, then bounced towards him like an excited toddler and flung her arms around him. She kissed him before he could present her with the red roses he held behind his back.

"Are those for me?" she asked coyly.

"Nah. They're for the cook, of course!"

Mikki grabbed the flowers from him and pulled him inside the foyer.

"Gran! Look who's come for breakfast!" Mikki giggled, as her hand entwined with Faris' long tan fingers.

"Hello, Mrs. Vanderhorn," he said as he walked toward the kitchen to give her a hug, eyeing the now clean and sparkling tile floor as he walked by. "Good job on the floor. Your granddaughter has stolen your flowers. Do you have a vase?"

"That girl!" said Emily. "And please call me Emily." She reached under the sink and pulled out a tall glass container that she began filling with tap water.

"It smells great in here. I'm starving!" exclaimed Faris, seeing the plates full of crisp bacon and browned sausage sitting on the food warmer. Mikki placed the flowers near the sink and went back to the table outside.

"How's your head? Still sore?" asked Emily, pulling him into the kitchen and gently examining the scab on his scalp.

"It's fine, really fine. I don't even notice it any more."

"Go join Mikki on the balcony. She's just finishing up. Here, take these napkins and placemats out to her." Emily had requisitioned the flowers and was expertly trimming the stems. "And thanks, they're lovely," she said, as she began placing them into the waiting vase.

Faris balanced the table items on his arm, butler-style, and proceeded to the open French doors, joining Mikki beside the table.

"Hey, I'm impressed with your culinary helpfulness!" said Mikki, with a smile aimed at Faris.

"Your grandmother made me do it," he whispered and grabbed her around the waist with his unencumbered arm. He kissed her on the cheek and then set the linens on the table. "I know, no messing around with the help, right?"

"She'll never know," she murmured, poking him with her elbow as she placed the forks onto the folded napkins and finished arranging the table set for two.

"Don't tell me the cook's not eating with us?" asked Faris.

"She's going somewhere. She was kinda vague. Who knows. But we'll be all alone for the rest of the day. My grandmother said she had a lunch date and then she and Mom are going shopping."

"Shopping? Should we call your dad and warn him?"

"Ha ha. He's used to that. I told you, he lives in New York and we only get to see him once in a while. In fact, you'll meet him soon, probably right before the shower. Also, Dad told me to buy any dress I wanted for the wedding and charge it to him. He misses out on everything that happens around here, but at least he can get away for this."

"Maybe we'll go to New York some time and visit him?"

"He'd love that. We girls go a couple of times a year, but I'm sure he's ecstatic about the prospect of adding a man to the family."

"Even a guy who met Osama?" he asked.

"He'll get used to it, once he gets a chance to meet and know you. He's coming to Florida this weekend for a prolonged vacation with all of us. Hey, by the way, what do you think about a honeymoon cruise?"

"Great, but I have to find Kami first."

Mikki leaned forward to be closer and then said quietly, "Of course, and that's what I want to talk about this morning. That, and can my grandmother come along?"

"On the cruise? Sure! As long as she brings those knitting needles and acts as bodyguard for us. Uh... she won't be staying in our cabin, will she?"

"Not on your life. We'd each book our own cabins. They have a super deal on a balcony suite on the new Pinnacle. It's an Italian ship and sounds gorgeous. I've never been on a cruise, have you?"

"Just with my first two wives."

Mikki just stared at him, hands on hips and silent, and then pulled out her finger gun and shot him.

"Just kidding, Mikki dearest. You're my one and only," Faris said, holding his hand over his heart to cover his wound.

"I'd better be the last one, too."

"Yes, ma'am."

The table was set and the sun was overhead. The sea breeze kept the veranda cooler than down on the sandy beach where a couple was walking hand-in-hand. Mikki went to help Emily carry the trays of food to the table and Faris followed along. Steaming cheese blintzes with strawberries and freshly whipped cream on the side, sliced grapefruit, and the platter of breakfast meats were ready. Faris carried a tray of two mugs and the carafe of coffee while the women brought the food outside.

"This smells great! Thank you," said Faris, hugging Emily as she removed her pink apron embroidered with a large flamingo. "I wish you'd join us, though."

"Places to go, people to do, you know," said Emily, wiping her hands on the balled-up apron. "I ate earlier while I cooked. Just enjoy!"

"Thanks Gran, you're the best," said Mikki, sitting down as Faris pushed her chair toward the table. "What time will you be back?"

"Later."

"Hmm. Okay," said Mikki, watching Emily reenter the house. Seconds later, Emily did an about face and pointed her cane at Faris.

"And don't let her drive your car! Did she tell you she wrecked her Bimmer last night?"

"Gran, I was getting to that," said Mikki, throwing up her hands, exasperated.

Faris sat back in his chair, hands gripping the arms, amused. "Don't worry, I've got that part about the driving. Not good, huh?"

Emily gave him a grave shake of her head, then smiled and disappeared into the kitchen. Mikki yelled after her, "Tattletale," and then, "We'll do the kitchen clean-up!"

"Well, that gives me a great idea about a wedding gift for my new bride," said a grinning Faris.

Mikki looked at him, squinting her eyes and planting her elbows firmly on the table, and said, "If you say driving lessons, you're a dead man."

CHAPTER FORTY

Faris was contentedly crunching a piece of bacon, when suddenly Mikki tossed her napkin on top of her plate and sat back in her chair.

"What?" he stammered, putting the half-eaten bacon back on his plate.

"We have to talk."

"You're scaring me again."

"That's just it. You're going to have to become more fearless."

"What the hell does that mean?"

"Oh sorry, I'm not berating your testosterone or anything. It's just that I have things to tell you. About myself. About my grandmother."

"Your grandmother?"

"Oh yeah," Mikki sighed, "my grandmother."

"Go on," urged Faris, tentatively again picking up the piece of bacon.

"She's not who you think. She's a dangerous and scary, calculating killer."

Faris' blank open-mouthed expression momentarily gave way to a loud laugh of relief. He thought Mikki was joking, playing with his mind. She was talking about the old lady with a cane and apron who just served him a delicious breakfast? Sure there was the one time attack on Aziz...but? Was there another grandmother or what in the world was Mikki saying?

"You laugh?"

"I laugh. And you? You're a dangerous and scary killer, too?"

"Yep. But I was going to gently lead you that way. Now that you mention it, I have to confess. I am a highly trained and efficient assassin, ready at an instant's notice to accomplish my mission."

"I think you're ready for the crazy house. Certifiable."

"Faris. Please listen. I'm not kidding."

He took Mikki's hand and said, "Go ahead. I'm listening." He was patting her hand in an annoyingly patronizing manner.

Mikki, undeterred, began slowly, telling him about her grandmother's store and her other business. She proceeded to explain how she rescued Emily from a hospital in Citrus City two years ago after her stroke. She gingerly touched on the murder investigation surrounding Emily's stay at the hospital.

"Here she was in a hospital bed, just diagnosed with lung cancer, and this cop kept coming around and asking questions. My grandmother was a suspect in a murder of another patient in the hospital. He was hospitalized for a gunshot wound received during a shoot-out with police. Tyrone Dupris was wanted for the murder of a little girl, among other things. The girl, Shakira, was the granddaughter of one of my grandmother's good friends. Granny had left home to try to find Dupris as a favor to her friend. She succeeded in locating him, but was injured in an accident and then became sick on top of that. This bad guy turns up dead in his hospital bed on another floor and somehow they blamed my grandmother."

"Well, they wouldn't have known that she was looking for him, so why would they blame her?"

Mikki swallowed hard. "Because she did it."

"Pardon me?"

"She was freaking guilty. Not only that, she was posing as a street person...a bag lady with an assumed name. But she did it. She killed him right there in the hospital. Got by the armed guard and everything."

"Whoa," was all the stunned Faris could say. His full and complete attention had turned from breakfast to Mikki. "Wow and how, I guess I should say?"

A barely concealed grin formed in the corner of Mikki's mouth. "She stuffed peanut butter up his butt." She smiled as she waited for the response. This was kind of fun, she thought.

"What the...?" Faris stammered. There was a moment of silence and then he began to laugh and laugh. "No shit?" he asked.

"No, it was peanut butter, I said! He was allergic! I'll tell you all the hilarious details later." Mikki laughed with relief at seeing his reaction. She was hoping he had a good sense of humor. He was going to need it to be in this family.

"And then what else?" asked Faris, when he could finally speak. He was wiping his eyes with his white handkerchief. "I know there's more."

"I'm going to tell you all of it, but if you back out of the wedding, we'll hunt you down and..."

"I get it. Just go on. It's getting good," he said.

"Well, there was a nosy chick trying to get Granny in trouble so I had to take care of her. She overdosed on insulin and died," stated Mikki, feeling braver.

"She was a diabetic?"

"No, she just overdosed on insulin. I had the feeling she might be targeting lonely and old sick patients...maybe getting them to fit her in their wills. She made me very nervous."

To Faris' credit, there was only a small pause of hesitation after that one. "Okay. I got that one, too," he said.

"That was more like collateral damage, but there's more. My grandmother had a stroke in the hospital and almost died. My mom, my sister, and I got Gran out of the hospital with the help of a nurse and one of the doctors. Neither of them knew anything about Granny offing the bad guy, though. The doctor supplied Gran's medication list and the nurse found us a gurney to roll her out of there. Granny was comatose at the time and this cop was just hanging around waiting to cause trouble for all of us. So we heisted her out of there from ICU during the night. The doc helped because he liked me and the nurse helped because she liked the doctor and wanted me out of there. You know...less competition?"

"You're a very bad girl."

"Yes, but you still like me, right?"

"I'm definitely afraid to say anything to the contrary

right now."

"You should be."

"How did your little old grandmother get in the business of tracking down bad dudes? That doesn't seem a likely occupation for a shop owner on Worth Avenue."

"She had a rough childhood and a mean step-father. She got rid of him, too."

"Got rid of?"

"Yeah, when she was nine, she killed him. Then she moved in with an uncle in the Secret Service and next thing she knew she grew up and was one of the first female agents and a sharpshooter, too. She was a sniper expert and ended up shooting one of the other agents."

"Oh great. At least she's not biased."

"Oh no, he was a bad guy too. He had planned on assassinating the First Lady at a charity rally. He wasn't a good guy at all. No one knew that Gran had planned to shoot him, but she quit shortly after that. Some of the guys began looking at her funny. No one sat at her table during lunch or something like that."

"Uh huh." Faris had picked up a sausage with his fingers and took a bite, swirling the remains in his fingers, lost in thought.

"Are you with me?"

Faris nodded and popped the rest of the sausage in his mouth, washing it down with lukewarm coffee. "Yep, any more coffee?"

Mikki got up to get another carafe of fresh brew and wondered if Faris would take off running and screaming out the driveway before she could get back. She got fresh cream from the refrigerator and was relieved to see him still sitting there, gazing out at the ocean. She returned and filled his mug and hers. She saw him glance at his watch and still wondered if he was planning a getaway.

Faris saw her look of concern and said, "The horse…just watching the time so we don't miss Aljazar's arrival. Continue, please."

"Anyway, after she quit the Secret Service, grandmother

got married and my mom, Susan, was born. She took Susan everywhere with her. They traveled and saw the world. Grandpa worked in the Mideast, so I didn't see him much. When I was a teen, I discovered the so-called panic room here at the house. It's full of weapons, spy ware, disguises, alternative identifications, and just all kinds of stuff. I knew Gran had a pilot's license and also her scuba certification. That was when I knew that not all grandmothers are like her. I thought at the time that my grandfather was the espionage expert. Little did I know. I realized something was up, but kept my mouth shut. I didn't even tell my sister and we've always been close."

"So your sister and mom still know nothing about all this?"

"In desperation I joined forces with them at Citrus City because I needed help getting my grandmother out of there secretly. I told them Gran had stupidly become a private investigator and was being looked at as a suspect in the murder of the guy she had been tracking. They agreed that to save the family name from the gutters and help Gran, we had to get her out of there. They think all is cool now since Gran has recuperated from her stroke and is going back to work off and on at the store. She has a full-time manager there now, and we girls help out once in a while too."

"So what's the current deal?"

"I found I liked the adrenalin rush. I wanted to help Gran. She knows a lot about fighting, tracking, weapons, spying, and all that."

"And all that means killing, too," said Faris. It wasn't a question. It was a statement.

"Yes. She once was in the military in covert operations. She told me some stories from her time behind enemy lines in Korea. She's pretty much done it all."

"Whew. I can say I'm pretty surprised…and impressed, though I did have my suspicions."

"She's taught me a lot, but of course, I've got a long way to go. I've been to all the martial art classes and rank pretty high for just getting started, but then I've got a good tutor right here at home. No one suspects anything, I don't think. I'm just a girl who likes to keep in shape and is able to protect my own ass in case of attack in the parking lot."

"I do recall that kick toward my kidney in the airport. I'm still a little sore."

"I was being gentle. You're just so cute!" explained Mikki. "And thanks for not bashing my head in or breaking my leg or something while defending yourself. I know you were being gentle, too."

"I never would hurt the beautiful woman that has intrigued me from the moment I laid eyes on her." Faris reached for her hand across the table and gave it a quick squeeze. "So where do we go from here? Why are you telling me all this now?"

"I'm telling you because Gran said I could, and also I want to be with you. I don't want to sit here alone worrying about you when I could help. I wanted you to know I'm not some pansy girl who needs smelling salts at the sight of blood or the sound of gunfire."

"I think I had that part already figured out," said Faris, making a show of rubbing his side. "I would love to have this trained killer chick accompany me on my search. I've got to find Kami and the guys who tried bombing the plane. With your red hair and green eyes, although quite beautiful, I doubt if you will be much help in infiltrating an Arab safe house. Perhaps you'll have value in some other manner."

His gaze lowered to Mikki's breasts, his eyes full of mischief. She met his staring eyes with the darkening green of her own until he gave in. "Okay, okay, I would love to have you along. Two heads are better than one and all that bunk. I just didn't want to have to worry about you getting hurt or leaving your grandmother alone here in this house. Now I know that both of those concerns are invalid."

"We've managed so far."

"Apparently the cars haven't fared so well? Tell me about your grandmother's Jaguar. I understand that you wrecked her car. In fact, your driving skills seem to be a continuing theme around here."

"It wasn't my fault."

"So, defend yourself. Give me your side of the story," said Faris.

"I would and I will, but look at the time! We've got to clean up here and get to the stables. Your horse will arrive in two hours and you never know when those vans will actually show up. The driver has probably been in touch with the barn manager, but we've got to get there early."

"A reprieve has been granted. Let's get busy on the kitchen," said Faris, standing and stacking up dirty dishes and cups to carry inside the house. "It's starting to get hot out here anyway."

CHAPTER FORTY-ONE

Shared kitchen duty was quickly completed. The pink marble counter tops were gleaming before the couple locked up and headed for Faris' car. He opened the sunroof and Mikki leaned back onto the headrest and closed her eyes. She was happy, although she knew there was lots to do and they had to find Kami soon before it was too late. Mikki had bad vibes about that situation and hoped Faris was prepared for the worst. But for now, she was with the man she would soon marry, it was a beautiful day, and they were going to see some horses. The day had great potential.

"Faris?" Mikki said, stroking his right hand, which was resting on her knee. "I have a confession."

"There's more?" Faris asked, as he glanced sideways at his fiancée.

"Just a little thing. I taped our first date's dinner conversation and I didn't want to but I knew Gran would be able to find out stuff when I got home and I didn't know you then and it was going to be evidence," Mikki blurted, rapid-fire.

"Slow down. You taped our dinner date? How?"

"Voice activated recorder in my purse, of course."

"Of course. And how did Emily like our date?"

"I never had her listen to it. I erased it. You're safe now."

"That's a relief. I'd hate for the tape of all my confessions to fall into the wrong hands. That would be my death warrant when I'm trying to work undercover with terrorists. Why the change of heart, evil spy woman?"

"Because when I got home, I found that Gran had followed me around on the date and also had completely checked you out on the Internet and on our hacked security sites."

"Great. Anything else? Did I pass?"

"Yeah, you passed."

Faris just shook his head and mumbled something

unintelligible as he drove. But then he squeezed her knee and laughed. They had arrived at the stables.

As the Aston Martin bumped over the grassy area that led to the barns, Faris couldn't help but comment, "Wonder what happened to the fence at the entrance?"

"Oh," retorted Mikki. "Very funny."

Faris peered over the top of his sunglasses innocently. "Think we ought to pay for it to be fixed?"

"I'll take care of it. Thanks for your concern."

Faris' smile faded as he pulled into a parking spot near the charred rubble of the barn that used to house Mikki's horse. He saw that the fire damage had been very bad. There was nothing left of the building. They were very lucky that no horses had been burned alive in that horrible inferno. The sprinkler system had given rescuers precious time to evacuate all the animals. But support poles and rafters built to survive a major hurricane had been no match for the gasoline inspired flames. The heavy lumber was now no more than large, broken shards of charcoal lying in piles of still smoking damp ash. The stench of smoke was everywhere. He knew Mikki had been through a nightmare and he put his arm around her shoulder to comfort her as they walked through the scene. Mikki's tears were forming again, but she quickly wiped them away.

"I'm fine," Mikki said, as if reading his mind. "It's over and we all did our best. It could have been much, much worse. Thanks for pulling the alarm. Don't feel bad about not rescuing horses. Help was arriving. You, well, we still have to find Kami and the rest of them. Gran will help us, you'll see."

"I know. I don't see the transport van. Let's go find Clown and the other displaced animals. Where did they put them?"

"This way," said Mikki, wiping her nose on a tissue and then taking his hand as they walked toward the temporary tent barn at the back of the equestrian center.

Clown raised his head from the hay in the corner of his new stall to nicker at Mikki. The bandage was clean and fresh and his mane and tail had been combed to remove stuck-on straw and wood shavings from his bedding. Mikki was relieved to see that Clown seemed quite comfortable in his new digs. She poked through her bag of supplies and brought out some pieces of carrot. The crinkling of the plastic bag got the horse's attention and he turned toward Mikki for the offering in her hand. The couple patted the horse and gave him a good look in the now sunlit barn. Mikki didn't see any more cuts or burns that needed attention.

"I think Julianne has been here taking care of him. She was sleeping on a cot, keeping an eye on a client's horse, when the fire started. She stayed all night. I hope she got some sleep. I owe her big time for all she did to help Clown. She was the one who told me she saw you at the scene, and of course, she suspected the worst."

"I would never do anything like that. I love animals."

"I know, but it did cause a moment of panic. I've really just met you, but I feel like I've been waiting for you my whole life."

Faris turned her away from her horse and hugged her, kissing her mouth passionately.

"Me, too," was all he could say.

"Heylooo! Woooo! The happy couple!" exclaimed Julianne, who had appeared in the dusty aisle way between the metal pipe stalls. "You're not going to flop down in the hay now or anything are you? If so, let me get that new pile of manure out of the way!"

"Oops! Sorry, Jules," said a reddening Mikki. "Julianne, please formally meet Faris Al Busaid. Faris, Julianne Connery, one of my very bestest friends!"

Julianne reached out her hand to be shaken, but Faris took the proffered appendage and kissed it. "Glad to meet you. You are almost, I said almost, as lovely as my bride-to-be!" said Faris.

"Yeah, and you should see her when she cleans up," added Mikki. Julianne smiled at the complement, apparently forgetting her concerns about Faris the night before.

"Look!" exclaimed Julianne, as she pointed at the north entrance. A large green horse transport van was pulling through the trailer entrance. "Let's go see the new horse!"

The three of them hurried towards the truck and pointed the driver, airport style, in the right direction to park near the temporary tent. Two men in coveralls stepped from the cab and brought a clipboard and briefcase with papers to give to Faris. He began signing forms as the girls helped the other man lower the ramp at the rear of the van. The stallion was the only horse inside the four-stall interior and he was instantly alert and trying to see what was outside his stall. The bay stallion began loudly announcing his arrival to all the fillies and mares as soon as he smelled them. The confident trumpeting of a stallion was easy to distinguish from the usual neighing of genderless geldings. Grazing horse heads popped up immediately from their grass mowing detail. Some fillies answered back, calling and trotting toward their fences to get a better look. The older matrons watched curiously, blades of half-eaten grass still hanging from their whiskery lips. But hearing the stallion's continued calling, even they began to walk toward the fence lines, eyeing the van and waiting for a glimpse of the new arrival.

Like a rock star, Aljazar appeared from the dark interior of the van, pausing before he walked down the ramp onto the clay road. He stood tall and masculine on his stage, muscles rippling under a gleaming coat of burnt umber. His satin-soft black mane and tail were streaming toward the ground in waves, like cascading, shimmering fluid. He danced lightly in the sunlight, eyes wide, nostrils flaring, excited to be off the truck, and enchanted by the delicious smells of other horses.

His entourage became instant and adoring new fans. The beauty of the Arabian horse had stunned them into temporary silence, but finally the adoration was put into words.

"He's fantastic! I would marry you just to get my hands on the horse!" exclaimed Mikki, as she walked around the prancing stallion.

"Me, too!" announced Julianne, now at Aljazar's neck

and rubbing him. The horse seemed to calm with human touch. His eyes, though fiery and brilliant, softened as he nuzzled the women gently. His head lowered and he seemed almost docile as he permitted Mikki and Julianne to rub his ears and coo baby talk to him.

"Welcome, Aljazar!" said Faris, approaching his horse and running his hands up and down his legs, checking for abnormal heat or swelling. The stallion was in fine shape and had weathered his trip like the true champion that he was. "Good boy, good boy," murmured Faris as he beamed with pleasure and pride.

"He's definitely amazing. I can't wait to see what he can do...besides run a race, that is, and breed mares. He'll definitely have a full book for breeding mares. Wait 'til everyone sees him. You'll have to hire a full time body guard," said Mikki, still admiring the horse.

"That's why the bad guys knew they could hurt me by doing something to Aljazar. Destroy something good, kill something beautiful and innocent...that's the way these guys play. You must know I'm not like them, never was, never will be."

Mikki went to him and hugged him hard. Julianne stood silent and calm. She knew her friend had picked a winner.

CHAPTER FORTY-TWO

Faris paid the transporters and the trio put the stallion in a stall with a thick layer of bedding. Aljazar had settled down and was resting quietly, yet remained alert and inquisitive about his new surroundings. He had nose-to-nose contact with Clown and amazingly neither one did the squeal and stomp horse greeting. It was more like two old buddies greeting each other after a long time apart.

"Maybe they knew each other in ancient times," pondered Julianne as she watched the two horses, now stalled side by side. "I imagine them running over ancient Saharan sand dunes, leading bands of mares, and looking for water at an oasis."

"Clown? My Clown? More likely he was back at the camp waiting for the Prince's favorite harem girl to feed him peppermints…or Coco Krispies, or something! There may have been a wild stallion that he dreamed about becoming, but the real Clown would have been happily living a life of luxury. Probably lazing about in the pool in the oasis, and then rolling in the sand just so his servant girls could brush him again. Huh, Clown? Isn't that how you do it here?" asked Mikki as she rubbed his forehead and twirled his forelock with her fingers.

Clown stared at Mikki and blinked his big, brown eyes quizzically. Then, as if to answer his mistress, his muzzle began searching her shirt for treats. She found a peppermint in her pocket and unwrapped it. His ears went to forward alert position and he began snuffling her hands in earnest to pick up the candy from her palm.

"I suppose you'll be spoiling Aljazar, too?" asked Faris.

"Of course. Do you think I'm biased? There isn't a prejudiced bone in my body," answered Mikki as she unwrapped another candy for the stallion.

Julianne had to return to her training duties and wanted

to call again about Minnie Mee and her foal. The morning's report had been good, she told Mikki and Faris. The miniature horses would hopefully come home after surgery on the foal's leg tomorrow morning. The owner was there with them at the equine hospital supervising their care and giving them extra attention.

Mikki and Faris had just sat down on a bale of hay in the aisle between the stalls when Mikki's cell phone rang.

"Oh, now what," she said aloud, before she answered. She spoke for a few moments and then clicked off the phone. "Hmm. That's funny. Granny said Mom called her looking for Brigetta. She went to work last night at the hospital and said she was going to sleep most of today. But when Mom went to wake her up to get ready for dinner, she wasn't in her room."

"Is that unusual?" Faris said, instantly concerned, but trying hard not to show his alarm.

"Yeah. She never just takes off without letting Mom know where she's going. I'm going to call Mom and see if I can find out anything else."

Mikki flipped open her cell phone and pushed the directory code for her mother.

"Mom? What's going on? Have you heard from Brigetta? What? She wasn't in her bed?" Mikki repeated what she was learning so Faris could hear what she knew. "And now she's not back for dinner and she has to work tonight? There's no note or anything? What did she say yesterday?" There was a pause while Mikki listened to Susan. Suddenly Mikki's face went white and she said, "What? Say that again!" Mikki's eyes grew wild and the pupils became dark. "Oh my God," she continued. "Hold on a second."

Mikki held the phone to her belly to block her conversation and grabbed Faris' arm.

"Do you have a brother?"

"No. There's only Kami and myself. Why?" answered Faris, his face tight with attention.

"Mom says Brigetta told her yesterday that a new doctor

at the hospital, a radiologist, came up to her and congratulated her on her sister's upcoming wedding. He said he was your brother!"

"Shit," murmured Faris under his breath.

"Worse yet, Mom said Brig was infatuated with him. A good-looking dude. They were to meet for coffee after work early this morning."

Faris was pacing now and whispered to Mikki, "Hang up. We've got to get going. Let's go to my condo and see if there's a message. That was the last place I saw Kamila, so I'm sure they know how to reach me there. Not even Kamila has my cell phone number. Quick! Let's go!"

"I've got to call Gran. I'll phone her from the car."

Mikki quickly said goodbye to her mother and grabbed Faris' hand. Both of them ran from the stables and left the horses staring after them, still licking pieces of stuck-on peppermints off their lips. Faris gunned the engine of the Aston Martin and dust billowed from behind the car as they bounced over the rutted dirt road towards the highway.

CHAPTER FORTY-THREE

Emily did not take the news well that her granddaughter might be at the mercy of terrorists...terrorists who didn't mind conceiving a baby just to use as a bomb. Rage, not panic, surged through every thought, every crevice of her brain. These guys would pay and it wouldn't be pretty. Even Guinea worms were too kind, too neat for these guys. They were going down ugly. But first she would find Brigetta and assure her safety. If one blond hair was even slightly out of place ... Emily couldn't even think about that. She grabbed her cane and tossed it aside, almost running up the stairs to the workroom. She surveyed the weaponry and every piece of special assault equipment she had accumulated over the years. She would sit in her chair and think. When the phone rang, she would be ready. She might be old, but mentally she was a Girl Scout, always prepared.

Faris and Mikki arrived at his condo and parked at the north side of the complex. They would approach from the garden wall behind the apartment. If Sajid and Hassad had taken Brigetta, they wouldn't be here. But someone else might be here, waiting for them to arrive, waiting in ambush. Faris held up his arm to stop Mikki while he surveyed the back of the condo. Nothing seemed out of place. In his mind he wanted to have Mikki wait down the block, but instead he motioned her to the right as he circled to the left. Both crept silently, holding automatic handguns at the ready. They went through the backyard and circled to the front. Faris peered in through the corner window of his study. The door was open to the living room and he could see the ceiling fan turning lazy circles. No one was visible. Faris signaled Mikki to stay near the bushes and watch the front entrance. He returned to the deck at the rear and opened the sliding door with his key. He entered silently and carefully, his weapon leading the way, until he was sure the condo was vacant. He went to the front door and called to Mikki to come in.

Both of them holstered their weapons and Faris went to the answering machine. He was positive there would be a message. The red message light was blinking and they listened.

"They will soon both be dead. Be happy you have traded the lives of these stupid women for the passengers of the plane. I'm sure they will all thank you," said a man's voice with a strong Farsi accent. Then there was a loud thud, a scream, and more banging and scraping noises. Then the recording ended with an ominous dial tone.

Mikki and Faris looked at each other in silence and then stared at the recorder. Faris said, "Wait, there's more. Another message," and pushed the play button again. This time there was a woman's voice, soft and pleading. It was Kami.

"Faris, come to the Luxor Airport. He is going to kill the blond girl. He wants you here. Be here at precisely nine o'clock," the voice said. "The private airport. Where the rich and famous keep their little jets. Hurry. Come alone or he will kill me, too." Faris noted the sound and tone of his sister's voice.

That was the end of the message recorded at 4 P.M. It was now 6:30. Mikki was more scared than she had ever been in her life. She looked at her watch and then at Faris' face, as a terrifying realization came over her. Her relationship with Faris had endangered her family. She was hurtling back to earth as this reality struck like a comet from the sky. When this was over, however it ended, she would have to end her relationship with Faris. There would be no wedding, no honeymoon, and no man in her life. A blissful life with this man was just a dream, a pleasant dream, but just fantasy. It was as if Faris could read her mind.

"I won't let anything happen to her. Trust me. I'd die first before I'd let anything happen to your sister," said Faris calmly, his face not betraying his own inner rage. But Mikki could sense the barely controlled power in his body that was coiled like a snake ready to strike and kill. She felt a sudden thin and dangerous chill hanging on his words. Strangely, his anger calmed her.

"I trust you with *my* life. Hurry!" said Mikki, grabbing his hand and pulling him toward the door, cell phone in hand, madly dialing. Mikki bit her lip as she dialed her grandmother, thinking that she couldn't really say that she trusted Faris with her family's lives. She suddenly felt an infinite sadness, an unwelcome addition to the fear and anxiety already on board in her mind.

"Hold on. I need to get some ammo and some extra firepower. I never bring a knife to a gunfight and I don't believe in living in an under-gunned home. Go to the cabinet in the kitchen in the other condo. Just take the hidden passageway and head for the kitchen. There's lots of ammo. Just bring what you can carry. I'll run upstairs to the gun safe and be right back," Faris ordered, as he headed for the steps. He tossed Mikki a small duffle and she ran off hunkering down through the closet to the other condo. Faris pounded back down the stairs in three minutes with a combat bag containing two Surefire flashlights and belts with pockets for an extra pistol and AR-15 magazines. Slung over his shoulder were three AR-15 rifles equipped with Short Dot Scopes. To round out his arsenal there was a Bushmaster .308, and a 9mm complete A4 rifle. As he hit the bottom stairs still running, Mikki returned with the cartridges in her bag. She stopped and stared as Faris dropped his load on the floor to place everything into the duffle.

"I knew I took all those courses on Urban Operations, Hostage Rescue, and High Risk Environment Personal Safety Detail for a reason," Faris said, huffing from the exertion of running up and down the stairs, retrieving the heavy equipment.

"Well, believe it or not, I took the Anti-terrorism Driving course and was second in my class," said Mikki in an impetuous moment of verbal competition.

"Let's go," said Faris, rolling his eyes as he hoisted the heavy bag. Mikki took a strap and together they heaved the bag to his car.

"First stop, we go get Gran. I talked to her and she's

ready," panted Mikki, as they stuffed the arsenal into the trunk. Her grandmother was the one person in the world she knew and trusted in a life or death situation like this one.

CHAPTER FORTY-FOUR

Faris felt a moment of hesitation cross his mind, but knew it was useless. Emily Vanderhorn was going along with them. Well, he thought, she could wait in the car and dial 911 if shit hit the fan. She might make a good lookout, even at almost eighty years old. No doubt she was a feisty old broad.

Mikki watched Faris' mouth open briefly to speak in disagreement and then close. Good, she thought. She needed Granny along. Another family member needed to be there. After all, it was her sister that was being threatened. If anything happened to Brigetta, she would never forgive herself.

"You might even need me to drive."

"That's where we draw the line. Death by terrorists is honorable. Me being driven to death by my fiancée' is just stupidity."

Mikki glared at him and hugged herself defiantly in the car until they reached the Pink Flamingo. It was 7:30 P.M. The garage was open and the Aston Martin jerked to a stop inside. Pacing in front of the elevator door in full combat regalia was Emily. She was hardly recognizable when compared to the little old lady busy in the kitchen this morning. Now she looked like a miniature S.W.A.T member, ready for battle. She wore a khaki-colored jump suit that resembled a relic from WWII. Over her flight suit were crisscrossed belts, bandoliers of bullets slung Mexican bandito style across her chest. She carried a tactical police pump shotgun with adjustable sights. On her right hip was an automatic handgun in a holster. Mikki and Faris might have stood gawking at this apparition, but were warned by the seething fury emanating from that small but dangerous-looking woman. Her face was a glowering mask of rage, her lips were thin lines of anger, and her nostrils flared as she spoke.

"I'm ready," said Emily through clenched teeth, with a calm demeanor that could have been recognized as serene acceptance by someone who didn't know her. But her granddaughter knew her all too well. Her grandmother's icy steel blue eyes revealed her inner being. Emily Vanderhorn had flipped her switch to hunt and kill mode.

"Well...let's get going," stammered Faris, opening the door for the old lady. He had backed all the way to the car, unable to turn his back on all those furious guns and bullets. Emily jumped into the back seat like a twenty-year-old and Mikki reentered the front passenger side. As they rode along, the evening sky began to turn ominously black and gray while flashes of distant lightning warned of the coming threat.

Perfect, thought Emily. *I love a good storm.*

CHAPTER FORTY-FIVE

There was a quick discussion in the car about their destination, but the plan would depend on the layout of the building. Emily handed Faris a chip to insert into his handheld GPS. This was the electronic unit needed to connect to the tracking device planted on Sajid at the airport. Mikki had forgotten about this valuable piece of espionage equipment. Faris slid the flat, one-inch piece of wire circuits and plastic into the loading slot of his mapped location system. He punched in the directory address for Luxor Airport and a blinking yellow star noting the location appeared on the screen. They sped along in the car until they were three blocks away from their destination. The area offered cover near high weeds adjacent to the runways. Darkness had come rapidly because of the approaching thunderstorm. The windshield wipers battled huge drops of rain now splattering noisily on the car. Faris parked their vehicle in a grove of scrub trees and the three jumped out, racing towards the trunk to gather their supplies.

Faris wanted to direct Emily to wait in the car. He planned to tell her they might need a driver or someone to call emergency services if things went bad. But one look at those intense sapphire eyes made him change his mind. Her gray hair was already wet and strings of dampness framed her face. She didn't seem to notice her physical environment. In fact, Faris could swear that the rain had helped Emily grow taller and stronger right before his eyes, like a carnivorous humanoid plant. There was no doubt that she was a woman on a mission. There would be no stopping her now. Emily grabbed her own equipment and took the GPS back from Faris and Mikki.

"Faris needs to go in first. They know him. Mikki will be your back up. I'll take care of any guards and then I'll watch in case anyone gets out of the buildings. They have to be in one of the hangers. In the darkness, we'll use the chirping system as we approach," directed Emily, handing each of them a small metal clicker that looked like a kid's novelty item. "The paratroopers used these over sixty years ago and they'll still be of value tonight. Remember D-Day? This may look like a toy, but it saved soldiers lives in the war. If you come across a sound in the night, hear someone in the midst of enemy territory? No talking. Use the clicker. It makes a small 'cricket' noise and if you don't hear it back, shoot to kill. That means it's not one of us. It worked for our boys back then, and it'll work for us today. Remember to use the clicker. There's going to be patrol out here somewhere. They're expecting us. Let's get in there and get the girls out."

Faris patted his weapons in the dark and felt for the ammo. Emily had taken charge and he was ready to go. Mikki, looking at the GPS in Emily's palm, said, "There! Look there!" She pointed to a moving red dot that was glowing inside a schematic of the building that was housing airplane maintenance. "Is that Sajid?"

The three of them stood in the rain staring at the GPS and Emily smiled and nodded. "He probably thought it was a spider bite, but the tiny implant will show us every move. I just touched my hand to the back of his arm in the airport, and asked him to check his watch for the time. As he jerked his arm away from my grasp, the tiny transmitter was injected automatically, easy as pie. He's a very rude man who wouldn't bother to tell an old lady the time. If I would've known he wanted to play this dirty, we would have gone after him a long time ago. Time to stop playing nice. He's going down, way down," announced Emily, with another flare of barely controlled temper.

"Faris, you need to figure out how to get in the building with Mikki. I'll stay outside until there's no further reason to…meaning all the bad guys have fallen down dead out here." Emily then patted both of them on the back and gave their necks, one by one, a hard squeeze to get them on their way.

"Ready?" Faris asked Mikki. She nodded and they ran

off through the hard rain. Emily watched the GPS for a moment. Quickly two blue dots from the newly implanted devices appeared and were moving away from her and toward the maintenance hanger. Emily wasn't about to let those two out of her sight tonight.

Emily moved quickly towards the road and soon was approaching from the main driveway to the suspect building. When close to the open gate, but hidden in the palmettos near the chain link fence, Emily pulled out her scoped weapon and peered through the night lens. There was a ladder to the north side of the roof beside one of the heavy truck access doors. Two men waited in the rain near the supply entrance ramp. They stood beneath the roof overhang, trying to stay dry. One was smoking and the other carried what appeared to be a mobile walkie unit. *Easy pickin's*, thought Emily as she reached into her vest for her handgun's silencer and quickly screwed the attachment into place. She couldn't use the rifle from here, and besides, it would make way too much noise. She edged along the palm fronds by the fencing easily. She felt as agile as a gymnast tonight. There was no time for arthritis pain or the disability of a past stroke. This was do or die. Nothing was more important to her than this. Certainly not her own discomfort. This favor would be done for her granddaughter, for her whole family. She felt alive and murderously alert. Emily loved the sensation the extra adrenalin was giving her, but she hated the thought that her granddaughters' lives depended on her success.

The pouring rain hampered the guards' vision, but they had a pair of night goggles they were passing back and forth. Also, at unscheduled intervals, the frequent bolts of lightning were surprisingly illuminating. In order for Emily to remain unseen, she had to be perfectly still when there was enough light for visibility. The men were stupidly standing near an emergency floodlight that kept tripping off and on when they stepped out of their dark dry spot to take a closer look around. That spotlight was her warning system, but could also be a tattletale to her position. She needed to get to the corner on the east side of the building where a small plane sat awaiting repair. There was a huge bolt and flash from the sky that hit close by, causing the startled men to quickly duck back into the recess of the building. At the distraction, Emily didn't shrink back but ran full force and low to the ground until she reached the parked jet. She belly-crawled quickly beneath the aircraft and waited. She could hear them talking now. All Arabic and nothing understandable, except that she knew they hadn't seen her make the run. Lying on the relatively dry concrete below the jet, she squirmed forward and positioned herself in the prone position. Emily flipped the safety on the gun, rotated the suppressor onto the barrel, and positioned her elbows to act as a bipod for balance. She hoped her sniper skills wouldn't fail her now. It had been a long time, but she had never missed before. This was a handgun, not a rifle, but the men were close. Two targets and both must go down. She waited and steadily squeezed the trigger...once, twice.

CHAPTER FORTY-SIX

Both men crumpled without a sound, like puppets with cut strings. Emily rolled out from beneath the plane and ran up the five steps to the loading ramp at the garage. She felt for carotid pulses. They were both dead. Each man sported a small black hole near his temple. She gave each body a couple of kicks, sending them one by one over the edge of the ramp into the rain and hard concrete below. Working entirely on adrenalin now, Emily reached down and rubbed her right knee. The old injury was issuing a warning reminder as she looked up through the rain at the metal ladder leading to the roof. The fall in Citrus City two years ago had changed her life. She shuddered just once, grabbed her weapons and jumped to the first rail of the ladder. She began to climb, full of resolve. The knee was issuing criticisms in the form of painful throbbing, but Emily only looked up and continued to climb to the highest rung. She flipped herself and her weapons over the edge onto the rain-soaked puddles on the tarred roof. She'd made it to the flat surface of the building top. She didn't fall this time. *Nearly eighty years old and I can still climb a damned ladder.*

Her self-congratulations didn't last long enough for Emily to even catch her breath. She thought of Brigetta, Mikki, and Faris. *Move, old woman, get moving! No time to reminisce about past adventures.* Looking around she saw humming ventilation units with fans. She edged along the perimeter, looking down. More men would probably be waiting in ambush inside where it's dry. They probably weren't seasoned combat militants, just wannabee murderers of innocent people...men, women, and children. No real bravery there. They didn't even want to get wet in a little bit of rain. Running in a quick circular reconnaissance from her rooftop perch, she saw no one else outside the building. She heard something rustle behind her and immediately reached for the clicker on her lanyard. She clicked. No response. She drew her weapon and turned, ready to fire. The beam of her mini flashlight showed rat eyes scurrying across the tarpaper. She exhaled and immediately checked the GPS. Mikki and Faris were little blue dots near windows on the south end of the building. It looked like they were trying to enter through a door near some crates at the back. Emily decided there was no way to enter the building through the roof. She leaned over the back edge and was going to motion at Mikki and Faris when suddenly a door opened below her to the right and a man started shouting. He couldn't find the two guards stationed at the garage, but he would soon. He called to the others inside and Emily watched the GPS as the red dot also came to the man's position. They all began yelling and jumped back into the building, slamming the heavy metal door. They had seen the two bodies lying in the rain.

Now the three rescuers had to move fast. The element of surprise was gone and *the bad guys are gonna be mad at us for messing up their plans*, thought Emily. After the commotion and the yelling, Emily ran to one of the ducts, lifted the cover, and jammed her baton into the fan. The motor stopped and with the cover off, Emily could see into the main room of the hanger. She used her body to shield the rain from the unit, but it was still splashing down around her, making it impossible to hear the conversation inside. Horrified, she saw Brigetta sitting huddled against a support beam, arms tied behind her back. She was alive, but her face was scratched and her mouth was bleeding. Her clothes were torn and she was trying to cover herself by drawing her knees up to her chest. Emily saw that Brigetta was shaking and terrified...or furious. One of the men came to her and started yelling and making gestures Emily couldn't understand. Which one was Sajid? He was tall, but it was hard to tell much from her vantage point. They all wore jeans and T-shirts. Their shaved beards had grown back to short, rough stubble. She finally recognized Hassad and Sajid. They were talking to each other in the corner and then shouted at the three others to position themselves for the anticipated attack. Emily knew they would kill Brigetta in anger, especially if they thought they were going to get caught or killed. Where was Kamila? Was she dead? Emily couldn't see her in the room, but the rain was slowing. Emily checked the GPS once again. The two blue dots were still near the building but hadn't yet entered. Emily couldn't just passively watch what would happen next, so she ran and nearly catapulted down the ladder. Hitting the ground softly and circling the building with a jog trot, she saw the parachute training plane, twin propellers already revved and rotating, the whirring aluminum blades shiny and dangerous. A pilot was on the ground doing a pre-flight check. Emily suddenly knew their sinister plan and there was little time to reach Faris and Mikki.

CHAPTER FORTY-SEVEN

Faris found a dirty window at the rear of the hanger that had a broken glass panel. He pushed a rag-covered hand through it and as glass shards tinkled to the floor, he released the lock. Amazingly the old window slid up easily and Faris motioned to Mikki with just a nod of his head. He climbed through and helped Mikki pull herself into what was apparently a tool room. They now had a perfect view from the room's doorway, down a hall, and into the main hanger. There were no planes in the hanger that was dimly lit with flickering florescent bulbs hung from chains. Faris counted five men inside the building. Brigetta was tied to a post. Kamila was standing among the men, talking to them.

Suddenly the giant roll-up door screeched in ascension, slowly revealing a plane right outside, ready to fly. Faris and Mikki looked at each other.

"They're getting away!" whispered Mikki. "We've got to go now!"

Faris nodded and reached for an extra clip of ammunition, pulling his automatic from its holster. Mikki had already drawn her weapon and was inching forward when a man in a black sweatshirt and jeans raced to Brigetta. Mikki gasped out loud when she saw the knife. The man slashed Brigetta's bindings and jerked her up, shouting orders.

"Move, move, now!" he screamed at her and the other men bolted after them. The pilot drew the plane close to the door and the deafening roar of the vibrating engines filled the building. Mikki and Faris began to run towards the group, guns drawn. The men turned and began firing at them. Mikki went left and Faris went right, crouching and trying to reach the plane. The man in black was shoving Brigetta up the step and into the body of the plane. Mikki was screaming her sister's name, but was helpless as bullets whizzed by her head. She scanned the other side of the room for Faris. She heard two shots and the guard on Faris' side of the building went down, sprawled on his back and bleeding. She saw Faris run for the plane but he encountered another round of bullets aimed in his direction. The man in black, Kamila, and one other man had boarded the plane and were pulling the door closed. The plane was turning and heading towards the tarmac.

"Run, Faris!" Mikki screamed as a bullet whizzed perilously close to her right ear. Faris ran to the hanger entry, but Sajid, Hassad, and the other man had disappeared into the rain-soaked night. Shots being fired kept Mikki and Faris in the building. They didn't have time to follow the men now. Mikki now worried about Emily. Was she engaged in a shoot-out in the darkness surrounding the hangar? Was she injured? Sudden loud whirring of the plane's ancient engine drowned out everything else. The plane was pulling away, so Mikki and Faris sprinted as fast as they could after the plane, slipping and sliding through the pools of rainwater, firing their rifles at the engines and wings. There was precious cargo in the fuselage that they didn't want to damage.

Mikki stopped far out on the runway, totally out of breath and sobbing. Faris went to her and put his arms around her. This didn't look good for the girls still trapped by their sadistic captors. Mikki tore herself from Faris and began to pace as the distant plane jerked and bounced once and then left the runway; its navigation lights becoming twinkling stars reflecting on the wet pavement.

"Brigetta!" Mikki screamed, in a frenzied futile effort. She sank to her knees in the puddles on the blacktop, feeling very lost. Faris couldn't console her, but he crouched with her as they watched the sky.

"It's coming back!" shouted Mikki. "What's going on?"

They both jumped up as Faris saw the plane, too, and pulled his binoculars from his belt. He switched on his powerful mag light and pointed it skyward.

"Oh, no," he whispered.

"What?" demanded Mikki, "What's going on?"

He said nothing at first, but Mikki's fingernails were digging into his forearm.

"They've opened the jump door."

"Huh? The jump door?" gasped Mikki, as fear, stark and vivid, glittered in her eyes. Mikki began to tremble as fearful images forced their way into her mind.

"Oh, my God," said Faris, tension building, causing his fists to ball up reflexively. "They're going to do it!" A cold knot formed in his stomach as painful as a punch.

Mikki breathed in short, shallow pants as a figure screamed and began to fall from the plane. Mikki mouthed, "Open, open, open!" But there was no parachute to open. To add to the macabre sight, a small flare had been attached to the falling, flailing body that glowed, pink and fiery, lighting the way to the ground.

The silence loomed between them like heavy fog on this rainy night. Mikki was crying inconsolably now and chanting her sister's name over and over. Faris knew this was the end of their relationship. Helpless, he had caused the death of Mikki's sister by mere association. This was too much. Someone would pay. As vengeful plans spun through his brain, he heard Mikki scream again. Someone else had been pushed from the plane and again no parachute opened. Another flare traced the body's landing to a wooded area just past the airport.

Mikki, feeling like a hand was closing around her throat, began to run towards the woods. Her mood suddenly veered sharply to anger as she seethed with mounting grief and rage. As she ran she thought, this will just kill Granny Em. I'm glad she's still watching the front of the building and not here to see this. Hopefully she's shot a few more terrorists. But Brigetta is dead and it's all my fault. I'm so stupid.

Faris, running too, reached for her hand as she stumbled up to the chain link fence near the trees, but she jerked her hand away. She didn't dare speak or even look at him. He helped her mount the fence and clamored over it behind her. This was not going to be good, he thought, and he shuddered inwardly at the mental impression of what was ahead. It would be so hard to lose Mikki. He had never loved anyone like he loved this tough and interesting woman. He ached with defeat as he followed Mikki into the trees with his spotlight.

CHAPTER FORTY-EIGHT

Feeling braver, he took her arm and pulled her towards him. He didn't want her to see this. Mikki's response was like that of a captured panther. She screamed and swung blindly at him, needing somewhere to vent her misery. Dodging her swings, he pulled her in closer and closer, until she was spent and hot tears flowed freely down her face. She wept loudly, rocking back and forth in his embrace as the deep sobs imploded her body. Finally she pulled herself away with a choking cry.

"I still love you, Faris, but we just can't be together. I can never endanger my family again. It's my fault because I thought Gran and I would be invincible and adding you to help us would be great. Well, it's not great. I can't do this!" Mikki moaned, still shaking, but calmer.

"I understand, Mikki. I love you, but the last thing I ever wanted was for anyone we love to get hurt," murmured Faris, trying to remain strong and upright.

Suddenly the silence of the night was broken by the sound of a plane. Were the bastards daring to return? Mikki and Faris scrambled their way through the brambles back to the fence. The jump plane was circling and tilting its wings! The bastards were taunting them with a wing wave! Both Mikki and Faris scrambled back over the fence. Amazingly the plane was in a landing pattern! They would get them this time and there would be no survivors.

The touchdown was a little rocky but the small plane bumped to a sliding stop near the main office. Mikki and Faris began to run back, fueled by fury and anticipation. When they reached the plane, their guns were drawn and they really wanted to use them, to use them and every single round of ammunition they had brought with them. In the dark they could still see that the plane's door was closed, but the small pilot's window was being pushed open little by little. An arm reached out the window, causing Mikki and

Faris to aim their weapons, but the hand was waving a white handkerchief!

"What?" breathed Mikki, and Faris just stared. Quickly Mikki said, "Maybe the pilot was hijacked and he found a way to come back and surrender?"

"Doubtful," said Faris, still pointing the barrel of his gun in the general direction of the plane's closed jump door.

Before they could come up with any other solution, the door popped loose and the step-up automatically slid into position. An arm poked around the corner of the doorway. They heard, "click, click, click." Finally Faris had the wits to grab the clicker from his pocket and click back. Then, on the dark tarmac, a smiling pilot appeared in the doorway with a wave, gesturing to them like it was a presidential landing complete with a welcoming military band.

Mikki and then Faris lowered their weapons. Their bodies stiffened with surprise and then relaxed with recognition. The pilot wore a khaki flight suit and when the headphones came off there was a mass of curly gray hair. Granny Em.

Mikki was too startled to speak. Faris stood still, looking blank. He gave Mikki a sideways glance of disbelief. Emily jumped down the step and bounced to the ground, wiping her hands on her pants.

"Greetings, Earthlings," said Emily, grinning cheerfully. Then she turned and motioned toward the opening and Brigetta appeared, crying, but smiling too. Her torn shirt and scratched face were temporarily forgotten. They ran to Brigetta and Faris reached for her hands to help her down the steps. Mikki grabbed her sister and was crying again, except this time they were happy tears. Faris was full of questions, but didn't dare to be the first one to speak. Emily saw the concern on his face. Where was his sister? The answers would come soon enough. Emily motioned Faris to her side.

"Kamila is in the plane. She's okay, but she's been a bad girl. Therefore she's shackled to one of the fuselage support beams," whispered Emily, when Faris was close enough to hear her. "The bad guys wanted to try night sky diving. But they didn't realize they would be the ones doing the jumping.

Then they forgot to take the class on packing their own chutes."

"I see," said Faris, still confused but calm now. "I'll take Kamila with me?"

"Yes. She's your sister. We've got 'family first' rules. I figure this is your problem and you need to deal with it. She may have been brainwashed or maybe not. She helped lure Brigetta into the hands of Sajid and Hassad and the rest of them. If you don't take her outta my life, I'm pretty sure she won't survive another day. You know what I mean?"

"Actually, I had my own suspicions, but I wanted to talk to her first. One way or the other, she'll be out of the picture. I promise."

"And I'll be holding you to that promise, young man. No one, but no one, messes with my family. Not now, not ever. I think you can understand that," said Emily, composure and dignity etched into her face. Emily ran her fingers through her mass of damp hair. Mikki was still hugging Brigetta so hard that her younger sister was struggling for air.

"Mikki, we've got to go. The airport is closed and soon someone will be wondering why all the lights and commotion is going on over here. Faris is taking his sister out of the plane and going home." Emily tossed a set of keys into the air. "I found these in someone's pocket. They won't be needing them anymore. I'm sure we can figure out which car they belong to. We'll drive back to town, dump the car in a lot somewhere, and get a taxi back home."

Faris started for the plane and reached into his utility belt for the handcuff key he always carried. When he disappeared into the plane, the women walked away and Emily pushed the remote entry on the key ring. They easily found the green H3 Hummer that flashed and beeped a welcome to its new passengers. Emily thought even the SUV would be glad to be rid of its previous owners. As the three women got into the vehicle, Emily suddenly felt drained. This was a happy ending for her latest adventure, but she had to admit, she was way too old for this kind of wild and crazy escapade.

CHAPTER FORTY-NINE

As Mikki settled into the driver's seat of the H3, somewhat surprised that Emily had asked her to drive, she began to relax. She had lots of questions, Brigetta had lots of questions. But it had been a long, terror-filled night and everyone just wanted to get out of there and back home. Mikki drove to the Cinema Ten parking lot where late night movies were still being shown. The lot was half-full and she slipped the car between a Ford pickup and a Honda Civic. As they walked away, Mikki pulled out her cell phone and dialed for a cab. It would pick them up at a nearby Applebee's restaurant. The cab would arrive in about ten minutes, so they began to walk faster. They sat outside the closing restaurant on a waiting area bench, hoping no one would see them there. They looked like dirty refugees who needed showers and a good shampoo. The cab arrived and took them to Sunburst Coffee Shop and Grille as directed. The Mini Cooper was still parked where Brigetta had left it. The little car sat alone under a light in the lot. Its bright red color, still wet from the rain, seemed to glare ferociously, as if the car was angered by the abandonment and neglect.

Brigetta suddenly realized she had no keys, no purse, nothing. Nothing but her own precious life for which she was eternally grateful. She looked forlornly at Mikki and Emily.

"Sorry guys. Must've lost the keys somewhere. We can call Mom to bring the extra set. I need to call her now that we're safe anyway."

"No," said Mikki calmly. "Too many questions we can't answer right now. We'll get the little sucker started."

Brigetta watched open-mouthed as her sister pulled a little plastic case from a leg pocket in her military cargo pants. Mikki found a small metal tool and jimmied the door lock. The door locks popped up in unison. Mikki squeezed into the driver's seat and began using another tool on the ignition. Within seconds, the car seemed to breathe with relief as the engine hummed to life. The women fell silent once again on the drive to the Pink Flamingo. They were all disoriented and needed to sort things out, but all three were totally exhausted.

In twenty minutes, the Pink Flamingo's security lights could be seen along the coastal road. As Mikki approached the house, she punched in the programmed security codes for the gate and garage into her cell phone that doubled as a transmitter. As they drove into the garage and home, there was a collective sigh of relief. In the kitchen, Emily started a pot of coffee and then turned to go to her bedroom to shower and change. As she saw Brigetta reach for the phone in the kitchen, she put her hand on Brigetta's arm.
"Only say that you're safe. You're at the Pink Flamingo and all is fine. Just tell her you'll explain everything later. And no, she isn't to come over, all hysterical or anything. Reassure her, that's it. We have to get our story straight first. We don't want to panic Susan."
"I'm sure she's already called Dad in New York about a hundred times. He's probably on his way here now to kill someone," Brigetta responded.
"Probably, but she can't come over right now. We have to clean up. We have to talk. Okay?" said Emily, with Mikki wildly nodding her head in agreement.
"Okay," said Brigetta slowly, "I guess we do need to talk first." Brigetta dialed and got Susan on the first ring. She did a superb job with her mother. She was staying the night at Granny Em's and would tell her all about her "getting lost" in the morning. Yes, she would call her dad and tell him she was fine and sorry she had upset them both.
Mikki urged Brigetta off the phone by demonstrating cutting movements at her neck and 'wind it up' circles with her other hand. Both girls went to Mikki's room to clean up. Brigetta stripped and tossed her slacks and blouse into the trash. The bra and panties went into the washing machine with Mikki's grimy outfit. Mikki had plenty of clothes for

Brigetta to borrow, so she tossed her a pair of shortie pajamas and a towel, briskly pointing towards the shower.

"Go. Go clean up," she ordered, with a sense of urgency.

"What? Do you think you smell like freshly baked bread or something?" Brigetta retorted, but she was grinning. She grabbed up the pajamas and went to the bathroom.

"I'm next, little Miss Stinky," announced Mikki, as she dug through her dresser for more pajamas and something for her sister to wear in the morning. Their mom had seen most of the clothes the girls wore, so probably wouldn't notice a change in outfits. Maybe. Some times her mother was a surprise waiting to happen.

Mikki heard the shower running upstairs and wondered what her grandmother was thinking as she stood under the steaming water. Mikki's mind was spinning. What had happened to Brigetta during her capture? What was she thinking about her rescue and rescuers? Where was Faris now? What would happen to Kamila? Would she be back to haunt them again? What about the men who got away? Did they think they had disposed of the women when they saw the free-falling bodies? She hoped so. But she knew this wasn't over. The what or who that was over was Faris. It couldn't work.

Mikki sat on the bed with a plop, holding herself with her arms in a cocoon of anguish, willing the tears not to fall. After all, her sister was safe. She just had to resign herself to the fact that she and Faris were not meant to be a couple. His sister was a terrorist and maybe his whole family was dangerous. She knew he cared about her and she loved him to death. That was it. To death. Mikki just couldn't take another chance like this. Family came first. Always.

CHAPTER FIFTY

"Want another cookie, Gran?" asked Brigetta, now cleaned up and her scratches barely visible. She had towel-dried her long blond hair and woven it into a tidy braid. Her freshly scrubbed face looked young and innocent. She usually only wore make-up when they went out for an evening of clubbing or to a party. But now shadows deepened under her eyes where fatigue had settled. Emily had made them some decaf and served it to the girls. Brigetta sipped her coffee and passed the peanut butter cookies to Emily.

"Sure, I'm kind of hungry," said Emily, taking two more cookies to put on her plate.

"You sure love these peanut cookies," said Brigetta, picking another one for herself. "Seems like that's all you like to bake."

Mikki was in the kitchen getting another cup of coffee. Emily sat with Brigetta on the couch. Mikki said, as she opened the refrigerator, "Yeah, that's her favorite, all right." Then she got giddy with laughter and Emily grinned at their secret.

"I don't get it. What's so funny?" asked Brigetta, taking her coffee cup to the kitchen, dumping the remains in the sink and getting some tea.

Mikki and Emily just shrugged and looked smug. Mikki decided it was time to change the subject. It was late or early, actually, as the clock read 2 A.M. They were all somewhat revived by caffeine and sugar. They sat circled in the living room, sipping the hot drinks prepared by Emily.

"Well, tell us what happened. Who was this guy who conned you into meeting him? He said he was Faris' brother?"

"Yeah, he was a new doc at the hospital, a radiologist, and he was nice looking. Seemed very charming, like Faris, you know? We talked and he seemed to know all about you and Faris and that the wedding was next week and all that. I agreed to meet him for coffee. I thought I was safe enough since I drove my own car to the café."

"Go on," insisted Emily, even though she could see a few tears of humiliation forming in her granddaughter's tired eyes. This would be a gentle interrogation, but Emily needed answers.

"Since I wear scrubs supplied by the hospital, after my shift I put on my street clothes and drove to the coffee shop. He was there, all smiles. Now that I look back on it, it seems a little funny."

"What?" asked Mikki.

"Well, he was a radiologist and they usually work during the day. Yet he was there on the night shift and found me in the pediatric unit. I was inserting a new IV in a little boy who had been having repeated seizures. The doctor had on the typical green scrubs and had a nametag. Dr. Numair Al-Busaid. He seemed to be for real. In fact, he helped me get the IV line inserted and definitely knew what he was doing. I never doubted he was a real doctor. I never thought anything suspicious about him."

"What happened when you got to Sunburst Café?" urged Emily, who was getting weary and stifled a yawn.

"He stood up, welcomed me, and asked what kind of coffee I'd like. He went to the counter, brought two coffees back, and sat down with me at a table near the back. We were talking about the hospital cafeteria when a van drove up by the side door. It was a dark blue panel van. You know, the kind with no windows. He smiled and said, 'Oh, here's my cousin! He wants to meet you, too.' When I said to have him come in and join us, Dr. Busaid, or whatever his real name is, said, 'his wife is handicapped and in a wheelchair. Could you just step out for a minute and say hello?' There was this little warning bell in my head that I foolishly didn't heed. I walked to the side door and he opened it for me. I stepped outside and the driver greeted me like an old friend. I heard a woman's voice in the back of the van and figured it was the wife. The doctor opened the side door and I peeked inside. A young woman wearing a black burqa, I think that's what you call it, was in a wheelchair. She was clear in the back of the van, which I thought was unusual but she beckoned me to her. As I leaned in, someone pulled me, the doc pushed me, and something covered my face. I think it was ether. I didn't even have a chance to fight or scream. Things went all sparkly and then black."

"Geez, Brig. I'd have been scared shitless," said Mikki, reaching for her sister's hand.

"It was over so quick, there was no time to be anything but surprised at the time. I felt real nauseous when I came out of the stupor and threw up on the concrete where I sat. I was already tied up at the building I later found out was a hangar at Luxor Airport. I had no idea what they wanted but knew right away they planned to kill me. The men disappeared into an office for a while. The other woman stayed and kept looking at me, like she was scared. I couldn't tell if she wanted to help and was afraid, or whether she was just afraid I would get away. They left me there all day, no food, no water, no potty break. Then later, towards evening, they said Faris was coming over to see me and it would all be over soon. I didn't have a real good feeling about that."

"That was when Faris got the message on his answer machine. We'd been at the stables all afternoon playing meet and greet with his stallion. Mom had called earlier looking for you, so we checked his house just to make sure there were no calls there," said Mikki.

"How did you know how to find me?" asked Brigetta, needing some puzzle pieces of her own to fit together.

"The men, and also I think it was Kamila, called and said to come to the airport and that both of you women were going to die."

"Oh, that's just swell," said Brigetta numbly, sitting back on her chair, and pushing the coffee cup away.

"So we grabbed up Gran and hopped into Faris' car to come get you."

"Somehow it doesn't seem like it was that simple, but I'm sure happy you came. It's all a little blurry to me. Maybe it'll be more clear in the morning. I'm alive and right now I've got to go to bed." With a long exhausted sigh, she stood up. Her muscles were beginning to veto further movement and she felt drained. She needed sleep.

Mikki and Emily got up and hugged Brigetta, each giving her a little kiss on the cheek and wishing her a goodnight.

"Thanks for saving my ass, you guys. Good night."

CHAPTER FIFTY-ONE

"Do you think she'll be okay?" asked Mikki, as she watched her sister head for the guest room downstairs. "She's not going to have post traumatic stress syndrome or something, is she?"

"I gave her a little something to help her relax and sleep," said Emily.

"Gran? What? You didn't!" whispered Mikki, hands steepled in a prayer position.

"It's not a sleeping pill, just a little something that will make the muscle soreness go away. And maybe a few of the memories…"

"You should be ashamed of yourself. You drugged my little sister!"

"It seemed to be a kind thing to do. In the morning we'll fill in all the missing blanks with our own version of the story and it'll become gospel to her. She'll be just a little foggy. She'll remember the ordeal, but not the fear or pain parts."

"Or the parts about how we got her out of there?" questioned Mikki.

"Exactly," answered Emily, leaning back on her comfy couch and rubbing her belly full of peanut butter cookies.

"Anything else you care to share with me?" asked Mikki.

"Hmmm. You might as well take the tracking chip off your neck. I think I know where you are right now. We'll let Faris keep his for the time being."

Mikki reflexively slapped at the back of her neck and felt a small bump just below her hairline. She scratched at it and felt a tiny piece of metal come loose that she grasped with her fingernails. Bringing it close to her eyes, she stared at it and then set it on her napkin.

Taking all this in stride, she asked, "How did you get that in there? Faris has one, too?"

"Automatic microchip injector. It fits on my finger and fires with pressure. You preload it and put in on your forefinger, like this," said Emily as she demonstrated the concept on her hand. "When you're ready to use it, you move the device to your fingertip and quickly press it into your victim's skin. Voila! Instant tracking. You can follow the chip with any GPS that has an exterior load to accept the program."

"You said 'victim,'" Mikki said. "I heard that part."

"Okay, victim or person or granddaughter or whoever. There, do you like that better?"

"Fabulously."

"Good."

"So Faris still has his?" asked Mikki, her mind swirling as she spoke his name. She wondered if she would ever get over him. No other could replace him.

"As long as he doesn't start rubbing his neck," said Emily, "it will stay there for a few weeks. Then the body tends to push all foreign objects out of the skin...just like a splinter. Sajid still has his too."

"I only wish it would be that easy to push my foreign object out of mind."

"I take it you mean Faris?"

"Yeah, but let's not talk about him. Now I know there can't be any 'us' and all those fantasy dreams are over. I can't believe I was such a dummy over a man."

"You weren't a dummy. You aren't a dummy. You gave him a chance. You had to do that for yourself and for him. He does really care for you. I see the confusion in your face and memories that are still alive. Those won't go away in a day or two. Some things were meant to be and others are not. You still don't know what will happen with that."

"Oh, I do know. I know his image is etched on my brain right now, but it'll fade. There've been others, maybe there'll be another man, another time."

"You're starting to sound like an old classical movie. A bit maudlin, don't you think? You're just a child in real life."

"But he was my favorite, ever. The best man for me, I know it. Just like you're my favorite grandma, Brig is my favorite sister, Mom is my...."

"Enough," interrupted Emily. "We are your only grandmother, your only sister and mother. Enough of this favorite crap. He's your favorite until the next one comes along."

"No Gran, you don't understand. He's it. He's the one."

"There, dopey girl. You've said it yourself. Now what are we going to do about it?" challenged Emily.

"You tricked me. You tricked me into saying all that."

"Yeah, I made you see the light. You love 'Mr. Favorite-of-all-time, he's-the-best, yahoo-yippee.' Let's see what happens next. He's no idiot. He'll be back."

"I told him we were over."

"So?" exclaimed Emily, throwing up her arms. "I'm going to bed. I was going to tell you about how I commandeered the plane, but we'll talk about that in the morning after we get Brigetta back to your mother." Emily rose to go to bed and then turned toward Mikki, saying, "Oh, by the way, you and Brigetta are my favorite granddaughters, too."

"Ha ha. Only granddaughters, you mean," said Mikki.

"Bedtime for me now," said Emily in dismissal, as she twirled her hand lasso-like toward her bedroom suite.

"Okay. Me, too," yawned Mikki, pressing both hands over her eyes that were burning with weariness and the earlier floods of salty tears. She sat alone for a few moments, bare feet planted on the coffee table. There was still a dull ache of desire for Faris as she recalled his face, his muscular body. Unbidden memories haunted her. She remembered his gentle and loving touch, his inscrutable expression, his boyish grin. Was Faris lost forever? Where was he right now? She needed to think, but now she needed rest. She closed her eyes and filtered the thoughts that scrambled her mind. Soon she was asleep on the big, cushy chair, softly snoring as her chin rested limply on her chest.

CHAPTER FIFTY-TWO

Mikki awakened to the musical sound of her cell phone playing "It's My Life" and looked under pillows and in her purse to quell the interruption. Finding the phone, she thought, now what? She said hello without checking caller ID.

"Mikki?" said Faris, hesitantly. Mikki knew he was judging her mood by the tone of her voice. This was too soon. She didn't know what to say to him.

"Hi," was the word she managed to mutter in response. She was still not fully awake and her eyelids felt like ground glass on her eyes. "What's up?" That was a brilliant greeting, but it was the best she could muster up at this time of the morning. It was 6:55 according to the clock on the fireplace mantle. Everyone had had only a few hours of sleep.

"Do you still hate me?" Faris ventured.

"Faris, don't be ridiculous. Are you trying to make me feel sorry for you? Because I feel sorry for both of us. We love each other. There. I said it for the two of us. That hasn't changed at all. You have to realize that our backgrounds are just way too different. It's not going to work. I thought I was clear on that yesterday."

"I was hoping you'd miss me by now."

"Well, if it's any consolation, I do. I do and I will. Please, take care of your sister and go your own way. It's best for everyone."

"There's still bad guys out there. No one will be safe until they're caught and disposed of. Remember the ones who got away? Sajid, Hassad, and Dr. Bad, among others?"

Mikki heard her sister stirring around in the bathroom below and knew she'd soon be coming up the stairs. She heard Granny Em's TV tuned to the news in her suite. Everyone would be up and wanting coffee and breakfast.

"Mikki, are you there?" Faris prompted.

"Of course, but everyone's getting up. I've got to go. Please, just don't call me for a while. I need to think. Goodbye, Faris." Mikki disconnected the call before she could hear him say another word.

This was just too hard. Willing away another barrage of tears, Mikki dragged herself to the kitchen letting her nose lead the way to the automatically brewed carafe of morning coffee. She pulled cups from the cupboard and opened a refrigerated tube of cinnamon rolls to put into the oven. She unlocked the French doors to the balcony and inhaled. What more could she ask for, she thought, as the aroma of ground coffee beans meshed with the morning ocean air. The breeze was warming and humid, but pleasant. Seagulls were calling and circling. She saw some dolphins herding fish toward the shoreline where they would soon become dolphin breakfast. The dolphins were rolling with the waves and circling in the churning water full of jumping fish. Don't worry little fishes, you're not the only ones trapped. I can't get away either. But mine is a love trap…need to give him up, don't want to give him up. Just then a flock of pelicans swooped down, landing among the school of encircled whiting and began to scoop them from the sea in their long, pouched beaks. The dolphins didn't seem to mind sharing their catch and continued to feast on the swimming and leaping bounty. The fish had no way out.

Brigetta's blond head appeared as she climbed the stairs. She was bouncing up the steps, looking much more lively and alert this morning. Mikki was glad someone was feeling better.

"Hey," said Brigetta, circling the kitchen like a buzzard. "Is there any flavored creamer?" She was scratching her stomach as she walked toward the refrigerator, pajama bottoms hanging low and sloppy. She was pulling some leftover bacon from a plastic container with one hand and wrapping her other fingers around the French vanilla creamer on the refrigerator door.

"You know, there's one thing that continues on forever with our family. What is that? An insatiable appetite!

Nothing stops our munching gene from operating. Not kidnapping, not terrorists, not even near-death experiences, huh, Brig?" Mikki was finally able to smile, seeing her sister alive and well and apparently back to normal. Whatever drugs Gran had given her didn't seem to have any ill effects.

"I'm hungry, that's all. I haven't eaten anything but cookies since the bad guys snatched me up. I think they were trying to starve me. Plus they wouldn't let me pee. Bastards."

The door to Emily's bedroom opened and a fully dressed Gran came out to the kitchen. She was smiling way too big for early morning. Something was up. Emily winked and grinned at Mikki who was puzzled and just stared at her. A bell rang and Mikki retrieved the sweet rolls from the oven and spread sticky icing over them. She placed them on a plate and grabbed napkins. They would all sit on the balcony while it was still morning, cool and breezy. The rain clouds were gone and it was going to be a beautiful day. Emily loved to sit outside at the beachfront home. It was how she rejuvenated. Emily breathed in and closed her eyes. She exhaled slowly, taking her time, eyes still shut. The two younger women figured she was meditating or praying or something and by the time Emily opened her eyes, they were fully indulging themselves. Delicious cinnamon rolls right from the oven were hard to pass up. Emily grinned as she helped herself to a roll and more coffee.

"Who called?" asked Emily, brows raised in question. She stopped chewing as she waited for the answer.

Mikki sighed and shook her head. She really didn't want to talk about it, about him.

Brigetta had no such qualms. "It was Faris, wasn't it? Is he coming over? I heard he loves Gran's cheese blintzes. You should feed him too. The poor man was also up all night."

"Brig, what do you remember about last night?" asked Mikki, avoiding the subject.

"I got tossed in a van, kidnapped, tied up in a hanger, we fly around in a plane and when we landed the bad guys were gone. Right?"

"Exactly. You've got it," replied Mikki.

"But that's not all. You three came to rescue me and somehow Gran was flying the freaking plane. I can't really figure that out, but she flew me away from the men who captured me. Why were you flying the plane?" asked Brigetta, staring at Emily.

"We told you that Kamila's husband had called Faris to say where you were and we came to get you. They were going to fly you away and hide you somewhere, but Gran got to the plane first. When you got on, she took off. Meanwhile the bad guys ran away, because Faris and I were pretty mad and…uh…were going to call the cops. Yep, they all just ran off. We're pretty scary people, I guess," stated Mikki, hoping her story wouldn't freefall like those men last night.

Brigetta chewed and stared at the other women for a few seconds. No one said anything. Then abruptly, Brigetta got up and announced, "I'm gonna have some Cheerios. Got any bananas?"

When Brigetta left for the kitchen, Mikki yanked on Emily's robe. "Is she alright? She isn't going bananas, is she? She's not going to suddenly remember all this shit and go postal at the hospital later or something, is she?" Mikki whispered to Emily.

Emily shook her head. "She's fine. The scary stuff has just been made more acceptable. She feels calm and rested. She doesn't really care that all the pieces don't exactly fit since she can't remember it clearly. She's safe. She's happy. Let her alone. Let her eat."

Brigetta returned with a bowl of cereal and then said sheepishly, "Gee, did you guys want some too?"

"Nah," Mikki replied and Emily shook her head. "In fact, I'm going to shower and get moving. I need to go to the office today. There's a new road contract we need to start. Are you going to work today, Brig?"

"Tonight. I'm still on nights, remember? Man, sometimes you don't have any memory at all. And yes, I'm going in. And yes, I'll be extremely careful. I can't believe the guys you ran off last night would dare to return to the state of

Florida, let alone my hospital. But I'll be careful. I'll have Ryder to drive me back and forth. God, I'd better call him. He's probably still worried." Brigetta jumped up, wiping away her milk mustache, and went inside.

Mikki and Emily exchanged looks and quietly sipped their coffees. Finally Mikki said, "I'll tail her all day and all night. I'm not taking any chances."

"No, I think she'll be okay. Those guys might be evil, but they're not dumb."

"I'm getting dressed and ready to go. In any case, I'll check on her at my lunch break and then after work I'll go to Mom's to see how she's doing. I also want to monitor what she says to Mom. No sense in having everyone freak out, but Mom needs to take safety precautions, too."

Brigetta appeared in Mikki's new Capri's, her favorite Gucci sandals, and her brand new halter-top. "Bye, everyone. Thanks for saving my life! Good thing we all decided to leave car keys here…just in case," she said, as she waved to them at the elevator door, grabbing the extra set of keys hanging at the exit. The doors closed before Mikki could protest the loss of her new clothes.

"Damn! She could've taken something I was tired of," complained Mikki. Then she shrugged and turned to Emily who was wiping her mouth on a napkin.. "By the way, what was the Cheshire Cat routine all about earlier this morning? Do you have something to tell me?"

CHAPTER FIFTY-THREE

"That's cute. Cheshire cat. I'll have to remember that," said Emily, her forefinger tapping her chin pensively.

"Crap. You're just going into one of your easily recognizable stalling routines," said Mikki, still sitting at the table, but her hands were on her hips.

"Okay, you know me too well. I can't have any fun."

"Fun? You probably think the last few days have been fun."

"Well, I'm a little tired, but I did enjoy some of the scary stuff."

"Out with it. Why were you giving me the big secret grins?"

"You know how every morning I like to wake up slowly by turning on the TV and watching for a while? Well, guess what made CNN breaking news this morning?"

"I know you can't wait to tell me."

"I could hardly contain myself until Brigetta left!"

"And?"

"There was a report that some guy went bonkers in a Queens neighborhood in New York City. I guess Homeland has been keeping an eye on two or three houses in this particular area, maybe because of Al Quada having a big interest in the nearby big airports. Both JFK and LaGuardia are close by. Anyway, all of a sudden, people reported hearing screaming, their description on CNN was 'blood-curdling shrieks,' early this morning. The home where the questionable yelling was heard, apparently summoning Allah, was a two-story bungalow in an ordinary residential area. The screaming was so horrible that all the lights came on in the nearby houses and the Homeland agents worried about being discovered in their surveillance spot. Of course, only the U.S. news media would report all this and blow the whole stakeout."

"True."

"So everyone's hair is already standing on end and suddenly this man, clad only in red boxer briefs, comes flying out the front door yelling and cursing in Arabic! Then to the agents' surprise, two more partially dressed men who are carrying some kind of assault rifles follow him. The Homeland guys think they've been had and draw their weapons in defense from their positions, but stay hidden. From the story, I think they might have been in the house across the street that gave them an excellent view to all this. The guys with the rifles are aiming at the first dude who is still screaming in terror at the top of his lung capacity. Now the punch line. Guess why they're aiming at their fellow Jihadist?"

"Uh…Al Quada doesn't allow men to wear red underpants? I don't know. Tell me!"

"The worms! My freaking worms were emerging! Isn't that great? He's one of the guys I gave the water to in the airport! The parasitic larvae have grown up big and strong and want to get out, go forth, and multiply! I love it!"

"So freaking cool, Gran!" said Mikki, raising her right hand in a pump of fisted triumph. "So what happened next?"

"One of the agents ran up to the house to see close up what was going on. He reported that the yelling man had huge red welts all over him. The agent said he originally thought that the other guys had beaten him up or something and now he was trying to run away. They were wondering if they should rescue him, grab him up for interrogation, or what, when one of the red swellings, which turned out to be a big red blister, erupted! This giant worm's head — the newscaster reported snake's head — pops out of this guy's stomach, right near the belly button. Then everyone starts screaming! I mean picture all the neighbors from the little quiet row of houses are standing outside and The Alien is suddenly among them! The rifle dudes are horrified, not only that their bud has been taken over by the devil himself, but that all the neighbors know, too. Damn, I wish I could've been there."

"Me, too!" added Mikki, pouting as she thought of this missed opportunity.

"Probably by now, the neighbors who haven't passed out are all dialing their cell phones for the Star or National Enquirer to get the reward for the story!"

"So some nice couple gets the money for the first non-hoax, truly interesting, and real-life story!"

"Listen, there's more. So next, more blisters are popping open and worms are coming out all over and kind of sticking up like they're looking around…total freak city. They're crawling out and the guy is swatting at them and mashing them against his body and screaming even louder. Don't you just love it?"

"Yeah," answered Mikki excitedly, bouncing up and down in her chair now, like a toddler. "Gran! Probably someone took photos or even a video on their phone!"

"I'm getting to that. Don't spoil my story."

"Sorry."

"The agents are now both outside and running towards the worm man who is now on the ground and writhing around, pale and in shock, but still screaming. As the Homeland guys approach, the two gunmen raise their rifles and aim. The agents quickly back off, but the rifles are fired at the worm man. They killed their own devil-possessed demon man. Finally there's silence and the men throw down their rifles, praying and cursing simultaneously. The agents rush them, cuff them, and toss them to the ground. The horde has cautiously moved in to view the downed man and sees that the worms are still emerging and now crawling towards the crowd on the rain-soaked street. They all run off like a herd of wildebeests being pursued by marauding lions just as the black and whites arrive, sirens blaring. Wouldn't this make a great movie?"

"I'd go see it. Go on," said Mikki. "Was he dead?"

"Unfortunately his suffering was over. He was dead. The good news is that now we know where at least one of those bad guys was hiding out. They never stray too far from the nest."

"I'd bet the rest of the gang are all now in New York, or on their way. Wouldn't you guess that?" asked Mikki.

"I'd say that group is staying close to Kamila's baby. She came from New York City and the baby will be in foster care somewhere there. They'll use the baby's location as bait to draw Faris and or Kami back to the child."

"What do you think Faris will do with Kamila?" asked Mikki, now serious and pensive.

"I don't know. I honestly don't know."

"I don't either, but it's real important to me. I can never marry him now, too much has happened, and I was too scared. Nothing can happen to my family, not ever."

"I would never say never. Too much can happen to change your mind. You're still young, just wait and see. We still have a lot of work to do."

Mikki just shrugged and got up to take the dishes to the kitchen. Emily followed carrying the carafe on a glass tray.

"I'll help you clean up the kitchen then I really do need to get to the office," said Mikki. "I've got to get started on that project. My team is counting on me to present some drawings. I'll wash, you dry. There's not enough to start loading the dishwasher."

Mikki pulled out the top rack of the dishwasher and saw some of Gran's antique crystal wine glasses sitting there ready to be washed. She took them out and smelled them. Gran's best vintage from the cellar downstairs? And what were her best Haviland plates doing on the bottom rack? She had imported them from France and never put this stuff in the dishwasher. Mikki eyed her grandmother's back suspiciously. Emily felt her stare as she pulled a dishtowel from a drawer. She turned to face her granddaughter.

"What?"

"Are we celebrating something?"

"Like?"

"Like now you're wining and dining with the best china and crystal? And why was this stuff in the dishwasher and not hand washed?"

"Well now, aren't we the little mother? Remember the last time you started checking up on me? In Citrus City?"

"Yeah. I saved your little ass, if I recall."

"Phooey."

"So what's up? I still worry about you since the stroke. God only knows why."

"I'm fine. More than fine. But if you must know, I had company. Good friends of mine. I do have some of those, you know? You're not the only very popular, sought-out, gorgeous, highly entertaining, Ms. Personality in our family, you know!"

"I do know that. Okay, I guess you're still coherent. But there's one more thing you need to detail. We always critique our adventures. How did you commandeer that plane? I still can't believe you did that!"

CHAPTER FIFTY-FOUR

Emily exhaled and pulled the expensive tableware from the dishwasher and gave it to Mikki to wash. She didn't remember putting it in there. Did she drink too much or was it just the excitement of the moment? Either way, it was none of her granddaughter's business. Yes, it wasn't quite fair that she knew every last detail about Mikki, but some of her own business was meant to remain clandestine and secret. Emily dried plates and exuberantly began to chat about her last evening's coup.

"You see, Mikki, it's all about experience and experiences. You need to get out more and see things, do things...I mean a variety of things...and meet lots of people. Learn to read them, know how they think, what they're going to do. That all comes with time and age! Yep, someday you'll be as good as me, maybe better, but now you're really a greenhorn. Can't even drive yet!"

"Ooh, not that again," said Mikki, exasperated. "Someday, you'll be so amazed at my newly honed driving skills, I'll blow your mind right outta your skull."

"Ha! That's what I'm afraid of!"

"Funny. You'll see, though, you'll see," said Mikki, flinging fingers full of soapy dishwater at her grandmother's head.

"Back to me. I was wonderful last night," Emily began.

"Of course," said Mikki, with a shrug. She used her forefinger to scrape the last icing off the platter and onto her tongue before she plunged the plate into the dishwater. "Yummmm."

"Yes, I was that good. When I saw the plane I immediately knew what they were planning. It was a parachute jump plane, one used for training. Now, I asked my brilliant self, why would they want that versus, say, a Lear jet? A jet could be used for a quick getaway to the Caribbean, Cuba, or some other escape. Even for a kidnapping. But why the jump plane? They were going to toss the girls out and then get away. When we arrived and they weren't able to kill or capture us, they must've thought they could still toss Brigetta out and then fly away. And they knew they could hurt us big time with the death of Brigetta. I'm not sure if they were planning to toss Kamila or not. I think that was a play-it-by-ear sort of thing. She was going along with what they were doing, but I don't think she was part of the planning. She had to do what they wanted or die. The only thing that came to mind was the old Patty Hearst case. But Kamila was not to be trusted, because even she didn't know what she was doing or why.

"After I off'd the two bad guys guarding the building, I went up on the roof...with excellent ladder climbing expertise, by the way, and could see Brigetta through the fan vent. But I couldn't get down there from a roof entrance. I had to climb back down the ladder. When I circled the building, I saw the plane and figured it out. Their pilot was doing a pre-check, so I nonchalantly went over to him. He saw me and quickly approached. He thought I'd be an easy target, small and short, an old lady in an old flight suit. As he reached over to grab me, I swung upwards with my baton and smashed him right on the nose. I hit him as hard as I ever hit anyone. His nasal bone fractured into splinters, all of them heading toward soft brain tissue. You know that move. Easy if you know where and when to hit. Hit hard, come from below, and give it all you got. He went down. The hard part was getting his body out of there before the hangar door rolled open. I was so hyped up that I did it, though. He was a heavy son of a bitch. Then I pulled off his headset and put it on, running for the pilot's seat. I just kept thinking about you and Brigetta in the building and my body knew to give me that extra jolt. I was high and energized, an old lady fightin' machine!"

"Why didn't you wait for Faris and me?" asked Mikki.

"You were just entering the rear of the building. You wouldn't have made it in time. The key was to get in the plane and get it moving, so they couldn't see me and figure out their guy was gone. The rain helped out a lot."

"And you knew where we were because of the tracking chips, right?"

"You're catching on!"

"Go on."

"This was the tricky part. I had been in one or two jump planes before, but never had actually flown this particular type of plane. I had jumped twice in Korea, but that was billions of years ago. I had no plan of hurling out of this plane, especially if I had to count on a parachute someone else had packed. I had no idea if they had rigged them so they wouldn't open to trick the girls or what other evil deeds they could have thought up.

"Like I said, I've had some flying experience, but not with that plane, and no planes for a long time. You wouldn't want me to land a 747 if the pilots suddenly became incapacitated, but I looked at the controls. It was an old plane, so that actually helped me. No new fandangle stuff to worry about and the small airport meant no control tower to watch me or try to radio me as to what the hell I was doing. I got the engine started and figured out the controls pretty easily. As the engine idled and warmed up, my idea of a preflight check was to check the damned parachutes. I was already convinced that no matter what, I was not using one of these and neither was your sister. So I took several and hid the rest. I stuck my knife in each one that I'd saved and twisted and cut hard 'til the whole thing looked like a mass of Susan's overcooked linguini."

"That big of a mess, huh?" quipped Mikki.

"Yep. Those chutes would only work with sauce on them and certainly not for floating gracefully from a plane.

"I had just finished making the pasta when the two sleazy goons boarded with Kamila and Brigetta. I think they were Pakistani or Iranian. Big mean guys but dumb-looking. I didn't look at them directly and as soon as they were on board and in the process of shutting the plane door, I started to taxi. Taking off was easy. With a ball cap and headphones, I wasn't easily recognizable. Brigetta had started crying, but Kamila looked hopeful, like she thought there was someway she might come out of this alive.

"Once we had reached a nice altitude for cruising, I turned my automatic handgun toward the big guys and watched their expressions change. They thought about rushing me, but the gun looked imposing, even if I didn't, and I had the general impression that neither one had the faintest idea of how to fly the plane. Brigetta didn't recognize me at first and then I saw her face change. She smiled but, smart girl that she is, didn't let on to our little secret. The bad guys never knew who I was.

"I threw the specially rigged parachutes to the goons and told them to strap them on real tight. They looked at each other and grinned, like I was stupidly letting them jump their way to freedom. I told them to strap the girls into their seats and then open the jump door. One hesitated, I shot. The flare from the gun lit up the interior of that plane like an operating room...at least that's what Brigetta said later. He wasn't hurt, but scared poopless. Then I thought of the bonus attraction. I had seen some show jump flares in a box in the plane's fore storage area. I gave a flare to each man and told him to attach it to his belt so they'd be found on the ground in case they landed in the trees or something. They had the chutes on and with the door open, wind was coming in that plane and blowing stuff around. They were hanging on tight, let me tell you. Meanwhile I was circling back toward the airfield. I lit the flares with a BIC lighter I found in the pilot's console. I wanted to give their pals on the ground the show they were waiting for. I yelled at them to jump! They didn't go. I pointed the gun once more, aimed and ready to fire, and screamed for both of them to go together. The one grabbed the other one's shoulder and pushed. He went out of that plane screaming like a little girl. The wind covered up his screams once he left the plane, so out went the other guy, flare burning away. I got up and shut the jump door. Brig unbuckled and I waved her back in silence. I didn't want Kamila to know that we knew each other. That wouldn't be safe. Then I realized that you and Faris might be watching and also believe that Brig and Kami had been pushed from the plane. I wanted to get back down quickly and set you straight before you went into a panicked shock."

"That had already happened. I thought Brig was dead and it was all my fault. It was the worst and happiest day in my life."

"I know. I'm sorry. There was no way to tell you what was happening. If I hadn't moved quickly, the guys in the hangar would've noticed something was wrong. I was just hoping they were gone when I touched down and it would just be you and Faris."

"Your landing was a little bouncy, Gran," Mikki criticized, grinning.

"Landing is what pilots are always judged on...the stupid landing. Hey, I got down, didn't I? Let's talk about landing, because I'm signing you up for flying lessons. Like I said, you need more life experiences. Not just fighting lessons and what I can teach you at home. You have to experience new things."

"You're right again. I was trying to experience love and I sure screwed up that life experience."

"You'll catch on. Let's talk about my landing. More airplanes are damaged during landing than any other phase of flight. Did you know that?" Without waiting for an answer, Emily continued, "and most pilots would rather no one watch that part of their flight. No one is perfect nor does it perfectly every time. The secret is a consistent approach. That was a problem since I had never flown that plane. You need to figure your speed for the base leg, in which the speed is slowed to 1.4 times the stall speed in landing configuration. The flaps are lowered to the next setting. As you fly down final, you'll have your last chance to run your GUMPS check."

"Huh? What's that," said Mikki, yawning.

"Am I boring you, darling? You'll need to know this stuff! The GUMPS is gas, undercarriage, mixture, prop, and speed...to be sure that everything's set for the landing."

Mikki was taking the used dishcloth and towel to the laundry room. She called back, "I'm listening."

"Okay, I get it. You'll be more excited about it when you're taking your first solo. There's nothing more satisfying than to hear that small, welcome chirp that says you've done the landing perfectly. Pilots just don't expect to hear that too often, even those with plenty of experience."

"I get it. You did a great job. Brig is alive and well. I love you and you continue to amaze me. Really! But, I've got to go to work and soon. I can't be late again. And you don't want me to get another speeding ticket, do you?"

"Lord have mercy. Did you pay the ticket yet? Please drive carefully."

"I'll pay it. Gotta get my shower. Try to behave yourself today while I'm gone, okay?"

"Sure thing, dear. You know me, your little ole granny. I'll probably be off to sewing circle...oh no, today is quilting. Must go get my little old self in the tubbie right now!"

"Gran."

"What?"

"You know what. Seeya later? We'll get dressed and go out somewhere nice for dinner, okay? That is if you don't have a Red Hat meeting or something."

"Sure, bye Mikki. And today I'm actually going for a walk on the beach."

"Good...I think."

CHAPTER FIFTY-FIVE

On the way to work, one hand on the steering wheel of her damaged car and one hand on the horn, Mikki thought about her grandmother. Last week Emily still needed a cane to help herself get up and down the stairs. This week, with all the excitement and near-death experiences, she was able to climb a ladder in the pouring rain while carrying an arsenal of equipment. She had jumped an assassin younger and maybe meaner than herself, single-handedly killed bad guys, hijacked a plane and had flown it away. The family had been encouraging Emily to stay home more, rest more, and spend more time dusting porcelain figurines at her gift shop. Maybe they were all wrong. What Emily needed was an exciting reason to get out of bed in the morning. A reason to toss away the cane and strengthen her muscles. The thing that nearly had killed Emily was the stay in the nursing home two years ago. She's never forgiven us for that one...but what else could we have done? She had a stroke, for God's sake!

Mikki weaved through traffic and bounced over the curbing into her employer's parking lot downtown. Some guy honked at her and gave her the one finger salute as she cut him off. Mikki just laughed and waved back as if happy to see an old friend. Idiot! He's probably thinking he would like to meet me on some deserted alley, but boy, wouldn't he be surprised! Yeah, Gran and I are a lot alike.

Grabbing her briefcase and laptop from the rear seat, Mikki walked briskly to the office. She was actually on time and ready for work. She had a meeting at 10 A.M., so she would have time to first get another cup of brew. At noon she would call her mom to check on Brigetta.

Mikki was so engrossed in her work after the meeting that she didn't even realize the time...almost 5 P.M. Did she have time to run out to the stables and check on Clown? She glanced at her watch, gauging the traffic and how much time she would spend at the barn. While still calculating, her cell phone rang. It was Brigetta.

"Hey," Mikki answered, without much enthusiasm. Hearing her sister's voice reminded her of the events of the last few days...and her breakup with Faris.

"Well, don't sound so happy to hear from me!" said Brigetta.

"I am happy you called. Really happy you're okay and able to make the call, actually," answered Mikki.

"I'm fine and I'm happy and have some things to tell you before you hear it from anyone else."

"What?" answered Mikki, now more curious and attentive.

"First, I've decided to take some self-defense classes. Maybe I'll come with you?"

"Fine," answered Mikki. "And?"

"And...I had a quiet but informative lunch with a mutual friend today."

"Do I have to guess who it was?" asked Mikki, now listening carefully.

"Faris! Your Faris. I have stolen him from you. At least for a half hour lunch. Now he's yours again," said Brigetta. Mikki could tell Brigetta was silently giggling.

"Why? Why did you have lunch with him?" exclaimed Mikki.

"Geez, Mik, don't get your panties in a wringer. I said you could have him back! He called and wanted to ask some stuff about Kamila and how she was during my kidnapping. He wanted a total breakdown of what happened and everything she said and did. I think he's trying to figure out if her story is true or not. We talked about lots of stuff about the kidnapping plot and all that."

"Faris and I are not together. We're not getting married. I'm not jealous, that's not it. I don't want you around him or his family. It's not safe. You should have figured that out by now. I'm not kidding here, little sister."

"So you're not jealous, you're just pissed?" asked Brigetta.

"Just be careful. Don't go to work tonight. Don't try to date any brothers, sisters, cousins, anyone that even resembles Faris or his family."

"I have to go to work tonight. I have a job. I have things to do at the hospital. I'm needed. Faris and I talked about it. I'll be safe, we'll all be safe. But hey, you broke up? You gave up that gorgeous guy who is obviously madly in love with you? Because you guys had to come and rescue me? Oh no, you're not pinning this on me. No way!" Brigetta's voice had gone up an excited octave or two.

"That's not it. Just…it just won't work, okay?"

"Why not? I'm upset. I want him for a brother-in-law. You're nuts. You need him. He needs you. Sooo…?"

"I don't want to talk about it now. Seriously," said Mikki with an unfamiliar firmness.

"Does Granny know? Did you cancel the wedding? Geez, it's only in a few days? I've already picked out a perfect dress!"

"I'm hanging up now," announced Mikki.

"I already have a date!"

But Brigetta just heard a dial tone in response. Mikki was already speed dialing her grandmother. She wanted to know if she could get the GPS and use it to locate Faris and also see if she could find Sajid's location. There was no answer at the Pink Flamingo. She dialed Emily's cell phone and got voice mail. She didn't leave a message, instead she decided to make a quick trip to Palm Pines to check on Clown. Julianne was such an angel for helping her take care of Clown's wound. At least she could show up and check on her poor horse.

CHAPTER FIFTY-SIX

Mikki sat in her car for a moment near the barns. She knew that Faris might be here. He had every right to be here, since his horse was stalled next to Clown. She didn't see his car. She was afraid of running into him right now. She was still worried about the threat to her family by association with Faris. There were still bad guys on the loose. Sajid, Hassad, Dr. Bad, and Worm Man #2 and maybe more. Mikki looked around for anything out of the ordinary. New faces, new vehicles, anything out of place. She was about to open her car door when someone tapped softly at the driver's side window. Mikki nearly jumped out of her jeans. Reflexively, she reached toward her purse…and weapon. But it was Faris, grinning like a kid at Christmas.

"Hi. I didn't mean to scare you. Nice to know you aren't totally fearless," said Faris.

"You scared the crap out of me. My mind was looking for bad guys and…"

Faris didn't let her finish. "You would've seen me if your side mirror wasn't bent crooked. Hit any fences lately? You were looking in your rearview mirror. Don't tell me you were putting on lipstick just for me?"

"You can't be that dumb. Of course not!" stammered Mikki, opening her car door into his knee as she spoke. "What are you doing here?"

"Ow! Uh, remember Alajazar? And Clown? Our horses live here and so we need to visit them. Isn't that why you're here?"

"Of course," said Mikki, slamming the car door so hard the convertible top billowed up like a balloon at the impact.

"Let's walk to the stalls like normal people, okay?" said Faris, becoming uncharacteristically angry at Mikki's dismissive attitude.

"Testosterone spill on Aisle Nine. Sure. Fine," said Mikki as she walked briskly away. Faris trailed like a lost puppy.

"You know this is not all my fault. Yes, Kamila is my sister, but you and your grandmother chose to get involved by helping her out at the airport. Kami brought both of us into the picture and it's proven dangerous for everyone, even the innocent horses. I'm worried about leaving Aljazar here and your horse has already paid a price. Now you want to cancel our wedding and don't even want to see or talk to me any more. Sorry, but I just don't buy all this. You're being unfair."

Mikki suddenly stopped and turned around. Faris saw the tears streaming before she had a chance to wipe them with her hands. "You're right, you're right, okay? But I just am so scared with those guys out there still running around wanting to do terrible things to the people I love. Sure, I told you I still love you, but we can't be together."

"Well, now who's the dumb one? We seem to work best together, as a team. We can certainly do more as a twosome or threesome, as your grandmother has demonstrated to me, than either one of us by ourselves."

Mikki was silently holding back more sobs. In the one instant she leaned forward to him, he reached for her and pulled her hard to his chest. It felt good and right. They fit together as one. Mikki sobbed aloud for a long time as he held her.

Mikki finally spoke, "Maybe after I know those men are all gone for good. That there's no more threat to my family. Maybe then. I really don't know if I can give you up, Faris. Guess I'm not as tough as I thought." Mikki was wiping her eyes and was holding on to Faris around his waist like she never wanted to let him go.

"Come on, let's go see the horses," said Faris as his arm reached around her shoulders and pulled her along, offering his handkerchief from his pocket.

Julianne wasn't there, but the horses each had two new flakes of alfalfa and timothy hay and were chewing contentedly, eyes half-closed with enjoyment. Both nickered a welcome and went right back to the serious business of eating hay.

"Let's get some brushes and do some grooming," said Mikki. "I have a few minutes and then I've got to get home. I have a dinner date tonight and can't be late again."

"What! You're an engaged woman! You can't have a dinner date with anyone but me!" Faris exclaimed.

"With my grandmother!" answered Mikki. "Hmmm, did I say that to get a reaction?"

"Of course you did," said Faris, as he followed her to the tack room. He showed Mikki his newly purchased tack box, enameled navy blue with gold pin striping. It had 'Aljazar' written in English on the front and then in Arabic on the top. It was beautifully made of heavy metal with a cedar lining. Inside were a plethora of new brushes, hoof picks, fly sprays, a first aid kit, leather polish, and assorted other items necessary for horse ownership.

They picked up a small carrying box of grooming supplies for their horses and returned to the stalls for some brushing, combing, and polishing. Horse therapy…the best psychiatrist could never even come close. The horses were in equine heaven as they had all the itchy spots scratched and the stems of errant straw bedding removed from their manes and tails. When Faris and Mikki were finished, they were sweaty but satisfied with the results of their work. The horses were gleaming and seemed as relaxed as if they'd been to a spa.

Gathering up the supplies, Faris dared to bring up the terrorists again, "I know where Sajid is staying. He's gone back to New York. Your sister gave me some good information about Kami and what went on during her capture. Did Brigetta tell you anything?"

"No, in fact she seemed kind of vague on the whole thing. Like some of it hadn't really registered in her mind. She did tell me about your lunch though and the discussion about Kami. What will you do about her? Send her back to Saudi to your mother?"

"That's been handled already. I'll tell you more later. This isn't really the place to talk and I'll have more to say about everything tomorrow. Do you have another hour to give me?"

"Hey! What do you have in mind? I'm definitely not going back to your bedroom."

"No, not that. Not today anyway. Actually I have some important business myself to take care of tonight. Just go wash up in the lounge and get your hands nice and clean. We're going for a drive into town."

Mikki didn't argue since she loved surprises, as long as they were good ones, like maybe ice cream. She didn't really want to eat anything though, since she was planning on a quiet dinner with Emily. If they went to a café, she could at least have a salad or something. She didn't want to disappoint him.

They rode together in the Aston Martin and parked in front of Tiffany & Co., almost next door to FAVORS. "That's my grandmother's store," she explained, pointing at the well-designed window in front. Mikki wanted to look in and wave at Sarah, one of Emily's managers, but Faris pulled her along.

"It's time we got you a ring, so you can remember you're engaged," he said, his smile both boyish and insistent.

Mikki grabbed him around his neck and kissed him right in front of the store.

"Now, that I love," said Faris, kissing her back. "You know in some places in Saudi we'd be arrested for that by the religious police."

"No way!" exclaimed Mikki, still bouncy with excitement.

"They're much less assertive in Riyadh now, but they're armed...with thin wooden canes and they go around telling people how to dress, what to cover up, how to act...especially the women. When Abdullah ascended the throne, women were given a few more rights of personal expression. Now you can see uncovered hair, but believe me, the women have their scarves handy. There are some new abaya shops now that cater to the younger women. Some of the previously shapeless black robes are now seen with elaborate beadwork and logos from the modern world like Rolling Stones and a marijuana leaf. The women don't know what they are, but just like the design!" Faris laughed. "Those rules are another reason I love America. I'll never go back unless it's to see my mother or attend her funeral. Very sad in a way, because it's a wonderful country full of ancient history."

"I would go with you...to see your mother, if she would want to see me," said Mikki, head tilting down, suddenly unsure of herself.

"My mother is very old country in some ways, but very modern in others. She would embrace you as my wife. She finally accepted my choice when I changed to a Christian religion. Whew, that was the really big thing. She'll never accept Christianity, but she still loves me as her son."

"I would like to meet her someday," said Mikki, holding Faris' hand.

"You will. Come on! Let's go in!" said Faris, opening the door and bowing at her as he waved her through the entrance to Tiffany's. "If you don't find something here, we can try Cartier just down the block."

CHAPTER FIFTY-SEVEN

At 7 P.M. Mikki burst through the elevator door to find an already dressed Emily sipping a Manhattan in her favorite corner chair. She was watching Jeopardy and seemed intent on the double jeopardy answers.

"Gran! Guess what! Guess, guess, guess!" Mikki shouted as she ran to hug the surprised woman whose cocktail was teetering precariously on the arm of the chair.

"Dare I ask?" ventured Emily, looking up at her beaming granddaughter.

"The wedding is on! We got rings! We went to Tiffany's and I got platinum and it's a pave' diamond wedding band and it's beautiful and so sparkly and it's getting sized!" Mikki finally paused long enough to breathe.

"Mikki, I'm so happy for you and I must say you never, ever, cease to totally amaze me!" said Emily, smiling and getting up to squeeze her granddaughter. "Gee, I hope the lucky man is still the Faris dude you just broke up with, huh? Huh?"

"Of course! We'll get married and we're going to get the last bad guys together. I told him if we go to the Caribbean on a cruise for our honeymoon, we'd get the engagement ring then! A little backwards, but I saw some gorgeous stuff in catalogs and on-line from St. Martins jewelry stores and other island spots. I just love those rings with Tanzanite and diamonds and Australian opals. Wow, those are really beautiful! I love the color! Those rings are so 'islandy,' don't you think, Gran?"

"I think I've never seen you happier except for the free Bon Jovi tickets you won in ninth grade. I'm really happy for you, darling. I really am. I'm excited now, too, so let's move forward with the party plans!"

"We can talk about the final arrangement during dinner, okay?"

"Sure, are you going to change clothes, I hope? I see horsehair on your shirt. Did you wear that to Tiffany & Co.? Those are my neighbors down on Worth Avenue, you know? Don't want to make a bad impression with my smell-like-a-horse granddaughter."

"We tried to clean up," said Mikki, brushing madly at her shirt and noticing the missed dirt under her fingernails. "Okay, I'm off for a quick shower and I promise, I'll be unrecognizable when I come back upstairs."

"Hurry up. I'm hungry," called Emily.

She heard Mikki's voice calling from her room, "By the way, Faris was grooming his horse, too, before we went shopping, so we both looked like misfits. It wasn't just me!"

Soon the two women were in the white custom Jaguar heading for the country club adjacent to the polo grounds. They could have a nice dinner and also talk to the manager about the set-up of the room for the big party.

The doorman ushered them in and they were immediately taken to a table that had a nice viewing window over the pastures and a corner of the polo field.

"Do you have a table that will afford us a better view of the playing field?" asked Emily as she saw where the maitre d' was taking them. "I hear there's an evening match tonight."

"Surely, I would be glad to seat you by the tiered window section, or would you prefer to be right by the window?"

Mikki said nothing, a little surprised that Emily wanted to sit by the window. Mikki really wanted a cozier atmosphere so they could talk more intimately.

But Emily said, "By the window please," and discreetly slipped the man a twenty-dollar bill for his effort. They were seated and napkins unfurled and draped upon their laps as the beverage server and wine steward approached for their orders. "I just love the window and the view, don't you? Shall we order champagne?"

"How about some Asti Spumante?" answered Mikki. "I really like the taste of that. Should we have that for the wedding? Several bottles on each table?"

"Whatever the bride wishes!" said Emily with a flourish of her hand, and ordered the Asti from the steward. "Shall we get appetizers? After all, this is a special time and I'm truly in a good mood."

They decided on lobster bisque and fresh bread with seasoned dipping oil to start. Their entrees were excellent but it seemed to Mikki that she didn't have her grandmother's full attention. She caught Emily looking out the window absently while she seemed to be thinking. Was she worried about Brigetta tonight? Maybe she had agreed to go out with her just to keep her company. There were still many issues at hand that commanded attention and Emily seemed lost in those thoughts. She was smiling though, and seemed genuinely happy about the wedding plans.

"Gran? Is something bothering you?" Mikki asked after her last forkful of seared tuna steak. "You seem somewhere else. Is everything okay? Are you worried about Brig?"

"Yes, I'm a little worried about Brig, but I think all that's under control. Let's just see how things go and what happens next." They went back to watching the polo match as they finished their dinners. They both vetoed dessert since the meals had been sumptuous.

Everything was set for the party and Mikki felt dreamy as they drove home in the starry humid evening. There were just the smallest of gnawings at the back of her mind. No one could relax until the threats were contained. Such a beautiful night should not be wasted worrying about the bad guys. Mikki wanted just one night of normal bride-to-be happiness. It almost worked like that.

CHAPTER FIFTY-EIGHT

Mikki tried to call Faris on his cell phone on the way home, but there was no answer. He must have turned off the phone, she thought. Brigetta was at work and it was too late to call her mom. She wanted to talk to family. To tell someone else about the wedding, the party, her ring, her Faris. Once back home, Emily had gone to bed early and Mikki could hear her in her room talking on her phone. There was nothing good to munch on in the kitchen and checking the pantry was of no value either in squelching her appetite for more... more of something. She decided to go to bed, maybe watch a little television in her room.

She clicked on her TV for the late evening news as she tossed her new dress on the bed. She had just slipped under the sheets when she saw the rolling news banner under the regional CBS anchor...more breaking news. Maybe the other worm man has met his doom! Worm Man #2!

Newswoman Sandra Ocasio spoke as the camera drew in for a close-up. "Tonight we have a report of a most unusual and strangely macabre story at our local hospital. Apparently a man whose body was in a locker at the morgue was not dead but in some sort of a coma. He was found to be alive only when the coroner and his assistant began to do an autopsy! Let's cut now to the interview with the clearly shaken pathologist, Dr. Ramon Ramirez."

After a moment of blurry fuzz and some static, a man in blue disposable paper coveralls appeared on the screen. He was wearing a surgical hat, paper shoe covers, and small horn-rimmed glasses. His eyes were wide with excitement as he tried to remain calm. A white lab coat was worn as a cover-up for the blood stains on the doctor's blue morgue uniform. Two clear plastic face shields sat on the table where the body had been. Dr. Ramirez was fiddling with a microphone on his neck and then began to speak. His voice came out in a squeak. Then he cleared his throat.

"Tonight, as I began an autopsy on a patient who had the toe tag Clement R. Smith, I realized that the body on the morgue table, well... the patient, was still alive. Unfortunately, he is now deceased," said Dr. Ramirez, in accented English.

The interviewer in the basement morgue as well as the hospital attorney and public relations officer all stood staring at the doctor. The television reporter asked, "How could this possibly happen? Aren't the deceased declared dead by a doctor before they ever come to the morgue at the hospital? Was he a patient in a room upstairs? What did he die from?"

"Mr. Smith was scheduled for an autopsy because his family had requested it. We believe that patient died from a massive aortic rupture. The man was pronounced dead by his attending physician after resuscitation attempts had failed. Bodies are normally held in refrigeration until we can perform the autopsy. Today I was out of town for my son's graduation and had to catch up tonight. So the diener, or morgue attendant, Mr. Swathner, got the body tagged Mr. Smith from the cooler and placed him on the steel table over there," says Dr. Ramirez, pointing at a steel table in the center of the morgue.

"The body's tag was double-checked and Mr. Swathner did the weight and measurements. There was no sign of life or movement, of course. Sometimes when you first start doing this job, you imagine movement, little flutterings of the eyes or fingertips, but you learn to ignore them. So then Mr. Swathner placed the body block under the trunk section. The block raises it and splays out the arms and neck for the best exposure of the chest. I then checked for a wristband and found it had been cut, which was kind of unusual, but it was still around the man's wrist, secured with tape. I guessed they had to cut it to access an artery or something. Don't know about that. While I went to prepare my tools and specimen containers, Mr. Swathner began the 'Y' cut."

At this point, the hospital PR representative began to make cutting motions at his throat, but the cameraman and reporter were urging the doctor on. Gore sells. Encouraged and made confident by his rising celebrity, the doctor continued his explanation of the autopsy. Mikki stared at the screen, transfixed by the scene at the hospital where her sister worked.

"The 'Y' is a deep cut that extends from the front of each shoulder all the way to the pubic bone…right here," said Dr. Ramirez, now smiling and pointing immodestly at his lower anatomy. "Then we use an electric saw to open the rib cage, so that it's no longer attached to the rest of the skeleton. Next the chest plate is pulled back with the help of a scalpel and we would ordinarily remove the organs of the chest…the heart and lungs.

"Mr. Swathner noticed and reported to me a small amount of blood seepage from the wound. Sometimes there's a little bit of drainage even from a dead body, so we didn't think too much of that. Then it happened," the doctor continued, with a theatrical whisper and then a sweeping dramatic wave of his arm. "I was preparing to remove the heart when I nicked a large vessel and it began bleeding profusely! It was pumping out blood! Surprised, I looked closely. I saw that the heart had a faint quiver and was actually beating, very quickly…more like a tremor, but it was alive and beating! Of course, we stopped right away and called a Code Blue. That brings our immediate emergency personnel to the spot as fast as they can get there. They have a cart and all the medications and equipment to try to save a dying or distressed patient.

"The code docs and nurses were there in less than a minute, as surprised as we were that they were being called to the morgue. They thought maybe it was me, that I'd had a heart attack or sawed off my arm or something. But now, unfortunately, this guy is really dead. It was strange. I thought I saw him open his eyes and look at me before he died. I didn't mean to kill him," said Dr. Ramirez, now breaking down and blubbering like an idiot, after realizing how his rambling must have sounded. Dr. Ramirez looked at the hospital administrators for help and the Palm Beach

Memorial Public Relations spokesperson was the first to speak up.

"Some of this matter is confidential due to the HIPPA rules and regulations. But I must tell you that we were shocked when we realized the actual identity of the body. Someone had switched the body tags and this was not Mr. Smith. Mr. Smith's remains had been placed into another refrigerated locker. We don't know where the other body came from and therefore we've notified law enforcement."

At this point, the Sheriff of Palm Beach County appeared from the dark recesses of the hospital basement. He flashed his election-winning smile for the TV audience and coughed to clear his throat, trying to appear very concerned and serious. His office hadn't had something this weird and interesting for many years.

"We now know the identity of the person on the morgue slab," said Sheriff Palmero. "He is a Dr. Numair Al-Thani who has been seen here in this hospital, but does not practice here on a regular basis. I can tell you that because of the unusual circumstances of his death, we are suspecting foul play, possibly a homicide."

The video fades away and Ms. Ocasio said, "A most unusual and frightening circumstance. We'll have more on this in our morning edition tomorrow. I hope this doesn't give any of you nightmares tonight. And now to Maxwell Cower for our five day forecast..."

Mikki was sitting ramrod straight up in her bed. She had a very weird feeling about this and her perceptual abilities had never been doubted. Not knowing what else to do, Mikki yelled at the top of her lungs, "GRAN!"

CHAPTER FIFTY-NINE

Emily shot out of her bed like her sheets were on fire when she heard Mikki scream her name. Her first thought was home invasion! so on the way out of her room she grabbed the Glock from under her pillow. She raced down the stairs almost tripping and carrying her weapon at the ready. Mikki stood at her doorway, uninjured and gleefully jumping up and down. The child's gone mad…must be the stress. Granny Em tried to catch her breath, waiting for an explanation.

"Look! Look at the TV!" Mikki demanded, as she poked at buttons on the replay remote. After a quick rewind on the DVR, the newscast played again for Emily. The two women sat on the end of the bed staring at the screen.

"Well?" asked Mikki, hardly able to sit still. "Do you think that was our Dr. Bad? Remember Brigetta said he gave her the name Dr. Numair Al-Busaid. This guy's real name must be Al-Thani…the guy who had the undead autopsy! Call Brig at the hospital on her cell! We have to find out what she's heard!"

"Mikki, she's in Pediatrics. She's working. She's not allowed to carry her cell phone around like she's at some shopping mall, for heaven's sake."

"We have to tell her. Geez, what if his own people did him in just so he wouldn't draw any more suspicion? I can't believe he'd be dumb enough to go back to the hospital again, though, with Brigetta there to point him out. I would think all of them would be in New York by now or trying to get out of the country."

"You'd think so, wouldn't you?" said Emily, drumming her fingers on her chin. "You're right. Something is weird and not just the autopsy. How did the body get to the morgue? Was he drugged? Injured? Lots of questions…"

"They'll be doing a real post-mortem now, right? Since they think it may be a homicide? I'm sure the coroner will have a statement on cause of death, but we might not get the answer from the media. If the hospital and law enforcement are smart, they'll leave the loose-lipped reporters out of it until they get it all figured out."

"Maybe Brig will know something when she gets home," said Emily, looking at the clock on Mikki's bedside table. "We'd better get to sleep now. Don't you have to work again tomorrow?"

"Sorry I scared you. I was just so excited," said Mikki.

"You're lucky you're not shot full of holes. I was cocked and ready to make Swiss cheese out of somebody," said Emily, smoothing the hair away from Mikki's face as they embraced.

"I know you better than that. You'd shoot alright, but you'd make sure of your target. I remember that was one of the first things you ever taught me about gun handling."

After Emily left to go back upstairs to her room, Mikki dialed the Pediatric nurses' station on the fourth floor of the hospital. She couldn't wait. She needed to talk to her sister tonight. The desk clerk answered on the second ring.

"Pediatric Surgical Unit," said a calm and pleasant voice, accustomed to speaking to traumatized and panicked parents.

"May I speak with Brigetta Walsh? I'm sorry to bother her at work, but I really need to speak with her," asked Mikki.

"Brigetta isn't here right now. Who's calling?" questioned the voice.

"It's her sister, Mikki Walsh. When she's back to your area, could you have her call me at home? It's urgent."

"Oh, that's not what I meant. She's not on break or doing a procedure or anything. She's not here. She called in and said she won't be coming in until tomorrow night."

"What?" exclaimed Mikki, fingers tightening on the handset of her phone. "When did she report off?"

"Hmmmm, maybe around one or two o'clock this afternoon. It was still day shift, because Nancy, the nursing supervisor, had to call in Shauna to take her place. And

Shauna was here on time, right at seven o'clock, so she must've been called in plenty of time to change her plans, get a shower, and to clock in on time. Is something wrong?"

"Uh, no. I just thought she said she was coming in. She said she wasn't feeling well last night, though. Thanks for the information," stammered Mikki, as she slowly reset the phone on its charger, her mind whirring like a pinwheel in a tornado.

CHAPTER SIXTY

As Mikki thought about calling her mother and sending her into a giant freak-out, the bedside phone rang again. Mikki grabbed it quickly before her grandmother could pick it up. It could've been Faris, but it wasn't. It was Brigetta.

"Hey! I hear you've been checking up on me?" asked Brigetta, sounding a little breathless.

"How did you know, and where are you? Have you been running?" Mikki blurted out.

"And the inquisition begins…" said Brigetta slowly, as mock seriousness crept into her lowered voice. "Next comes the torture…haha…we will make you talk!"

Mikki smiled as relief came sweeping over her and the momentary sense of panic subsided. "You are certifiable. Do they know about your mental health status at the Florida nursing license division?"

"I'm just happy. Must've been something I ate or drank last night," said Brigetta with just a hint of sarcasm in her voice. "But Fourth Floor called to check on me, since they got a little worried when you called. They said you sounded 'concerned' when you found out I wasn't at work. I thought I'd better call you, being the dedicated sister that I am."

"I think the terrorists did something to your head. Why didn't you tell me you weren't going to work. The last thing I heard was that you had to go and you have a job to do, and the next thing I know…you've called off sick. What was I supposed to think? This wasn't like you at all. Didn't you think I might be a little bit nervous because of what happened last night?"

"I really didn't think you'd be checking up on me and I had some things to do…that's all. You may be my sister, but you're not in on all my little secrets, you know."

"What? Another man? Hopefully not some stranger this time," Mikki warned.

"Glad you asked. Yes, another man. One I feel safe with and won't take advantage of my lust, my youth, my nympho complex!"

"You are really wound up tonight, little sister. Is it Ryder? Or some other guy? Not another doctor, I hope. We've had enough of them for now, okay?"

"Yep, okay. Well, I'm fine, gotta go. Mom just got home from her night out with the ladies. I think they went to a movie. Wonder if Dad knows about the wine tasting party last week? She was half-tipsy when she got home. Luckily she wasn't the group's designated driver that time. Poor Mom, I'll bet she's lonely for Dad. That's why she stays so busy. I think in another year that she'll move to New York to be with him. She loves the museums and theatre and their city penthouse is close to everything."

"She also loves the warm, sunny weather here in Florida. New York at Christmas might be fun, but ice, snow, and cold northern winds…not for me, anyway."

"Yeah, you're probably planning some vacations to some very hot desert in the future. Like after you get married. I can't wait to see your ring! And I'm so glad your wedding is back on. Wouldn't want to leave my new designer gown dangling in the closet forever!"

"Hold on. How did you know that Faris and I went ring shopping? How did you know that the big event was still happening?"

"You must have told me, or Faris did, I don't know," stammered Brigetta.

"You had lunch with Faris today. Then we spoke this afternoon and I said the wedding was off. I remember that quite well. Faris and I didn't talk until this afternoon at the stables. Tonight Gran and I went out to dinner at the club and I haven't told anyone anything."

"Of course not. Everyone still assumes the wedding is on because there was no announcement otherwise. You are so paranoid. Settle down. I'm speaking to you as a nurse. You are too stressed out. You probably haven't even decided on a dress for your wedding which just happens to be in three days."

"A dress? Omigod! I have nothing to wear! Tomorrow we shop! Grab Mom and meet Gran and I at the Worth Avenue Gucci Courtyard. We'll have a nice lunch and shop until I find something pretty. I don't want a traditional white gown..."

"Whoa! Not jodhpur boots and riding breeches, I hope?"

"Ha ha. I want something different and totally awesome. Something summery, maybe blue or turquoise or maybe emerald green. Long but sleek and stylish. But I don't care if it's right off the shelf. It doesn't have to be custom made or fitted. I'm really a perfect 7/8 if the length is good."

"Well, it definitely isn't going to be custom made in three days. You do have that part right. But I'm sure we can find something perfect tomorrow. Maybe I'll just take a few vacation days so I can help you. I'm your maid of honor, right?"

"Sure. I'm glad you at least have your dress. We'll all get dresses tomorrow...Gran, Mom and me. You can do the critique and you can buy lunch for all of us!"

"Mom's calling me. I gotta go. Love you!" said Brigetta and then she was gone.

Mikki went right to the computer to do some window-shopping on line. She was so excited now about the wedding that nothing else seemed quite so important as finding the perfect dress. She wanted Faris' eyes to pop when he saw her walk down the aisle. He was so confident that she would still marry him that he had gone ahead with the plans for the ceremony. First Methodist of the Palms. Reverend James R. Hodge will officiate. They had decided on the music in the car this afternoon, while Emily and Yolanda had taken care of flowers, decorations, and food. It would be a great time and she couldn't wait to become Mrs. Faris Al-Busaid. She totally forgot to ask Brigetta if the morgue man was the doctor who had helped in her abduction. Since Brigetta hadn't been at the hospital and hadn't mentioned it, Mikki knew her sister would find out all the details in the morning.

Mikki saw a gorgeous plum-colored satin gown and began clicking her mouse to see how and if it could be purchased at her favorite boutique. Then she saw a vintage wedding gown and it was beautiful, too. Mikki stayed up two more hours traveling the on-line shopping world before sleep overcame dress hunting madness.

CHAPTER SIXTY-ONE

The shopping day was a complete success and each decided on a new dress or two for the big occasions. They were ready for the wedding and the before and after parties. For the wedding day, Susan chose a mint-green mother-of-the-bride gown and Emily opted for a long silvery tunic with tight stretchy pants. Mikki's favorite and final selection was an elegant soft silk strapless evening gown. She chose a green that was almost the same color as her eyes. The shirred bodice was lightly embellished with pearls, sequins, and beads. The simple straight skirt unfolded into a spectacular fan-like train…ideal for a wedding day. Mikki decided to play it safe and opted for the optional pearl-beaded tiny straps that would act as safeguards against wardrobe malfunction. It was beautiful and perfect for her big day.

At lunch the women were all suggesting hair-dos and wanted to go home and try them out on each other. They went to the Pink Flamingo and called the Fantasy Faces studio to arrange for James to do their make-up on Friday morning. Mikki looked at her fingernails and deemed them hopeless. She would run to Walgreen's and buy some glue-on French tips tomorrow. The cuticles could be shaped up, but she wasn't expecting a miracle. She was so happy and enthusiastic about her wedding that she hadn't thought about the groom in several hours. By cocktail time, the ladies were still giggling, planning, and having quality girl time. Mikki was starting to feel like a normal twenty-five year old woman. She needed this. This party, this family, and her new and wonderful favorite man of all time.

Finishing up some of Brigetta's famous Mojitas and Emily's homemade Parmesan cheese crackers, Susan stood up and took Brigetta by the arm.

"Come on, let's go. Your father arrives in the morning and we need to do some grocery shopping tonight. We're also in charge of buying the champagne for the reception and we'll stop at Fazio's for that. Good thing we brought my SUV or we wouldn't have room," said Susan, smiling widely and glancing back at Mikki.

"Bye Mom, and thanks for all your help," said Mikki, kissing her mother on the cheek.

"I wouldn't have missed it for anything. I'm just glad you and Faris are happy and safe," stated Susan, patting Mikki on the head, like her daughter was an errant toddler. "Your grandmother and I wouldn't know what to do without both of you girls."

Mikki's cell phone buzzed in her pocket and the caller ID told her it was Faris.

"Gotta go, Mom. Bye, Brig. We'll talk later," Mikki said, pointing at her sister, as she waved them off and went to the veranda to take the call, plopping onto a chaise lounge.

"Faris! I'm so glad to hear from you! I got a dress! We're really getting married! I'm so happy and excited, just like a normal crazy bride!"

"You'll be gorgeous and I can't wait to see you. The ring is finished and I picked it up this afternoon. Maybe you should try it on so there's no surprises at the church?"

"Want to come over?" asked Mikki, hopefully. She would love nothing more right now than to relax on the balcony with her man and another Mojita cocktail. Even from the veranda Mikki could hear Emily singing some off key opera in her shower. It was so nice to be together as a family, happy and full of hope for the future.

"I was thinking I might get you dinner and then home to my place where I would take advantage of you. I don't want you to get out of practice before the wedding," said Faris, smiling.

Mikki could feel his charm right through the phone and wasn't going to fight the urge to see him, to experience him. She had waited long enough for Faris to appear in her life and now there was no time to waste. She would appreciate and be grateful for every second of their time together. She was dying of curiosity, though, about Dr. Bad.

"Did you hear or see the news? I've been dying to talk to Brigetta about it, but she hasn't been back to work to hear the scoop. Is Dr. Bad dead?"

"One less bad guy to worry about. We won't be crying over him, will we?" asked Faris.

"So it was him for sure?"

"Oh yeah, the bastard's dead as any corpse can be. Not many people can go to hell and brag that they watched their own autopsy while still alive. And just think, Dr. Thani and I were just having dinner a few hours before his untimely demise."

Mikki jerked up ramrod straight from the chaise and thought for a moment. "You didn't!" she ventured.

"I did. You're talking about the dinner, right?" asked Faris. "It was very nice. He had some sort of fish and rice. Maybe the food was bad, not prepared correctly or something."

"Gee, I doubt that would put him into a near death state. What did you do to him? Where did you eat? Some greasy spoon?"

"Yep. My condo," Faris chuckled.

"Uh oh. Remind me not to have you cook me dinner after we're married. We'd better talk about this later. What time will you pick me up? Or should I meet you somewhere?"

"This is kind of funny sounding now, but I was really thinking about making some shish kabobs on the grill and a salad at my condo. I promise not to give you bad food, really! I don't know what'll happen to you after the meal, though. I can't guarantee that I'll be on my best behavior. We can practice all aspects of being married. Cooking and…"

Mikki laughed and said she'd drive over to the condo. This made sense because they could talk privately and have some quality time alone. Alone? Wait a minute! Was Kamila still there? Mikki doubted she would feel comfortable if Kami was still there lurking about and passing judgment…like she was one to talk. At least she hadn't birthed a baby girl for the sole purpose of importing an undetectable bomb onto a plane. Yeah, Kami was something else. But she was Faris' sister. Mikki knew she would have to accept that.

"Faris? What about your sister? Will she be there?" said Mikki, cautiously.

"You won't see her again. She's gone. We'll talk more later, okay?" Faris answered.

Mikki quickly showered, excited by the thought of her night ahead with Faris. She wondered what being married to him would be like. How would their lives work? Mikki was an engineer and had a career. Faris was covertly with U.S. intelligence, but had a wealthy family and didn't really need to work. Would they be a team joining their forces to do favors, to fight terror, to make the world a more fair and better place to live? It would be the three of them, Faris, Mikki, and Emily, against evil forces. Or maybe they would all retire from bad guy chasing. Mikki and Faris could raise a family. Gran was getting too old for this anyway. She had pulled off a giant coup at the airport, but she was now nearly eighty years old. It's time she slowed down and spent more time at ladies' luncheons and style shows and less time being cocked and loaded.

In less than forty-five minutes, Mikki had packed an overnight bag, complete with make-up, toiletries and hair products, fresh underwear, and a peach-colored silk nightgown she never wore much at home. This time she was prepared to stay at the condo. This wouldn't be another night where she was covered with mud and had no clean clothes or hair conditioner. She packed two new outfits just in case. Well, maybe he'll take me out for breakfast and I'll have to look stunning!

CHAPTER SIXTY-TWO

Mikki was wearing white sandals, turquoise Capri's, and a matching polka dot cotton blouse when she knocked at the door. She heard a bolt turn and Faris appeared. His dark hair was still damp and tousled from his shower. A comma of curl drooped sexily toward his right eyebrow. He wore a pair of faded blue jeans and a plain white polo shirt. He stood, barefoot, in the doorway and looked at Mikki's stuffed travel bag. He smiled and said, "Are you moving in today?"

"This is just the beginning, dear. A few things to hold me over for the night. You should see me when I travel out of the country or even out of the zip code."

"I can't wait for that to happen…our honeymoon!"

"A cruise then? And Gran can come, too? I'd feel guilty leaving her all alone."

He nodded, took her bag, and then pulled her to him for a kiss. "Shall we start with dessert?" he asked, as his hands began roving up and down her back and then to her curvy and firm bottom.

"I love dessert. What'd you have in mind? Chocolate? Strawberry? Whipped cream and cherries?" murmured Mikki, as she wrapped both arms around him. She drank in his scent as she rested her head on his powerful chest, listening to his heart. He smelled wonderful, a manly combination of citrus, musk, and spices. Mikki put her nose into his shirt and took several deep breaths. "You smell pretty good. My favorite dessert is you," Mikki said, her voice growing husky and low.

"I knew it. You find me irresistible. But we must eat first or my culinary skills will be wasted. I have marinated the kabobs, tossed the salad, and uncorked the wine. We shall follow proper decorum and have a lovely dinner and conversation before I ravage your wanton and lustful body."

"Darn. Oh well, let's have the wine!"

Faris poured some Riesling into her glass and they toasted each other before sipping. Faris had also bought some fresh sushi from the market down the street. They were sitting at his kitchen bar, munching maki rolls with wasabi dip, and drinking wine, when Mikki blurted out, "So where's Kami? So what happened to Dr. Bad?"

"Big questions…long answers," Faris replied. "Where do I begin? There should be no secrets between man and wife, so I'll tell you everything, if you tell me everything."

"I think I've already done that."

"No, I want to know how your eighty-year-old grandmother hijacked that plane and knocked off all the bad guys while we just basically stood around and looked flaccid."

"The best way to explain it? Well, let's just say you're only beginning to know my grandmother. Although I worry about her and I don't know if I can leave her to live alone, I could tell you more tales, but not tonight. For now, I'll tell you about Monday night…" Mikki explained what Emily had told her about the parachutes, the men, and the rescue. Faris just listened and nodded, as if he heard this kind of story every day.

"So is she finished with them? The bad guys, I mean?"

"Hell, no. Gran won't be finished until all is settled and life again seems fair and just. That's her thing. She had a rough childhood and ever since then, she's been a real tiger in everything she's ever done. And trust me, she's done a lot."

"Okay, I'll tell you about Kamila. You women can scratch her off your hit list."

Mikki took in a big breath, concerned about what he was about to reveal, "You didn't do something to her, did you?" She had put down her glass and was looking into his eyes for an answer.

"No, she's my sister. She's messed up, but you can't blame her entirely. She was in an arranged marriage to a guy who turned out to hate America and Americans. Pretty funny for a man who made a nice living here. Made his life here…the restaurant, their big apartment, fancy cars. What a hypocrite. What an idiot. We still need to get him…big time."

"So where is Kami, then?" asked Mikki, taking another sip of wine.

"Well, I weighed all my options. Kami was brainwashed into believing a lot of crap that these guys were dishing out, but they didn't care a bit about her or the newborn baby. She went along with them, but did try to fight back when there was a chance to get away. I took all that into consideration. I could've turned her over to Homeland Security, the FBI, or some other government law enforcement agency. She would've never seen the light of day again, but our family name might be ruined…for me, for us. I didn't want that. Kami and I had a long talk and this time I handcuffed her to the bed in her room. This morning, I met with another agent who also works covert operations. They took her and are flying her back to Saudi at 11 P.M. tonight in an Army cargo plane that delivers supplies to the troops in the Mid East. They have no other way of secretly transporting her out of the country. She'll go back to our mother and back to the old ways. She's never to return to the U.S. again."

"What if she comes back? What if Sajid goes there and gets her? It shouldn't be too hard for him to figure out she's there. I'm sure he has lots of friends in the Riyadh area."

"You're right about that. Things are going to be handled and we'll just have to take that chance. This way seemed to give us the best chance and a chance for her to make another life. I trust the agent who helped me. He'll make sure that everything is taken care of."

"I'm glad you helped your sister. That's the way our family works, too. Family loyalty is top of the list. But, I must confess, I'm glad she's gone to Saudi. I felt weird and uncomfortable around her, like she wanted me out of the picture and was constantly trying to ruin our relationship. When Brigetta was kidnapped, it almost worked. It almost broke us up. I'm sorry, I just don't like your sister and don't think we ever would have been able to bond or form any sense of trust between us."

"I know. It's over," said Faris, reaching across the counter for Mikki's hand. "Don't worry, I understand entirely." Then hesitatingly he added, "I'm not sure I should tell you this, but I will in the interest of truth. It was Kamila's idea to kidnap your sister."

Mikki's face burned red with pent-up anger, then finally she gulped the last of her wine and setting the glass down a little too hard, she said, "That bitch!"

CHAPTER SIXTY-THREE

Mikki looked at Faris and felt embarrassed, yet relieved, to be able to vent emotionally with this man. "I'm sorry. She terrorized our family. She was ready to blow up that plane with women, children, and babies! And the baby bomb? She knew about all that. I just can't feel too sorry for her...even though she's your sister. You're nothing like her. You're kind and thoughtful and gentle and ...very handsome."

Faris had come to her side and was holding her. "I know you feel that way, and you have every right to those feelings. Please know that you can say anything to me and we'll always talk it out. Even if we're fighting, arguing, let's say that we'll always talk. I just can't stand that silent treatment stuff."

Mikki was so overwhelmed that she felt her eyes begin to get watery. So she said nothing, but hugged him back. Using a cocktail napkin to blot her eyes, she released herself from his grip and said, "Okay, one problem solved. Now I want to know about Dr. Bad and how that problem went away."

"Actually Kami helped me on that one. She told me that Dr. Thani was the doctor who implanted the bomb into the switched baby. They took the baby to the Miami hospital where he has privileges and in the middle of the night they secretly accessed one of the operating rooms. The baby wasn't doing well anyway by then because she couldn't suck, Kami said. She had some 'genetic defects' is how she put it."

"So that made it okay to blow the kid up with another hundred or so passengers?" Mikki interrupted, anger flaring again. "Grrrr..."

"Calm down. Let me finish. So when Kami told him your sister worked at the hospital in town here, he arranged for one of his patients to be admitted there for surgery. That would give him an excuse to wander around Palm Beach

Memorial looking for Brigetta. He's not a radiologist, he's a general surgeon. He had some background in radiology in Pakistan before he came to the states. He probably didn't want to be linked to the baby bomb surgery, so he said 'radiologist' as his introduction to Brigetta. You notice he didn't want to give up his lifestyle of the rich and famous to board that plane with the rest of them? He agreed to try to get Brigetta to come with him and or meet him somewhere and they arranged to capture her."

"Poor Brigetta. She's so naïve and innocent. I wish I could've warned her in some way without telling her the whole story about Gran and I and what we do. That discovery would be a huge shock to her, especially right now. She seems to be recuperating from her ordeal just fine now, though. Amazingly well, actually. I always thought of her as intelligent but much more timid than I ever was. But, go on."

"I'd better tell you something first. Your sister was well aware that your grandmother had tried to drug her. She had dumped her coffee out that night. She told me that you two always forget she's a nurse. She knew as soon as she tasted the drink that it was doped up. She's a smart cookie and she may know more than you think. She's also much more brave and vindictive than you give her credit for."

"Hmmm. I always said to watch out for those quiet ones," said Mikki, soaking in Faris' commentary.

"Anyway, Kamila told me Dr. Bad was Dr. Thani so I made preparations and went looking for him. He was still in town because of his medical practice while the others had flown the coop. I called him and identified myself as Sajid's other brother, Ahmed, who I think is actually in England somewhere going to college. See the irony in that? He was claiming to be my brother and hadn't even met me and I used Ahmed's name to fool him. I said I had received cash from the Al Quada cell in South Florida so he could be paid for all his work. The greedy bastard quickly dropped everything to meet me for a late dinner. I didn't want to bring him here to the condo, so I arranged to meet him at Kenny's...the seafood place on the Boulevard?"

Mikki nodded. She knew the place. Very expensive, very upscale.

"I recommended the pecan-crusted grouper and prayed he wouldn't order a steak or something outlandishly non-seafood. I was thinking, please order fish!" said Faris as he continued his story. He ordered the grouper, probably because he wanted to get on with the main event...his cash reward for being a good terrorist, kidnapper, and baby bomb maker. He was nervous and kept glancing around like he was watching for the cops or CIA or something to come swooping down on him and whisk him away. He also kept looking at my satchel and bag. I'm sure he thought they contained many American dollars just for him. He told me he had put his house up for sale and as soon as the 2.5 million dollars for the sale was in his account, he was moving to his villa at St. Barts. He had lots of plans. Too bad for Dr. Bad.

"As he was eating his fish, I asked if he would like dessert and he said he was a little light-headed. If it were you, I would've said it was the booze! But he was Muslim and there was no wine or liquor. Then he complained that his chest bothered him and he seemed to be having some respiratory problem. Being helpful, like I always am, I said I'd take him to the emergency room at Palm Beach Memorial. He said if I could just follow him there, he could drive himself. I thought, good, that way his car will be in his own temporary space in the doctor's parking lot.

"He barely made it to the lot, but parked the car sideways in his space. I don't think he was thinking clearly at this point. I parked at the curb and ran to help him out of the car. I half carried him to the designated hospital door at the back of the main building. It was pretty dark and no one saw us at the employee's small rear door by the supply room. I swiped his physician's ID to gain entry. Once there, I headed down the stairway. He protested at first but I just kept reassuring him that he'd be fine. Within minutes I was mostly dragging him and luckily the place was deserted. I saw the sign for the morgue and again swiped his card to get in. Getting him on the table was easy. He wasn't that heavy, just long and tall, all arms and legs."

"So you were the one who put him in the morgue? What was wrong with him?" Mikki interrupted again, wanting to know all the answers at once.

"I'm getting to that. You don't have a lot of patience. We're going to have to work on that, aren't we?" Mikki just twirled her hand urging him on and clamped her lips tightly together. "Next I got the Ketamine out of my pants pocket. My hands were a little shaky but the syringe was prefilled. I was only going to use that if necessary because it could cause a fatal blood pressure and breathing problem."

Mikki couldn't help herself. She had questions! "So why were you worried about killing him with the Ketamine?"

"Patience… I didn't want to kill him. Not then. I wanted him to experience the dead zone without being dead. I wanted him to see and hear and feel. Ketamine, I learned, stimulates rather than depresses the circulatory system. I wanted him to be recognized as a dead person. In effect, I had made him a zombie."

"What are you talking about? Now I'm worried about your mental state! What are you saying?" exclaimed Mikki, her eyes dancing with confused excitement.

"Surely you've seen the documentaries? About the people in Africa who rise from the dead to become zombies? You've heard of that?"

"Yeah…" answered Mikki tentatively.

"Well, it's real. Well, sort of. Here's how it works. Tetrodotoxin is a poison that causes various symptoms, starting with difficulty breathing. It progresses to full paralysis. These people are sometimes declared dead but recover and then walk around life with the 'zombie' glassy-eyed stare. They're able to follow simple orders but not much else. Sometimes they're found working in fields in Africa like slaves."

"So you wanted to make him our slave?"

"No, I wanted him to appear dead. These victims really look dead, apparently. There were two Japanese guys that scientists used for a case history. Both were poisoned by tetrodotoxin and were declared dead, but physically recovered before burial. I guess that the body, if buried, must be exhumed within eight hours or the person asphyxiates in the grave."

"I think you've been watching too much Discovery channel."

"No, really. There's been lots of research on this. In fact, that research led to the discovery of curare, an arrow poison from the Amazon. It's now used to paralyze muscles in surgery.

"But the reason I had the Ketamine was the fail safe idea. I didn't know how much of the poison I could get Dr. Bad to swallow. The Ketamine would do something similar but is shorter acting and if I needed to dispatch him quickly, I could have given him the second syringeful I still had in my possession."

"So you just handed him the poison pill and said eat this?"

"Mikki...are you being sarcastic? Anyway, the tetrodotoxin is found in puffer fish. I'm sure you've heard of being poisoned by improperly prepared puffer fish? That would be enough for me not to order it. When he ordered the fish for dinner, I was ready with the Hell's Kitchen puffer plate special in my satchel. It took some shopping to find it in the Asian markets, but I cooked it my way, covered it with toasted breading, and kept it warm in a hot food server.

"I watched anxiously for the waiter who would bring our food. Then I called Dr. Bad on his pager. I had preset my cell phone to dial his number, so all I had to do was push the call button. His pager started making annoying sounds and everyone looked our way. He cursed something in Pakistani and moved to shut it off. I had asked for a booth in the back, luckily. When the doctor reached for his cell phone, I suggested he take it out to the cloakroom, so as not to disturb the other diners.

"He grumbled, but left the table. The waiter arrived, left the plates, and I doctored the doctor's food. I took his grouper and put it in the hot plate, thinking 'I'll have this for lunch tomorrow,' and replaced it with the puffer fish. I scraped the pecan topping onto the puffer fish and made sure the veggies were neatly arranged. Martha Stewart would have been so proud of me."

"Yeah, at least she wasn't in jail for murder," said Mikki, reaching for the wine bottle. "You sure this sushi is good? No raw puffer fish, right?"

"Well, there is the part about the Ketamine being used as a date rape drug," said Faris, emptying his glass and getting up to pour their refills. "But I want you to know that you'll never have to use that on me. I'm pretty easy…at least when it comes to you."

"I love to prey on sweet, innocent men. You don't fall into that category. You're more the dangerously rugged type," she crooned, as she crept up behind him and rubbed his neck.

"You keep that up and you may never hear the rest of the story," said Faris, moaning with the pleasure of his neck massage.

"You force me to stop. Go on," said Mikki, again taking her seat.

"Just for your info, I wasn't totally sure this would work on Al Thani. I had read that the zombie-makers also used the Bufo marinus, a huge New World toad that is a veritable chemical factory. There are hallucinogens, powerful anesthetics, and chemicals in that toad that affect the heart and nervous system. Since I haven't seen many Bufos around lately to squeeze toxins from, I tried the Ketamine as a back up. I wasn't sure of the dose, but had a premeasured syringe. If all else failed and my patient died before the autopsy, at least he wouldn't be bothering us anymore.

"But as soon as I flopped him onto the table, I knew it would work. There were no vital signs detectable, so I removed his clothes and took the tags from the only other body in the morgue and put them on Dr. Bad. I labeled the refrigerated door and he was all ready to have his 'procedure.' We moved his body to his new, though cramped, home in the morgue crypt. I heard him gurgle once and his eyes were fluttering, but he wasn't looking so good. Pale, staring, no visible breathing or heart rate, and it would only get worse, or better, depending on who is giving the account.

"I'm sure he had enough awareness to realize that he was in the morgue, but not enough to be sure if he was hallucinating or it was real. But he couldn't do a damned thing about it. He was totally paralyzed. He couldn't even blink his eyes or move his lips. When the knives and saws came out, he had his own rated 'R' for violence horror movie and he was the star victim. The coroner cuts him open, they find a beating heart, but he dies from shock and the wounds from the autopsy procedure. I guess they tried to put him back together, but like Humpty Dumpty, it was too late and too much damage. Now the body will undergo a real autopsy and I'm sure they'll find the toxicology panel of tests quite interesting. No one can connect any of us to him. At the restaurant, I paid with cash as we rushed out the door. I said 'the man isn't feeling well,' and we left. End of story."

"No, wait a minute. I was listening closely and you said, 'We' moved the body. Not just you. Someone else was there. Who was it?" asked Mikki, leaning forward on her elbows as she sat at the counter, "and how do you know so much about all the medical terms...like vital signs?"

"The Internet?" answered Faris, seeing if Mikki would believe that one.

"Wrong, try again. Like how did you get the prefilled syringe and know the dose to give?" demanded Mikki, still looking for answers to the puzzle.

"Alright. You might say I had a little help. Another hospital employee met me earlier in the day and helped me plan. Then she met me at the morgue at the appointed time. It was all quite cloak and dagger."

"She? She who? It can't be Kamila since she doesn't work at the hospital and I thought she was handcuffed until her departure later tonight."

"No, she doesn't know anything about medical procedures or medicine or drugs," Faris said, as he looked at her incredulously. "You don't know?"

Mikki thought for a moment and then stood up accusingly pointing her finger at Faris, "NO! You don't... you can't...mean my little sister?"

CHAPTER SIXTY-FOUR

"She forced me. The other choice she gave me was that she was going after these guys on her own since she had the name for the real Dr. Thani. In fact, she's the one who told me that the semi-dead guy would have no sense of touch, but he would be completely aware. His heartbeat would only be detectable on an electrocardiogram. She was more than a little ticked off about her abduction. I told her you'd be mad at me, but she didn't care," explained Faris, bracing himself for a verbal attack from Mikki.

But Mikki sat back down abruptly on the barstool and rested her elbows on the counter, thinking. Faris raised his eyebrows, questioning her unexpected silence.

"Well, she sure faked out both Gran and myself. We thought she'd accepted all of it and was living in a drugged state of happy forgetfulness," said Mikki, finally.

"Oh, no. She was very anxious for some revenge and she didn't care what happened to Dr. Bad, as long as it was painful and deadly. I didn't even tell her anything about the baby bomb. With her being a pediatric nurse, she may have really gone bonkers. She helped me with the info and medications I needed. All the while she was putting herself and her career at great risk. She waited for me in the basement at the empty morgue and together we set up Dr. Thani for his final medical procedure. This time he was the patient. The operation was a success but the patient died. Ever hear that one?"

"Yeah, of course. I'm not mad at you, Faris. I'm just shocked that Brigetta has such a vengeful heart within her cute little blond self. She was always the most compassionate and caring of all of us, kind of youthful naiveté. I'm just having a hard time accepting her in her new role. She called me about meeting you for lunch, but never mentioned a word. So that's also how she knew we were still getting married. You told her last night."

Faris nodded. He felt braver now and sat back down at the counter. "Let's eat," he said, "The shish kabobs are drunk with marinade, so I'll just put them on the grill. The salads are in the refrigerator. Want to get them for us? I set the table in the dining room."

Mikki got the salads and took them to the table. Faris had even bought flowers for the center of the table. It was an arrangement with orchids and some greenery at the base. The flowers looked so beautifully delicate, yet healthy and strong. Maybe Brigetta was similar to these plants, appearing much more fragile than she actually was.

The meal was great and had an Old World flavor. Faris had used a family recipe for the marinade on the lamb and it was tender and delicious. He had grown some of the vegetables in a small potted garden on his cedar deck. They drank more wine and sat outside until it grew dark. Mikki had brought along some cruise brochures and they talked about their wedding day, their honeymoon plans, and their dreams for the future. They were both a little drunk with happiness and Riesling when they went inside to the couch to watch some late evening news. Faris pulled her close and she curled into him. He was soon kissing her and making circling caresses on her shoulders. They made slow and passionate love there on the sofa and then, still naked, walked to the bedroom for more. This was what life was all about, thought Mikki, before she fell asleep in the warm security of his embrace.

CHAPTER SIXTY-FIVE

"Wake-up, lazy almost-wife. Today is the big party. We have to get you an engagement ring. We'll get another ring, if you still want one, when we go on our honeymoon. I've been thinking about our party tonight. All our family and friends will be there and here's my lovely fiancée with a naked ring finger. This won't do. Let's go back and get that big one you liked. The signature designer one? With all the clumps of diamonds all around it?"

"Clumps of diamonds? Gee, I don't remember that," said Mikki, sleepily as Faris grasped her hand and was nibbling at her left ring finger.

"You know what I mean...it was big and flashy," said Faris, now up and pulling the sheets off Mikki's recumbent body. Mikki giggled and hugged the white cotton trying to hide her naked body beneath. Faris locked her wrists and began to pull her out of the bed. Mikki was laughing so hard that she found it hard to fight back, but she scissored the sheets between her legs as he pulled and she thumped down to the thick lamb's wool rug on the floor, dragging the bedclothes off the bed with her. Faris continued to pull her and the sliding rug towards the bathroom, grinning with the depravity of his crime.

"It's time to shower and get your butt into your shopping clothes. We're getting a proper ring this morning, so don't argue. And besides, you need to help me pick out some clothes for my trousseau," said Faris, still laughing and pulling Mikki and the tangled mess.

"Stop! Okay, you win...I'm up!" squealed Mikki as her bare bottom suddenly hit the cold tile floor of the bathroom. Faris quit pulling, released her arms and got down on the floor with her.

"That was fun," he exclaimed, panting from the exertion of his efforts. "Let's do this every morning."

"Laugh now," warned Mikki, as she got him in a headlock, wrapping her naked belly around his back, "but paybacks are a bitch!" Then she brought her head around and kissed him hard. They didn't even notice the icy coolness as together they found the floor rather inviting.

After coffee and a bubble bath, Mikki called Emily to see if she needed help with the couple's shower at the club, but everything was under Yolanda's professional management.

"All we have to do is show up, darling. Are you coming home to change clothes, hopefully? Take a 'breather' from whatever you two are doing?"

"Well, what we're doing is having coffee, Gran. You have an evil mind. Then we're going shopping for some last minute new clothes. God, I hope there's a tailor open for alterations today! After shopping, I'll be back and get ready, then Faris will pick both of us up for the party. I'm so excited! Thanks, Gran for calling Yolanda and helping to arrange my celebration. We're so lucky this is coming together in such a short time. Faris will pick up the marriage license this afternoon too. I can't believe this is all real. We'll see you later!"

At 3 P.M. the Pink Flamingo's kitchen elevator door slid open and Mikki burst in, flashing something huge and brilliant on her finger. "It's now official. I have to get married since I have this big rock on my finger. Get your sunglasses, because it'll dazzle you into blindness!" Mikki exclaimed, scampering like a rabbit to Gran's favorite chair. Gran took Mikki's hand and touched the flashy ring. When the sunlight from the balcony hit the ring, brilliant rainbows of color disco-danced across the room.

"Did you know you could get a ring sized in a half hour? The store wants you to wait there while they do it. Then they sell you lots of other stuff. We got some diamond earrings for me and each lady in the family gets a pair, too."

"It's quite lovely and quite sparkly! Wow, is that an original? And diamond earrings, too? Congratulations to both of you! Where's Faris? Resting up?"

"We went back to his place so that I could get my car and he'll be back later to get us. Pray that nothing else happens before that! Speaking of which…wait until I tell you the latest about your other granddaughter and the saga of the autopsy table."

CHAPTER SIXTY-SIX

"So Faris has been a busy man, has he? And Kami is in Saudi now with her mother?" asked Emily, after listening to the latest news report from Mikki.

"Kami should have arrived early this morning. The cargo plane was to leave around 11 P.M. last night. I think that's what Faris told me. His mother knows most of the story and will keep her in line there. Kami won't be making any more trips to the states, so she'll be safe from the Feds and also her husband. That's how Faris wanted it and it seems fair, don't you think?"

"That's why we left it all up to him. His sister, his decision, his responsibility. Now I wonder what will happen to the little baby?"

Mikki was quiet for a minute, twirling the new ring on her finger and then she said, "I was wondering about that, too. Faris seems to have a plan, but I don't know anything more about it. We didn't discuss that last night. I must confess, we were too happy talking about the wedding, our marriage, and our honeymoon. Oh yeah, we need to get busy on the cruise, Gran. Do you want a balcony cabin? That's what we're reserving for us. We'll talk more about it when the wedding's over and we have time to regroup. I don't feel comfortable leaving until we know where Sajid and Hassad have gone and what they're up to now."

"Right. I don't want to spend the rest of my life looking over my shoulder, either," said Emily. "In fact, I'm going up to the Pink Room and check our security notices and news channels to see if there's anything exciting going on. Then we'd better get beautiful before your handsome young man comes to pick us up. Hope he doesn't mind being shared. George was out of town on a movie set and couldn't be here as my date tonight, so I'm solo again."

Mikki was completely dressed and putting on her new diamond earrings when Emily tapped softly at the door.

"Mikki?" Emily said quietly.

Mikki opened the door, wondering what was wrong. Granny Em was hardly ever this quiet. Emily wasn't dressed yet and she looked worried.

"What's happened?" Mikki squeaked. "Is everyone okay? Is someone hurt? What's going on?"

"I don't mean to alarm you, but yes, something's happened. General Bleckman has just announced a terror attack at the Army base in Riyadh. A cargo plane, landing at the base, was shot down today by a ground-fired missile. There's a video of a large fire and lots of smoke at the airstrip. You can't see much, just flames, smoke, and explosions, people running all around."

"Omigod! Do you think it was Kami's plane? Do you think it was hit because someone found out she was onboard? Oh, no! Poor Faris! He'll be so upset! Should we cancel the party?"

"Let's let Faris make that decision after we find out more. I'm going to finish getting ready and you should too. He'll be here in forty-five minutes to pick us up. His friends and some of his family will be waiting at the party for us. Let's just go to the Club and enjoy the festivities. We'll watch the news when we get home."

"Okay, there's not much we can do anyway except give him our love and support. Let's play it by ear," said Mikki, feeling a little guilty now that Faris' sister was probably dead and she was so happy that her sister was still very much alive.

The front doorbell rang and Faris was there looking like a fashion model for GQ. He looked at both women and saw something in their faces he couldn't quite recognize. Maybe they were just worried that nothing would fall together as it should tonight. After all, they would be meeting his aunt, uncle, three cousins, and several of his friends this evening. Just a case of premarital jitters, he supposed.

"You ladies are the most beautiful on earth," he said as he stood back and looked at them. They both twirled in circles, allowing him to see their flowing knee-length dresses and sparkling jewelry. They had both picked silky evening dresses with sleeveless tops and V-necked bodices. Mikki wore a matching silk scarf and let her auburn hair fall in loose ringlets to her shoulders. They both wore evening sandals; Mikki's were plain gold high-heels and Emily's were silver flats with tiny rhinestones on the straps.

Smiling, they each came to take an arm of their escort. Faris felt their apprehension fading as he led them down the marble stairway to his car.

"You don't look so bad yourself, Mr. Busaid," said Emily, and Mikki just squeezed his arm. Mikki looked into his eyes and he felt immediate protectiveness. She looked so vulnerable and sweet. He knew she wasn't either one, actually. She was really a thief, stealing his beating heart right from his chest. He had gladly let her have it.

Mikki put her head on his arm when they got into the car and drove off. *Until death do us part*, she thought.

CHAPTER SIXTY-SEVEN

The party was already buzzing with conversation when they arrived. The clinking of glasses heralding their arrival mixed with excited voices as people found their assigned seats for dinner. Gifts were stacked high on the bridal table and Asti Spumante was flowing from a bubbling fountain nearby. Mikki and Faris mingled with friends and were introduced all around the room. Mikki met Faris' family who had flown from Chicago and Atlanta to be with Faris for the wedding. At least he had some family here, thought Mikki, still worrying about the news of the plane crash. Faris seemed calm and relaxed even in this crowd of people he mostly didn't know.

"Dad! Dad!" Mikki yelled across the room and Michael Walsh immediately spotted his jumping, screaming daughter. Michael, who had just arrived, pulled his wife along and came to her side, giving her a big hug and kissing her cheek. He grabbed Faris' hand and shook it heartily.

"My man! Good luck to you with this one! Hasn't anyone warned you about her? She always was the uncontrollable daughter, you know," said Michael, still one arm around Mikki and still gripping Faris' arm.

"That's what I'm hearing, but I'm willing to take my chances. I'll probably have to lock her in a castle somewhere and only let her out once in a while to ride her horse," answered Faris, smiling broadly.

"The horse is definitely the key. You've got that part right. She'll do anything for that beast. She's his servant, from what I understand. Cleans his stall, but won't clean her own bedroom. You know all this about her, right?" asked Michael, winking at Faris.

"No, but it's too late now. She's grown on me and I can't live without her. I'll just have to try to train her or something," said Faris.

"Good luck with that," said Susan and Michael in unison. Then they all laughed, even Mikki.

Faris took Susan's arm and Michael escorted Mikki to the head table for their dinner. The food from Caribbean Soul would be, as usual, fantastic. Yolanda and her family sat at a table near the buffet, so Yolanda could make sure her staff was serving the carefully prepared meal perfectly.

Just as they were seated, Faris suddenly stared at the country club's glass door entrance and said, "I can't believe it!"

A tall seventy-ish man in a white dishdasha robe and white flowing shora headpiece, complete with egal band, had just exited a white stretch limousine in front of the building. The aristocratic Arab looked like he had just arrived from a desert oasis as he and his entourage merged smoothly into the hall. He was following two men who had opened the glass doors for him. He made a path directly toward the bridal table. Emily squealed, jumped up from her seat, and ran towards him.

Mikki stared open-mouthed as Faris stood up and also hurried to the handsome man. Emily reached him first and hugged him tightly. Faris also hugged him and kissed him on the cheek. There was much excited chatter and men's back patting. Feeling left out, Mikki rose to join them.

"Uncle Radi, this is my fiancée, Mikelle Walsh,"

said Faris, beaming with pleasure and pride.

Uncle Radi took her hand and bowed gracefully to her, his dark eyes appreciating the young beautiful woman. Emily meanwhile seemed stuck to Radi's left side, her arm entwined in his.

"I so hoped you'd make it," said Emily, flushed with excitement, as she gazed up at the graying, but handsome Arab.

More than a little confused, Mikki, eyebrows arched, asked her grandmother, "So you know Faris' uncle Radi?"

By now, Brigetta, Susan, and Michael had all swarmed the visitor, curious and ready to welcome him.

"All you silly people," said Emily, "of course! You all have heard me speak of Prince Shahid? The Sheik who is totally mad about me? The one I visited frequently in my younger days?" Emily gave Radi a conspiratorial wink and the rest of the family just stood there absorbing what she'd said, shocked into dumb silence.

Mikki was first to get it. This was the sheik Emily always talked about...the same one in Emily's stories who had always lusted after her and wanted her to join his harem? Oh my God! He's for real! This was so shocking that it was hilarious! Mikki began to giggle and couldn't stop. Faris' uncle was the infamous sheik. Amazing!

Composing herself in an effort to be polite, Mikki said, "So glad to be able to finally meet you in person! We've heard so much about you!"

Faris was also surprised to find his uncle knew Emily and that their relationship had been so long and close. No wonder Emily knew all about him and felt safe letting her granddaughter be with him. She'd called Radi in Saudi. His uncle would have given him glowing recommendations, after all he'd already given him his prize stallion. It truly was a very small world.

Radi Shahid joined them at the head table sitting beside Emily and the two chatted amiably all through the meal. Radi told the family he could hardly turn down the wedding trip to the U.S.A. after getting invitations from first Faris and then Emily.

After the dinner and during the serving of the desserts, Mikki and Faris began opening some of the presents. The shower gifts were unusual and fabulous. There was everything from a steel-drawer tool cabinet for their garage to gift certificates from Beach Travel Company. When Mikki opened a large box and found an ironing board, she asked, "What's this for?" and got a big laugh from her guests. Faris just grinned, totally amused. Julianne and a group from the stables joined together and got the couple a gift card from a local feed and tack store. There were the usual gag gifts among the treasures from all the well wishers, and Mikki and Faris saw that everyone was having a good time.

At 9 P.M. the band began to play and everyone was on the dance floor. This was the first time Mikki and Faris had ever danced together. Mikki felt like a princess and this was all a fairytale that she hoped would never end. Holding him close, it was easy to forget the bad memories of the past and focus on her new life with her new man.

At midnight the crowd began to break up, since many guests had to return to work in the morning. Tomorrow's wedding was just for family and then the big post wedding reception would be held at the Pink Flamingo. Mikki was tired and just wanted to go home. Emily was supervising the gifts. She had hired a storage company to load up the gifts and take them to their building for safe keeping until the new couple decided where they would be living. Faris said goodbye to his aunt and uncle from Chicago and also Radi. He said he'd see them tomorrow afternoon. Mikki motioned him over after he walked his relatives to their rented cars.

"Hi, babe, ready to go home?" Faris asked, as he walked toward Mikki and Emily.

"Faris, Gran and I need to talk to you. Something's happened that you need to know."

CHAPTER SIXTY-EIGHT

"What's that?" Faris asked. "You forgot to pay the caterer? My new suit won't be ready in the morning?"

"No, it's a bit worse than that. It's about Kamila. Or at least we think it's about Kami," said Mikki, a rare solemn expression on her face. Emily nodded, but said nothing. She was watching Faris.

"On the news there was a cargo plane crash...In Riyadh. We think it was Kami's plane," Mikki blurted out, waiting for his response.

"You heard then," said Faris. "I got a call this morning about that."

"You knew? You never said anything?" asked Mikki.

"I didn't know when the news release would come out, and I didn't want to interrupt our day with that."

"That seems a little callous. That's your only sister we're talking about," said Mikki.

"Well, it brings up another situation that I was waiting to spring on you later," said Faris.

"Which is?" asked Mikki.

Emily was very curious now, but wondered if she was intruding on their conversation, so she added, "Maybe we should get going home. We can have a little after dinner drink there and you two can talk. I'm really tired and need to get to bed. My old legs aren't what they used to be."

"Oh, sorry, Gran. It's been a long, but wonderful day. Thank you so much for everything. Did you see the pile of gifts? Thank goodness so many people decided on gift cards or we would spend a fortune storing all those presents," said Mikki. She turned to Faris and said, "Are you ready? Gran's right, it's not really a good place to talk."

Soon they were all sitting in the living room area and had taken off their shoes, rubbing their tired feet on the thick woolly throw rugs. Mikki made them some spiced tea and they shared some leftover pecan cookies. The sea air was coming into the room from the open doors to the balcony. The temperature was still warm, but the ocean breezes were cooling and pleasant.

"I can't believe I'm still eating. If this keeps up, I'll have to diet before the cruise," said Faris, rubbing his belly and eating another cookie.

"I'm hitting the sack," announced Emily, as she rose from her favorite chair. "It was so nice to see Prince Radi again." She made a point of staring hard at each of the unbelievers in the living room.

"You don't have to leave," said Faris. "Please stay while we talk about the plane crash and I tell you what I know."

Emily sat back down and waited. The last phone call of the evening could be delayed a little longer.

"Kami will be pronounced dead soon, and if all goes well, hopefully Sajid will be captured or killed in the next few days. I applied for temporary custody of the baby. Little Sofah needs to have a family…just not her biological parents. As her uncle, who will soon be a married man, I would have a good chance of assuming temporary parenthood. This is all providing my wife agrees to taking a baby."

Faris watched Mikki who answered without hesitation, "Sure, let's do it! We'll be a real family!"

"It's not that easy. Sofah's father will probably still be trying to snatch the baby. Why? Who knows? So he can try to use her in some other horrible plot? To raise her to be another terrorist, perhaps a human suicide bomber? We have to stop that. It would be impossible for him to ever legally be able to take the baby, since he's a wanted man. But that won't stop him. He won't want anyone else to have his child. Now that he thinks Kami is gone forever, he can concentrate on finding Sofah."

"What should we do?" asked Emily.

"This morning, when the Pentagon got word of the crash, I petitioned the New York court to grant me custody based on familial rights. I think my request will be granted.

The tough part will be getting access to the baby and bringing her home safely to Florida."

"Hmmm, so that's why we're getting married? Not just for love, but a baby rescue operation? I'm all for it! Let's do it! You'll make a great father. I'm not sure about my motherhood abilities, but Brigetta and Gran will help, right?"

"I'm gonna be a great grandmother? Woowoo! I'll have a tiny baby to hold and nurture and mold her into a perfect little person? When do we leave to pick her up?"

"I'm happy you two are so receptive, but if all goes well, Mikki and I will have to appear in the court in New York and state our case for granting custody to us. Then if we get approval, we'll pick her up at the foster home…the whereabouts of which is a big mysterious secret right now…and bring her back here."

"We'll have plenty of room at the condo," said Mikki excitedly. "She can have a bassinette in our room and then she can take the guest room as a nursery and then we'll decorate it in My Little Pony pastels and cut-outs and it'll be soooo cute!"

Emily and Faris stared at the motor-mouthed Mikki and then looked at each other and then wagged their heads in unison.

"We've created a monster," said Emily. "Mikki, slow down. Try to think and speak s-l-o-w-l-y."

"I am. I'm just excited. I'm going to be a mother!" said Mikki, still rosy-cheeked and delighted. "It's so weird that I was just thinking about that the other night, thinking how great it would be to be a parent with Faris. To have children, our own family to take care of and love."

"Actually, I wasn't sure you'd be that happy about it. And remember, it'll be temporary. She'll probably go back to Saudi eventually and live with my mother, to be raised in the same world that is her heritage. Only it'll be a modern Arab world, with modern education for women and plenty of the important things…like shopping!"

"You mean I'm going to get all attached to this little girl and then they'll take her away to the Middle East? I'm getting sad already," said Emily, again getting off the chair to go to bed. "Really Faris, that's great. I'll back you however I possibly can to make sure the baby is safe and happy."

"Goodnight, Gran," said Mikki as she got up and hugged her grandmother. Then she pulled Faris to the balcony and they sat listening to the ocean waves lapping the shore. It was so peaceful. Mikki thought of the many times she and Emily had sat on this same balcony and shared thoughts. Now she had Faris. Please God, don't let anything happen to him.

The couple sat in silence, sipping tea. Mikki reached out, lacing his fingers with her own. She could stay like this forever as she watched him. His eyes were half-closed and he was humming or chanting quietly. His sexy eyes opened and he gazed back at her. Lightly he touched a loose tendril of hair on her cheek.

"There's something else I have to tell you."

Mikki's lips trembled slightly as he eased towards her for a kiss.

"What else?" she murmured.

"I will always love you, no matter what."

They kissed and sat silent again, watching the moonlight dancing on the incoming tide.

"Faris, just one thing. You don't seem that upset about Kami. Gran and I were worried that you would be very distraught and maybe even feel guilty about her death. I was hoping that it wouldn't spoil our wedding and our special times together, but you seem so nonchalant. So cool…so uncaring," Mikki ventured.

"You know me better than that. I'm a very caring person. Sure, I have mixed feelings about Kami, but she's not a lost cause. There's hope for her. She needs time with the right people. You know, she didn't want to go at first. There was a lot of crying and defensiveness, but I stood hard and firm. I forced her to go to an intensive debriefing with our government. They arranged the transportation after they talked to her. Everything's taken care of."

"What do you mean?" asked Mikki, completely confused.

"Kami's not dead. There was no crash. Don't tell me you believe everything you see on the news channels. She's alive and well, and living in Saudi Arabia with my mother."

"So, it was all a ruse to throw Sajid and Hassad off her tail until we can get them?"

"Yes. The explosions on TV were set off to create a lot of smoke and flames. The scene wasn't even near the airport. It was a Special Units operation away from town that filmed the video for the news. But Kami is now dead for all intent and purposes. The death certificate will be created by the Army surgeon in charge and sent to me as next of kin."

"You've been even busier that I thought. Congratulations on the successful completion of that operation, Commander."

"Right now, I'm commanding myself to get home and get some sleep. I've got things to do in the morning and still meet you at the church at 2 P.M., my lovely one."

"You could sleep here..." Mikki whispered, reaching into his shirt and rubbing his chest. "Gran's asleep and my room's right downstairs."

"You're such a little scoundrel, trying to misdirect me from my mission. I must go, though the temptation is mighty."

"You are such a bull shitter," said Mikki. "But you're right, we need our strength to do our thing tomorrow. Gran has scheduled massages, hair styling and make-up for all of us ladies tomorrow morning."

"Oh right, that sounds like a lot of work. I'll be thinking of you. That's why I'm leaving so you'll look rested and festive for our wedding pictures tomorrow."

"Geez, I forgot about photos! Hope Gran and Yolanda came up with someone good."

CHAPTER SIXTY-NINE

"Ummm, does that ever feel good," groaned Brigetta as one of the masseuses was expertly rubbing her aching shoulder muscles.

Susan sat in a terry robe waiting her turn on the massage table. Mikki and Brigetta were already in the capable hands of the two Swedish women doing the massages, getting the full treatment of aromatherapy, hot rock treatments on their backs, and moist warm towels wrapping their feet in preparation for foot massage and pedicure. Emily was also robed and in her favorite chair, as a manicurist worked on her fingernails. When Tova saw Mikki's 'stable boy' hands, she quickly applied a thick layer of cuticle cream and moisturizing gloves. She had shaken her head and said something about needing extra time for those nails. So Mikki reclined on the other massage table while Solvig applied emollients to her legs and rubbed the calves and ankles.

The spa professionals had brought their own music that was not only relaxing and pleasant, but gave a sense of timing to the girls as they worked. As the section of angelic harp music ended, the massage tables were cleaned and prepared for the next two women.

"I feel like rubber," breathed Brigetta. "I don't think there's any way I can walk down the aisle. Find another maid of honor."

"Another Mimosa and we'll all be done for," said Susan, stripping and getting onto the table. "I hope we have time for a little nap."

"I'm going to the south deck and get in some nude sun bathing. Gotta get rid of these strap marks," said Emily. "We could all catch a nap out there. Our lunch is being catered in today. With food and a little down time, we'll be ready to leave for the church about 12:30 P.M. I told the limo driver to stop and pick up the dresses before that. Everything will be ready at the church."

"I still can't believe my little girl is getting married," said Susan, as the masseuse began working on her scalp and face.

The women were rosy-cheeked and looking refreshed and rested when the limo arrived at the church. Susan had arranged the music and went to check on the instrumentalists and singers who were setting up at the front of the church.

The others went to the chapel meeting room that was used as a dressing area for weddings. The flowers were there and the church was decorated with lilies and red roses. Groomsmen were waiting at the entrance, laughing and shoving each other boyishly while looking handsome in their gray suits and red ties.

The dressing room was full of mirrors and tables for last minute primping and lipstick touch-ups. The music had begun and the atmosphere changed. This was it, thought Mikki. She felt a little nauseated and wished she hadn't eaten so many canapés at lunch. The two Mimosas at breakfast weren't helping her stomach either. The sudden reality of marriage was causing her some uneasiness. Old fears and uncertainties rose like bile into her throat. She ran for the bathroom and Brigetta followed.

"Don't toss your cookies, Mik. It'll give you bad breath all day!" Brigetta admonished. "Be brave. I hear everyone gets these jitters."

Mikki was pale and looked somehow older than a few minutes ago. "I'll be fine. Too much food, drink, and excitement."

"Here, have a cracker," ordered Brigetta as she unwrapped cellophane from a duo of Saltines. "Trust me, this'll help."

Mikki took the package and broke off a small bite, mustering courage to put it to her lips.

"Come on, eat it! I'm a nurse, I know how to deal with this stuff," Brigetta ordered.

Mikki sat down on a lounge chair in the ladies restroom area and ate the crackers. Brigetta ran to a vending machine in the teen room and bought a can of ginger ale. Mikki took several sips and laughed as the bubbles made her sneeze. Amazingly, she felt better. She still was nervous, but the queasy feeling was gone.

Susan appeared at the door. "Are you all right?" she asked, brow furrowed with concern and choking an embroidered hanky to death with her hands. Mikki nodded and suddenly looked rosy again.

"Then come on! They're playing your song," urged Susan, helping Mikki to her feet.

Mikki's nervousness vanished as soon as she saw the wide grin of the man she loved, waiting at the front of the church. She smiled back at him and fought tears of happiness. She dared not look at her escort as they walked down the aisle. Her father was gripping her hand and also trying hard not to cry. Her mother and Granny Em stood to the left of the aisle and were enthralled by the beauty of the young bride and the emotionally moving music. They both dabbed tears, as Brigetta handed out fresh Kleenex. The ceremony was simple and beautiful with thankfully, no interruptions, terrorist attacks, or shots fired. The newlyweds kissed and went outside where everyone released butterflies into the summery Florida afternoon. They had done it. They were man and wife. After a quick photo session, Faris was beaming with pride as he accompanied his new bride to the waiting limo. The car was dressed for celebration with streamers, signs, and noisy cans hung from the bumpers. Honking and good wishes were loud and hearty, as the wedding party took the long way back to the Pink Flamingo.

There would be an hour of down time for just family and more photos before the rest of the guests arrived. Michael and Susan were on the deck talking, happier than Mikki had seen them for a long while. It was so rare for her Dad to be in Florida for more than a few days. He had arranged to spend ten days at home with his family. Mikki had spent as much time talking to him as she could, but now had another agenda on her mind. While he was home, perhaps she and

Faris could use his apartment as a base for their trip to New York. She would ask him later.

There were beach photos with the Atlantic as a majestic background, photos taken at the massive front foyer, and more relaxed, unposed candid shots in the living areas of the grand home. Everyone was happy and relaxed. Brigetta was again dating Ryder, who seemed totally captivated by her long legs peeking from the slit in her satin-skirted gown. Faris was pulling at his tie and talking with his friends who had already removed theirs. Two bartenders had set up shop in the game room that was doubling as a dance hall for the more ambitious. Kids got flavored Cokes and had plugged in the jukebox so they could dance to the latest music.

Faris and Mikki shared intimate glances but knew they were expected to mingle and greet all their guests, some of whom had driven or flown quite some distance to be here for the celebration. They would have time together later. The night would belong to only them.

The clean-up crew was finishing up. Black plastic garbage bags were packed with party debris and being taken to a truck waiting in the front driveway. By morning, no one would know there had been a wedding reception at the home. There were only three security guards still in place around the grounds and they would soon be dismissed. It was time to get things back to normal, thought Emily. One of the little fledglings was leaving the nest, but she wouldn't fly far.

Emily wanted to make a phone call, so excused herself to her bedroom. The rest of the family was hugging and saying goodbye. During this time, Faris had told them about his sister being in a plane crash and that he and Mikki were going to apply for custody of Kami's baby girl. Susan was shocked that Mikki and Faris would be taking on so much responsibility this early in their marriage, but she and Brigetta offered babysitting services if the newlyweds were able to bring the baby to Florida.

"I love kids," said Brigetta. "What a better babysitter could you ask for? I'm a pediatric nurse and CPR certified. I know all about babies, even though I've never raised one myself. But then I've got Mom to consult for that part."

When Emily reappeared she was wearing pajamas and a robe.

"Gee, I guess she's telling us it's time to leave?" said Susan, staring at her mother's outfit. "The pink fuzzy flamingo slippers are a nice touch, Mom."

"She loves those things," said Mikki, "and it's time to go. Faris and I are going to his condo for the night. We really haven't decided on a permanent home for the two of us as yet, but tonight we're playing house at his place!"

"Let's go," said Faris, making a big show of snatching up his keys, grabbing Mikki's arm, and running for the door. "Our honeymoon has officially begun!"

CHAPTER SEVENTY

"I can't believe I'm an old married woman...in bed with the most handsome man on earth," murmured Mikki, so sleepy she could hardly speak anymore. She lay next to Faris and had entwined her legs with his. She loved feeling the hairy, manly muscles of his thighs as she moved against him.

"Me, too," mumbled Faris, as he began to snore, his arms wrapped tightly around his bride. They had slept about four hours when their cocoon of comfort was cracked open by the ringing of the phone.

"Whaaa? What time is it?" babbled Mikki, trying to think where she was and what was going on.

Faris was sitting straight up and had flipped on the bedside lamp. Mikki squinted to see the time and watched him through heavily lidded eyes. Faris was talking fast and some of it was in Arabic. Oh, no, thought Mikki, now what? It was 5 A.M. As Faris hung up the phone, he flopped angrily back on the pillows, staring straight up at the ceiling.

"What's wrong?" asked Mikki, sitting up and scanning his face.

"Sofah. They've kidnapped her from the foster home. We've got to go to New York right away. They've issued an Amber Alert, but Children's Services and the agents in charge doubt they'll try to drive her out of town. There are too many places to hide in the city."

"That explains why Sajid and his goons have been so quiet. They heard about the wedding and rather than disrupt that, they planned to get the baby before we could. Did they say what happened?"

"The foster mom had taken all her kids to the park last evening after dinner and had Sofah in a stroller. There were two Homeland Agents assigned to guard the baby. They're supposed to be there, but be unobtrusively on watch. The first one apparently took a piss break and never came back from the men's' room in the park. The second one was distracted by a purse snatching and ran off to help. When he came back, he found the foster mom on the ground and bleeding and all the kids screaming in panic. One little boy had fallen off the swing and had a broken arm. The stroller was empty. He found the other agent in the bathroom in a pool of blood. He'd been shot twice in the head. Bastards!"

Faris rubbed his temples with his palms. It would be so much easier to just distance himself from all this and spend a quiet honeymoon with his wife. He couldn't do that. Mikki put her hand on his arm to console him. He looked at Mikki, frowning. "I've got to go. Maybe you should stay here and see what you can turn up on your grandmother's computers."

"No way. I'm going. Gran will give us the heads up on anything she finds on her end. Let's get up and get moving. Drive or fly?" she asked, with no more hesitation than if she had said 'paper or plastic' at a grocery store.

"We'll drive, but we'll rent an SUV that won't be recognizable to any of them. We may have to get in close to retrieve Sofah. We'll need some clothes for our court appearance. First thing is to get full custody, so we'll have legal right to the baby when we find her. Then whatever happens, happens. We won't come home until she's safe."

"I'll call Gran and tell her what's going on while you shower. Then I'll shower while you pack. Then we'll get going. I need more clothes."

"Oh, I don't know," said Faris staring at the naked body in front of him, finally smiling.

CHAPTER SEVENTY-ONE

The rental agency delivered a white Lincoln Navigator to the door of Faris' condo. He signed for it and tossed their luggage inside. Mikki was still talking to Emily as she walked to the car, cell phone propped against her ear, carrying her makeup bag and a duffle.

"Gran said we should be careful and that everything will work out. We should take our time getting there and enjoy the travel time. She said go to the court first, like you said, and get all the paperwork completed so we can bring Sofah back to Florida. Then she's reminding us that the cruise, our honeymoon, leaves next Saturday."

"Yeah, like we'd forget all about that."

"As if. She also agreed to go ahead and board the ship and not wait for us, just in case we're delayed...which hopefully, we won't be. I told her that would be good and even if we miss the embarkation at Miami, we can catch up at the first island port by plane. Also, she conned Brigetta and Mom into babysitting for us during the week we'll be gone."

"This baby will only change our lifestyle briefly, Mikki. I plan on starting our honeymoon year with lots of time for just each other."

"Right, but remember, your niece is just a tiny baby and she needs us right now."

"Trust me, my mother is dying to get her hands on that little girl...her first grandbaby? She'll be under her total supervision. Kami will just be along for the ride...and the dirty diapers!" Faris chuckled.

"Should we stop at Wal-Mart and buy a car seat?" asked Mikki.

"Well, I'm definitely confidant that we'll get Sofah, but I really want to get moving," answered Faris as he drove the vehicle out of the gated exit. "Maybe we'll see somewhere to shop once we're on the road. Right now I'm just worried about Sofah and getting her back safely."

"I told Gran that we'd call her in a couple of days to keep her posted. She didn't really seem all that concerned. It was almost like saying goodbye as we left for some sort of vacation."

They agreed to take turns driving, though Faris didn't sleep the first time Mikki was at the wheel. She glanced at his wide-open eyes and foot placed strategically on the imaginary brake pedal on the passenger side. But to his credit, he said nothing as his white knuckles clenched the door handle. His tense and stiff body language said it all.

"Okay, that does it. I'm telling you how I wrecked Gran's Jag."

Faris sat straight up immediately and watched her face. "Really? We're going to discuss the big taboo subject of your driving?"

"No, it's not a discussion. It's an explanation, so here it is."

"Please…I can't wait," said Faris, wringing his hands in mock anticipation.

"Do you like animals? I mean other than the horses? Like dogs, cats?"

"Sure."

"Well, then you'll understand and I'll be forever vindicated. One day, I'm driving Gran's car to the grocery to pick up a few things. I decided to check and see if my car was finished at the shop. They were rotating tires and changing the oil and all that stuff. On the road to the auto mechanic, I see these teenage boys laughing and throwing something around. As I pass them, I look closer and see that the thing being thrown is a little puppy! Worse yet, there's a box of puppies on the edge of the road and as I pass, they begin putting the puppies into a black garbage bag. I pulled over to the curb and looking out the Jag's rear window, I see one of the boys take a tied bag with two or three puppies in it and toss it into the street. They're all laughing hysterically like this is really funny? Then I see a brown UPS truck heading towards the squirming bag lying in the street. You can guess that I'm about nuts with rage and terror as I slammed the car into reverse, backed over the curb, and did a smoking rubber burn…squealing the tires, as the car raced back towards the boys. Now, remember those driving techniques I told you I learned? Well, have you seen the car video that was circling the Internet where trained drivers could skid a car from a fast circle into a parallel parking place? That was me on that day. I slammed the brakes, did a sliding donut, and skidded into place sideways in front of the UPS truck. Big Brown's driver reacted reflexively, his tires squealed and braked, but the truck hit the Jag in the passenger side. I didn't care, I jumped out, grabbed that bag of puppies and put them in the car. Then I ran and caught two of the little monsters and body slammed them together until their poor little noses were bleeding. Aww, too bad, I thought. I was furiously shrieking like a wild woman! I flew like a banshee after the other two, so startled that they were easy to catch. I got all four of the little idiots who were lucky I didn't kill them right then and there. I grabbed some duct tape from the trunk of Gran's car and taped them all together into a circle, back to back, around a stop sign. Two were crying, but all were speechless with fear of being eaten alive by this insane crazy woman, let me tell you.

"As an eight-legged creature hooked to a street sign, they weren't going too far, too fast, so I went to check on the puppies. One had an obviously broken leg from the hard landing in the street and all were whimpering, shaking, and cowering in the bag. Poor little things! They were so cute, too. Little fluffy black balls of silky curly hair. I think they were little Poodles or something like that. I called the Sheriff and let the boys sit and stew until the officer came. He called Animal Protective Services who came for the puppies. I didn't know where they got the dogs, but the Animal Welfare Officer who came to get them said that they were reported stolen from a kennel in the neighborhood. Nice kids, huh?"

"Super, grade A delinquents," replied Faris with a big sigh.

"The poor UPS driver wasn't hurt, but I guess I scared the shit out of him, too. But it all worked out. I caused the accident and I paid for the damages...so it was my fault. But I'd do it all again without a minute's hesitation. The puppies were checked and treated by a vet and returned to their owner. She called to thank me and to tell me the poor little guys weren't even weaned yet...only five weeks old! Ooh, nothing makes me madder than the torture of innocent animals...and they were just little babies. So sad...then this thing with the baby bomb. What's this world coming to?"

"That's why the world needs people like us. What happened to the boys?"

"They went to the Juvenile Detention Center for a while. One of the parents was a real asshole and tried to blame everyone but his own son and threatened to sue me! But I was there in the courtroom and convinced the judge of the wanton cruelty of the act. I cried and said how the tiny puppies were thrown in the road to be mashed just for the boys' afternoon entertainment. And how I just happened along at the right time. What else had they done or planned? Geez, Judge, what will they do next if they're not corrected now? The other boys seemed sincerely repentant and all of the kids were released to the parents. As they left the courtroom, I finger-signed each of those kids 'I'll be watching you with two eyes' and my best 'if looks could kill' face."

"That would scare me."

"It should. But do you understand about my driving record now? A few fender benders for a good cause?"

"How about the speeding ticket?"

"Oh crap. I forgot to pay for the ticket before we left!"

CHAPTER SEVENTY-TWO

When Mikki and Faris arrived in New York City and after settling into Michael's apartment, they went directly to the courthouse to speak with the District Attorney. Their court date was arranged for the next morning at 10 A.M. They were told that Judge Hartley had already been briefed on Sofah's case and planned to grant the Al Busaid's their request for temporary custody. The judge was also aware that the baby had been kidnapped, but was willing to award the child to them in her absence.

After settling into Michael's Manhattan apartment, Mikki and Faris needed to go to the foster home and talk to the mother to get more details about the infant's abduction. Faris was given the address only after he showed his government C.I.A. identification.

"This is almost as exciting as your driving, Mik," said Faris, nudging Mikki's arm in the back of the cab, as the driver darted through traffic like a hungry mouse in a maze.

Mikki glared at him. Shortly they arrived at the cheese, which was in the form of a two-story row house in a nice neighborhood. Mikki looked around before they approached the porch. The home was well kept and there was a small cluster of potted plants on the porch railing. There was a school, a day care, a church, and a nursing home in close proximity. The solid wooden door was open, but a screen protected the home from insects. They heard Sesame Street and children's laughter through the door. They peered inside and knocked loud enough to be heard over the television noise inside.

A grandmotherly woman in an apron and flowered housedress came to the door, wiping her hands on a dishtowel. Her forehead was damp from the heat and she looked tired, but she smiled widely and pushed open the door, motioning them to come in. The three toddlers on the floor in front of the TV jumped up and excitedly skipped to them.

"Hi! Are you a policeman? Are you a police lady? Did you come to see us? Wanna watch Big Bird? He's funny! Did you find the baby? Where's the baby?" The children had a million questions, but were told to finish their sandwiches and sit back down. Mrs. Hannah Blayton introduced herself when things got quiet. Mikki and Faris followed her to the kitchen where she motioned for them to sit at an old enameled table. Mrs. Blayton sat steaming coffee mugs in front of them and then sat down with them.

"What else can I tell you?" she asked. "I've told the police everything several times. I'm just eternally grateful we all came out alive. Poor Sofah, such a sweet, sweet baby. I hope she's okay. Do you know why they took her? Detective Zambrino said you were coming and that you're her relatives."

"We've been granted temporary custody or we'll have it tomorrow. I'm her uncle," explained Faris. "This is my new bride, Mikki."

"Oh, congratulations! When did you get married?"

"Just a few days ago," answered Mikki. "Now we need to find Sofah and take her back with us to Florida. Eventually she'll go to Saudi Arabia to live with her grandmother. She'll have a great home there with Faris' parents."

Mrs. Blayton, looked skeptically at Faris and then back to Mikki. "I don't think I'd want to live there as a woman…or even as a man. I'm sorry, that's just what I think. The whole Mid East is nuts and just not safe!"

"My family is very modern and Sofah will have the best of everything…a great education and the chance to have a normal life. A life away from her father and other zealots."

"So it was her father who took her?" asked Mrs. Blayton, stirring her coffee.

"We're guessing that, but we need your full description of the events that day to help us track him and, hopefully, the baby."

"I'll tell you what I know, but it's not much. It all happened so fast, before I could do or say anything. I couldn't even open my mouth to scream and it was over. I was on the ground, the kids were screaming, and Sofah was gone."

"Tell us what happened from the beginning, if you don't mind," said Faris, his hands cradling the steaming porcelain mug.

"I had the kids at the park after dinner. It was a lovely evening to be outside. They were all playing on the swing set and I was sitting with Sofah at the picnic table, setting out some chocolate pudding snacks from my cooler. She was in her stroller right next to me. Suddenly, all the kids were looking past me to my right, their mouths hanging open and staring. That was something new and unusual so I turned to see what they were looking at. There were three men with hooded masks and some kind of rifles. They came toward me and pointed their guns at me. I was terrified! But just as suddenly and without a sound, one of them grabbed Sofah from the stroller and took off running. When I tried to stand and cry out, another one pushed me to the ground, real hard. See my elbow? William was standing on a swing and he fell off when he got scared. He's the one who has the broken arm. They told me one of the two agents guarding me was killed! I was terrified!"

Mikki examined Mrs. Blayton's right elbow that was scabbed, scraped, and bruised.

"I had an X-ray, but it wasn't broken or anything. Just a hard hit and a bruise. Anyway, the kids started bawling when they saw me fall and the men took off. In a flash, they were gone. Not a word was spoken. An ambulance took William to the hospital. The men were gone and so was Sofah. I couldn't really understand why they wanted her. I knew it was a secret that she was with me. I hadn't told anyone, so how did they know?"

"These guys have their ways. But we have our ways, too, and we'll find her and take her home. Anything else you can think of?" asked Faris.

"No, but people are really concerned about the baby. Just this morning a detective came over, one of those plain clothes guys? And also some people from the neighborhood. An old couple from assisted living. Said they'd heard about the kidnapping and came to tell me everything will be all right and if needed, they'd send out the AARP vigilantes or something. That was kinda funny, but I can't really say everything will be all right. Everyone around here seems to be behind me, but maybe they'll take away my license to foster kids. This was a big screw up for me. I should've been more careful," said Mrs. Blayton, pulling out a Kleenex from her apron pocket and dabbing at her eyes.

"Who was the cop? Did he give you ID? You've got to be careful now. You're the only witness, I think," said Faris.

"He was for real. Showed me a police badge. A young guy. I forget his name, but he was Italian. Looked scary to me. Kinda handsome, but dangerous looking. I'd be frightened if he came looking for me even for a traffic ticket," said Mrs. Blayton.

Faris dared a quick glance at Mikki, but she chose to ignore the remark about the traffic ticket. "Well, with everyone working together, maybe we can find Sofah quickly," said Mikki.

"The agency told me her mother is dead, killed in a plane crash or something. So why would anyone want a little baby? Why would they take her?"

"I hesitate to even try to answer that question for you. We just know we have to find her quickly before anything happens to her," said Mikki, rising from the kitchen chair.

"Oh, no! They aren't going to hurt her, are they? Why, why, why?" cried Mrs. Blayton as tears started anew.

"Nothing will happen to my niece," said Faris. "We promise you."

CHAPTER SEVENTY-THREE

The Al Quada safe house in Queens remained quiet since the Night of the Worm Man and the arrest of his shooters. The remaining four men had quickly relocated to a rented apartment in an old warehouse section of Harlem. There, the baby with them remained passive and calm, sucking formula from bottles purchased at Walgreen's. She didn't seem to care about the long time between clean Pampers or that she'd worn the same one-piece pink pajamas for days. But the dark, dank windowless walls were starting to grate on the nerves of the two guards assigned as babysitters tonight. The other men had gone to get dinner at a nearby Taco Bell.

"We're going to get killed. This is stupid," muttered the youngest one to the other in Arabic. "Why do we need this baby? She has no value. We should kill the child and send the head to our enemies. That would make a statement."

"Sajid is the father. It's up to him what we do. He plans to lure Kamila's brother and trap him. He'll get him this time. This time Sajid holds all the cards, as they say in America," said the second man.

"In the meantime, we're hiding here in this hole, like filthy dogs. Spending our time guarding a baby. I say, leave her here. She'll be here when we get back…if these rats don't carry her away," laughed the first man.

"Yes, the rats. This America isn't so great, shootings every night, even in the day and drugs everywhere. These people look at us like they want us dead as we walk on the street. Those blank faces, staring with cold black eyes. Like they're dead and don't care about anything. I hate them all. White, black, yellow…infidels. All are Americans to hate."

"What about the guy who gave you dollars for gas money this morning?"

"Stupid, but an infidel all the same to me."

"Someone's coming. Quiet!" said the young man, glancing quickly at the sleeping, contented baby.

It was Sajid and Hassad, carrying two bags of tacos and a two-liter bottle of Coke. Sajid went immediately to his infant daughter and saw she was asleep. His appraisal was quick and he showed no affection toward the child. He spoke to the men.

"Eat these. Tomorrow they'll come. They've been to the court and have gained custody of my child. This won't happen. She'll die before she ever sees Faris Al Busaid and the red-haired slut. In the morning, they'll be scouring the city, turning every stone, using all the government agencies at their disposal…but they won't get the baby. We'll find them first and smash them like a train in a collapsing tunnel. They have nowhere to run to escape us."

"What is the plan, Sajid?"

"They're staying at the woman's father's apartment in Manhattan," Sajid laughed. "I hope they're enjoying their honeymoon, because tomorrow they'll have togetherness forever, starting with their funeral. I'm going to call them in their bedroom to give them a pleasant awakening. Then we'll take the baby to Central Park and give her to them."

"What? Give them the baby after all this? I thought you said…"

Sajid and Hassad just grinned at each other and then Hassad handed the brown paper sack to Sajid who dumped it ceremoniously onto a metal table. "Tonight we put together the baby's toy," said Hassad, pointing at the contents of the sack. The men smiled as they gathered in a circle around the small table. Slowly Hassad picked up the contents, one by one, like show and tell at kindergarten. Nail polish remover, peroxide, a stopwatch, four nine-volt batteries, a small bottle of sulfuric acid, and a yellow rubber duck made an ominous appearance on the tabletop.

The men said nothing, but all were smiling, standing in a circle with arms crossed, smug with victory. Though very difficult to work with and very sensitive, the items represented only one thing. An excellent and volatile bomb.

TATP, Triacetone Triperoxide…the "Mother of Satan" bomb.

Oddly, the men were startled when, for the first time in the small dingy apartment, Sofah began to cry.

CHAPTER SEVENTY-FOUR

Faris didn't sleep well. Even making love to his new bride hadn't quelled a sense of anxiety that had been building since their arrival in New York. He'd been sitting in a chair and staring for hours out the bedroom window ever since dawn revealed a gray, misty morning in the city. Finally he returned to the bed and watched Mikki sleep. He had felt her tossing and turning into the night, and knew her slumber was also fitful and restless like his. He was quiet, letting her rest as long as possible. He hoped this wasn't a mistake, bringing his new wife along on this dangerous mission. He had promised his mother and Kamila he would bring Sofah to safety and this he would accomplish. But he'd die before he would let anything happen to Mikki. Trusting, loving, adventurous, beautiful Mikki. She could be dangerous in her own right, but her inexperience made her a questionable asset in this equation. He would have rather done this alone and not have to worry about his new wife being injured or killed. He didn't really have that choice now. They were in this together as a team.

The bedside phone rang, jarring Mikki awake. Faris stopped her hand from grabbing the receiver as he placed the recorder near the handset and pushed the button for speakerphone. He knew Sajid would find them. It had been merely a matter of when.

"Hello," Faris said brusquely, as he motioned to Mikki to keep quiet and listen.

"Pick up the baby at the duck pond. You can have her. Central Park. She'll be on a bench. 11 A.M. Do not be late," was the message before the line was disconnected.

"What the hell? What duck pond? How will we find it? Crap, it's ten o'clock now! We've got to get there before they do! We've got to get moving!" exclaimed Faris, as he yanked the covers off Mikki and ran to the bathroom. Mikki jumped up and followed him.

As Mikki picked up her purse, the phone rang again. They had to answer. There might be a change in location. This time Mikki answered as Faris pushed the recorder on.

"Hello?" said Mikki, expecting anything and anyone.

"Hi, dear. Are you up and ready for breakfast this morning?" It was Emily.

Mikki exhaled quickly and explained what had happened and where they were going. "Gran, we've really got to move quickly. This isn't the time for a chat. Time's running out. As for the cruise, just be sure you're aboard and we'll see you there. We're going to grab Sofah and leave right away for Florida. Okay?"

"Just be careful. And the most likely duck pond is on the east end of the big pond. Go there and look for Sofah. Don't hurry, you'll just make mistakes. She'll be fine."

"Bye, Gran," said Mikki as she hung up. "I don't get it. Gran still thinks we're on some vacation. It's almost like she's planning to slow us up. She keeps saying that Sofah will be fine. Yeah, like the terrorist dudes are just gonna hand her over, like they're returning an overdue library book. Sometimes I wonder about the woman. Let's go!"

In less than a half hour since the first phone call, they were dressed in jeans and running shoes and hailing a cab in front of the apartment building. Their rented car remained securely parked beneath them in the valet parking lot. It was much more convenient to travel the city in a taxi than trying to bash their way through traffic on their own. It was also more anonymous. There was no cab in sight. Mikki saw a green taxi halfway up the block, parked at the curb. They ran towards it. The driver wasn't there, but keys were in the ignition and the motor was running. Mikki didn't hesitate. She ran to the driver's side and jumped in. Faris hopped in the other side and looked around for the driver. Suddenly Mikki floored the gas pedal and Faris covered his eyes as his skull slammed backwards into the headrest. Within minutes Faris was flung sideways as Mikki executed a perfect sliding stop into a parking spot by the park.

Daring to exhale, he said, "That was pretty good. Scary, but pretty good."

"I told you I could drive!"

There was no time to talk. They began to run. Faris was still watching his Rolex when they arrived at the east side of the park.

The park was busy for a cloudy Wednesday morning. Nannies were pushing strollers along the paved walkways and small children were running here and there like gerbils suddenly given freedom from their cages. Dog walkers with tangles of leashes and were being pulled this way and that way, while trying to drag the stragglers along behind. Two boys who looked to be of school age were playing catch in a clearing near some trees. Leaving Mikki behind, Faris walked over to them.

"We're allowed to be out of school! It's still summer for three more days!"

"I'm not a truant officer, guys. I just have a question."

"Well, we're not gay, either!"

"What?" said Faris, taken back in surprise. "Oh, no. I just want to ask you something. That's my wife over there and we're a little lost."

Both boys looked back and forth between Faris and Mikki and were still eyeing them suspiciously. At least their parents had trained these kids, Faris thought.

"We just need to know about the duck pond, a duck pond with benches. Where is it? We're supposed to meet someone there and don't know where it is," said Faris, frustrated by the delay.

"Oh," said the boy in a gray T-shirt with the Yankees insignia. "You do know that there's like a bunch of ponds around here and like six thousand benches in our park." Sighing, he continued, "Take that path there and bear left. You'll find it. I think it's the one you mean. It's pretty far, though." He pointed with his finger the direction they should take.

Faris thanked him quickly and he and Mikki began to jog down the path.

"Do I look like a pervert or something?" ventured Faris, huffing as he picked up speed.

Passing on this opportunity to poke fun at him, Mikki said, "Not in the least, babe."

After a steady pace for fifteen minutes, they were beginning to feel like they were on an endurance run. Emily had given them the wrong direction. The pond was west, not east, and they had stopped the taxi far from the duck pond they sought. Finally it was like they were suddenly in a lost forest with plants and marsh and lots of water birds, including lots of ducks. It would've been lovely if they hadn't been on such an urgent errand. There were kids and adults feeding remnants of their sandwiches to quacking and squabbling white and brown ducks. Some birds were in the water, but the braver ones had advanced to the shore and were steadily approaching the people feeding them. One of the toddlers got scared and ran to hide behind his mom's legs, but the ducks kept circling them, quacking louder and louder.

"Gee, think we need to do a rescue here?" panted Mikki, as she stopped to look around and catch her breath.

"Nah, I think those are just the annoying AFLAC ducks. All quack, but no bite…hopefully. Did you notice there are no benches here? The caller said 'bench,' right?" asked Faris.

"Faris, look over there!" exclaimed Mikki, pointing across the pond to the other side of the water where a row of benches curled in a semi-circle bordering a sandy beach. She squinted her eyes and tried to see over the shimmering reflections of clouds over the water.

"There's a bench with something on it. Is it Sofah?"

Faris pulled out his mini folding binoculars and adjusted them to his eyes, turning the focus knobs. He stared, not saying anything.

"Well? What's going on?"

"You won't believe this," he stammered, handing her the binoculars, and grabbing her hand, ready to run.

Mikki pushed the lenses to her eyes and squeezed them together to fit her face. She saw a pink-blanketed something sitting in an infant carrier alone on the bench. A curious couple had seen the baby and was approaching, looking around for her parents.

"Shit! Let's go!" yelled Mikki, "Which way?"

"You're considering going through the water?" asked Faris, his eyes wide and wary.

"Well, which is fastest, running all the way around or swimming?" Mikki asked, as if his question was ridiculous. The next thing Faris knew, they were both pulling off their shoes and sticking them into their shirts. People were staring at them. No swimming was allowed. Ducks even stopped scavenging for food to hustle back toward the water, well away from the wading couple.

"You're not allowed in the water," said a tiny voice. A small, blond girl about five years old, pointed an accusing finger at them.

"It's okay, we're mermaids," Mikki answered, as she and Faris splashed and thrashed their way from shore, wading deeper and deeper.

"Mommy!" yelled the little girl. But Mommy was dialing her cell phone for the swimming police.

CHAPTER SEVENTY-FIVE

As the muddy water reached their knees and their feet began to suck them down like doomed dinosaurs in the sticky mud, neither Mikki nor Faris continued to believe that crossing the pond was a good idea. The one good thing was that their illegal wading might bring help in the form of more law enforcement. Holding hands for balance, they stopped and stood staring straight ahead at the scene developing beyond their reach on the opposite shore.

A man was running towards the couple as the woman was bending to pick up the baby. His hands were waving in a threatening manner. As he reached the couple and struggled to take back the infant carrier, another man appeared and fired a weapon he'd pulled from his belt. The first man dropped where he stood. Mikki and Faris stood helpless, hearing people screaming after the sound of the shot.

"Oh, no!" they said in unison. Standing in the water, they were as ineffective as if they had been bound in straight jackets. Helpless from their vantage point, they could do nothing to interfere with the evolving scene. Faris had reflexively drawn his weapon, but a handgun was useless at this range. Mikki and Faris were only spectators in an audience.

The woman huddled back down on the bench after the shot, shielding the baby, as the man with her examined something in the plastic baby carrier. Then the shooter saw something, briefly saluted the couple on the bench, turned quickly and was gone. He ran into the trees and more shots were heard. Just as suddenly, another man who was hiding behind marsh bushes, jumped into the water, flailing and screaming as if he had hydrophobia. The startled woman on the bench stared at the man for just a second, then snatched up the baby from the carrier and ran up the hill toward the jogging path. The couple hurried away from the danger, arms around each other for support, carrying the baby between them. They disappeared as sirens were heard approaching from the distance. At least someone had the sense to call 911 and not the swimming police. Everyone was gone from the scene but the man in the water and the fallen man lying still on the grass. Faris grabbed Mikki's hand and they struggled back out of the mud and, barefoot, began to race around the lake towards the spot they last saw Sofah. As they ran, they wondered what they'd seen, what had happened? Where was Sofah?

It took a good six minutes of running full speed to reach the beach on the other side. A small crowd had gathered in the area and was gawking at the man on the ground. He had a red circular bullet wound in his left temple and lay face down ten feet from the bench. Meanwhile, the man was in deep water and still screaming and splashing. Mikki recognized his face from the airport, pulled her weapon, and ordered him out of the pond. Still cursing and yelling, he made his way to shallow water. Familiar red, raw blisters were now revealed, oozing with fresh blood, and containing the emerging heads of super-sized guinea worms anxious to begin their new lives in the outside world. The gathering crowd watching the man emerging from the water had also seen the local news from Queens. Faris flashed his ID badge to try to calm them, but it was futile. They knew about the 'snake people' and were not hanging around to catch that particular disease, which now believed to be contagious and spreading! The stampede began with hysteria and then full force running, and in seconds the crowd was nonexistent. Mikki went farther into the water to force Worm Man #2 out at gunpoint. Faris stepped into the muck to help.

"The devil! Ahhhh!" the man cried, still squirming and writhing. As the victim tried to cool his burning skin lesions in the pond, more worms erupted en mass, released from the water-exposed blisters to propagate. Unfortunately for the creepy crawlers, their life cycle wouldn't be complete here in New York with its sub-freezing winter temperatures.

"Yep, it's the devil," offered Faris in no consolation. He pulled handcuffs from his belt and snapped them to the man's red ulcerated wrists. Mikki stood back, her pistol's barrel aimed toward the man. She was repulsed and unwilling to touch him, even to assist Faris. The man was securely handcuffed to the bench when officers arrived. Faris pulled the police aside and gave them a quick synopsis of events, leaving Mikki to guard the Worm Man in his misery. Several ambulances had been dispatched to the scene. A large, swarthy-looking man reappeared from the trees and, huffing and puffing, went to Mikki. He was a New York detective and first on the scene. He'd shot the man on the ground, a reported kidnapper and subject of his search.

"My name is Salvo," he said, as he grabbed Mikki roughly and gave her a hug.

"H'llo," Mikki stammered, surprised. Was this how New York officers greeted their crime witnesses? Very friendly, indeed! Was Salvo his first name or last name?

Then the officer explained how he chased two men into the adjoining woods after they'd drawn weapons on him from the trees. Salvo said he'd shot and killed one, but the other escaped. He just returned to check on the baby, but the infant was gone. The man moaning and chanting on the bench was almost drowning out their conversation. Glancing back, the plainclothesman saw the baby carrier on the bench and picked it up. Examining it carefully, he went back to Worm Man #2 and offered him the toy duck from the carrier.

"Quit your bellyaching, you big cry baby!" he said to the Worm Man. The man stopped shrieking long enough to try to jump away from the little yellow toy.

"No, no, no!" he screamed, "Put down! Down please!"

"Hmmmm, are we afraid of the little bitty ducky? It's just a baby's toy!" Then Salvo just smiled and placed the rubber duck beneath him on the ground below the bench. The officer backed away slowly, still grinning. The Worm Man leaped and pulled at his tethered handcuffs, wrists bleeding from the effort. He suddenly became still and silent. Now crying silently, he was afraid to move. The officer went back to speak to Faris and then motioned Mikki away from the sobbing man. Hands on their holstered weapons, they ran low and quick, off into the woods.

"Faris!" Mikki called after him. The paramedics and police were rolling the dead man into a black plastic body bag. When Mikki saw his face, or what was left of it, she recognized Hassad, Sajid's brother. If there was one man dead in the woods, who remained alive? If it was Sajid, he was very dangerous, even with a dozen police officers swarming the scene. And the baby was gone! Where was Sofah? This had gone all wrong. She wanted to call Gran right now.

She pulled out her cell phone, luckily still dry from the near plunge into the water. She walked far away from the now silent Worm Man so he couldn't hear her conversation. As she dialed the Pink Flamingo, she looked down at herself. Mud was dripping from the hems of her new Hudson jeans and grassy marsh plants were stuck between her recently pedicured toes. Geez, at least this time there were no gators for this, her latest trip to the marshlands.

Come on, Gran, where the hell are you? There was no answer at the Pink Flamingo. Where could she have gone, wondered Mikki, as she began punching out the numbers for Emily's cell phone.

"Helllloo!" came a singsong voice into the phone.

"The baby was taken from the pickup location and we don't know to where or by who!" said Mikki, as calmly as she could.

"I believe it's 'by whom,'" answered Emily.

"What! Gran, have you lost your marbles? We're in crisis here and you're worrying about my grammar?"

"Okay, okay. Slow down. Are the police there? Where is Sajid?"

"Huh? Well, Faris and this cop are looking for him."

"What does the cop look like?" asked Emily.

"What the....? Gran. What does that matter?"

"Please answer."

Sighing with exasperation, Mikki said, "He's probably Italian. Looks tough to me...you know, good looks, but rough around the edges. Dark hair, dark eyes, kinda mean and dangerous. He wears the 'don't cross me' badge very well, if you know what I mean. Gran, he gave me a hug!"

"Good, everything is under control. I keep telling you, you've got to relax. Call me back later. I've got to pack for the cruise." Mikki could swear she heard lots of people and a loud speaker announcing something in the background, but it was muffled, like Emily had her hand over the receiver.

"Gran…what…" Mikki started, but abruptly and without warning, she heard the silence of and ended call.

CHAPTER SEVENTY-SIX

Mikki was jolted from thoughts when two shots rang out from the nearby wooded area. Within a minute after the shots, Mikki's cell phone rang again. "Gran?" Mikki answered, but it wasn't Gran, it was Faris.

"What are you doing right now?" he said quickly.

"I just hung up from another very strange conversation with my dear grandmother. Why? Where'd you think I'd be?" Mikki answered, a bit miffed.

"Don't make any more calls on your cell. In fact, move away from the dude on the bench. He's secure, right? And the baby toy is still under his butt?"

"Yeeah," Mikki answered slowly in two syllables.

"Is anyone else around?"

"Nooo," she slowly answered again, slowly backing farther away from the bench.

"Go to the pond now! Quick and for once, no arguing or questions!"

Mikki scooted to the water and hesitated only an instant as she viewed the drying, sticky mud on her jeans. She was in the water as Faris said, "Dive!" For once, without question, she dove head first under the brown cloudy muck.

As her face felt the cool impact and receptors in her nose logged into the fishy odor of lake water, she felt, more than heard, the huge explosion. Instinctively she dove farther beneath the surface and when she came up for air, the acrid smell of smoke and burned flesh assaulted her senses. Intuitively she knew what had happened. The rubber duck had been rigged to explode and Sajid had triggered the detonator. Mikki fought her way out of the water as the murky lake bottom tried to possess her feet. The sucking sensation was slowing her down, but she fought against it until she felt firm and sandy shore beneath her toes. The smoke was so thick that she coughed and gagged for breath. She could only see enough to continue in the direction of the shoreline and not into deeper water. She twisted her ankle as she stepped on something in the shallow water. It felt more firm than hard, not a rock. She reached down, feeling for the object, and grasped something, something...the stump of a foot! She jerked her hand back with a little squeal and splashed forward to find breathable air and her shoes.

She saw her new, but almost unrecognizable, Reeboks on the grass and grabbed them, running toward the trees as fast as she could in her bare feet. Faris was coming the other way.

"Are you okay?" he said as he reached her, the worried look soon replaced by something resembling amusement.

"Say one word and you die," said Mikki, pointing her forefinger into a gun-like stance, trigger ready.

"You're beautiful!" he offered, but his attempt to stifle his smile gave him away. Then he slowly backed away, holding his two forefingers crossed in front of him as if warding off a vampire curse.

"Now you die," yelled Mikki running after him, catching him, and wrapping herself around him tightly. He laughed and tried to pull her off. She was quite a sight. Red hair now dripping with brownish-gray gunk and weeds, clothes wet and muddy, bare feet black with gooey filth. She released him and stood with her hands on her hips. "Why didn't you tell me to run for the trees, you idiot? No, go in the water, Mikki, get in the mucky damned pond, Mikki.," she admonished him.

"Are you really mad?" he whispered, daring to come closer once more.

"Damn straight," she harrumphed haughtily. The tiniest crinkle of a smile at the corner of her mouth gave her away and suddenly she burst out laughing. She grabbed him again for a kiss. Faris wasn't sure if the display of affection was for him or to him. He was now also a muddy disaster.

"What happened? Where's Sajid?" said Mikki, pulling away from Faris and wishing they were back at the apartment in the shower.

"He's dead. Salvo and I cornered him in a grotto of elms where he was down with a shoulder wound. That Salvo's a pretty good shot...two dead. Sajid had the detonator, but he knew that Sofah was no longer on the bench. He hoped for a last chance to hurt me by killing Sofah and whoever had taken her. Only Salvo guessed the bomb's true location. The duck toy full of liquid explosives sat under our Worm Man. Once I knew you were out of the way, we thought what better way to end his suffering. Sajid knew he was caught and we told him we'd shoot him if he used the detonator. He didn't care anymore. He wasn't going without his last hurrah. So boom... he killed his own guy. Then I shot him. Sweet."

"Salvo? The cop? Where is he now?" asked Mikki.

"Took off to see if anyone found the couple with the baby. Who knows who they were and what they were thinking. They almost got themselves blown up. Luckily for them they left the baby carrier and the toy duck behind."

"That liquid stuff is really volatile, isn't it? If it would've been dropped or thrown...I don't even want to think about it."

"Right. Very sensitive and hard to work with for terrorists, but it makes a good bomb."

"Wasn't that why, after the 'shoe bomber,' the airports weren't allowing any liquids over a certain quantity in the carry-ons? They thought the terrorists would meet and mix their own cocktails right on the plane to take it down."

"Correct. Let's get out of here. We need to clean up and find the baby."

Mikki and Faris put on their wet shoes and after speaking with the law officers, they headed for the apartment. They needed hot showers and something to eat before they looked for Sofah.

Within minutes Mikki was luxuriating in a warm bubble bath and soaking her freshly shampooed hair in conditioner when she heard Faris answer the phone. Now what, she thought? They had tried to call Gran at home again, but there was no answer. No luck on her cell phone either. Mikki would try later, after she and Faris had rested and decided on the next step in finding Sofah.

Mikki, languishing in soapy bubbles, heard distant knocking at the apartment's front door and decided that that was enough bath time. She toweled her clean hair and let it hang loose to dry as she put on a short silk robe she'd packed. Securing the robe at her waist she went to the living room area of the suite. Faris was tipping a waiter from Bella Lunesta, a restaurant right down the street. The smiling man, in a white starched uniform, unloaded a cart carrying silver-lidded lunch entrees and a bottle of Asti Spumante in an ice bucket. The dining room table was set and Mikki inhaled the delicious aromas. She was famished and grateful for his thoughtfulness, but worried if they had time to eat all this.

Faris was beaming and in a surprisingly good mood. He pointed towards the champagne and held up a glass with a question on his face.

"Sure, but just a small glass," answered Mikki. "What are we toasting? Not getting killed or sending the bad guys to meet the promised seventy-two virgins?"

"We have a baby on the way!" Faris announced with a grin.

"You're giving birth? Gee, that's great. That will save me a lot of trouble later!"

"No, silly girl. The phone call! They've found Sofah and she's fine!"

Mikki put down her glass and ran to Faris and hugged him. Tears of relief and joy fell freely down her cheeks as she clung to her husband.

"Omigod, I'm so happy for you, for us. It's over! We can begin our lives! Thank God!"

"Yes, thank God," Faris said, wiping his own eyes. This was the second happiest day of his life. The bad guys were all dead, Kami was safely in Saudi, and the baby would soon arrive at Michael's apartment. Faris explained that the couple in the park had noticed the baby alone and after all the trouble began, they deposited her at a nearby fire department. The fire captain called the police.

"Uh, oh," said Faris.

"What?" said Mikki with new alarm.

"Do we know how to take care of a baby?"

"We'll learn. Everybody has to learn. We'll eat breakfast and then run out to a store and get baby stuff. It'll be fun!" said Mikki, sounding more confident than she really felt.

Faris looked at her for a moment and said, "You're wonderful, you know?"

"Yeah, that's what I'm told," said Mikki, now heading for the trays of food. "Look what's under here! Eggs benedict, bacon, au gratin potatoes....let's eat!"

CHAPTER SEVENTY-SEVEN

Mikki and Faris finished lunch and were dressed and packed in record time. Mikki wore the same brown Prada suit and beige silk blouse that she wore to court, since her destroyed jeans were in the bathroom trashcan. Faris chose tan pleated linen pants and a white cotton open-necked shirt. They were ready to meet Sofah. The baby had been through a lot in her first few weeks of life and now, legally at least, she was an orphan.

Faris was nervous about seeing the baby for the first time and Mikki had little experience with infants. They consoled themselves with the fact that most new parents, even with their own brand new baby, were beginners in the realm of childcare. Faris had checked and rechecked the apartment for belongings left behind. The plan was for Mikki to go to nearby Babyland and pick up their list of items. Over their meal they'd talked about what would be needed for the car trip with Sofah. But when it was time for Mikki to go shopping, Faris had begged her to stay until Sofah had arrived.

"Don't leave me alone with the baby," he'd begged. "I won't know what to do! What if she cries or throws up or poops her pants? I won't know how to handle it!"

"Faris, it can't be that difficult. A cat living in an alley can take care of her kittens and no one issued her a manual, did they?" replied Mikki, who was sitting on the edge of the bed, filing the broken edges on her nails.

"Easy for you to say, you're a woman...you're the female cat! It's supposed to come naturally to you!"

"Well, if it makes you feel any better, that makes me even more nervous. What if I fail this womanly task? What if I'm just not mommy material?" Mikki had put down the nail file and sat staring at him in question.

"Okay, you'll be great. We'll be great. Just like riding a bike...or a horse. You just have to get the rhythm of the whole thing and then practice," said Faris. "Okay, go ahead and do the shopping. I do want to get out of here before rush hour. We can make it out of the city and then stop for dinner and a good hotel. Do you think we'll get any sleep tonight?"

"You mean because of the baby? We're both so tired, we'd probably sleep through a nuclear holocaust. Heaven forbid. I don't even want to say stuff like that."

Just then, there was a knock at the door and Mikki jumped up to look through the security peephole. Sofah had arrived!

Two social workers from the Child Protective Agency, accompanied by a uniformed police officer, stood in the doorway. The woman in a navy blue suit held a baby carrier containing Sofah, who was covered by a yellow-striped flannel blanket.

"We thought we'd bring you some supplies. We understand you're driving all the way back to Florida?" said the younger woman with blond curly hair. In her arms were two huge shopping bags of baby items.

"Oh, come in, come in," said Mikki, waving them through the doorway from the hall.

"Yes, please come in," said Faris, staring at all the supplies. "We're so anxious to meet my niece. It's been a long hard road for all involved and we want to bring her some normalcy as soon as possible."

Mikki reached for the baby carrier and took it to the couch. To Mikki and Faris, it was like opening a Christmas package in a flannel wrapper. Gently Mikki pulled back the coverlet from the baby's face. There, wearing yellow pony print pajamas, was the most adorable baby Mikki had ever seen. Tousled curly black hair framed an impish face with rosy Santa Claus cheeks. Faris bent to look closer and when he did, Sofah opened those fabulous sapphire eyes to flirt with him. The baby's long black lashes fluttered as her eyes grew wide to focus on her uncle. Sofah was openly studying him with what appeared to be great concentration. Then suddenly, she smiled and began to squirm. Mikki's eyes filled with tears as she fell in love for the second time. Faris reached for one of the actively churning arms and caught the little hand. Sofah's response was to tightly grasp his finger and make attempts at cooing. Her feet were kicking with excitement and her mouth began to make sucking noises. Faris was enthralled by all of this. He almost reached in to pick her up and then pulled back.

"She won't break, sir," said the officer.

"Sure, go ahead and pick her up. She loves attention and she is such a good baby. You won't have a bit of trouble," said the woman in the blue suit. "I'm Nedda, by the way." She reached for Mikki's extended hand and then turned to Faris. "You're the uncle, right?"

"That's me. I'm the uncle. I'm Faris Al Busaid and this is my wife, Mikki. We've been working hard to make sure this baby was safe. It's such a relief to finally see her in person. I think I'd like to hold her, if you promise she won't break," said Faris, grinning. He reached into the carrier and Nedda showed him how to cradle the baby in his arms.

"I think I like how that looks," said Mikki, standing by his side and stroking Sofah's soft hair. "She is so very sweet. And Faris, you look so fatherly holding her! Very sexy!"

Mikki and Faris were both quite smitten by their new charge, instantly in love with the tiny little girl. Nedda and Brooke demonstrated all the baby items and how to mix the formula for the bottles while they were traveling. Soon they were confident enough to embark on their trip, so Faris called Valet Parking for the Lincoln to be brought to the front of the hotel. They signed all the paperwork for custody of the baby. Sofah was legally theirs for now. It was time to start for home. Mikki carried Sofah and they left for the lobby, Faris pulling along the wheeled suitcase and Mikki's duffle hiked over his shoulder. They were, at last, a family going home.

CHAPTER SEVENTY-EIGHT

Their trip was without incident and the baby was wonderful. She slept almost all night during their first hotel stop. She really only awakened because her new temporary parents kept turning on the light to check on her. Was she still breathing, was she okay? Sofah was fine and only fussed a little at the frequent diaper changes and repeated attempts to feed her when she wasn't hungry. She just wanted to cuddle and sleep. The second night on the road, Mikki and Faris were so tired that they just wanted the same thing. Sofah slept soundly in the portable bassinette and the newlyweds slept entwined on the king-sized hotel bed. Everyone needed the rest and awakened rested and fresh on Friday morning.

"Do you think we'll make the cruise?" asked Mikki hopefully, as she gathered the baby's things together and set them by the door. Faris had been shaving while Mikki gave Sofah her early morning bottle. This motherhood thing was starting to grow on her, but she also wanted a honeymoon cruise with her new husband. Mikki had finally been able to reach Granny Em on the cell phone last evening and gave her all the latest and greatest happenings. They had agreed to just meet aboard the ship whenever they got there. But now, when she tried dialing the house again this morning, there was no answer. Maybe she was outside giving her plants a last minute soaking before tomorrow morning. Mikki would just have to assume everything was okay.

"No problemo, darling," Faris answered. "It's cruise time! Have you set up everything with our babysitters? God, that sounds weird. One week into the marriage and we're getting babysitters! I love it!"

"Me too, I love it. But yes, I talked to mom a few minutes ago and she is soooo excited she can hardly stand it. Brigetta has supplied the house with thermometers, baby wipes, baby scales, local emergency numbers, and has even contacted a pediatrician to be on call the whole week we're gone. I read my sister the list of Sofah's vaccinations and she said we're good. No shots needed for another month. Brig has taken a whole week of vacation to bond with her new baby, she says. We may have a problem prying our baby away from them when we get back!"

"Not another kidnapping!" exclaimed Faris as he came from the bathroom, looking handsome and ready to leave. "I don't think I can handle another one of those."

"Luckily, I know where these two women live. It'll be pretty easy to track them down."

The remaining car trip was easy, no detours and no accidents to hold them up. In a few more hours they would be crossing the state line into Florida. First they would take Sofah to Susan's house and get her settled in. There would be lots of explaining about the custody hearing, but they didn't need to know all the rest of the drama. Sofah was with them now and safe, and that's all that mattered.

At 8 P.M, their car pulled into Susan's driveway and Brigetta was standing impatiently tapping her toe in the driveway. She waved and jumped up and down like a mad woman when she saw them pull up.

"Give her to me, give her to me!" squealed Brigetta, blond hair tied back into a bun, nanny style. "Come on, you sweet little girl," she murmured as she scooped up Sofah into her arms and walked away.

"Uh, hey Brig, aren't you forgetting something? Like hello to your sister, how are you to your sister? And what about Faris…hellooo?" said Mikki, as she and Faris were left standing beside the car with the doors hanging open.

"Oh yeah, hi," was all that was heard as Brigetta took the baby inside, which was followed by a scream of happiness from Susan and the slam of the screen door.

Mikki and Faris just stood staring and then turned to each other and shrugged their shoulders.

"They're your family, dear," said Faris, with another of his famous boyish grins. "Poor Sofah, just an unloved waif left on the doorstep. Ha! Come on, let's start hauling our version of Babyland into the house. Then I'm taking my wife home to pack for our honeymoon!"

CHAPTER SEVENTY-NINE

The next morning, the newlyweds drove to the cruise ship port in Mikki's wedding gift from Faris. It had been waiting at the condo when they arrived home late last night. A new Vantage Roadster, the Aston Martin convertible with the 4.3-liter V8 engine. It was the shiniest silver Mikki had ever seen! She couldn't believe Faris had bought her a car like this! He knew about her driving record and loved her anyway. She laughed out loud at his trust and confidence! She didn't want to drive it to the parking terminal at the port this morning, but Faris insisted that a car was no fun if it only sat in the garage. Mikki thought about calling Emily to say they'd pick her up, but Faris just laughed and reminded her that her new car sat only two people.

"We're going to drive it everywhere! That's why I pay the big bucks for the insurance, so get in... the driver's seat! Anyway, I've hired a private security guard to keep an eye on the car while we're gone. We're honeymooning at last!" After a last quick call to Julianne at the barn to check on their horses and make a promise to ride together when they returned, they were on their way to Port of Miami.

The new owner drove the car cautiously, the top down and her red hair tousled by the wind. Mikki lacked the confidence to be anything but careful with her new car, so she was terrified when flashing lights appeared in her rear view mirror. Oh no, she thought, pulling the car to a stop. What could be wrong?

The officer walked to the car while talking into his mobile radio. He seemed to be checking something on his clipboard.

"Do you think they tracked us down about stealing the taxi in New York? Crap, crap, crap," Mikki muttered. Faris didn't answer, unsure of what to say to that.

"Mikelle Walsh Busaid? I have you registered as the owner of this car?"

"Yes, it's mine. Here's my driver's license. We haven't stolen it and we weren't speeding," answered Mikki.

"Not speeding?" said the policeman. "Get out of the car! You're under arrest!"

"What?" shouted Mikki, dumbfounded and scared.

Faris stepped in the conversation as the cop opened Mikki's door and began tugging her arm to pull her out.

"What's going on? We're driving well below the speed limit."

"Like I said, not speeding *today*. Appears that'll be a first for this young lady. She didn't pay or appear for her last speeding ticket, so we have an arrest warrant," explained the officer as he reached for handcuffs from his belt. "You can't just walk away from your tickets, ya know?"

"May I talk with you Officer Holstrom? May I get out of the car?" asked Faris, now flashing his C.I.A. credentials.

Officer Holstrom peered at the badge and ID and walked to the other side of the car. Faris got out of the car and the two men had a brief discussion, occasionally glancing back at Mikki who was close to tears. Finally the policeman tipped his hand in salute and went back to his patrol car. Faris got back in the Aston Martin and said, "Drive. Don't talk or ask questions, just drive."

Mikki's hands shook as she gripped the wheel, too terrified to move, but gradually she crept back into traffic.

"Are we going to the jail?" she asked.

"Hell, no. Why would you want to spend your honeymoon in jail?" Faris smiled and put his hand on her thigh. "Everything's fine. I told him you were in my custody. I was letting you drive your new car one more time before we put you in San Quentin to serve your life sentence."

"For murdering my husband, you mean?" Mikki said, staring at him as they stopped at Beach Boulevard for a red light.

"Okay, so it wasn't exactly like that. I pulled rank on him, flashed my badge, and promised we'd stop at the courthouse as soon as we got back from our trip."

"Thank you. That sounds a little better."

The ship was even more gorgeous in person than all the colorful brochures had proclaimed. The Pinnacle had been billed as the largest luxury liner to travel the seas thus far. Created in an Italian shipyard, she looked trim for her hefty mountain-sized weight of two hundred twenty-five thousand tons. Perhaps it was The Pinnacle's length that gave her the sleek profile of a reigning queen in charge of her watery world. Mikki and Faris held their balcony suite boarding passes tightly as they entered the embarkation building at the pier. They showed their passports and tickets to ship officials. As they wound their way around the main security lines to the VIP boarding area, Mikki looked around for Emily, while Faris made a brief stop to speak with the chief security officer. It was 11 A.M. and the ship had allowed the early arrivals to access their cabins. The gathering crowd was excited and friends were calling to friends in the passenger holding area.

"I'll bet Granny's already on board," said Mikki when Faris rejoined her. She was looking through her handbag and pulled out a notepad. "She's in Cabin 925, at the ship's stern. We're on the port side, number 1095, nearer the bow. I figured she'd be early. Remember the brunch buffet for early boarders? She'll be there on the 'eating deck' for sure."

"She'll be really surprised that we made it this early, right?" asked Faris, wrapping his arm around his new bride and pulling her close. He looked into Mikki's eyes. She was happy and at ease at last. He could see a new warm glow in her face. The traumas of the last few weeks were over. He was relieved that finally they could relax and enjoy each other. The worst was over and they both needed this vacation. Exhausted after their late arrival back to Palm Beach yesterday, Mikki decided not to try more calls, but to surprise her grandmother on the ship. Mikki had insisted before she and Faris left town that Emily go ahead with the cruise even if they weren't back in time to join her. At the time they weren't even sure if they would come back alive.

"She'll be ecstatic to see us! We're home and we're safe! Anyway, who would want to take a cruise through the Caribbean by themselves!"

"Well, I don't know. Your grandmother seems quite capable of being able to entertain herself independently," said Faris with a shrug and a knowing grin, "but it'll be fun to see her face when she sees us!"

They crossed the gangway to the interior of the ship and were immediately greeted by a deck steward from Portugal in a starched uniform. He smiled in greeting as he looked at their tickets to check their cabin number. When the crisply dressed officer saw they had booked one of the two penthouse suites, his expression changed from ordinary politeness to instant respect and rapt attention.

"Welcome aboard, Mr. and Mrs. Busaid," he said in perfect English, as he motioned for them to follow him to the amidships elevators. Mikki swore he clicked his heels together. "I'll show you to your room. Right this way, please." He bowed slightly and asked to carry Mikki's small but heavy carry-on bag.

Mikki took Faris' arm and then followed the steward towards one of six glass-enclosed elevators, all of which were gleaming with highly polished brass and chrome. Mikki's eyes were bright and sparkling green as she viewed her new surroundings. Faris watched her with approval. Her auburn hair hung loose and cascaded down her shoulders to her island print cotton halter dress. The blues, greens and yellows of the summery dress accentuated her body and long, tan legs. Sterling silver hoop earrings and low-heeled Jimmy Choo sandals completed her look. As she absorbed her new environment, Mikki felt like a princess on a floating ocean palace. Modernistic chandeliers and fountains were everywhere in the eight-story atrium of colored glass and majestic metal sculptures. Cascading water tinkled and bubbled everywhere, almost in unison to the music that she heard coming from the welcoming piano bar on a floor far below. Mikki looked down over the upper railing of the huge atrium, viewing the lower levels. Emily was nowhere to be seen. Down the many levels of circular stairways, there was a small orchestra consisting of men wearing white tuxedos. They were playing violins and other string instruments. A female accompanist, who wore a long white gown, played the harp, strumming an angelic, soothing melody. Mikki felt this was so peaceful compared to the previous two weeks that it might be a dream. If so, she didn't want to pinch herself back to reality.

As they rose in one of the glass elevator shafts, they could see a plaza of shops and even an old-fashioned ice cream parlor. Mikki squeezed Faris' arm and looked up at him. He, too, was beaming with anticipation. They were going to enjoy this trip. The last few weeks had been harrowing at best. A full week of fun in the sun, fantastic food, exotic islands to visit, and most of all, each other.

Mikki never again thought about her quick decision to marry Faris. She appraised him in his Mexican *guayabera* embroidered shirt she had bought him for their honeymoon. The short-sleeved aqua blue shirt was paired with casual white pants. He wore comfortable sandals with no socks. Now he looked very Caribbean and she could picture him on a deck chair at a beach in San Juan. All he needed was a Cuban cigar. He was perfect. Here he was on a honeymoon trip with his new wife and he was willing to share her with her grandmother. What a guy, she thought. And handsome, and smart, and...everything! She had finally chosen and she'd picked a winner!

The steward was leading them down a long corridor on Deck 10 that seemed to never end...a long tunnel of lights and doors that at first looked like an optical illusion of depth perception. Faris and Mikki looked at each other and raised their eyebrows in concord. Miles of hallways meant they might have to spend lots of time in their room. This long path was too far and too long to walk more than once or twice a day. They were still chuckling as the steward opened their cabin door and bid them to enter with a sweep of his arm.

"Wow!" they said in duet.

The aroma of fresh cut flowers filled the air. A multitude of bouquets were arranged in their cabin. While Mikki read the card on the largest vase, Faris said, "There's so many flowers, you'd think we were dead!"

"No, they're congrats for our wedding and bon voyage for the honeymoon. This one's from Gran, so I know she's got to be aboard."

The sliding doors leading to the living room's balcony were ceiling high and the rest of the wall was glass. Their corner suite had a private separate bedroom with a king-sized bed. European-styled, the crisp white sheets and comforter were simple and classically elegant. The furniture looked like it came from the islands, taffy-colored wicker and bamboo headboard and night tables. Caribbean artwork decorated the walls. Their feet were sinking into a full inch thickness of pale peach luxurious carpet. After walking on the cloud-like rug, Mikki fought the urge to take her shoes off and get comfortable.

Their room attendant appeared immediately from the hall and introduced himself. His name was Felipe and he announced that he would be taking care of them and their suite of rooms during their cruise. He explained where everything was located in the cabin and gave details as to how to access the safe and how to order room service. He reminded the newlyweds of the mandatory muster station drill that must be executed before they could sail. Felipe told them that the life jackets were located in the walk-in closet on the top shelf. Faris tipped the steward and turned toward Mikki. Felipe discreetly slipped away through the cabin door.

"Well, shall we?" she whispered sexily into his ear, grabbing his hand and pulling him toward the fresh and inviting bed.

He was intoxicated with her, but said with practical reluctance, "Since we're responsible adults, shouldn't we find Emily first? She needs to know we're safely on board."

"Spoil sport," pouted Mikki, lower lip sticking out as she plopped with a bounce onto the bed. She thought briefly about enticing him by lolling sexily on the white comforter, but then she jumped right up again and said, "You're right, husband...this time! Let's go!" Then she grabbed the notepaper with her grandmother's cabin number and pulled him again, this time towards the door.

They walked hand-in-hand towards the nearest stairway and descended the colorful carpeted steps down one flight to the Deck 9. Now they needed to find the cabin number.

"I wonder why Gran didn't want to get a penthouse suite like we did?" Mikki asked Faris. "She is sooo used to big, big, big. I mean her bedroom at home would be bigger than nine or ten of these balcony cabins. Where will she put all her stuff?"

"Well, from what you've told me about all your grandmother's travels, she probably knows how to pack light," suggested Faris, as he thought of all the places those hit-chick jobs may have taken Mrs. Vanderhorn. Once more he studied Mikki's face, still trying to picture his own lovely bride with a laser-scoped assault rifle in her hands. At least she looked safe enough to him right now.

"My grandmother always dresses for the occasion and this is one big wonderful occasion. I'm sure she has full-length evening gowns, matching jewelry for every swimsuit, and shoes to match every single outfit...of which I'm sure there are too many to count. Oh yeah, plus the extra empty suitcases for 'purchases' she might *need!*"

"I see. So she has half as many suitcases as you brought? Is that what you're saying? I felt guilty giving the porter a twenty for all of our bags. Some of them must weigh a hundred pounds!" said Faris.

"You are such an exaggerator, Mr. Busaid. I only brought the essentials," answered Mikki.

"Remind me not to take you on a world tour or something," said Faris. Then he added, as another thought crossed his mind, "You didn't dare bring any ...hmm... *hardware,* did you? I mean that's not why our stuff is so heavy, is it?"

"Be serious, love, how could I get that *stuff* through the security measures here in port?" answered Mikki, waving a finger at him.

"You'd think of a way. But don't worry, I don't think there are any pirates, and if there are, I'll walk the plank for you."

"Thanks a lot."

"Hey! Here's Emily's room!" announced Faris, waving his arm at a door.

"It's a *cabin,* darling," corrected Mikki, as she giggled and raised her hand to knock on the door. She read the brass plaque. *Owner's Suite! Okay, now that makes sense.* There was only one door for the whole stern of the ship on this floor. Emily had the entire back of the ship on Deck 9 all to herself! Mikki couldn't wait to see Emily's private balcony! She tapped three times and waited. No answer. Three more taps, louder this time. Nothing happened. "Shit. She's not in there. Probably chowing down on lobster salad upstairs and flirting with the waiters."

"Well, shall we join her there or...," whispered Faris, as he grabbed her tightly in the now vacant hallway and mashed her body against Emily's door, "shall we go back to the room?"

Mikki breathlessly answered, "Let's go back to..." Her sentence stopped mid-word. She held her finger to her mouth, shushing him. "Shhh! Listen!"

They both put their ears to the door just as a porter carrying a tray passed and eyed them suspiciously. They both stood erect and Mikki suddenly looked scared.

"There's people in there! I can hear them! What if they're robbing Granny?"

"You're right! I hear voices and things being moved around!" Faris agreed.

Mikki pounded on the door and said loudly, not wanting to yell just yet, "Granny! Are you in there? Are you all right?" Mikki saw Faris draw a small automatic weapon from a holster under his shirt and she pulled back in surprise.

"Where'd that come from? How'd you get it on board?" she sputtered, confused.

"Stand back!" he commanded and backed up, preparing to kick the door and break the lock. Just before his foot was about to connect to the wooden entrance, the door opened just a little. Faris froze in mid-kick and fought to regain his balance. Emily peeked through the narrow gap.

"Gran? Are you okay?" asked Mikki, cautiously trying to see around her grandmother to find the source of all the commotion she'd heard. Emily stood blocking the door and appeared strangely disheveled. Her hairdo, usually tousled but neatly under control, was now a poster demonstration for major bed head. Emily grinned sheepishly, as she slid around the corner of the door into the hallway to hug them both. She was wearing a white robe embroidered with the cruise line insignia on the breast pocket.

"I was taking a nap," explained Emily, watching carefully as she saw Faris replace his handgun under his shirt. "Who were you planning to shoot?" She was looking at Faris, and self-consciously rewrapping the belt of her robe.

Mikki jumped right in to the conversation and explained further, "We knocked and knocked, but no one answered. Then we heard the noises. It sounded like someone was rifling your room. We decided to save your ass or at least all your stuff."

Faris was quiet and pensive. There was something funny going on here. Emily was hiding something. Was she in trouble?

"And since when do you take naps before lunch?" demanded Mikki. "I know you weren't expecting us, but I figured you'd be up on the pool deck looking for the chocolate fountain. We thought we'd surprise you."

"Well, you did. And I'm very glad to see you, so could you go away?"

"Gran, what...?" queried Mikki and started to shove her way into the room. "Something is wrong here. We're coming in."

"Suit yourself," said Emily with resignation. She aimed a sly smile and a wink at Faris who was no longer really worried.

Faris and Mikki entered the room and left Emily standing by her open door. Faris looked around and held his hand over his chest where he could feel the confidence of his weapon, just in case. Once inside, their attention was diverted to the glamorous surroundings. The cabin was the size of a small house and beautifully decorated!

"Geez, Gran. This place is huge! And gorgeous! No wonder you didn't want to let us see you in the lap of luxury," said Mikki, eyes roving around the fantastic Owner's Suite. "Your room is three times the size of ours and ours is humongous. But, of course, I still like ours better. It has Faris in it! Or at least it will soon have Faris in it!"

Just as Faris was pulling Mikki toward him for an affirmative hug, the sliding wooden door to the master bedroom opened and a handsome gentleman with damp silvery white hair stepped through the opening. He wore the same type terry robe provided by the cruise line and apparently nothing else. He'd been showering. Mikki and Faris were frozen in place, owl-eyed and speechless, gaping at the stranger. Undaunted, the smiling man rushed to them with an outstretched hand.

"*Buon giorno!* I'm Dante Delano, my darling Emily's very good friend," he said as he took Mikki's hand and kissed it. "Salvo said you were beautiful and he's always right about women!" He then shook Faris' hand, pulled him close and hugged him like old family. Then he went to Emily and placed his arm possessively around her shoulder. Mikki and Faris were still staring in quiet shock. Salvo? Salvo Delano, the cop… and this was…?

"*Your Emily?* You're Julianne's grandfather?" stammered Mikki at last, when the silence began to be uncomfortable. Dante nodded, still grinning widely. Then at last, Mikki smiled and her shoulders sagged with relief. "I'm stunned, but thrilled and excited, too! This is great!"

"I was hoping you'd say that, but I was afraid to tell you at first. Figured you'd make some kind of joke out of it," said Emily. "Maybe I wanted to surprise you, too! Plus, I haven't seen either of you for some time. Dante and I are 'shacking up,' you might say."

"Yes, but I'm going to talk her into marrying me, you'll see!" Dante interjected. "Maybe the Captain can do the job, after all this is an Italian vessel! It's bound to be full of love, just like me!"

"We knew you'd make it on time to the cruise, since we were just about a day in front of you, but we came home by air! You didn't recognize me as I grabbed Sofah off that bench? I knew the duck was gonna blow and so Dante and I booked out of there with the little darling, dropping Sofah at the Central Park fire station and then came home."

"So you were the couple in the park?" asked Mikki, accusation in her tone.

"Yep. We were hanging around the foster mom's too, getting the scoop before we tackled the park. Dante and his grandson have lots of New York *connections*...the type of connections that are not all law enforcement related. Remember *The Godfather?* We found out where the bad guys took Sofah and where she'd be dropped. Our plan was to casually drop by and scoop her up...just some dumb old people on a stroll through the park. Meanwhile, Salvo was ready and waiting for those goons to try to stop us," explained Emily.

Emily and Dante's arms wrapped around each other so tightly, they seemed to be conjoined at the navel, their bodies a mass of smiles and arms and white fluffy terrycloth. Mikki grinned widely as she recognized their happiness had homogenized with her own. She summoned the still dumbfounded Faris towards her and said, "I should've known somehow you had to get yourself involved, Gran. Come on, husband, and let's get out of here. We have serious business to attend to in our own suite."

Faris kissed her and patted her butt, recovering quickly, and said, "Now you're talking. Let's go! We need to leave this love nest behind and find other entertainment."

Mikki was now beaming with pleasure, but she did, however, remember her manners. "Nice meeting you, Dante." Then turning to her grandmother, she said, "We *will* see you at dinner this evening, *right?*"

There was no answer, but Emily and Dante ushered the younger couple to the door and said in unison, *"Ciao!"* Then Emily continued, "Sure, we can't miss the gala welcome dinner…and next time you want to check on me, try the phone. They do have them on the ship, you know."

With waves and promises to meet at dinner, the couples went their separate ways for now. While Emily and Dante watched, Faris hoisted Mikki over his shoulder before she could react and began carrying his laughing bride away, fireman style.

"Don't drop her!" warned Emily with exaggerated concern, as the young couple disappeared around the corner toward the staircase.

Turning to Dante, Emily whispered, "They're gone!" Grinning conspiratorially, the seniors, in their twin robes, quietly evaporated back into their suite.

Emily went to the phone in the salon beside the sofa and pushed some buttons. "Hold Calls" mode was set. Dante placed the "Do Not Disturb" placard on their exterior doorknob and shut the door with a firm click. Emily heard the security locks being snapped into place. Soon Dante was in front of her. Emily smiled at the tan and still virile-looking man who was untying the belt to her robe and gently pulling it from her shoulders. Emily had waited a long time for her vacation and she planned to start her adventure right now.

CHAPTER EIGHTY

Once back at their suite, Mikki and Faris locked their doors, too. They took quick showers and glanced at the robes hanging behind the bathroom door. They decided naked skin was even more comfortable than the luxury robes. They fell into the wonderful bed clutching each other, limbs entwined like kudzu vines. They made love quickly and lay easily in each other's arm afterwards, still warm and damp from the shower and love.

Faris spoke first as he ran his fingers along the tendrils of hair framing Mikki's face. "This is more than great. It all seems worth it now. All the turmoil, all the close calls. Sofah is ours for now and we have a little family. I wouldn't mind having a few kids of our own. I saw how you are with Sofah. I can see you'll be good with children and she'll adore you."

"Do you miss your sister?" asked Mikki, running her fingers along the back of his neck as they lay face to face under the now rumpled sheet.

"I'm sad that I couldn't do more for her. I couldn't save her downfall. Poor Kami. She never really had a chance. Once she married Sajid, she thought coming to America would be her chance to find happiness. Instead Sajid and his family led her down a dark and evil path. She wasn't brave enough to find a way to escape them. I should have been there for her somehow."

"Faris, you're a wonderful guy. I'm sure there was nothing else you could do. Who knew that anyone could be so callous as to conceive a baby for the soul purpose of getting a bomb on an airplane. You know, Kami could have helped herself. She could've called you earlier. She was ready to go through with their plan. She only had second thoughts after the baby was born."

"I know. She's a brainwashed nut case. I couldn't really trust her, but she's family and I had to try to help her."

"Kiss me, my wonderful man," commanded Mikki as she increased the pressure on her fingers to push his face to hers.

"Whatever you wish, my darling, but I can't be responsible for anything that might happen next."

"Well, before you pull out the big guns, babe, there is one thing," whispered Mikki, now close to his ear.

"What?" he pulled himself up on one elbow and stared at her. "Something good?"

"Oh yeah."

"Well?"

"I'm late."

"You're always late."

"No. I'm *late!* I mean L. A. T. E.," she spelled it out for him.

Now he sat straight up in bed. "You're late? As in *late?*"

Mikki just stared at him with a lop-sided grin as she gleefully watched his expression. She knew he would be happy about this and he was.

"Omigod!" he finally stammered. "We're having a baby? You're saying my baby is in there?" He had tossed back the sheet and was poking gently at her tan flat belly.

She nodded and he reached for her and squeezed her hard, then stopped abruptly. "Are you okay? Should we? Do we…?"

"Everything is fine…more than fine. Are you happy?"

"Ecstatic is more like it. This has been a day for surprises. You told me before you told your grandmother?"

"Of course! She will be the great-grandmother, but you're the daddy!"

"I'm amazed!"

"I can't wait to tell her though."

"Oh no. We're not going back there again…now?"

"Nope. Trust me, her doors are locked and the phone is turned off. I know how she operates. Didn't you notice how she practically shoved us out the door? She doesn't know what big news she's missing."

"She doesn't seem to be missing too much if you ask me. But I am…" Faris pulled Mikki to him and enjoyed the sensation of her legs wrapping around his body as they cuddled again in their cocoon of sheets. "Right now, I want my wife all to myself, before she gets too big and round to walk!"

"Faris Busaid, keep talking like that and you could find yourself going overboard before the shrimp cocktails tonight."

"You're scaring me again with all that dangerous talk. I'm starting to like it, so I'm going to have to shut you up for good." Faris kissed her mouth gently and with his free hand reached for the phone. With a flick of his thumb, he assured their privacy. No more calls from anyone. A late dinner would be a much better time for conversation.